Margaret Oliphant

Lady William

Margaret Oliphant

Lady William

ISBN/EAN: 9783337119096

Printed in Europe, USA, Canada, Australia, Japan

Cover: Foto ©Raphael Reischuk / pixelio.de

More available books at **www.hansebooks.com**

BY

MRS. OLIPHANT

London

MACMILLAN AND CO.

AND NEW YORK

1894

THE village of Watcham is not a village in the ordinary sense of the word, and yet it is a very pretty place, with a charming picturesque aspect, and of which people say, 'What a pretty village!' when they come upon its little landing-place on the riverside, or drive through its old-fashioned green, where some of the surrounding houses look as if they had come out of the seventeenth century, and some as if they had come out of the picture-books of Mr. Randolph Caldecott. It is a village of genteel little houses where a great many people live who have pretensions, but are poor : and some who have no pretensions and yet are poor all the same, and find the little, fresh, airy villa houses, with their small rooms and little gardens, a wonderful relief from London, even from the suburbs which are almost as rural as Watcham. Watcham, however, has various advantages over Hampstead or Wimbledon. It is close by the river, where a little quiet boating may be had without any fear of plunging into the mob of excursionists from London on one side, who make some portions of that river hideous, or the more elegant mob of society on the other, who do not add to its charm. But I need not linger on the attractions of this little place, with which the reader will, no doubt, if he (or she) has patience enough, become well acquainted in time.

The church in Watcham is a pretty church of very old foundation, low in stature and small in size, its porch covered with climbing roses, its modest little spire rising out of a mantle of ivy. Inside I have always felt that there was a faint breath of generations past, perhaps not so desirable as the traces of them left on the walls—which mingled with the breath of the congregation, and the whiff of incense, which was now and then added to the composite atmosphere. For the Rector was 'High,' and, though he never laid himself open to troublesome proceedings, was watched with great attention by a little band of parishioners very anxious to be aggrieved, who kept an eye upon all he did, in the hope of some day catching him at an unguarded moment, in the act of lighting a candle or donning a vestment which exceeded the rubric. But Mr. Plowden was quite aware of this watch, and delighted in keeping his critics up to the highest mark of vigilance without ever giving them the occasion they desired. The Rectory was an old red-brick house showing rather high and narrow above its garden wall, and the Plowden family consisted, besides the Rector, of his wife, a son, and two daughters, to whose credit the floral decorations, for which the church was famous, were laid, undeservedly, by the strangers and visitors who frequented the place—though this was always indignantly contradicted by the inhabitants, to whom it was well known that Miss Grey was the real artist who made the church so beautiful, and seemed to invent flowers when none were to be had by other persons, for the adornment of the little sanctuary. There were a few houses dotted about in their gardens in the neighbourhood of the church which contained the aristocracy of the place. These were generally very small, but, on the other hand, they were very refined, and contained old china and dainty pieces of old furniture such as might have made a dozen connoisseurs happy. They, however, were inhabited chiefly by ladies, though there was an old soldier and an old clergyman among them who stood out very strongly on the feminine background. The old clergyman, indeed, was no better than an old lady himself, and so considered in the place, which sent him on errands, and set but little store by his opinion ; but the General ! the General was very different. He had seen a great deal of service ; and on occasions when he went at strictly-regulated intervals to a levée or other great function, with all his medals upon his ancient bosom, he was a sight to see. It was believed generally in the village that he had won several victories with his own right hand, and the sword which hung in his room was believed to have been bathed in blood on many terrible occasions ; but, as was to be expected, the old soldier bore no terrible aspect, but was very amiable and gentle to his neighbours. The Archdeacon, of whom nobody stood in any awe, was on occasion ten times more severe.

It will be perceived that society in Watcham was not without dignitaries. But the person who was of highest rank in the place, whom all the ladies had to acknowledge as unmistakably their superior, who had the undoubted right to walk out of a room and into a room before them all, was a lady who lived in one of the

smallest of those little houses which were as Belgravia to the
population of the village.   Such a little house!   It had a pretty
little garden all round it, with a privet hedge and green gate, which
in their insignificance, yet complete enclosure and privacy, were a
sort of symbol of their owner and her position.   For it could not
be denied that she was Lady William, sister-in-law to a marquis,
connected (by marriage) with half the aristocracy; and yet not
only was she very poor, but she was of herself, so to speak,
nobody, which was the exasperating particular in the tale.   Nobody
at all, the Rector's sister, once a governess, whose elevation by her
marriage—and such a marriage!—over the heads of the best
people in Watcham was an affront which they never got over,
though these ladies were too well bred to make any quarrel, or to
be anything but observant of the necessities of the situation.   I do
not pretend for a moment that it was ever suggested to Lady
William in any way that her precedence annoyed her neighbours,
and that to have to walk humbly behind that governess-woman, as
Mrs. FitzStephen, the General's wife, had hastily called her on her
return to Watcham, was an accident of fate which made them
furious.   She was a woman full of perception, however, and she
was quite aware of the fact, and derived from it a certain amusement.   Above all was Lady William amused by it in respect to her
sister-in-law, Mrs. Plowden, who, as a married woman, and the
Rector's wife, not to speak of her own connections, had been vastly
superior to Emily Plowden in her earlier days when that young
woman was a governess and of no consequence at all.   The first
time Lady William dined at the General's, and was taken out
by him before all the rest, the sight of Mrs. Plowden's face was
almost too much for her gravity.   Her elevation had cost her dear,
and had brought her little, except that empty honour; but she was
a woman with a fine sense of the ludicrous, and that moment
compensated her for many troubles.   She was the first lady in
Watcham, where she had received many snubs once upon a time,
and this was at once a balm and an amusement to her of the most
agreeable kind.

But Lady William was very poor.   They were none of them
rich in that little society, but Lady William had less than any, less
even than Miss Grey.   The small annuity given her by her
husband's family, given very grudgingly, and sometimes in arrears,
was all she had to depend upon.   She had, as people said severely,
as if it had been her fault, nothing of her own.   The Plowdens
were not rich, and all that Emily Plowden had had been bestowed
upon a prodigal brother, who had disappeared in the wilds of

Australia, and never had been heard of more. What she had thus lost would not have added fifty pounds a year to her income; but fifty pounds a year when you have only two hundred is a great addition, and she was very much reproached for having made this sacrifice 'to that good-for-nothing boy,' the neighbours said. I am afraid she thought it very foolish herself when she came to be what she was, middle-aged, with Mab growing up, and so little, so very little, nothing at all, so to speak, to keep her little household upon. Sometimes she would calculate to herself how much better off she would have been if she had still possessed the interest of her thousand pounds which poor Ned had carried with him, and which probably only enabled him to ruin himself more quickly. Sometimes she would amuse herself by speculating how much it would have brought in. Thirty-five pounds perhaps, or possibly forty-five if she had been very lucky : and how many comforts that might have got during the year ; or she might have taken a little off it— two hundred pounds or so—for Mab's education. And Mab had really got no education, poor child. However, these were nothing but speculations, and had no bitterness in them. She did not grudge her money to poor Ned. Poor Ned ! How often is there one in a family who is never spoken of but with that prefix, and how often he is the one who is the best beloved !

Lady William was quite worthy in externals of her elevation, being of what is called an aristocratic appearance, though it is an appearance which is to be found impartially in all classes, and I have often seen a young woman in a shop who was much more like a duchess than the owners of that title sometimes are. Perhaps it would be better to say that Lady William was conventionally correct in every way, with a rather tall and slight figure, an oval face, a deportment which strangers thought distinguished, and fine hands and feet, which are always considered to betoken gentle blood. But Mab, alas ! who ought to have possessed more of these attractions, had none of them. She was rather short, and at seventeen she was certainly too stout. Stumpy was what Mrs. Plowden at the Rectory said, and there can be no doubt that there was truth in that unlovely phrase. Her nose turned up, her face was round and her features blunt, her hair no colour in particular. As for waist the poor girl had none, and her feet were good useful beetle-crushers, which she encased by preference in square-toed shoes without heels. In short, it was impossible even for Mab herself to entertain any illusions as to her personal appearance. She was a plain and homely girl. 'Ah !' said the people who disliked the Plowdens, and those who did not know anything about

it, except that her mother had been a governess; 'the common
blood bursting out.' But, as a matter of fact, it was the noble
family to which her father belonged whom Mab resembled. She
was as like the present Marquis as it was possible for a girl to be
like an elderly man. None of his daughters (heaven be praised,
they said) were half so like him as the niece whom he barely acknowledged. Mab was the very quintessence of that distinguished
man. She had very light hair of a faint greenish tinge, eyes
equally light, but bluish. To see her beside her graceful mother
was wonderful. And she did not show her blood like the Princess
in the fairy tale by feeling the pea that was underneath two
mattresses. Mab might have lain upon peas, and she would never
have been any the wiser. Her perceptions were not delicate. She
was not sensitive. In short she was the most perfectly robust and
contented little soul there was in Watcham, and met all her little
privations with a broad smile.

You could not imagine a more minute drawing-room than that
in which this mother and daughter spent the greater part of their
life. There was nothing poetical or romantic about the house.
The door was exactly in the middle, with a window on each side,
which indicated the two sitting-rooms, and three windows which
represented as many bedrooms above. The reader will perceive
that it was the rudimentary house designed by infantile art in its
first command of a slate or other pencil with which to express its
ideas. The narrow passage into which the outer door opened, and
from which you entered the sitting-rooms, was scarcely capable of
containing two persons at once. By dint of having the smallest
specimens possible of those pieces of furniture, Lady William had
contrived to have a sofa and a piano in the drawing-room. There
were also some low chairs and two or three of those little tables
which are so useful in this tea-drinking age, but which are chiefly
remarkable as handy things to throw down. You could scarcely
throw down Lady William's tables, however, for there was not
room enough for them to fall. The ladies were sitting together in
this little room with a large basket on the floor between them, in
which it was their habit to put their work if it was not suitable to
be beheld by visitors. They were both engaged at this particular
moment in the making of a dress, of a kind which is generally
described by novelists as 'some kind of light woollen material.'
Shopkeepers say simply 'material,' leaving the light woollen to the
imagination. I think, as I love to be particular, that it was *biège*.
There was a fashion-book, or perhaps a copy of the *Lady's Pictorial*
—but I think the scene occurred before the commencement of that

excellent periodical—lying among the folds of the stuff, half hidden
by them. And this was Mab's spring dress, which her mother
was making, aided by the less skilled yet patient efforts of Mab
herself. 'Do you think you like that sleeve?' Lady William was
saying, looking at it in her hand, with her head a little on one side,
as an artist looks at his picture; 'these puffs are apt to look a little
fantastic, especially when they are home-made——'

'You mean when they are on a fat little girl like me, mother.'

'Well, Mab, you are a little—stout,' Lady William said. She
did not take it so lightly as Mab did, but half resented, half
lamented, this unfortunate development.

'Don't say stout, please,' said Mab. 'Stout sounds such a
determined thing. Call me fat, mother : it's nicer—it might be
accidental : or I might, as Mrs. FitzStephen says, fine down.'

Lady William shook her head with a suppressed sigh. She
knew Mab would not fine down. 'Never mind about words,' she
said, 'but tell me——'

Here she was interrupted by a rattle of small shots, as of
pebbles, on the door. She knew very well what it was. It was
the knuckles of Patty, the little girl who was groom of the
chambers, and head footman, and kitchenmaid, and general aid to
the woman-of-all-work at the cottage. She opened the door when
she had delivered this volley, and thrust in a curly head at about
the height of the keyhole. 'Please, my lydy,' she said, breathless,
'it's Missis and the young lydies from the Rectory. I thought as
you'd like to know——'

'Are they coming here, Patty?'

'Leastways, I think so, my lydy,' Patty said.

'Thank you, Patty; as soon as you've let them in, bring tea.'

There was no thought of closing the door to these privileged
visitors. But the dress was carefully and swiftly disposed of in
the big basket, which was thrust under the sofa. 'They've
nothing to do with your new frock,' said Lady William, in an
apologetic parenthesis. Mab, who required no apology, who had
seen this little feat of legerdemain accomplished more often than
she could count, required no explanation ; but she did not take up
any other work. Lady William, on the other hand, had a piece of
knitting provided for such occasions, and was working at it as if it
were the chief occupation of her life when the Rectory ladies were
ushered in. Mrs. Plowden had reversed the order which ruled in
Lady William's house, for it was she who was short and stout,
while her daughters were of the Plowden type, long and thin, like,
and yet not like, their aunt, who was slim and tall, words that

mean the same thing with a difference.   The three figures came in like an army, filling the small room.

'Well, Emily, busy, as usual?' Mrs. Plowden said, a little breathless from her walk.   'And Mab idle, as usual?' she added, after she had taken breath.

'Just as we always are, aunt,' said Mab with a laugh, conscious of the half-finished dress.

'You might come, now and then, to the Sewing Society, Mabel,' said Emmy, her cousin.   'It's quite amusing, and it would show you how nice a quiet hour's sewing can be.'

'But Mab does not like parish things—and neither do I,' said the other, the heterodox daughter, under her breath.

'I wonder,' said Mrs. Plowden, 'that you don't set her in some way of employing herself systematically, Emily.   Doing things by fits and starts loses half of the advantage.   What should I ever have done with Emmy and Florry if I had not gone on in the most systematic way?'

'And look what examples we are,' said Florry, as usual under her breath.

'Haven't we made up our minds to agree to differ on these points?' said Lady William.   'I am sure you had something more amusing to tell me than the way you brought up your girls and how I have spoiled Mab.'

'I don't know if you will think it amusing.   There was something else I had to tell you.   Have you heard that Mrs. Swinford and her son have come back to the Hall?'

'The Swinfords!' said Lady William, with a start of excitement.   'Have they come back?   I thought they were never coming back any more.'

'I don't know what reason you had for such an idea.   I never heard of it, and as James is the clergyman, and knows most about his parishioners—but, at all events, they have come back: and I want to know what your ideas are about calling.   People stood a little aloof, I have always been told; but it's a long time ago, and naturally the people here will take great notice of what you and I do, Emily.   It will all depend upon what we do how Mrs. Swinford is received.   Do you think you shall call?'

'Call!' cried Lady William.   A little colour had come upon her face, a little agitation into her usual calm.   The exclamation seemed like a kind of reply, but whether it meant 'Call! of course I shall call!' or 'Call! how could you expect me to do such a thing?' her sister-in-law could not tell; neither did she follow up that monosyllable with any further elucidation.   She said, after a momentary pause, ' How long it is ago, and how many things have happened since then !'

' That is very true—but it's always like that when people have been away for more than twenty years. Half the people that were living then are dead, of course : and other things—why, none of the children were born.'

' Nor dreamt of,' said Lady William. It gave her a great deal to think about; but after a while Mrs. Plowden grew tired of waiting for some definite response to her question, and took up the theme on her own account.

' As I am a new person here since her time it would be silly of me to keep up old prejudices. I know nothing about any old story. I am quite justified in saying so, for, of course, I was not even here. We had only a curacy, and your father was still alive : James did not get the living till a year after : and then, of course, I was a very young woman, thinking of none of these things. Your mother had a prejudice—but why should I take up her prejudices ? And they are rich, and the son is an agreeable young man, people say ; and probably they will entertain a good deal. It would be sinning against a merciful Providence if one refused to take advantage of what is brought to your very door. Everybody says that they will entertain, and probably a great deal.'

' And Leo will want a wife,' said Lady William.

' Good gracious, Emily ! don't talk in that way before my girls ! I keep all such ideas out of their minds. But what I meant to say was, if you think of going don't you think we might go together ? It would have a very good effect, and be an example for the parish. I suppose they have got quite French being so long away, and I have been so long out of the way of speaking it that —— But you are quite a linguist, Emily.'

' You don't suppose Mrs. Swinford will have forgotten her native tongue ?' Lady William said, with a laugh.

' Well, if you think not—oh ! I suppose not ; but one gets so rusty in a language one never uses. Look at me ! I spoke both French and German like a native when I left school ; but, for want of practice, you could put me out completely by a single question. So I think, as you have always kept it up, I should feel more comfortable. And as they can't all go, suppose we take the eldest. You and I and Emmy—three are quite enough to make a call. Don't you see ?'

' I see,' Lady William said ; but it was not for a long time that Mrs. Plowden could get her to say more.

'THE Swinfords come back,' Lady William said to herself, as she sat on the little sofa in the twilight by the light of the little fire. She had been very silent after the Plowdens withdrew, saying little except on the subject of the frock, which was resumed as soon as these ladies were gone. And when Mab went out, as she had a way of doing when the light began to fail, Lady William put the work away, and sat down in the corner of the sofa, which was the cosiest spot in the little room, almost out of reach of the draught. This is an extremely difficult thing to attain in small rooms where the doors and windows are at right angles, and you never can get far enough off from one of them to avoid the stream of cold air which pours in under the door, or from the window, or somewhere else in the sweet uncertainty of cottage architecture. But that end of the sofa was nearly out of the way from them all : and there she sat when she did not go out, at that wistful hour when it is neither night nor day. Lady William was not old enough to like that wistful hour. She was young enough to prefer taking a run with Mab, being, though she was Mab's mother, quite as elastic and strong, and as fond of fresh air and exercise as she : and she was philosopher enough to take care not to think more than was absolutely necessary ; for I do not disguise that there were episodes in her past life which were not pleasant to go back upon, and that the future, when she gazed into it closely, was too precarious and alarming to inspect. But to-day Lady William's mind had been stirred, and so many things had come up which forced themselves to be remembered that she had no resource but to allow herself to think. The Swinfords ! They were the great people of the place. Their house was close to Watcham, its gates opening upon the road a little beyond the village —and they had in her early days exercised a great influence upon Emily Plowden's life. A flood of recollections poured back upon her, a succession of scenes one after another—scenes in the house, in the park, and in the conservatory, all about the place. She remembered even the looks of certain eyes, glances that had been cast at herself, or even at others, swift changes of aspect, vicissitudes of sun and shade which were more rapid than the shadows upon the hills. What a thing it is to recollect over twenty years and more the way one look succeeded another on a face, perhaps gone into dulness and decay, or perhaps only changed out of knowledge, but equally separated from us and the scenes in which we remembered it! Lady William sat and recollected, and saw again the very light of the days that were past, how it came through a long window and fell upon—sometimes her own face, which was as changed as any of the others, sometimes other faces fixed in eager regard upon hers. How strange to think that she was the girl that stood then on the threshold of life, so full of many emotions, so easily touched one way or another, smiles and tears chasing each other over her face. And to think it was all over, and everything connected with that time was as a dream! She had met her husband there; a great many things had befallen her there; and now here was Jane Plowden coming to ask her to call —to call, of all things in the world, on Mrs. Swinford, as if she were an ordinary neighbour, as if there was nothing between them that could not be told over the tea-table among the afternoon visitors! And she had consented to do it, which was more strange still— half for the wonder of it, half because now they had come back, she was curious to see how things looked across the abyss which separated now from then. Oh, as she thought of it there rose a hundred things she wanted to know! Her busy fancy figured how the patroness of her youth would look; what she would say; the questions she would ask. 'So you have settled in Watcham again—in Watcham, after all? And you have a little girl? And you never see or hear of——'Oh, but that is impossible—you must hear of them constantly, for it is in the papers.' All these things she heard Mrs. Swinford say with the little foreign accent which was one of that lady's peculiarities. Then Lady William paused with a foreboding and asked herself whether she could not avoid the meeting—whether she could have a bad headache, or go off on a visit, or simply sit still and refuse to move. Alas! going off on a visit is not so easy—you want money for that, and there was nowhere she could go except for a day or two. Neither would a bad headache last beyond a day: and as for sitting still, that would be equally ineffectual, for if she did not go to Mrs. Swinford, Mrs. Swinford would probably come to her. She considered

that but one of two things could be done—either to go away altogether from Watcham while the Swinfords remained there, which
was, of course, impossible—or to call with Jane as was proposed
to her. She laughed at this softly, with a little secret fright, yet
sense of the ludicrous—to call with Jane ! walking in over the
ashes of volcanoes (so to speak), over the dragons' teeth that had
been sown in their time and produced such harvests, with that in-
carnation of the commonplace by her side. No doubt the ashes
would be covered with Persian carpets, and Jane would think of
nothing but the future parties to be given there, and whether perhaps young Mr. Swinford—— Lady William could not be supposed
to be particularly happy during this review of the things that had
been and the things that would have to be, but she laughed to
herself again. That eternal question could never be left out, she
said to herself.

'What are you laughing at, mother ?' said Mab, as she came
in, bringing with her a rush of cold, and that smell of the fresh
air which changes the whole atmosphere of a little room in a
moment. Her whole person was breathing it out. Her hat,
which she took off when she came in, was full of it, sending the
mingled fragrance and chill into every corner of the tiny little fire-
lit room. Lady William shivered a little.

'You have brought in the draught with you, Mab, like a gale
at sea.'

' I am sorry,' said the girl, turning back to shut the door. And
she came to the fire and knelt down before it, and repeated, with
the pertinacity of youth, ' What were you laughing at, mother ?'

'Nothing very much—chiefly at Aunt Jane and this new thing
she has got in her head !'

'Oh, Aunt Jane,' said Mab carelessly, as if that was a subject
already exhausted. Then, however, she added, still pertinacious,
' but what is the new thing she has got into her head ?'

Lady William thought of a certain baby in a book who wanted
to see ' the wheels go wound,' and laughed a little once more.

'How do you know that I can tell you ?' she said.

'Don't you tell me everything, mammy ?' said Mab, rubbing
her head against her mother's arm like an affectionate puppy : and
Lady William stroked her child's hair, which glistened with a drop
or two of cold dew upon it from the dripping branches outside.

'You have pretty hair, Mab,' she said softly, with praise, which
was a caress.

'Have I ? Oh, I don't think there's anything pretty about
me,' said the girl. ' What a little fool I was not to take after you,

mother! It is you who are the pretty one: and Emmy has the impudence to be a little like you—Emmy, and not me! But never mind. What has Aunt Jane got in her head?'

'The pertinacious child! She has this in her head, that she wants to drag me to-morrow to go with her and call at the Hall.'

'Oh, is that all?' said Mab. She felt that her lively curiosity, which was a pleasant sensation, had been wasted. But then she added, 'Is there anything that makes it of importance that she should call at the Hall?'

How the child swept over the ashes of the volcanoes, raising a little pungent dust, which got into her mother's throat: but she laughed a little, for Aunt Jane was always fair game.

'Do you remember the Bennets in *Pride and Prejudice*,' she said, 'and the commotion there was when Mr. Bingley first came?'

These ladies were great readers of novels, which held perhaps the first place among the amusements of their lives: and they were happy enough to possess an old edition of Miss Austen, which kept them, as much perhaps from their good luck as from good taste, familiar with all she has added to our knowledge of life, and fully prepared with an example for most emergencies that could occur in their little world.

'Yes,' said Mab, a little wondering. And then she said, 'Oh, I see. Aunt Jane is like Mrs. Bennet, and Emmy— But Emmy is not half so nice as Jane. And Mr. Bingley is— Oh, I see, I see——'

'Don't see too much,' said Lady William, 'for it is all in embryo; but I should not wonder if your aunt were at present in her imagination arranging Emmy's trousseau, and thinking over what hymns should be sung at the wedding. "The voice that breathed o'er Eden" is a little common. It was sung for Susan Green only last week, who said, "No, my lady; we ain't got nothing to do with gardens nor apples, nor folks going about without no clo'es."'

It is very probable that this story was told by the artful mother with the intention of throwing dust in the child's eyes and leading her away from a subject on which explanations were difficult; but, if so, she reckoned without her Mab. The girl owned the fact of the anecdote with a little laugh just proportioned to the occasion.

'Is Mr. Swinford quite—young?' said Mab doubtfully. 'And then there is his mother, who lives with him——'

'Well, yes, I suppose that is the right way of putting the case,' said Lady William. 'He lived with his mother when I knew them—and as for his age, I remember him a little boy.'

'Oh,' said Mab, with partial satisfaction, ' but you were young yourself then.   I think I saw somebody in the village just now who may have been—this gentleman.   He was in a big coat, all fur, and shiny shoes—fancy shiny shoes for going through the mud at Watcham!   And he was as old, I should think, as—as old as—Uncle James's last curate, the one who was *locum tenens*, and who did not stay—Oh, over thirty at the least.   Now Mr. Bingley cannot have been more than twenty-five.   I am sure he was not more than twenty-five—and I don't call that very young.'

'Leo Swinford must be over thirty, as you say.   He was about nine or ten when I was eighteen—a great difference then, but perhaps, as you say, not so great a difference now.   Who is that, Mab, at the gate ?'   It showed how Lady William had been roused and disturbed by this afternoon's intelligence that she should be thus moved by the idea of any one at the gate.

'If you please, my lady,' said Patty, the little maid, putting in her curly head once more ; 'it's a gentleman as I never see before.   Nayther the Rector, nor the Curate, nor the General, nor nobody as I know ; and he has got fur round his neck like a female,' said Patty, with a cough which covered a laugh.   'It's just like the thing as they call a victorine.   I never see it on nobody but a female before.'

'Let him come in, Patty,' said Lady William.   She gave a swift glance at the candles on the mantelpiece, and then she decided not to light them.   'Mab, get up and take a seat like a rational creature.   You will soon have your curiosity satisfied, it appears.'

She said to herself that she did not care for Leo Swinford, not a bit !   It was his mother, not he, who had affected her former life.   He had been a boy, and now he would be a man, just like the others.   It showed that they meant to be civil that she should send him so soon.   This was the only point of view in which Lady William regarded the visit ; but that was the point of view which affected her mind most.   She cared no more for Leo Swinford in himself than for any curate in the diocese—which was almost the only other specimen of young man which she was likely to see.   She drew back into her corner, which was so near the fire that it was deep in shade, the reflection going quickly through her mind that *her* first question would be, How does she look ? is she much altered ? does she look old ?   That was what his mother would want to know.   But she should be baulked in that desire at least.   The firelight flickered about, making a pleasant ruddy half-light in the little room.   It danced about Mab, coming and going, giving a

note of colour to her light hair, and showing the round youthful
curve of her cheeks without any insistence upon the overfulness of
her chubby, childish figure. It was very favourable to the child,
this ruddy, picturesque, uncertain light. These thoughts flashed
through Lady William's mind in the moment that elapsed before
Patty threw open the door again, and with a loud voice announcing, 'The gentleman, my lydy,' shut it again smartly upon
herself and the sudden chilly draught from outside. And then
the scene changed, and the principal figure became, not Lady
William and her thoughts any longer, but a solid shadow in the
midst of the firelight, a man, unaccustomed intruder here, bringing
with him a faint odour of cigars, and that sort of contradictory
atmosphere which comes into a feminine household with the very
breath of an unknown being of this unhabitual kind. It was an
embarrassing position for a stranger; at least, it would have been
an embarrassing position for most men. But Leo Swinford was
not one of those who allow themselves to be affected by circumstances. He made a bow vaguely directed towards the corner,
drawing his heels together after the manner of France, and then
spoke in the easiest tone, though his words expressed the embarrassment which he did not at all feel.

'I am under a double disadvantage,' he said, 'and how am
I to come out of it? I came prepared to say that I feared
you would not remember me, and now you cannot even see me.
Never mind. I am Leo Swinford, and you cannot have forgotten altogether that name.'

'No,' said Lady William. She held out to him from the shade
a hand which looked very white in the ruddy light. 'I heard
this afternoon that you had come home,' she said, 'and your name
was on our lips.'

'What a good thing for me,' he said, 'save that it does not
at all test your recollection, which I had pleased myself with
thoughts of trying. But it is all the same. Do not send for
lights, and as you cannot see me, next time we meet I can put
my question with equal force.'

'I see you very well,' said Lady William, 'and I should not
have known you. How could I? You were a child, and now you
are a man. And I was a girl, and now I am an old woman.
Your mother will see innumerable changes. How is she? It was
kind of her to send you to see me so soon.'

'Ah!' said the visitor, 'I said I was at a double disadvantage,
but it seems there are more. She did not send me to see you,
dear lady. I came on my proper feet, and by my proper will.

Mamma is not changed, but she no longer sends little Leo on her errands. He has certain instincts of his own.'

'Well, then, it was a kind instinct that brought you here,' said Lady William.

'I am not so sure of that — an instinct very kind to myself: I foresee little pleasure in the society of home, you will not be offended if I say so. But there was one quarter in which I knew I could indemnify myself, so long as you permit it, madame.'

He spoke very much like a Frenchman throughout, Mab thought, who sat breathlessly looking on, rather hostile but exceedingly curious, thinking it was as good as a play; but the 'madame' was altogether French, not that harsh 'madam' of the English, which comes at you like a stone, and which may mean more animosity than respect.

'We have not, indeed, much variety here,' said Lady William; 'you will soon exhaust our little resources. But then we are not very far from town, and I advise you to keep the house full. After Paris, Watcham! It is perhaps rather too much of a difference, unless you have a very strong head.'

'My head is indifferent strong. I can stand a good deal in the way of change, from ten degrees below zero to twenty over it. Ah! I forgot you go by that other impossible standard of Fahrenheit here. You have not presented me to the young lady whom I see by glimpses, as if we were all in a fairy tale.'

'My daughter, Mab; and, as you have already divined Mab, the gentleman whom we were talking of, and who remains in my mind ten years old, in a velvet suit, with lace, and, I believe, curls——'

He waved his hand. 'Spare me the curls, they were the *supplice* of my early days. Picture to yourself, Miss Mab—Mab! how curious to put Miss before that name! One might as well say Miss Titania.'

'One does sometimes in this day of fantastic names. There are Miss Enids and Miss Imogenes.'

'I was saying, picture to yourself a very plain little boy, with very common hair, exactly like every other little boy's, only worse —in long curls upon his wretched shoulders! they made my life a burden to me. Mamma is a most interesting woman—not at all like other people—I am exceptionally happy in having had such a companion for my life—but so long as I was a child there were drawbacks. By degrees things right themselves,' he added after a brief dramatic pause. 'I have no longer curls, nor am I sent to call, and we have solved the problem of having two independent rulers in one house.'

There was another pause, which Lady William did not herself wish to break. Perhaps his voice, the atmosphere about him, produced recollections that were too strong for her : or perhaps Leo Swinford by himself did not interest Lady William. It was Mab who blurted forth suddenly, with a juvenile instinct of relieving the tension of the silence, a piece of information.

'I saw you just now in the village, Mr. Swinford. I wondered if it was you. We don't see many strangers in the village—at least at this time of the year. I said to myself: unless it is some one from the Hall, I don't know who it can be.'

'Some one from the Hall is very vague, Miss Mab—Queen Mab, if I may say so. I hope you had heard of me, myself, an individual, before that vague conjecture arose.'

'No, I can't say I had,' said Mab bluntly. 'Mother said something to-day to Aunt Jane about Leo wanting a wife; but then, you see, I didn't know who Leo was.'

'If that is the only attitude in which I am to be presented to my new world! but I don't want a wife,' he added plaintively, addressing himself to the dark corner in which Lady William was seated. 'However, I am Leo,' he added, turning to the girl again with such a bow as Mab had never seen before.

III

MANY messages passed between the Rectory and the Cottage the next morning on the subject of the visit to the Hall. How shall we go? Would it be best to get the fly, as there is a prospect of rain? Would it do to go in the pony-carriage, as the clouds were making a lift? Finally, when the sun came out, would it be best to walk? Emmy and Florry Plowden were running to and fro all the morning with notes and messages. Emmy (who was going) was anxious and serious on this great subject. It would be such a pity to get wet. 'It is true it is nearly the end of the winter, and our dresses are not in their first freshness; but it is so disagreeable to go into a new house feeling mouldy and damp. First impressions are of so much consequence. Don't you think so, aunt? and Mrs. Swinford is Parisian, and accustomed to everything in the last fashion.'

'You might as well go draggled as not,' said Florence, 'if that is what you are thinking of: for she will see there is not much of the last fashion about you.'

'Aunt always looks as if she were the leader of the fashion wherever she goes,' said Emily proudly. She it was who was conscious of being the only one who was like her aunt.

'Thank you for such a pretty compliment,' said Lady William; 'but Florry is right, I am sorry to say. We shall all be so much below her standard at our best, that a little more or less doesn't matter. Still, without reference to Mrs. Swinford or her impressions, it is unpleasant to get wet.'

'Then you vote for the fly,' said Emmy with satisfaction, 'that is what I always thought you would do. One does not get blown about, one comes out fresh, without having one's hair all wild and marks of mud upon one's shoes. Thanks, Aunt Emily, you always decide for what is best.'

In an hour, however, they returned, Florry, who was not going,

C

leading the way. 'Mamma thinks as it's so much brighter our own pony-chaise will do. It's much nicer being in the air than boxed up in a fly. And she thinks it would make so much fuss, setting all the village talking, if the fly was ordered, and it was known everywhere that she was going to the Hall.'

'I thought she wished it to be known.'

'Oh, of course,' said Emmy, who was the aggrieved party, 'mamma wishes everything to be known. She says a clergyman's family should always live in a glass house and all that sort of thing. And to have the pony-chaise out, and everybody seeing where we are going, will be just the same thing.'

'At all events it's your own private carriage, and not a nasty hired fly,' said Florence. ' "Mrs. Plowden's carriage at the door," and you needn't explain it's a shandrydan.'

And the unfeeling girl laughed, as was her way : for it was not she who was going to have her fringe disarranged, and the locks at the back blown about by driving in the pony-carriage in the whistling March breeze.

'Tell your mother I think the pony-chaise will do quite well if she likes it ; everybody knows what sort of a carriage a country clergyman can afford to keep.'

'But you are not a country clergyman, Aunt Emily.'

'Heaven forbid !' that lady said.

Next time it was Emily alone who ran 'across,' as they called it. 'Mamma thinks on the whole we might walk. The roads have dried up beautifully, and it's not far. And walking is always correct in the country, isn't it, aunt ? '

'It is always correct anywhere, Emmy, when you have no other way to go.'

'Ah, but we have two other ways to go ! There is the fly, which I should prefer, as it protects one most, and there's our own pony-chaise. It cannot be supposed to be for the want of means of driving, Aunt Emily, if we pleased.'

'Of course not,' said Lady William with great gravity. 'And there is a gipsy van somewhere about. I have always thought I should like to drive about the country in a gipsy van.'

Emmy gave her aunt a look of reproach : but by this time her sister had arrived with Mrs. Plowden's ultimatum. 'If the sun comes out mamma will call for you at the door, if you will please to be ready by three ; but if it is overcast she will come in the fly. So that is all settled, I hope.'

Mab had maintained a great calm during all these searchings of heart. She was not going, and had she been going it would have been a matter of the greatest indifference to her, consciously a plain, and what is still more dreadful to the imagination, a fat girl, whether her hair was blown about or not, and what first impression Mrs. Swinford or even Leo Swinford might form of her. As for Leo Swinford, indeed, in face of the fact that he had called at the Cottage the night before, she felt for him something of that familiarity which breeds contempt: and how it could matter to anybody what he thought was to Mab's youthful soul a wonder not to be expressed.

'What are you so anxious about, after all?' she said. 'If your hair is untidy, what of that? Everybody in Watcham knows exactly how your hair looks, Emmy, whether it is just newly done and tidy, or whether it is hanging about your ears.'

'I hope it never hangs about my ears,' said Emmy primly, yet with indignation. If there was one thing upon which she prided herself, it was the tidiness in which she stood superior over all her peers.

'Oh, I've seen it, after an afternoon at tennis, just as wild as other people's,' said Mab, 'and everybody in the village has seen it too.'

'But then,' said the other sister, 'these are not people in the village; they're new people, and there's a great deal in a first impression—at least, so Emmy thinks.'

'A first impression—upon whom?' said Mab, with all the severity of her age. Seventeen, being as yet scarcely in it, is a severe critic of the ages over twenty which are in possession of the field.

There was a pause, which Florence broke by one of her disconcerting laughs.

'Mab, you are too much of a baby. Don't you know the Swinfords are going to entertain? Perhaps you don't know what that means. They are going to give all sorts of parties, and we'll not be asked if—we don't please.'

'Whom?' said Mab again.

And then there came another laugh from Florence, and an offended 'What can you mean, Mab? Mrs. Swinford, to be sure. It is only she who could invite girls to make the house pleasant, and,' said Emily, with a little dignity, 'it is as much for you as for me.'

'Oh! I thought it might be Leo Swinford,' said the audacious Mab, 'who wants a wife, mother says. But he says himself no, he doesn't want anything of the kind.'

'Mab!' said Lady William, in a warning tone from behind.

'He didn't say it in any secret,' said Mab, 'not the least.

He didn't tell you "But this is between ourselves," or "You won't mention it," or anything of the kind, as people say when they confide in you. He said it right out.'

'Who said it right out?' cried Emily. It was their turn to question now, and they looked at each other after they had looked, in consternation, at Mab—asking each other, with their eyes, awe-stricken, what could this little minx mean, and how did she know?

'As for Leo Swinford, I don't think anything at all of him,' said Mab. 'He was got up in a fur coat yesterday, when it was not cold at all, only blustering; and he had shiny shoes on and red socks showing, as if he were got up for the evening—to walk about the Watcham roads.'

'Do you mean to say,' said Emily severely, crushing these pretensions in the bud, 'that *you* have seen Mr. Swinford, Mab? And how did you know it was Mr. Swinford—it might have been some excursionist or other down here by a cheap train.'

'A Marshall and Snelgrove young man,' said Florence. 'Absurd! red socks and evening shoes and a fur coat.'

'And we have always understood Mr. Swinford was a gentleman,' Emily said. 'But it is not at all wonderful at Mab's age to take up such a foolish idea. For a new person in the village always looks as if there was an adventure behind him, doesn't he, aunt?—and Mab is such a child still.'

'However,' said Lady William, 'I don't know how it came about, but it was Leo Swinford, my dear. I knew him very well when he was a child, and he sought me out because, I suppose, he didn't know any one else here.'

There was another pause of consternation and disappointment: for to think that Mab had seen this new personage before any of them, and that he had seen Mab, was very disconcerting and disagreeable to these young ladies. But then they reflected that Mab did not count—a little fat, roundabout thing, looking even younger than her age, and that if it was ordained that they should be forestalled by any one, better Mab than another. The horrid little thing! But then it was a good sign for future intimacy that he knew Aunt Emily, and had come in this way at once to her house.

'I am sure,' said Emmy, 'he might have come to the Rectory. Papa would have been very glad to see him, and the clergyman is generally the first person—unless when there is a squire. And of course he is the squire himself. But then Aunt Emily is the highest in rank, everybody knows.'

'My rank had not much to do with it. All that Leo knows

of me was as Emily Plowden, the Rector's daughter, just as you are now, Emmy,' said Lady William, with a little laugh. She was going out of the room as she spoke, and turned her head to give them one glance from the door. If it occurred to Lady William that the second Emily Plowden was not precisely like the first, she did not give vent to that opinion. But it was a little ludicrous from her point of view to be told, as she was told so often, that Emily was 'her very image'—'just what I remember you at her age.' It was with, perhaps, a little glance of satire in her eyes that she flung this parting word at her niece. But the Emily Plowden of the present generation understood no jest. She blushed a little with conscious pleasure and pride, and threw up her head. Now, Lady William had a throat like a swan, but Emily's could be described no otherwise than as a long neck, at the top of which her head jerked forward with a motion not unlike the darting movement of a hen.

'So you have really seen him, Mab? Think of having a man, a real man, a young man in Watcham! Were you much excited? Had you presence of mind enough to note any particulars as to eyes and hair and height, and so forth—as well as the red socks and the shiny shoes?'

'Oh, he's fair, I think,' said Mab indifferently, 'a sort of no-coloured hair like mine, and the rest to correspond. He was very talky and jokey with mother, just as if she had been a young lady. But he said little to me.'

'It was not to be expected,' said Emily, 'that a gentleman and a man of the world like Mr. Swinford would find much to say to you; and I wonder that he should have remembered Aunt Emily. I have never heard that men like that cared much for old ladies: but no doubt it was because he knew nobody else, and just to pass the time.'

'Mother is not an old lady,' said Mab; 'if I were a man I should like her better than all of you girls put together. You are, on the whole, rather silly things. You don't talk out of your own heads, but watch other people's eyes to see what will please them. I don't call that talking! You never would have found out what would please that man if you had looked into his eyes for a year. Now mother never minds—she says what comes into her head: and if any one contradicts her she just goes on saying the other thing.'

This somewhat vague description seemed to make a certain impression upon the young ladies, who probably were able to fill up the outlines for themselves. Emily gave a little sigh.

'Conversation's quite a gift,' she said, 'and it's always difficult with a new person till you know their tastes. I suppose Mr. Swinford knows about pictures and that sort of thing, and unless you've somebody to tell you when you go to the exhibitions it's so hard to know which are really the good ones. Then books— Mudie never sends us any of the best. He puts all the common novels into the country parcels. At the Hall they will get everything that comes out.'

'He said nothing about books or pictures either,' said Mab— 'Yes, by the bye, he's going to lend mother some—but they're French ones——'

'French ones!' said the cousins; and then there was a pause of consternation. 'Papa once said if he had his will no French novel should ever come into the parish.'

'Ah!' said Mab, 'but then I suppose Mr. Swinford didn't write and ask uncle what he should bring.'

Emily remained gazing out of the window with a troubled air.

'We shall never know what to say if that is the sort of thing; and as for going to their parties, if they are all made up of—— Mamma, too, who never read a French book in her life. We had a little practice in the schoolroom, when we had Fräulein, don't you remember, Flo—— Who was it we read? It was all long speeches, and one could never make out what they were about.'

'And they sounded exactly like German when Fräulein read them. I never could tell which was which. But I know where the books are, and perhaps if you learned one of the speeches and said it to Mr. Swinford, he might like it, don't you know.'

'I was not, of course, thinking of Mr. Swinford, but of Mrs. Swinford,' said Emily, frowning.

'And you think you will get a chance of talking to her with mamma and Aunt Emily there?'

'Well,' said Emily, 'at least I can show her that I know my place, and how an English girl behaves.'

'I wish you would not wrangle,' said Mab; 'it was rather fun listening to mother and him: they said no speeches out of books—I believe after all what they said was chiefly chaff. Mother is a wonderful hand at chaff. She looks so quiet all the time, and goes on till you are nearly jumping. But he liked it, and laughed, and gave her as good. There was one thing he said,' added Mab demurely, 'which wasn't chaff, and which you might like to hear. He said at once he didn't want——'

'What! I'm sure I don't care what he wants or doesn't want

—a gardener perhaps? and papa has just heard of one he wanted
to recommend.'

'A wife!' cried Mab, her blue eyes quickening a little with
mischief. 'Mother asked if he did, and he said he didn't. Perhaps she had some one she wanted to recommend.'

'Perhaps,' said Florence, coming to her sister's aid; 'that is
the way in France, the parents arrange it all. I shouldn't mind
at all—that. I give my consent. It would be nice to be the
bride's relations and always about the house. If you'll promise to
ask nice people and always us to meet them—and be kind about
sending the carriage for us, and that sort of thing, for papa hates
a bill for flys—I shall give my consent.'

'Me!' cried Mab, indignant, 'I would not marry Leo Swinford, not if—— I'd rather marry the silliest of the curates.
I'd rather——' She stopped short breathless, unable to find a
stronger alternative.

'Then what a good thing for you,' said Florry, 'that he
doesn't want a wife!'

'If you think it is nice,' said Emily, 'for young girls to talk
about gentlemen, and whether they want wives or not, as if wives
were sold at the shop at so much a pound—I am not of that
kind of mind: and Aunt Emily would not like it any more than
mamma. Good-bye, you two. I have got to go home and get
ready, whatever you may have to do.'

And thus Emily retired with the honours of war. If there
was any one who had formed plans on the subject of Leo Swinford it was she; not plans, indeed, which are dreadful foreign
things, but just a floating idea such as an English girl might
entertain, that if a young man and a young woman are thrown
much together, why, then certain consequences might follow.
One never could tell what might happen, as Mrs. Plowden herself,
who was the very essence of propriety, did not hesitate to say.

THE road was a little muddy, but not much ; and it was quite possible by taking a little trouble in walking to keep your boots quite clean. Under the trees in the avenue this was not so easy, for it was more sheltered, and the wind could not get in to sweep through and through every opening. There is a pond, or lake, in the grounds, as everybody knows, which had been the delight of the neighbourhood for the skating in winter, all the long time the Swinfords had been absent.

'I wonder if they will still let us skate now they are at home,' said Emily, as they walked round the bank over the crisped and extremely living water, which did not look under the breeze as if it had ever been bound by chains of frost.

'Winter is a long way off,' said Mrs. Plowden, who was a little blown by her walk. She desired her companions to pause a little and look at the view. 'I don't want,' she said, panting, 'to go in out of breath. These sort of people have quite advantage enough over one in their fine houses without going in panting like a washer-woman.' She added, 'Winter's a long way off, and, as we never knew whether they gave permission at all, or if it was only Howell at the gate, I wouldn't say anything about it, Emmy, if I were you.'

Mrs. Plowden's loss of breath partly proceeded from the fact that she had been talking all the way. She had no want of sub-jects : the past history of Mrs. Swinford, whom they were going to visit, which she did not know ; but that made little difference ; and the character of her son, which nobody in Watcham knew ; and the precautions to be taken in arranging their intercourse with the family so as to get all that might be advantageous out of that intercourse without in any way compromising themselves in respect to that which might be unsatisfactory. 'If there should be any matrimonial entanglement,' said Mrs. Plowden, 'or that sort of thing, of course it would be for the girl's family to make every inquiry. But I daresay as he's half a Frenchman, and not at all one of our sort, nothing of that kind will happen : and it is time enough to take it into consideration when it does.'

'Quite time enough,' said Lady William, very decidedly, 'especially as nothing can be more unlikely.'

'That is just what I say. Of course when young people are thrown together one never knows what may happen : and it is to be hoped that Mr. Swinford may see how much better it would be to settle down with a nice English wife than to bring over a French mademoiselle, who never would understand English ways. But it will be time enough, don't you think so, Emily? for I always acknowledge you know better than me when it is anything French that is in question—with your languages, you know, and all that.'

'My languages won't help me much with Leo Swinford, who is just as English as I am—nor with his mother, who is cosmopolitan, and of no country at all.'

'That's just one of your sayings, Emily, for how could a woman be of no country at all? What I'm most concerned for is whether they will come to church : and I can see it's much on James's mind, though he never says anything ; for a great house like that, almost the only great house in the parish, sets such a dreadful example if they don't go to church. One hears of it all through the place. If the people at the Hall don't go, why should we? I tell them it's quite different—that the people at the Hall have many opportunities, and are deeply interested all the same, and all that ; whereas if poor people don't pay attention to their religious duties, what is to become of them? But often they don't seem to see it.'

'I shouldn't see it if I was in their place. I thought that in Christianity there was no respect of persons.'

'Oh ! my dear Emily, you ought to know better than to bring up that common argument against us, and your brother the Rector of the parish. Of course there's no respect of persons ! But if Mrs. Swinford comes to church she will be shown into the Hall pew, and old Mrs. Lloyd will just find a place for herself, if she is early enough, in the free seats. How could anybody do otherwise? We must be practical. Old Mary Lloyd would be very uncomfortable if she were to sit down with you or me. She is much more at home in the free seats. And with the poor people it is only their individual selves that are in question, whereas the great lady sets such an example : and there are all the servants and the servants' families, and one doesn't know how many——'

'I think you may set your mind at ease, Jane. Mrs. Swinford will come to church.'

'You take a load off my mind, Emily; but it is many, many years since you have seen her, and people change a great deal. I sometimes feel even myself, you know, an inclination to stay in bed on Sunday mornings. It is a thing to be crushed in the bud. If you give in to a headache once, there is no telling where it may land you in the end.'

'But, mamma dear,' said the sympathetic Emmy, 'your headaches are so bad!'

'Hum!' said Mrs. Plowden doubtfully. 'Yes, my headaches are bad sometimes: but it is a thing that one should set one's face against. It ought to be crushed in the bud—on Sundays, I mean; it does not matter so much on other days. And Mr. Swinford, Emily. I hear that you have seen him already. Now, I wonder what made him go to see you——'

'Why shouldn't he?' said Lady William, with a laugh.

'Oh, well, you know! I should have thought a gentleman would have looked up the Rector, or the Archdeacon, or the General, instead of a lady just living in a small way by herself, like you.'

'Mamma, you forget Aunt Emily's rank,' Emmy said in dismay.

'Oh, I never forget her rank!' cried Mrs. Plowden, with a little irritation. 'I hear enough of it, I am sure.'

'The Rector and the Archdeacon and the General are all very important persons. The only thing is that Leo Swinford did not know them, and he knew me.'

'I have always observed that people in that sort of position know everybody,' said Mrs. Plowden, 'and, my dear Emily, I don't want to seem censorious, but do you think it is quite *nice* to talk of a young man like that by his Christian name? *I* don't even know his Christian name. It may be Leonard or it may be Lionel, or it may be——'

'Oh! Leopold, mamma!'

'I don't see what you have got to do with it, Emmy. If your aunt knows him so well as that, *you* don't know him—and perhaps never will if he is that kind of man!'

'Don't you think,' said Lady William, with that perfect composure of which she was mistress, 'that we might stop for a moment again and look at the view——'

'Oh, if you feel the hill, Emily—it is a little steep—I don't mind sitting down for a moment, if you feel you want it. It is very pretty here,' said Mrs. Plowden, panting; 'the water—through the trees—and the lodge—in the distance—with the wisteria just beginning to shoot.'

The pause made here was a few minutes in duration, for Mrs. Plowden had heated herself much by her argument and by clambering up the ascent—which was, indeed, only a very gentle ascent. At last, however, the party reached the door.   As they came up sounds were audible inside, which disclosed themselves, when the door was hastily opened, as produced by a game of billiards, played by Mr. Leo Swinford, and—oh ! terrible sight—his butler : though for the first moment Mrs. Plowden's eager intelligence had not taken in this fact.   She said, politely, that she was afraid they had driven the gentleman away——

'Oh !' said Leo with a laugh, 'it's only Morris—let me fulfil his functions and take you to my mother.'   He offered the Rector's wife his arm, but she drew modestly back.

'My sister-in-law, Mr. Swinford.   Oh, I hope I know what is *comme-il-faut*.   I could not go before Lady William.'   Mrs. Plowden had a flash of exultation in thinking of that word—*comme-il-faut*.   It was something like an inspiration that brought it to her lips in the very nick of time.

The drawing-room at the Hall was a large room in three divisions, divided with pillars of sham marble with gilded capitals. It was too bright, notwithstanding the heaviness of the decorations. Large windows almost from the roof to the floor poured in floods of afternoon light, and shone pitiless upon the lady who rose languidly to meet her visitors, keeping her back to the light.   She was a tall woman, exceedingly worn and thin, but with a great deal of grace in her movements, though she was old.   Her age was the first thing which the eager rural visitors noted, for it was a sort of age which had never come under their observation before. She was dressed picturesquely in dark velvet with such folds and cunning lines as they had never dreamed of, and which plunged them into anxious questioning whether that might be the latest fashion.   If so, it was unlike anything that Miss Singer had in her books and papers, or even Madame Mantz, who was Miss Singer's great example in town ; and her hair, which had not a white thread in it, was uncovered.   No cap on her head ! and approaching seventy, Mrs. Plowden thought, making a rapid calculation upon the facts she knew.   Mrs. Swinford stepped forward a little with a faint cry of 'Emily' when Lady William appeared, and took her, with every appearance of cordiality, into her arms, and they kissed, or at least Mrs. Swinford touched Lady William's cheeks one after the other, while the Plowdens made a respectful circle round and looked on.   'This is indeed kind,' Mrs. Swinford said.   The ladies were so bent upon the aspect of the mistress of the Hall that they did not observe how pale Lady William was, or how little part she took in the embrace. 'And though, of course, she could not take us into her arms,' Mrs. Plowden said after, 'never having set eyes on us before, she was quite as cordial, and hoped she would see a great deal of us, and that it was so nice to feel that one was coming among people who felt like old friends.' 'I have heard so much of you through Emily,' was what Mrs. Swinford really did say ; to which Emily was so disagreeable as to make no reply. And then they all sat down, and Mrs. Plowden began to make conversation, as in duty bound.

'We are so glad to see you in your own house, Mrs. Swinford. The Rector has always said it was so cold like to feel that there was no one in the Hall. A squire's house makes such a difference. The poor people think so much of it, and the middle people are always looking out for an example ; and of course the higher class, it is yourself—so you being here is, if I may say so, of the greatest consequence to everybody, and I do hope it will be agreeable to you.'

'You are very good,' said Mrs. Swinford, with a motion of her head. 'It never occurred to me that it could be of any importance except to ourselves.'

'Oh, I assure you it is of the greatest consequence. What we want in England is the higher classes to set a good example, to keep back those horrid democratic ways, and show us how we ought to behave. We are very loyal to a good example in England, Mrs. Swinford. You have been so long away, perhaps you may not remember how in a well-ordered parish the people are taught to look up to those who are above them——'

'But suppose we do not set a good example?' said the lady, with a languid smile. She was looking at Lady William, who sat by, saying little, and who was in the full flood of the light, which she was quite able to bear. The elder woman, who was not, bestowed an interested attention upon the friend whom she had greeted so warmly—not even a look or movement, nor even a fold of the very plain black dress, which showed how little means of adornment the other possessed, yet how little it mattered to her whether she was adorned or not, escaped her. Mrs. Swinford was very deeply learned in all these arts, in all that tended to preserve beauty and enhance it. She had been a beauty herself in her day, and was very reluctant to part with it. She looked at her old friend with an eager, yet veiled attention, observing all that was in her favour, and the few things against her. Poorly dressed, but looking none the worse, the black being in its way a kind of veil

even of its own imperfections : the charm of the face enhanced by
sorrow and trouble and many experiences, the outlines uninjured,
the cheek almost as purely oval as in youth, the eyes as sweet, the
hair—it had a touch of gray, perhaps, but that is no harm to such
a woman, a woman not standing upon her appearance, perhaps not
thinking much of it—at least, giving herself the air of not thinking
of it at all. Mrs. Swinford did not believe that any woman was
ever indifferent to her appearance, or not thinking of it. It did
not matter much to herself at the present moment, when there was
no one she cared to affect or charm, no one worth the lifting of a
finger ; and yet she was not indifferent to her own aspect, and why
should Lady William be ? Lady William ? A strange smile
crossed the elder lady's face as she remembered what was now
Emily Plowden's name. She said to her in the middle of Mrs.
Plowden's speech, to which she paid no attention, with a way that
women of the world have, 'How strange it is to think of you,
Emily, by that name !'

The entire company pricked up its ears. Mrs. Plowden stopped
short, much discomfited, in her explanation of what was the
Rector's opinion, in which Mrs. Swinford had interrupted her with
such absolute indifference as to what she was saying. And Emmy
raised her long neck, remembering always keenly that it was she
who was now Emily Plowden ; and even young Mr. Swinford, who
had been talking to Lady William, raised his head with sudden
attention, glancing from her to his mother. Lady William herself
coloured suddenly, and with an unusual air asked, 'What name ?'

'What but your married name, my dear ?' Mrs. Swinford said,
and laughed low, but very distinctly, with her eyes fixed upon her
guest.

'Ah, yes,' said Lady William, returning the look, 'you are
more used to my husband's name than mine.'

Nobody had the least idea what this passage of arms meant—
not even Mr. Swinford, who kept looking from his mother to Lady
William with a questioning look. As for the other ladies, they
stared severely, and did not attempt to understand. Mrs. Swinford was a little rude, and so was Lady William. They did not
show the fine manners which ought to belong to fine ladies. On
the whole, Mrs. Plowden thought it might have been better for her
to make her first call alone. Mrs. Swinford had talked to her
quite sweetly, she said afterwards, but Emily and she did not seem
to be on such good terms. It is always a mistake, Mrs. Plowden
thought, to depend upon any one else in the way of introduction.
The Rector's wife in her own parish is the equal of any one. And

as for French, in which Emily was believed to be so superior, French was no more wanted, she reported to the Rector, 'than between you and me.'

'I daresay,' she said, when this little sensation was over, 'that you find our poor Emily much changed. Such a difference for her to come from the society in which she was, and everybody so superior, to our little village again : but, of course, all these things are little to the loss of a dear husband, which is the greatest a woman can have to bear——'

'You speak most eloquently, Mrs. Plowden,' said Mrs. Swinford, 'the very greatest a woman can be called upon to bear.'

'It is very kind of you,' said Lady William, 'to feel so much for me.'

'Yes, yes, the very greatest : and she has taken it so well. But naturally it makes a great difference. My daughter Emmy is considered by everybody to be extremely like her aunt,' said Mrs. Plowden, directing with a look the attention of the party to Emmy, who bridled and drew up her long neck with that little forward movement which was like a peck, but did not at all mean anything of the kind.

Mrs. Swinford gave poor Emmy a look—one of those full, undisguised looks which again women of the world alone permit themselves ; but she made no remark—which was very eloquent, more so than many remarks. She said, after a time, with the air of a person who has been puzzling her brains to keep up a conversation :

'You have other daughters ?' adding to her question a smile of great sweetness, as if there was nothing in the world she was more interested in.

'One,' said Mrs. Plowden, much gratified, 'Florence, named after another aunt, and more like my side of the house. And I have a son, who we hoped would have gone into the Church ; but he is like so many young men of the present day, he has religious difficulties. And the Rector thinks it is not right to force his inclinations, especially into a sacred profession. I have great confidence in my husband's judgment, but I don't quite agree with him on this point ; for I think if you only use a little pressure upon them when they are young, they are often most truly grateful to you afterwards, when they begin to understand the claims of life. I wonder,' said Mrs. Plowden, with a glance at Leo, who was once more leaning over Lady William's chair, 'whether you agree with me ? I should like to have the support of your opinion, for you must have experience in dealing with the young.'

Mrs. Swinford had delicately intimated her entire indifference to the homily of the clergyman's wife for some time past, but she was recalled by this appeal, which amused her.

'Yes,' she said, 'I have a son; but I do not think I have attempted to force his inclinations,' she added, after a pause.

'Ah, then you would agree with James! I am sorry, for it would have been a great support to me; but we must all judge for ourselves in these matters—and in such a question as entering a sacred profession——'

'Leo,' said Mrs. Swinford, 'we are forgetting: our habits are not yet quite English. Offer Lady William some tea.'

'Oh,' said Mrs. Plowden, with a start, 'let me pour it out! Or Emily will do so, I am sure, with pleasure, if you will permit. It is so awkward for a gentleman——'

'Pray do not trouble yourself. Leo can manage it very well, or he can ring for some one if he wants help. And you, Emily, have a daughter, too?'

'Yes, I have a daughter.'

'Quite young? She can scarcely be grown up. I do not remember many dates, but there are two or three—— Eighteen perhaps, or a little less, or more?'

'She will not be eighteen for some months.'

'And pretty? Like you? Do you see anything of the family? Do they take any notice of the child?'

'To tell the truth,' said Lady William, 'my child and I have been very happy in our cottage, and we have not thought much of any family—save our own very small family of two.'

She had flushed with suppressed anger, but with an evident desire to keep her feelings concealed, answered the questions very deliberately and in a tone of studied calm.

'Ah, I recognise you in that! always proud: but not prudent. One must not despise a family, especially when it has a fine title. You ought to consider, my dear Emily, how important it may be for the child; your excellent sister-in-law,' said Mrs. Swinford, turning with her wonted smile to Mrs. Plowden, 'thoroughly recognises that.'

Mrs. Plowden, thus unexpectedly referred to, was taken in an undignified moment, when she had just begun to sip her first mouthful of very hot tea. She had felt that a second interruption in the very midst of what she had been saying was too much to be forgiven; but on being appealed to in this marked manner she changed her mind, and perceived that it was only Mrs. Swinford's way. She swallowed the hot tea hastily, to her great discomfort, in her haste to respond.

'Indeed I do,' she said fervently, coughing a little. 'Indeed I do—— I tell Emily often I would put my pride in my pocket, and insist on having Mab invited to make acquaintance with her father's family. And she's such a Pakenham, more like the Marquis than any daughter he has.'

'Oh, she's such a Pakenham!' said Mrs. Swinford, with a faint laugh.

'I think, Jane,' said Lady William, 'that you are forgetting we walked here, and that it is time we were going back.'

'Oh, please, let these dear ladies finish their tea. Leo, Miss Plowden will take some cake. I am more interested than I can tell to hear that your child does not take after you, but is like the Pakenhams.' The laugh was very soft, quite low, most ladylike, and, indeed, what is called poetically, silver in tone. 'What an ill-advised little mortal!' she said.

'WELL,' said Florence to Mab, 'we two are left alone. We're the young ones, we have to keep out of the way. But I am sure the Swinfords would rather have seen you and me than Emmy. We are the youngest and we are the most amusing.'

'Oh, please speak for yourself,' said Mab, 'I am not amusing at all.'

Florence looked at her with an air of consideration. 'Well, perhaps that is true,' she said; 'you have a turn-up nose, and you ought to be lively, but appearances are very deceiving. I wonder what that army of observation will do to-day? I call them our army of observation because they have gone to spy out the land, and decide upon what are the proper lines of strategy. It's quite new to us in Watcham to have a squire's family: and then it is not even a common squire's family. They are such superior people, and their ways are so unlike ours. Shouldn't you say it would be a nice thing in Watcham to have people whose ways are not as our ways?'

'Oh, I don't know,' said Mab, with the indifference of extreme youth, 'we are well enough as we are.'

'It is easy for you to speak, with only Aunt Emily to think of, and your own way—and seventeen,' said Florry, with a sigh. 'I would give something to be seventeen again.'

'Why?' said Mab. 'It is the most ridiculous age—too old to be a child, too young to be anything else. One cares no more for dolls and that sort of thing, and one doesn't care either for what the old people talk about. How they go on and on and talk! as if anybody minded.'

'You shouldn't listen,' said Florry.

'Sometimes one can't help it. Sometimes there's a bit of story in it, and then it's nice—only in that case they say, 'You remember so-and-so: what a tragedy that was!' and then the other

D

wags his or her head, and they shut up, not reflecting that you're dying to know.'

'There's something of that sort about Mrs. Swinford,' said Florence; 'there was quite a talk about calling before mamma made up her mind. Mrs. FitzStephen came in about a week or two ago, and she said, "I have come to know what you're going to do?" And mamma said, without even asking what she meant, "I am very much perplexed, and I don't know in the least." And then papa, standing in front of the fire, with his coat-tails on his arms, you know, grumbles out—"You had better let it alone." "Let what alone?" mamma called out quickly, and he just stared and said nothing. At this mamma said, "They are sure to entertain a great deal; they are people that can't live without company." And Mrs. FitzStephen, she said, "Oh, I don't care for such company." And then mamma replied, with her grand Roman matron air, "You have no young people to think of, Mrs. FitzStephen."'

Florence was a tolerable mimic, and she 'did' those characters, with whom Mab was intimately acquainted, in an exceedingly broad style, and with considerable effect.

'Florry, you oughtn't to take off your own father and mother.'

'Who then?' cried Florry. 'I must take such as I have; I don't know such lots of people. Wait till the Swinfords come on the scene and I'll do them.'

'Ah, he's not so easy to do. The others you've known all your life, and they are all the same kind of people: but you never saw any one like—*that* gentleman. The General would give you no clue to him, nor anybody you know here. He is like nobody you ever saw; he is—I don't know what to say.'

'You are always thinking of that fur coat of his and patent leather shoes. I wonder if they will see him to-day? They had much better have taken you and me, Mab. Emmy may be the eldest, but she will never make any impression. A man like that will never look twice at her.'

'Why should he?' said Mab, raising her eyebrows, 'or what does it matter whether he does or not?'

'Oh, Mab, you silly little thing,' said Florence, 'you must know, however silly you may be, that it matters a great deal. Think only what it would matter! To have a girl settled like that—rich, able to do what she pleased, one's sister; only think; or still more if it was one's self. We've got twenty pounds a year each for our clothes, fancy! And Mrs. Swinford will have hundreds—she will have just as much as she likes, and whatever she likes, and a grand house where she could ask the Queen her-self: and power—power to get Jim settled somehow, to make him sure of his living: perhaps to get something better for papa, and save mamma some of the anxiety she has. And if anything happened to *them*, why, there would be a home for—for—the other one, don't you see? Oh!' said Florence, with a deep-drawn breath that seemed to come from the very depth of her being, 'it would matter so much that it is wicked, it is dreadful, to think that a man could make such a change in another creature's life only by looking at her and throwing his handkerchief. It's immoral to dangle a chance like that under a poor girl's very nose.'

Mab was not unimpressed with this terrible truth. She felt also that to contemplate the differences that might ensue if one of the daughters of the Rectory became Mrs. Swinford of the Hall was more than words could say. The very possibility caught at her breath. She made a momentary pause of awe, and then she said, ' But he never will, he never will!'

' Emmy, no,' said Florence; ' no—she's too—she's not enough —oh! she's impossible, and I can see that very well for myself. Emmy is—she's one's sister, and she is as nice as ever was. You know she is a nice girl! But she was never made for that; whereas if they had taken you and me——'

' Don't say me, please,' said Mab, reddening all over that blunt-featured and irregular little face, which was unfortunately so like the Pakenhams. The flush was quite hot, and discomposed her. ' I'm impossible, too—much more impossible,' she said.

' Oh! you stand upon your family,' said Florence, ' and upon your mother's position, and all that; but you may take my word for it, that if you were the Marquis's own daughter instead of a disrep—— I mean instead of his brother's, you would have to do the very same thing. If it is because you're not pretty, that's true enough; but there's never any telling what may take a man like that, and you've got plenty of " go " in you, Mab, though I don't want to flatter you: and even in looks a year or two may make a great difference——'

' Will you stop! will you stop, please!' said Mab; ' Florry, stop! You make me ashamed. You make me feel as if——'

' You were going in for it, too?' said Florence calmly. ' It makes me crazy, too, sometimes to think that—— But so long as girls are poor, and a man, just because they please him, can change everything for them—how can we help it? Even if you were to work, as people say, what difference would it make? I could perhaps make my living—and Emmy—— But dear,

dear, to think of the Hall beside any little breadwinning of
ours——'

'Don't talk so, *please*,' cried Mab, with a shiver. She was
not a visionary at all, nor had she any sentiment to speak of.
But she was very young, still something between a girl and a boy,
and ashamed to hear those revelations which she only half understood ; or, rather, did not understand at all.

'Well, one needn't talk,' said Florry, with a slight emphasis
on the word. 'But though you mayn't talk of it, you can't stop
a thing from being true.'

'Let's go out for a walk,' said Mab, 'a long walk, down by
the Baron's Wood and up by Durham Hill ; or let's go out on the
river for a pull. Let us do something—one can't stay quiet all
this bright afternoon.'

'I want so much to see them when they come back,' said
Florry. 'I want to know what they think of him—if they saw
him : and whether Emmy made any impression, and what happened.'

'What could happen ? Do you expect her to come home
engaged to him ?' said Mab. 'However well things may go, they
could not go so quickly as that.'

'I am not a fool,' said Florry, with indignation. She stood
at the little gate looking out wistfully along the road by which
the ladies had gone. The great trees hung over the wall which
bounded there the nearest corner of the demesne of the Swinfords ; the lodge and gate were just round the corner out of sight.
It was too soon to expect them to come back. 'Unless Mrs.
Swinford had been out,' said Florry. 'She might be out, you
know, and then they'd be back directly.'

'She never goes out,' said Mab ; 'it's too cold for her here.'

'Or she might not receive them very well, and then they
would only stay a few minutes. You are so indifferent, you don't
care a bit what has happened : and I am on pins and needles till
I know.'

'Then I shall go for a walk by myself.'

'Don't do that,' said Florry, putting out her hand to stay her
cousin. She stood thus for a moment with her head turned towards the Hall, but her hand clutching Mab, gazing in one direction
while her person inclined towards the other. She drew a long
breath, and turned at last from her fixed gaze. 'They must,' she
said, sighing again, 'have stayed to tea. Yes, I'll go on the
river if you like ; but let us go round home on the way and fetch
Jim.'

'Jim!' said Mab.   'He'll want to scull, and I prefer to scull myself.'

'Oh, he doesn't mind. He is as lazy as—— He'll steer and let us pull as long as ever you please. I don't know anybody so lazy as Jim.'

'We should be better by ourselves,' said Mab; 'not that heavy weight in the stern of the boat. When we go by ourselves it's no weight at all.'

'He'll steer,' said Florry; 'it's better to have some one to steer. And don't you see it will keep him out of mischief for one afternoon.'

'You have always another reason behind,' said Mab.   'It never is just the thing you think of, but something at the back of it.'

'Well,' said Florry soothingly, 'it's always so, don't you know, where there's a family. You are so lonely, you have no brothers and sisters. If you do well, then everything is all right. But our being right depends upon so many things: First, if papa is in good humour, and if Jim is going straight. Emmy and I have little questions between ourselves, of course, but these are the chief ones. Now, you have only Aunt Emily to think of, and she neither gets into rages nor goes wrong.'

'I should hope not,' said Mab, indignantly.

'It is all very well for you to throw up your head like that; but we cannot do it. We must manage the best we can. Mab, I do often wish there could be a change.'

This was said when she had at last torn herself away from the road to the Hall, and the two girls were walking towards the Rectory and the river.

'What sort of change?'

'Oh! anything. That Jim should go away, or that he should do something dreadful that couldn't be forgiven—or that Emmy should marry. I would even marry myself—any one! to make a change in the family and get away.'

'I should think, however bad things may be, that they would be worse if you were all separated and not knowing what happened to each other. And what is there so very bad? You are all happy enough for anything one can see.'

'That is the worst of it,' said Florry, 'we are all pretending about everything. It's just one big lie all round—and it isn't right to tell lies, or at least the Bible says so. There is papa breaks every one of the commandments, you know.'

'Florry, don't tell stories of Uncle James; I am very fond of him, and I won't have it.'

'It's true all the same. I don't say it's his fault, it's Jim's fault. Papa swears—he does, he can't help it, at Jim, and then pretends it's something else—the gardener, or the overseer, or the poor people, or even poor Dash—that makes him so angry. Isn't that lying? Then mamma pretends Jim has doubts and won't go in for the Church because of them, when she knows very well what it is really he has been sent down for. And Jim pretends that he is going back to Cambridge next term, and that he is quite friendly with all the dons, and came down to read—I've heard him say that.'

'It may not be true,' said Mab, doubtfully, 'but I shouldn't call that lying—why should we all go and tell that poor Jim has not been good? What have the other people to do with it? Mother says we're not called upon to give them any information—and she just says the same as you do: but that is not to lie.'

'We are all pretending, every one,' said Florry. 'Emmy and I are by way of knowing nothing at all. I believe Jim thinks we don't know anything. So we have to pretend not only to other people, but to him in our very own house, and papa too. I have heard papa say, "Thank Heaven, the girls at least know nothing," and mamma, the dreadful, dreadful liar that she is, thanks Heaven too, though she knows very well that we knew as soon as she did, and that she couldn't keep anything from us two. If you think of that, Mab, and just imagine how we go on pretending to each other, and to everybody.

'Now, if Jim were to go off to a ranche, as people advise, we should all be very wretched, and probably it would be his ruin, but it would be a little relief all the same. Or if Emmy were to get hold of this man—oh, it may be odious, and you may cry out, but it would be a great relief. There would be her wedding to think about, and her things, and altogether it would be a change for everybody; and then she could do something for Jim.'

'Her husband could, you mean?'

'It is the same thing: he would, for his own sake, not to have an idle brother always about. It is killing all of us. One could bear it, perhaps; but four all bearing it—all pretending something different, as I tell you; Emmy and I not to know; mamma and papa that it's another thing altogether that vexes them. Oh! we get exasperated sometimes to that degree, we could tear each other to pieces just to make a change.'

'You are so exaggerated, Florry; mother always says so. You make a mountain out of a molehill.'

'I just wish Aunt Emily had our molehill for a little while—

just for a little while — to see how she liked it. What a
lucky woman she is to have only a girl! Nothing very bad
can ever happen to you, Mab, or come to her through you.
You may be dull, perhaps, just two women, one opposite to the
other——'

'Dull! mother and I? Never. We don't know what it is to
be dull!'

'Ah, that's very well just now,' said Florence, 'you're only
seventeen; but wait a bit till you are older, especially if you don't
marry, and year goes on after year, and nothing ever happens.
See whether you are not dull then. I don't know which is worst,'
she added thoughtfully, 'to have men in the family that make you
miserable, or to have no men at all about to make any variety,
but just women together, who never do any harm, but kill you
with dulness. I really don't know which is the worst.'

Mab was a little overwhelmed by this point of view. She was
at the same time still indignant and resentful of the unexpected
accusation. 'When we begin to be dull,' she said, 'I'll let you
know—but I don't see any reason for being so miserable. Poor
Jim has never done anything so very bad. Sometimes he is
silly——'

'There you are quite wrong,' said Florence, with great decision
—'he is not silly: I wish he were, then one might think he didn't
know any better; but even papa allows he is very clever. It is
not from want of brains or sense either, if he would only be as good
as he knows how——'

'Oh, if that is your opinion! Mother thinks he is only weak,
and does what people ask him.'

'Aunt Emily is just as far out of it as you are. Does he ever
do anything that *we* ask him? There is papa at him for ever—is
he any the better for it? Weak! that is what people say, thinking it's a kind of an excuse. I call it strong—to resist everything
you ought to attend to, and take up everything you ought not.
How can that be weak?'

'I am sure I don't know,' said Mab; 'I don't understand
about boys. Jim is the only one I ever knew intimately. But
mother thinks if some one were to get hold of him in the right
sort of way——'

'What is the right sort of way? I suppose Aunt Emily thinks
papa doesn't know—nor any of us who have it to do; that is just
the way with people. You are always thinking of a thing, thinking, and puzzling, and troubling: and then somebody comes in who
has never spent ten minutes on it altogether, and says you are not

taking the right way! Perhaps we are not; but who are they to
pretend to know better? and since they are so wise, why don't they
tell us which is the right way?'

'I am sure,' cried Mab, 'I never meant to make you angry,
and mother is not one to interfere. She only said it to me. But
since you're so full of this, Florry, I think I had better go, and not
trouble you any more, for I only wanted some fun, and you are
thinking of nothing but trouble. I'll run down to the water, and
jump into a boat and have a little spin by myself.'

'Oh, Mab, don't,' cried Florence, clutching her once more.
'Here we are at our gate, just come in and ask him. He will
come far more readily for you than for me.'

But it was with an ill grace that Mab followed her cousin
through the Rectory kitchen garden, between the borders which
veiled the lines of potatoes and cabbages. It might be flattering to
suppose her capable of it, but she had not any desire to fill the
place of missionary and guiding influence to her cousin Jim.

THE Rectory was a red house standing in a garden, which its inhabitants, one and all, energetically declared not to be damp ; from which the stranger might gather that they were not so certain on the subject as it would be well to be. Its doors were quite level with the ground, so that you walked in, without the interval even of a step to raise you above the drippings of the rain : and as the drawing-room windows also opened down to the ground, it was rather a trying business in wet weather, and kept both the house-maid and the family much on the alert. The two girls went in through the open window, for the afternoon was quite bright and fair, and no fear of rain : but they found nobody in the drawing-room, which was low and rather dark, notwithstanding those two good-sized French windows, which somehow seemed to keep the light within themselves, and did not distribute it to the further side of the drab-coloured wall ; this, unornamented with pictures or any variety, afforded a dingy background for the somewhat dingy couches and easy-chairs, which were covered with brownish chintz, intended to keep clean, or in franker language, 'not to show the dirt' for as long a period as possible. Chintzes and wall papers, and even dresses, which were calculated not to show the dirt, were very popular at the time Mrs. Plowden married, as means of economy, and her daughters had been brought up in that tenet of faith. Accordingly everything in the room was more or less of this dingy drab complexion, which was not exhilarating to the spirits. There were signs that the room had been recently occupied by the untidiness of the loose cover of one of the sofas, which bore evident signs that some one had been lying there, and had jumped up hastily, and apparently fled, since the old novel he or she had been reading lay open on its face on the floor, and the antimacassars with which the sofa had been adorned were huddled up in limp bundles, and lay here and there where restless shoulders or limbs

had left them. Florence gave her cousin a look as she picked up
the book and spread out the forlorn adornments on the arm and
back of the sofa. 'They were put on quite fresh two days ago,
and look at them!' said poor Florry; they were chiefly in crochet,
and the work of her own hands.

'He has been here,' she said, 'and papa has called him to see
if he was at work. Papa might just as well let it alone, for
he is never at work; but that is what they will not learn,'
said Florence, impatient of the blindness of her parents. 'We,' she
added, 'have to put the room tidy after him a dozen times a day;
but I prefer him to be in the drawing-room, for at least he can't
smoke here——'

'If he is out,' said Mab, 'let us go, Florry: we have lost half
the afternoon already.'

'I don't believe he is out—he is being "jawed," as he calls it,
in papa's study: don't you hear them? Papa is at it hot! and
what good will it do? He will only say the same thing over
and over—I could say it all myself off by heart, everything papa
says—and, of course, so could Jim, and what good can that do?
Come and stop it, Mab. Jim will be so thankful to you: and
poor papa won't be sorry either,' Florence said, with a more sympathetic perception, 'for he knows it's useless; but when he
once begins he can't stop himself.'

'Oh,' said Mab, 'I can't go and disturb Uncle James.'

'When he'll be so thankful to be disturbed!' said Florry,
'and you much better than me, for you will have the air of not
knowing what it all means. No; don't go to the study door. Go
round by the garden, to the window where he can see you coming.
Walk slowly, and make a little noise to attract their attention, so
that you may not take them unawares. You might ring, or
whistle, or something—or call to Dash—and then papa would see
you, and have time to make up a face.'

These domestic diplomacies were unknown to Mab, but she
took to them with the natural instinct of femininity. There was
a certain element of fun, too, in stopping what she still called 'a
scolding,' and in getting the culprit off—even though the culprit
did not commend himself very warmly to her partiality. She
carried out the programme accordingly, while Florence waited just
out of sight of the study window. It was not a French window
like those in the drawing-room, and it looked out upon the dullest
portion of the surroundings—a bit of grass where the water lay
treacherous during the long winter months in the slight concave of
the ground, with shrubs cruelly green and unchanging around it,

and a dead wall which they only partially veiled behind. Mab began to call Dash loudly as she walked round the corner to this sanctuary, scattering the gravel with her feet.

The scene that might have been seen inside the Rector's window at that moment was this : a tall youth seated on a chair presenting nothing more responsive than the crown of his head, supported on his hands, to his father's remarks, and saying never a word ; while the Rector, who had risen from his own seat at his writing-table in his impatience, stood pouring out the vials of his wrath.   He was putting before Jim all the enormities of which he had been guilty—his debts, the expense he had been to his parents, the disappointment, the disgrace.   When, however, Mr. Plowden held up his hands to heaven and earth in grief and dis-appointment that it should be '*my* son' who had been sent down by his college, it is to be feared that Jim was making angry comments in his mind to the effect that all his father cared for was that—'not me, or anything about me.'   He knew the circum-stances very well—far better than his father could tell him ; and was it likely his conscience would be more tender for being dragged over the same ground again and again?   When the Rector cried, 'What is the use of talking to an impenitent cub like you?' his son felt deeply inclined to reply, 'There is none.'   He had, indeed, been wound up to the pitch of saying, 'Why do you go on like that when you're so sure it will make no difference?'—a pro-foundly sensible utterance, but one, perhaps, which it does still less good to say.

When 'Dash, Dash! come here, old fellow—get ready to come out for a walk,' sounded into the study, that home of anything but retired leisure, the Rector came to a sudden stop.   'There's some confounded visitor or other,' he said in vexation, but not without relief.

'It isn't a visitor, it's Mab.'

'Don't contradict me, sir!   Who is she but a visitor, a silly girl breaking in where your mother herself—— Don't think I've done with you because I'm interrupted.   Don't let me see you stir from your book till dinner.   Try whether you can't do something like your simple duty, for once in a way, just for the variety of the thing!   Eh!—yes, my dear, you can come in if you really want to, if you have anything to say to me, but you know I'm always busy.'

'Open the window, please, uncle,' said Mab.   'Is Jim there? We want him to come out with us, out on the river.   The weeds are coming up already in the backwater, and we don't want to risk going over the weir. It would be a wetting, and it might be a drowning, don't you know : and we want Jim.'

The weeds and the weir were the invention of the moment, and Mab felt rather proud of her skill; for of course the most obstinate of backwaters is not choked with weeds in March, and the girls, who were used to the river, were not so foolish at that season as to approach the weir. The Rector looked out upon his niece, of whom he was proud, with a look of helplessness ; for even from his sister he had kept the secret (knowing nothing of Florry's indiscretions) of the sad state of affairs with Jim.

'My dear,' he said, 'it is quite true that Jim is here : but he's busy, almost as busy as I am, reading up, don't you know, for his examination. You really must not tempt him to-day. I am sure you know the river so well, you will take care not to go near the weir.'

'But, Uncle James, it is getting near four o'clock, we shan't be more than an hour. Don't you think he will get on much better with his work when he comes back ?'

Jim had gradually expanded himself while this conversation was going on ; his father's back being turned he actually, not metaphorically, kicked up his heels a little in secret demonstration of his joy. Then he rose, and appeared exceedingly composed and respectful behind his father, who was leaning out of the open window. 'Since it is a question of the girls' comfort, sir,' said Jim, 'an hour won't make very much difference. I can get up that Sophocles just as well after dinner as now.'

'I don't put much faith in you after dinner,' said the Rector, without turning his head.

'Oh, but why shouldn't you, uncle ?' said Mab, 'I'll answer for him ! Of course he'll work ! Why there's nothing to do after dinner. Uncle says you may come, Jim.'

'I don't say anything of the kind,' said Mr. Plowden. But his eyes went from Mab outside to Jim within. They were both of them so young, and surely if there could be anything innocent in this world it would be an hour on the river with your sister and your cousin, both interested in keeping a boy straight. What was Sophocles after all (in which Jim took so little interest) in comparison with a more healthy rule of habit and purified nature ? If only he would but be good, what would it matter about Sophocles ? The Rector sighed with perplexity and impatience. It was all very well to attempt to keep Jim back, to say he was busy. Would all that keep him at his book a moment longer than his father's eye was on him ? And if Jim escaped and stole out by

himself, how could it be known whether his companions would be
as innocent as Mab and Florry? Was it not even a good point
in the boy, showing at bottom some traces of early innocence, that it
was with Florry and Mab that he wished to go? Mr. Plowden
turned in from the window and looked at his boy. He was the
only boy of the house, and no doubt he had been petted and
spoiled, and taught to think that everything was to give way to
him. The Rector looked at him with that longing of disappointed
love, the father's dreadful sense of impotence, the intolerable feeling that a touch given somewhere somehow, at the right moment,
might bring all right if he only could tell when and how to give
it. What did it matter that all his plans and arrangements should
be put out the moment he had made them, if the right effect could
be produced anyhow? Perhaps this little girl, with her childish
innocent mind—who could tell? And at least how innocent it all
was, the boy and the two girls! They would bring no harm to
him, and perhaps—who could tell?

'You will come home straight, Jim, and get to work again as
soon as you return?'

'Of course, sir,' said Jim, opening large eyes, as if he had
never departed from his word in his life. 'Of course, when I say
it I will do it. If you would but learn that it is the best thing
to trust a fellow,' he said, looking at the Rector with a grieved
disappointment which quite outdid Mr. Plowden's sentiments of
the same kind. The poor Rector could not restrain a laugh as
the young man hurried out of the room, leaving Sophocles just
ready to topple over, on the very edge of the table; but it was
not a cheerful laugh: though, perhaps, there was the chance that
little Mab, if she had only been a little prettier—— Prettiness,
however, as he knew, is not the only thing that matters in things
of this kind.

'You little brick!' cried Jim, as they hurried along. 'I
owe you one for that. What put it into your little head to come
and get me off to-day? for I was at the end of my patience,
and could not think of any excuse to get away.'

'What should you have done, Jim, if I had not come? read
your Greek?'

'Not if I know it,' said Jim. 'I should just have cut and
run, excuse or no excuse. A fellow can't be shut up all the
afternoon, and the sun shining. It's cruelty to animals. The
old Pater has forgotten that he was ever young.'

'But you will keep your promise, Jim, and go back and
learn up your Greek?'

'Oh, we'll see about that. Let's get our pull first. Oh, there's Flo! I thought you and I were going alone.'

'It was Florry who wanted you to come,' said Mab, with the frankness of extreme youth, 'not me. I like to do the pulling myself.'

'You shall if you like,' he said. 'I'm not fond of trouble. And it's not much fun you know, after all, to go out with your sister and your cousin. It's too much bread and butter. If I'd known that Flo was in it I shouldn't have come.'

'You can go back if you please—to your Greek.'

'Oh, catch me,' said the young man.

'But you will when we come back, Jim?'

'Perhaps I shall; not if you bully me. So I warn you. I should do my work all right and make up lost time if I wasn't bullied for ever and ever. Every one is at me. You heard what papa said. He ought to know how a man feels and shut up. But it's being so much among women, I suppose, makes a clergyman like that. If he wasn't a clergyman he wouldn't nag, he'd leave that to the women, and then I should feel that there was some one who understood. But how do you suppose a fellow is to do anything when from morning to night he hears nothing but "Are you going to your work, Jim? When do you begin your work? How are you getting on with your work?" and so forth. If I don't pass it will be the family's fault, it will not be mine. Mab, do you row stroke or bow?'

Mab jumped into the boat and took her place, without otherwise answering his question; but when they had floated out amid the reflections of the still river, she found that little tongue, which was not always under proper control.

'I like pulling,' she said, 'very much. I'd rather a great deal have an oar myself than sit still and let other people row me; and I like to bring mother out or—Aunt Jane.' She was about to say *even* Aunt Jane, but happily remembered that Aunt Jane was the mother of both her companions. 'But,' said Mab, with a long, slow stroke, to which Florence, very anxious to hear what was passing, kept time very badly, 'one thing I do hate is to pull an idle man.'

'By Jove!' burst from the lips of Jim. He had been listening very calmly up to the last two or three words, amused to hear little Mab's statement of what she liked and didn't like, but quite sure that she could say nothing that was derogatory to himself. 'I say, you little cat, why did you ask me to come out if you meant next moment to give me a scratch like this?'

'I told you it was Florry who wanted you and not me.'

'You might be civil at least,' said Jim, who had actually reddened under this assault. 'What did you come and butter up my father for, to let me go?'

'That was different,' said Mab. 'When it is against the old people, of course you are my own side; and then it was fun carrying you off as if you were something one had captured; and you looked so silly with uncle holding forth.' She broke into a laugh, while Jim grew redder and redder. 'But one thing I will never hold with,' said Mab, 'is that girls, who are not nearly so strong, should take and row a big heavy man.'

'Not so heavy,' cried Florence, pushing her head forward, neglecting her stroke entirely, and putting the boat out of trim. 'Oh, Mab, why should you reproach him too? He's no heavier than I am.'

'Shut up, Flo,' cried Jim indignantly, 'I'm close upon eleven stone, and that's the least a man should be of my size.'

'Well,' said Mab ('I'll pull you round, Florry, if you don't mind)—that is what I say; girls may do for themselves as much as they please, but to drag about a great heavy man, whether it is pulling in a boat or driving in a dog-cart, or whatever it is, is what I don't like. It is not what ought to be.'

'You are so old-fashioned, Mab,' said Florence anxiously from behind. 'You and Aunt Emily, you have the old anti-quated ways of thinking about women, that men should take care of them, and work for them, and all that, when perhaps it is the women that are most able to work, and take care of others too.'

'I have no antiquated ways,' said Mab. 'I have no ways at all. I don't think about women any more than about—other people. Mother and I have not got many men to take care of us, have we? But I say, it isn't our place to pull a heavy man. He should do that for us. I prefer to pull myself. Do, do, Florry, keep time! And I don't want your help, Jim. I am not talking of to-day; I am talking of things in general. It isn't nice; it doesn't look well; it's not the right thing. I don't want to have any man working for me; I'd much rather do it for myself. But he is the biggest and the strongest, and we oughtn't to be doing things for him. That's my opinion, without any reference to to-day.'

'You are not very civil,' said Jim. 'Why didn't you leave me at my Greek, Miss Mab? I might have done a lot, and been free after dinner. Now, instead of father's jawing, which

I'm used to. I have yours, which I'm not used to, and a slave in the evening as well. Hold hard a moment, till I shake off my coat and my boots, and I'll swim ashore.'

'Oh, Jim! it will be your death,' said the frightened Florence, starting from her seat, and once more putting the boat dreadfully out of trim.

'Be quiet, sit down!' cried Mab, 'or we shall have an accident. Do you hear? Jim is not going to do anything so silly. I was not speaking of him; I was only making a general remark. You can sit there and welcome so long as you steer against me, Jim: for I am pulling the boat round, can't you see, and Florry is not the least good.'

'Girls never are,' said Jim; 'the least little thing puts them out.'

'You see, Florry:' said Mab, 'it was on his account you were exciting yourself and behaving like one of the cockneys on Bank Holiday, and he doesn't mind. Let him alone. How far can we go to get back in daylight, Jim?'

Florence once more put in her word. 'We can go as far as the island,' she said.

'Coming back to-morrow morning?' said Jim. 'How should she know? Going up you can go as far as the lock, and going down you can go as far as the lock, but not a step more.'

'That's like an oracle,' said Mab.

'Well, so I am. If I don't know anything else, I know the river. I know it every step up to Oxford and down to London. I'm as good as the Thames Conservancy man. They'd better put me on if they want to look after all the backwaters and keep the riparians in order. That's what I could do. I may not be a dab at Sophocles, but there isn't a man knows the river better. You ask any man that knows me, either at Oxford or here.'

'Then why does not Uncle James try to get you an appointment on the river? It would be better than going out to the colonies.'

'Oh, they don't think so here. In the colonies nobody knows you. You may go about in a flannel shirt and knickerbockers, and a revolver in your belt; but if you stay at home they want some work for you that you can do in a black coat and top hat.'

'Couldn't you take care of the riparians and the backwaters in a top hat, if you liked?'

'Oh, they like a naval man,' said Jim; 'their uniform gives them a little dignity, don't you know, whereas I'm nobody.'

'But it is the same in everything. You can't be somebody all at once. You must begin low down,' said Mab, bending her little person over her oar with that slow, steady stroke which confused Florence. Florry was choppy and irregular—one time slow, the next fast; never able to hit the time which Mab gave her with such steady composure. 'The way to do,' said Mab, 'is to put everything else out of your head, as long as you are able to, and think of nothing but that. You should never mind what you like, or what you want, but just set your thoughts on what you are doing. Look at Florry; she wants to hear what we're saying, and she wants to defend you, Jim, that I mayn't say anything unpleasant; and the consequence is that if you were not steering against me with all your might, I should pull the boat round and round.'

'Florry is only a girl, and a bad specimen,' said Jim. 'You should have let me pull, and then you'd have seen something like pulling.'

'I am only a girl myself,' said Mab.

'But, then, you're a good specimen,' said the young man, with a laugh. 'You keep your eyes in the boat.'

'Which is what you don't do, Jim!'

'How do you know, you little thing, lecturing people older than yourself? I may not with Sophocles—but I do with other things.'

'Which other things?' said Mab.

But Jim made no reply; and here Florry interposed again with strokes shorter and more irregular than ever, to talk over her cousin's shoulder, and ask, though they were not half-way to the island, or even to the lock for that matter, whether it would be better to turn back and go home. They lay for a moment in midstream. Mab pausing on her steady oar to remonstrate, making a picture in the water, the boat floating as a bird floats in mid air, between the sky and the river, which reflected every line of cloud and stretch of blue. Some cows at the water's edge stood double, feeding, on the very brink, and the trees still bare, but all downy with life, pushing out a greenness here and there, seemed to stretch out of the water in reflection to meet the others on the bank. Watcham lay glorified, one white house above the rest lighting up all the river with its white shadow in the stream. The boat lay like a thing enchanted with the three figures shining in afternoon light, above and below.

E

JIM strolled down into the village when the boat came to shore. It was before the hour at which he had concluded he would go home, which, as was natural, was considerably later than the hour proposed by Mab. What was the good, he said to himself, of going in before dinner, or at least before the time which was necessary to get ready for dinner? In that hour, as everybody knows, very little can be done. Mrs. Plowden and the girls would be in the drawing-room talking about what had happened in the afternoon, and the Rector would not have come in. So it was quite a certainty in Jim's mind that no Sophocles would come of it if he had returned home when Florence did, as she begged him to do. He would not have worked; and, indeed, it would be a kind of breaking of his word if he had done so then, for had he not promised his father to work after dinner, which was quite a different thing? And it was more amusing to prowl along through the village on the outlook for anything that might happen, than to go in and listen to the girls chattering, probably about the Swinfords. And Jim was sick of the very name of the Swinfords. He had that distaste which a young man who has fallen into objectionable ways so often acquires of party-givings and society in what his mother called 'his own rank of life.' He flattered himself that what he did dislike was the conventionalities and stiffness of society, and that his own desire to see 'life' was a more original and natural sort of thing. He liked to hear what the people said when they were at their ease in inn parlours and tap-rooms. He liked, it is to be feared, what accompanied these sayings. And the more familiar he became in such localities, the more 'out of it' he felt in the drawing-rooms, and among the staid and quiet folk who represented society in Watcham. So that the Swinfords represented nothing but a succession of fresh annoyances to Jim. If they gave parties, as his mother and the girls hoped, he would be obliged to get himself up in gorgeous attire and take a part in these entertainments. There was a time when he, too, would have been excited by such a prospect; but that had departed after his first experiences of the life of the somewhat disreputable undergraduate, into which he had been so unfortunate as to fall. Now that he could not lounge into any resort where he could meet his peers in that class, Jim found his distaste for the home society grow upon him. He was tired to death of the girls. The old ladies bored him, which was not so wonderful. The correct old General and the clergymen about were old fogeys, which indeed was true enough. Where was the poor boy to find any one whom he could talk to with the freedom of those delightful but too brief terms at the University where he had been taught what life meant? It had been a shock to his own remaining scruples, and all the force of tradition, when he first strayed into the public-house. Oh no; not the public-house, but the little inn at Watcham, which was quite a pretty little house, all brilliant with flowers, and where people from town came down to stay in the summer; it was so nice, so quaint, so respectable, and so near the river. But it is a very different thing coming to stay at an inn for the sake of being near the river, and stealing in in the evening to the same place for society and amusement. There was nothing disreputable going on in the parlour of the 'Swinford Arms,' or the 'Blue Boar,' as it was vulgarly called, in reference to the Swinford crest, which presented that aspect to the common eye. The people who went there were respectable enough—the tradesmen in the village, good decent men who liked to see the papers and talk them over with the accompaniment of a glass of something, and a pipe: and the veterinary surgeon, who was a great deal about the country, and talked familiarly of Sir Thomas Barnes, and the Mortlocks of Well-wood, the great hunting people. It made a young man who felt acutely that he did not belong to the class of the tradesmen, more satisfied with himself to talk with a man who spoke of such people familiarly in a sort of hail-fellow well met way, even though he was only the vet. But by degrees as Jim acquired the habit of dropping in in the evenings to the 'Blue Boar,' he got to think that the village shopkeepers were very good fellows, and their opinions well worth hearing. So they were, indeed, as a matter of fact: solid, decent men, whose measured glass of something probably did them no harm, and whose wives were rather glad than otherwise that they had this little enlivenment in the evening of a little respectable society in the parlour of the 'Blue Boar,' which was itself as respectable as could be desired. But yet it was not respectable, alas! for Jim.

When the Rector first discovered that this was where his son went when he went out in the evenings to take a walk, as he said, Mr. Plowden's feelings would be difficult to describe. The misery, the shame, the acute and intolerable sense of downfall were perhaps exaggerated. But who can say what the descent is from the drawing-room of the Rectory to the parlour of the village public-house? which is what it really was, no doubt, though it was a most respectable little inn, and frequented in summer by the best of company. The first interview between the father and the son was very painful, but not without hope, for Jim himself was very well aware of all that it meant, and did not stand against his father's reproaches. 'I know it is not a place for the Rector's son,' he said, humbly enough. 'It's not a place for anybody's son,' the Rector said. 'Do you think even White and Slaughter would like their sons to go there?' This was an argument Jim was not prepared for, and he acknowledged with humility that he did not think they would. The Rector was very gentle with the boy that first time. He pointed out that for Slaughter and White, and even the vet., it was a sort of club where they went to meet their friends—and whether or not there might be any objections morally to their glass of something, yet at all events it was a very moderate indulgence, and went no further. 'I don't say it is quite right even for them; but that's a very different question,' Mr. Plowden said, and Jim acknowledged the self-evident truth. The Rector said nothing to his wife for that first time, nor for several times afterwards; but he could not conceal his anxiety when Jim disappeared in the evening, as, after a few very quiet and dull nights at home, he again began to do. When Mrs. Plowden heard she cried, almost with indignation, 'But why didn't you speak to him, James?' Speak to him! After two or three interviews poor Mr. Plowden soon began to recognise how little use there was in that.

Jim, accordingly, when he left the girls to stroll down the village street, did so against the remonstrances of Florry, who tried hard to persuade him to come back and hear what mamma and Emmy had been doing at the Hall, then offered herself to share his walk, with equal seriousness. 'I like a stroll by myself,' Jim said.

'It will very soon be dark, Jim; it is no fun walking in the dark.'

'Not for you. But let me alone; if I like it, that's enough, Flo.'

'Oh, Jim, mamma is so pleased when you come in early,' cried Florence, pleading; 'it does us all so much good. If you only saw the difference in poor papa's face when he knows you're in the drawing-room.'

'I shouldn't be in the drawing-room in any case. I've got my Greek to do.'

'Still better if you are at your Greek. Oh, Jim, do for once come home with me!'

'I'll come in in half an hour—will that satisfy you? I only want to shake myself up a bit after sitting there with nothing to do.'

'Well, mind you don't forget: in half an hour,' said Florence.

He went off waving his hand to her. Then thrusting his hands into his pockets, with that idle lounging step of the man who is ready for any mischief, but has none immediately in sight, he strolled away. Florence stood looking after him, with anxiety in every line of her face, until she remembered Mab looking on, whom it was necessary to keep from knowing if possible: and then the poor girl laughed. 'Isn't he lazy?' she said; 'and it does vex papa so. Papa thinks Jim should like Sophocles as much as he does, which is nonsense, isn't it? But Jim says that old people never can understand young ones, and perhaps it's true.'

'Mother always understands me,' said Mab, with a child's unhesitating confidence.

'Oh,' said Florence. Her secret thought was, 'What is there in you, you little thing, to understand?' She said after a moment, 'Boys are so different!' with a sigh.

'You should not nag at him so much,' said Mab, with a reflection of her mother's sentiments, who as yet knew little of Jim's case, and gave her opinion privately in the bosom of her own home that the boy was being driven out of his senses by never being left alone.

'I don't think we nag at him,' said Florence meekly: and then the two girls parted, Mab taking the way to the cottage, and Florry that which led to the Rectory. 'You don't want to hear what they have got to say?' Florry said, with a faint smile, before the other left her.

'I shall hear it from mother,' said Mab, 'and I don't know that I care.'

So the cousins separated—with thoughts so different. And Jim strolled away in the other direction with a thirst which was both physical and mental, in his whole being. It was physical, alas! and that was perhaps in its immediate development the worst: but it was also mental, a craving for something he knew not what; something that would supply the atmosphere, the novelty, he wanted, the something he had not got. He knew very well at other moments that the inn parlour, and the village society, and the pipes and the glass—in his own case so often repeated—would not give that. Ordinarily, he thought Oxford would give it and the society of the young men with whom he sometimes talked metaphysics, though usually it was only horses and racing, and boats and bumps, and the qualities of the different dogs of the circle, that they discussed ; but still, it was not to be denied that there was something in Jim's being which thirsted, as well as that fatal thirst in his body, which, alas ! it was so much more easy to satisfy. The drab-coloured house at home, with its habits fixed like iron ; the evening round the lamp ; the mother's prolonged talk about her neighbours, and about people she once knew, and about getting on ; his father's scanty, careless replies ; the girls' talk, which was very often about their dresses, and how things were worn now—all these had become wearisome to the young man : and he did not care at all for his Sophocles. He had found in Oxford that opening out of the restricted household circle for which his young being craved ; but it had not been the best of openings, and now poor Jim prowled down the village street, wanting that something which he could not tell how to attain to, neither what it was. He did not want to go to the 'Blue Boar.' He had never yet gone in daylight openly, but under cover of night, when the parlour window looked so bright in the dull village street. It wanted some courage to go now, in cold blood as it were, when there was no reason for it, and he felt all that it meant, the son of the Rectory going in, in the light of day, to the village public-house. He did not want to do it, if he could only find somewhere else to go.

It happened in this way that Jim was very ready to be led in any quarter where a little novelty or amusement was to be found. Not in any quarter ; for supposing he had at that moment met the good old General, whose company could do him nothing but good, who had told him, perhaps, that he had a young nephew, perhaps a pretty niece, to whom he wished to introduce the Rector's son, Jim would at once have found that he had to go back to his Greek : he would not have gone to the General's, nor to any house, as his mother said, 'in his own rank of life.' And why this should be I am quite unable to tell. Houses which were in his own rank of life did not seem to him to have what he wanted ; he would have felt sure in advance that the General's nephew would be a prig, or perhaps an insolent young soldier, thinking nobody was anybody who was out of the service ; and the General's niece, ugly and stupid. This he would have felt sure of, though he could not have told why. Neither can I tell why, nor any of those to whom it would be of the greatest advantage to make this all-important discovery. It would be even more important than finding out how to resist a deadly disease; and in the one case as in the other, there are many surprises and many experiments. But nobody as yet has been able to find out the way.

It was while he was thus moving along on the other side of the street, not desiring to go to the 'Blue Boar,' yet not knowing where else to go, and having within him an imperious wish to go somewhere, that Jim suddenly heard in the soft stillness of the evening air—for the wind had quite fallen as night came on—a pleasant voice saying, 'Good evening, Mr. Plowden'; a voice which was quite new to him, and which he could not associate with anybody in Watcham. He knew everybody in Watcham, great and small, so that it was not easy to take him by surprise. He turned round, startled, and saw a woman, a lady, standing in the half-light in the door of the house next to the schools, which was appropriated to the village schoolmistress. He knew there was a new schoolmistress, for he had heard it talked of, but he had not seen her, so that this was about the only person in Watcham whose voice he did not know. Jim stopped suddenly and made a clutch at his cap. I hope he would on any occasion have taken off his hat to the schoolmistress, but at all events this voice made it imperative, for it was a refined voice, the voice of a lady, or else an exceedingly good make-believe.

'Good evening,' he replied vaguely. He could not very well make out her face, but yet there was something in it which it appeared to him he had seen before.

'You do not remember me?' she said.

'You have newly come to the school, I suppose,' he said. 'I beg your pardon. I don't think I have seen you before.'

'You have seen me before, but not here, and if I were quite sure you did not remember me I should be very glad.'

'That is rather a queer thing to say,' said Jim.

'Perhaps; but it is a true thing. I wanted to ask you, if you did remember me, not to do so—at least, to say nothing about it.'

'This is more mysterious still.'

'Yes, I daresay it does sound mysterious; but it is important to me. I don't know whether to trust to you in this way, that if you remember me after you will say nothing about it; or to be frank and recall myself to your mind.'

'You had better let me judge,' said Jim.

Here was the something he wanted, perhaps—an adventure, a mystery; of all things in the world the least likely thing to find in Watcham village street.

The woman—lady he called her—gave a glance round to see if any one was looking, then suddenly stepping back, bade him come in. There was nothing in the house of the schoolmistress that looked like mystery. He knew it well enough. He had been there with his mother when he was a child. He had come with errands from her to the late mistress. The narrow passage and the tiny little sitting-room that opened off from it were as familiar to him as the Rectory. He walked into the parlour, which, however, startled him, as if it had been a new place which he had never seen before. How well he remembered the black haircloth sofa, the square table with its heavy woollen table-cover, which left so little room for coming or going. It was newly furnished, draped with curtains much more fresh than anything in the Rectory, a small sofa with pretty chintz, an easy-chair or two, the small tables which were not so common in those days. Jim did not notice those things in detail, but the general effect was such as to turn his head.

'Hullo!' he said, in his surprise.

'You see the difference in the room? No; I wouldn't have my predecessor's old things. I have done it almost all with my own hands. Isn't it nice?'

'It is very different,' said Jim. His home was dingy, but it was natural, and he had an undefined sense that this was not natural. There was something fictitious in the air of the little room with its poor, coarsely-papered walls—a sort of copy of a boudoir out of a novel, or on the stage. He was not very learned in such things, and yet it seemed to him to be part of a *décor* rather than a room to live in. In Mrs. Peters' time it was very ugly, but as honest as the day.

'Sit down,' she said, 'and let me give you a cup of tea; or perhaps—for I think I know gentlemen's tastes—there may be something else that you will like better. Sit down, at least, and I will try if I can find something to your taste; for I want to make a little bargain with you, Mr. Plowden, that may be for my advantage and yours, too. Sit down for a moment, and wait for me here.'

She vanished as she spoke, and left him much bewildered in the little bedizened room. It occurred to him during the moment he was left there that perhaps, on the whole, it would have been better had he gone after all to the parlour in the 'Blue Boar.' But his entertainer reappeared in a minute or two, bearing in her hands a tray, upon which stood a tall glass, foaming as nothing ever foamed in the 'Blue Boar.' I don't pretend to say what its contents were. They were foaming, and highly scented, and they pleased Jim Plowden, I am sorry to say, better than tea.

'That is something like what we had at Nuneham that lovely day. Don't you recollect me now?'

'Mrs. Brown!' cried Jim. It was not a name which said very much to the ordinary ear. It would, indeed, be difficult to say less. But the new schoolmistress made him a curtsey such as had never been seen in Watcham before.

'I am glad,' she said, 'that you remember me; though I ought to have been pleased and satisfied that you did not—for a woman, however she may came down in the world, never likes to think that she has been forgotten. I have recalled myself to your recollection, Mr. Plowden, in order to say that I hope you won't say anything to your father or any one of where we met last. I was then, if you remember, chaperon, to some young ladies.'

'Oh yes, indeed, I remember perfectly,' cried Jim, 'your nieces.'

'Well, yes, my nieces if you like; and I was not at all like a village schoolmistress, was I? Things happen so in this life; but it would do me no good, Mr. Plowden, with the Rector or the other good people, to know that I had been—well, helping you to squander your money at Oxford only last year.'

'You did not help me to squander my money, Mrs. Brown. I was only one of the guests. I had no money to squander; but I fear what you mean is that you have come down in the world. I am very sorry, I am as sorry as I can be. It is very different, this, from anything you have been accustomed to; but instead of saying nothing about it, which I can understand as a matter of pride, don't you think it would be better for me to tell my mother, who though she has her own ways which you might perhaps not care for, is very kind, and would, I am sure, try to make things as pleasant as she could and as little hard, and ask you up to the Rectory and all that?'

Mrs. Brown turned her back upon Jim, and he feared that she wept. But I don't think she wept, though when she turned round again she had her handkerchief to her eyes. She said, 'I am sure your mother is goodness itself, Mr. Plowden; but I am a proud woman, as you perceive. No, you must not breathe a word to your mother. I have one friend who knows all about me, and that is Mrs. Swinford, at the Hall; but except her and yourself I want nobody to know. Will you promise me that nobody shall know from you, Mr. Jim?'

How did she know his name, Jim? How did she remember him at all, a little, young, ignorant freshman much honoured to make one of the brilliant water party of which she and her nieces had been the soul? He was ready to have promised anything, everything she asked.

'SHE was nice enough to us,' said Mrs. Plowden, 'but very hoighty-toighty with your aunt. Did you observe that, Emmy? Poor Aunt Emily was very kind. She said in such a pretty way, "That is Emily Plowden now," and really Emmy looked so very like her at that moment—with the charm of youth, of course, added on—that nobody could help remarking it. Mr. Swinford looked from one to the other, making a little comparison I could see—and you may imagine in whose favour it was.'

'It was in my sister's favour, of course,' said the Rector. There was something in the way in which he emphasised the *my*, as if to mark the difference between his daughter, who was her mother's as well as his, and his sister who was all his own, that might have been amusing to a bystander, but to Mrs. Plowden was not amusing at all.

'It is most curious,' she said, 'the way you always stand up for your own family——'

'Whom do you mean by my own family? Emmy is my own family, I suppose?'

'You know very well what I mean. I mean your side of the house in opposition to mine. One would think that nobody born was ever equal to your people—not even your own children.'

'My own children are as God has made them,' said the Rector. He added, as if she had been somehow of a superior manufacture, 'But my sister Emily was the sweetest creature I ever saw when she was Emmy's age. Emmy is a good girl, and she is very nice-looking or she could not be supposed to be like my sister. But as for comparing the one to the other, my dear, it only shows how little you know.'

'Upon my word!' cried Mrs. Plowden, not without reason, 'I hope my Emmy may be compared to any one. Your sister had always a great deal too much intellectual pride about her to please me. She was not content to be nice-looking, which nobody ever denied, but she went in for being clever, too. I know you don't approve of women taking that sort of position, James. Indeed, you have said as much a hundred times—and now to go on raving about your sister, as if we haven't all had sisters that were out of the common in our day!'

'My dear, I didn't know there was anybody out of the common connected with you. My impression is I never heard you brag of that before—no more than poor Emily ever did about being more clever than the rest of us. Poor girl, it hasn't come to much in her case.'

'I am not one to be always blowing a trumpet about my family,' said Mrs. Plowden angrily; 'but if you think my brother Thurston is nobody——'

'Not in the least; he is a very nice fellow, and a Q.C.'

'Or my sister Florence!' said the Rector's wife, 'poor Florry's godmother—and the girl takes after her, I'm glad to say—and it's to her credit, whatever you may think.'

'Oh, your sister Florence!' said the Rector. This was a point that had been argued between them often before, for, as a matter of fact, though Emily Plowden was understood to have done very little good for herself by her distinguished marriage, yet it was a distinguished marriage, and one of which the Rector's wife herself was more proud than any one. She quoted Lady William in her own family in a way which made her brother who was a Q.C. and her sister who was Florence's godmother very angry. 'I wish you would not be always dinning that eternal Lady William into our ears,' was what these good people said. But at home, in face of her husband, Mrs. Plowden liked to show her independence, and that she and her brothers and sisters were as remarkable as he and his brothers and sisters any day.

'Well,' said Mrs. Plowden, 'they were really more nice to Emmy, though she is only my daughter, than they were to your sister Emily, James. I did not think that Emily was received as her rank demands. They were more civil to me, a simple clergyman's wife, than they were to her. Now, though one is always pleased, of course to be put in the first place, I don't think it was right. Oh! not Mr. Swinford, he was very attentive; but in such cases the man does not count, and the old lady——'

'Is she really an old lady, mamma?' said Florry, who had not yet found the opening for her anxious questions which she desired.

'Well—her son is not quite young. He is not like Jim; he

is a full-grown young man of the world. As for Mrs. Swinford, she is so curled and frizzed and powdered and everything done to her, that you can't tell how old she is. But it is always safe to say the old lady when there is a son quite old enough to marry. Of course she will be the old lady as soon as he gets a wife.'

'I am sure, mamma, it would not make you an old lady if Jim were to marry,' said Emmy, always exemplary in her sentiments.

'Jim!' Mrs. Plowden said, with a sort of shriek. And then she added : 'Poor Jim's not a landed proprietor like Mr. Swinford. He can never make me a Dowager, poor boy! And what chance has he of ever marrying? none that I know of, without any money, and not even a profession. Alas! there is a great difference between Leo Swinford and Jim.'

'Is Leo his name? What an odd name!'

'But pretty, don't you think—and so uncommon?' said Emmy.

Emmy had a slightly dazzled look about the eyes, as one that has seen visions. She had been into that fairy palace, and come into absolute contact with Prince Charming. Florry knew that the details of the interview were not likely to come out until they two came face to face in their room, with no father or mother in the way.

'By the way,' said the Rector, as if it had not been the prominent thing in his mind all the time, 'did Jim come back with you from the river, Flo?'

'He thought he would like a little stroll before he came back —for half an hour. He promised me faithfully he would come back in half an hour.'

'It is more than half an hour now,' said the Rector, with his watch in his hand ; and then he sighed and went away.

'Oh, children,' said Mrs. Plowden, when his steps had died out in the distance of the rambling house, 'how often must I tell you not to be so pointed with your half-hours? How can a young man tell, if he strolls out in the evening, exactly to a moment when he's to get back? He may meet a friend, or some little accident may happen, and he is kept, without any doing of his. And there is your father with his watch in his hand as if he had never been a young man himself. I don't want you, I am sure, to be anything but truthful—but if you could throw a little veil over such things! Now, however soon he may come, and how-ever right he may be, your father will never forget having looked at his watch. He will say you can never trust in his word be-cause of that half-hour.'

'I only said what he told me, mamma,' said Florence, half offended.

'As if there was any use in saying what he told you!' cried Mrs. Plowden, 'when you know that's Jim's weakness never to be sure when he is coming in; and to say in half an hour is just as easy as in—— Jim! why, here he is, as exact as clockwork. Run and tell your father, Florry: he can put his watch in his pocket. Oh, I am so glad! It is always a little triumph for us womenfolk who believe whatever you say, you troublesome Jim!'

'Do you believe whatever I say, mother?'

'Oh, more than I ought—more than I ought. And oh, Jim, if you only knew the pleasure of it, the pride of it! To see you walking in at your time as a gentleman should—and like a gentleman in every way!'

The words were, perhaps, capable of various interpretations; but the little party in the Rectory drawing-room knew precisely what they meant; and Jim knew very well that his mother, in the darkness of the room, where no lights as yet were lighted, was crying quietly to herself over his virtue and punctuality. It struck him with a sort of mingled shame and ridicule to think that, perhaps, had she known where he had been, she would not have been so much content. I may say that it was much more like an hour and a half than half an hour since he had left the two girls at the landing-place; so that he was not precisely a model of exactness after all.

When Jim came in all the other subjects in the world went out; and as he had no interest in the Hall and its inhabitants there was no further gossip about the Swinfords in the Rectory family that night, until, indeed, the evening was over, and the girls found themselves face to face in the room which they shared, which was a long and low one, under the eaves, with a number of small windows, and space enough to make up for a slanting roof on one side. It was indeed quite a large room, with two little beds, two little white-draped toilet tables, two sets of drawers, everything double, as the two were who had lived in it all their lives. All their little confidences had been made to each other there, all that had happened had been discussed; their whole life, which was not eventful, had passed in this dim chamber, where the light came in through greenish lattices, and under the shadow of the waving trees. They came upstairs, following each other very demurely, each with her candle, but when they were safe in their shelter, and had shut their door, each put down her candle on her own table, and they rushed together, seizing each other's hands.

'Oh, Emmy, tell me!' cried the one who had been left at home.

'There is nothing to tell, indeed,' said Emmy, 'except what you have heard already.'

'I have heard nothing about *him*,' said her sister.

'Oh, Flo, dear! all that nonsense was amusing enough as long as he was only a dream. He has been a dream for so long; but now he's a man, just like another.'

'Not like any other in the world, Em.'

'That is, to you and me; but, thank heaven, nobody knows except us two, and it is all over. He is like any other man, rather more nicely dressed, rather more careful of his clothes.'

'Oh, Emmy!'

'That doesn't sound like our hero, does it? I suppose it is because he is half French: red stockings and patent-leather shoes, as Mab said.'

'Well,' said Florry, 'if true hearts are more than coronets, they are certainly more than patent-leather shoes.'

'That is very true, but somehow it goes dreadfully against one's ideal. And, Flo, he is not—tall.'

Florence burst into a somewhat agitated laugh. 'What does that matter?' she said.

'Oh, nothing at all. I know that little men are just as nice, sometimes nicer, than big ones; but you know what we always thought: and he is not the least like it—not one little bit.'

Emmy looked as if she were going to cry; for the fact was that Mr. Swinford had been, by a piece of girlish romance not very uncommon among such unsophisticated girls as those of the Rectory, the hero of an entirely visionary castle in the air on the part of this young lady. Florence was more wise; she had the ideas of her century, and was very strongly convinced that for her sister to marry well was a thing most essential at the present crisis of the family fortunes; but she had been very indulgent to Emmy's romance, possibly from the conviction that this was the only way in which her sister could be moved to take such a step —and partly because she had herself a sentimental side, and was deeply convinced that no true marriage could be made without love.

'Well,' she said soothingly, 'never mind; he may be everything that is delightful in himself, even though he is short and not handsome.'

'I never said he was not handsome,' said Emmy, with some indignation, 'nor yet short. How exaggerated you are! I said he was not tall. He is very nice-looking. Not the way we used to think ; not dark-haired and with deep dark eyes as we used to imagine—and not fair either, which is perhaps better : but yet very nice—in his own way.'

'Brown !' cried Florence, 'sober, sensible, common brown—like most people.   After all, that must be the best and safest since Providence makes the most of us of that hue.'

'If you think he is common,' said Emmy indignantly, 'you are making the greatest mistake.   He is not heroic—in appearance : but unusual—to a degree.'   Emmy's powers of language were not great, but her feeling was unmistakable.   'I never saw any one at all like him,' she said.   'If he is not like a man in a poem or on the stage, he is just as little like the ordinary man you meet. Fancy, it was he who made the tea !   His mother said he always did it.   The way she calls Leo at every moment is the most curious thing.   She has a sweet voice, but it is so imperious, as if she never thought it possible that any one could resist her ; and, though it is quite low, he hears her before she has half called him, whatever he may be doing.'

'All that is very interesting,' said Florence, 'but'—she seized her sister's hands and looked anxiously into her face—'of course you can't see how things are to go the first time—but, Emmy, oh, tell me——!'

Emmy shook her head; she withdrew her hands; her eyes drooped before her sister's gaze.   'How can you ask ?' she said, 'how could anybody tell ?   He was very nice, of course—as he would have been to the housemaid if we had sent her, or to Mrs. Brown at the school.'

'Mamma said he was exceedingly nice to you, and not so nice to Aunt Emily.'

'Ah, that was Mrs. Swinford she was thinking of.   Mamma naturally thinks of her.   No, no, Flo, we must not deceive ourselves ; it was all the other way.   If there is any one here whom Mr. Swinford thinks it worth his while to talk to and make friends with, it will neither be you nor me.'

'Me, no !   I never thought of such a thing.   But why not you, Emmy ? and, if not you, who else ?'

Emmy clasped her hands together and shook her head.   She had been shaking it for at least a minute before she let the words 'Aunt Emily' drop from her lips, with an accent of something like despair.

'Aunt Emily !' said Florence in the profoundest surprise : her tone changed in a moment into one of disdain.   'Aunt Emily ! why, she is old enough to be—she is almost as old as mamma. She has nothing to do with it at all.'

'Do you remember,' said Emmy, with some solemnity, '*that* French novel which we found in Uncle Thurston's room?'

Florence nodded her head. It had been a fearful joy to find in their uncle's room anything so wildly wicked, so universally condemned, as a yellow French novel. It had not been so delightful in the attempt to read it—for the girls were far too innocent to understand the stimulating fare there placed before them. But it was a terrible and alarming memory in their lives.

'Well, the heroine in that was a widow,' cried Emmy. 'She was the one everybody thought of. And Mr. Swinford is quite French, and Aunt Emily doesn't look old, and she is really handsome. Don't you know when people want to be very complimentary to me they say I am like Aunt Emily?—only when they want to be very complimentary.'

'So you are; and the more he thinks of her the more he ought to turn to you, who are so like her.'

'Oh! do you think so? I, for my part, feel sure that he will like her best. She will be able to talk to him. She has been in Paris, where he comes from. She will be like the people he has been used to.'

'Oh! not like the people in Uncle Thurston's novel!'

'I did not mean that; but she can talk, and she is what people call elegant, and you'll see he'll think more of her than either of you or me.'

'It is impossible,' cried Florence, with the confidence of youth. 'A woman with a grown-up daughter!'

'Wait,' said Emmy oracularly, 'and you will see.'

IT was a day or two after these events before any new incident happened; and, indeed, the appearance of Mr. Swinford in the village of Watcham was not a very remarkable incident. For Watcham was not in the depths of the country, where the sight of a new face was in itself extraordinary. People from London were continually appearing in this little place. To be sure, it was too early in March for the shoals of men in flannels who were to be seen lounging about in summer; but still there were people who would come down 'to have a look at the river' even in the winter season, when the boats were laid up. And boating men, and indeed others, had a way of appearing at the 'Blue Boar' on visits from Saturday till Monday, and were very correct in their town costumes when they arrived, though afterwards falling into many eccentricities of apparel. Mr. Swinford might have been one of them, as he walked down on Saturday afternoon. He was not very fond of walking, having had a French rather than an English education. It had already been discovered that his usual way of going about was in an exceedingly smart dog-cart, which he drove in a way rather unusual to the aborigines, with a rein in each hand. I need not pause to point out that Leo Swinford, an Englishman educated in France, was not at all an Anglomane, but probably more French than most young Frenchmen whose desire would have been to look English—at least in everything that had to do with riding or driving. But on this occasion he walked, and might have been taken simply for one of the Saturday to Monday men. But no; Watcham was too clever for that. None of them were so point devise as the young master of the Hall. Though it is always a little muddy on this riverside road, he still had the *chaussure*, so much admired yet scorned by the young ladies who had discussed it—the red silk stockings and glistening patent-leather shoes which had filled Mab with wonder and disdain. He had a warm greatcoat buttoned over a white silk *cache-nez* which was round his throat. The cut of the coat, though excellent, was not like Bond Street—or is it Savile Row? I am of opinion that it had been made there, but it had acquired from the wearer a something, a little more shape than is common to a young Englishman, a *je ne sais quoi* of foreign and stranger. His hat, I suppose, was also an English hat, but somehow curled at the brim, as an Englishman's hat rarely does. The village got note of his arrival in some extraordinary way before he was within its bounds. People peeped over the little muslin blinds in the cottages; a woman or two bolder than the rest came out to the door to have a good look at him. Even the men in the bakers' and butchers' carts stopped and winked at each other; 'awful Frenchy,' they thought he was.

After a while it became apparent that this exquisite figure was bound for the Rectory; and some thrill running through the very path brought the news before he did to the Plowdens, who came together as by some electric current driving the different atoms towards each other. I have no doubt this is an impossible metaphor, and that electric currents have nothing to do with atoms; but the reader who knows better will, I hope, derive a little gratification from his smile at my ignorance. Anyhow, the ladies of the house flew as by an instinctive movement into the drawing-room. Mrs. Plowden was the first to get there; and the girls found her shaking up the sofa cushions, and drawing the chairs about—not to range them against the wall and make everything tidy as her grandmother would have done, but to give them that air of comfortable disorder which is the right thing nowadays. Emmy followed her mother's example with a little flutter and agitation, shaking up anew the sofa cushions which Mrs. Plowden had just arranged to the best advantage, while Florence gathered up a leaf or two which had fallen from the flower vases, and picked off a faded flower or two from the pots of narcissus and jonquils which were in the room. It might have been the Queen who was coming, though it was only a natty young man. Then the Rector appeared, a little anxious, rubbing his hands. 'What had I better do?' he said; 'shall I be here with you to receive him, or wait in my study? He may be coming only to call on me.'

This view of the subject filled the ladies with consternation, though they allowed there was a certain truth in it.

'You had better be in the study, anyhow, James,' Mrs. Plowden said; 'and if he asks for me, of course I will send for you;

if he is shown in to you instead, of course you will say, after you
have had your conversation, "You must come into the drawing-
room, Mr. Swinford ; my wife and daughters will be rejoiced to
see you ;" or words to that effect.'

'Oh, I don't suppose I shall be at a loss for words,' said the
Rector, who had no respect for his wife's style. He gave a glance
round the room ; not with any satisfaction, for he felt that it was
rather dingy, and that a stranger would not be likely to see what
he felt, being so accustomed to it, to be the real comfort of the
room. It was looking its best, however. The sunshine was bright
in the windows, the jonquils and narcissus filling it with the
fragrance of spring—a little too much, perhaps ; but then one
window was open, so that it was not overpowering. The green of
the lawn showed through that open window, just on a level with
the carpet ; but it was so bright outside that there was no chilling
suggestion in this. And the girls looked animated, with more
colour than usual, in their fervour of anticipation. The Rector
gave a little note of semi-satisfaction, semi-dissatisfaction peculiar
to men and fathers, and which is not in the least expressed by the
conventional Humph ! but I don't know what better synonym to
give than this time-honoured one ; and then he turned away and
shut himself into his study to await there the advent of the great
man. There was no reason why he should be deeply moved by
the coming of Leo Swinford. It would be well that the Rectory
and the Hall should maintain amicable relations, but that was all.
Mr. Plowden was not likely to be any the better whatever happened, except perhaps through the parish charities. There was
no better living or dignity of any kind to which this young man's
influence was likely to help him. Jim? Was there perhaps a
possibility that Leo, if he pleased, might do something for Jim?
or at least bring him into better society, make him turn to better
things, even if he did nothing more ? There was surely that possibility. One young man can do more for another, if he likes to
try, than any one else could do—if Jim would but allow himself
to be influenced. And surely he would in this case. He would
be flattered if Mr. Swinford sought him, if he was invited and
made welcome at the Hall. These thoughts were not very clearly
formed, as I set them down, in Mr. Plowden's head ; but they
flitted through his mind, as many an anxious parent will know
how. And this was what made his middle-aged bosom stir as he
sat and waited for Leo Swinford. Then a smile just crept about
his mouth as he remembered what his wife had been saying about,
perhaps, one of the girls. But the Rector shook his head. No,

no, that was not to be thought of. They were good girls—invaluable girls. But she might as well think of a prince for them as of Leo Swinford, who was a sort of prince in his way. No, not that; but perhaps Jim——

The question between the drawing-room and the study was now put to rest, for Mr. Swinford, when he had walked up briskly to the door, admired by the ladies from between the bars of the venetian blinds in the end window, asked for Mrs. Plowden, and was triumphantly ushered into the room by the parlourmaid, who secretly shared the excitement, wondering within herself *which* of the young ladies? And he was received and shaken hands with, and set in a comfortable chair; and a polite conversation began, before Mrs. Plowden, looking as if the matter had just occurred to her, in the midst of her inquiries for Mrs. Swinford, broke off, and said, 'Florry, my dear, your papa will be in the study; go and tell him that Mr. Swinford is here.'

'Can I go?' said the young man; 'it is a shame to disturb Miss Florry on my account; tell me which door, and I will beard the Rector in his den.'

'No, no! run, Flo; my husband will be so glad to see you here. I daresay you remember him in old times, though we were not here when you were a child. It was his father then who was Rector, and Lady William—I mean my sister-in-law Emily—was the young lady at home, as it might be one of my girls now.'

'I recollect it all very well,' said Leo, with a look and a smile which did not betray his sense that the girls now were not by any means what the Emily Plowden he remembered had been. He even paused, and said with a tone which naturally came into his voice when he spoke to a young woman—'I see now how like your daughter is to the Miss Plowden who used to play with me, and put up with me when I was a disagreeable little boy.'

'I am sure you never were a disagreeable little boy,' said Mrs. Plowden. 'I have often heard Emily speak of you. She was very fond of you as a child.'

'I hope she will not give up that good habit now I am a man. I hope, indeed, I am a little more bearable than I was then. I was a spoiled brat, I am afraid. Now, I am more aware of my deficiencies. Ah, Rector, how do you do? I am so glad to meet another old friend.'

'How do you do, Leo?' said the Rector. The girls admired and wondered, to hear that their father did not hesitate to call this fine gentleman by his Christian name. 'It is a very long time

since we met, and I don't know that I should have recognised
you : a boy of twelve, and a man of——'

'Thirty,' said Leo, with a laugh, 'don't spare me—though it
is a little hard in presence of these young ladies.   But it has not
made any such change in you, sir, and I should have known you
anywhere.'

'Twenty years is a long time.   What do you say, Jane?
Eighteen years : well, there's no great difference.   And so you
have come home at last, and I hope now you are at home you
mean to stay, and take up the duties of an English country gentleman, my dear fellow—which is your real vocation, you know, as
your father's son.'

'And what are those duties, my dear Rector,' said Leo, with
a laugh ; 'perhaps my ideas are rather muddled by my French
habits—to keep up a pack of fox-hounds, and ride wildly across
country : and provide a beef roasted whole for Christmas ?'

'Well, you can never go wrong about the beef at Christmas—
but I think we'll let you off the fox-hounds.   If you'll subscribe
to the hunt, that will be enough.'

'That is a comfort,' said the unaccustomed squire, 'for I am
not, I fear, a Nimrod at all.'

To hear the familiar way in which their father talked, laying
down the law, but not in the least in his imperative way, filled
the girls, and even Mrs. Plowden, with an admiration for the Rector
which was not invariable in his own house.   He was at once so
bold and so genial, so entirely at his ease with this gentleman,
who was so much out of their way, and beyond their usual range,
that they were at once astonished and proud—proud of their
father, who spoke to Leo as if he were no better than any other
young man in the place, and astonished that he should be able to
do so.   But Mrs. Plowden could not longer allow these two to
have it all their own way.

'It is so nice of Mrs. Swinford to give up her favourite place,
and to consent to come home, in order that you may live among
your own people—for it must be a sacrifice.   We can't say anything in favour of our English climate, I fear.   We all get on very
well, but then we are used to it—but Mrs. Swinford——'

'Oh, your mother is with you, of course,' the Rector said in
no such conciliatory tone.

'Yes, my mother is with me.   But, so far as that goes, Mrs.
Plowden, Paris, where we have chiefly lived, is no great improvement, that I know, upon England.   It's very cold, and now and
then it's foggy too : but she likes the society : you know it's

generally supposed to be more easy than in England. Not knowing England, except as a child, I can't tell ; but if you can manage
to be more conventional here than people are in France, I shall be
surprised. Of course, I should not have come, unless my mother
had seen the necessity : for I am all she has, you know,
now——'

'*Now*,' said the Rector, with pointed emphasis

At which Leo Swinford showed a little uneasy feeling. 'For
a great many years,' he said. 'You know my father died—shortly
after we left here.'

'I know,' said the Rector, very gravely. Then he added, in a
softened tone, 'It is a very long time ago.'

'Yes,' said the young man, more cheerfully, 'so long, that
almost my only experience of life is, that of being always with
my mother, her companion in everything. We have been a sort
of lovers,' he said, with a laugh ; 'everything in the world to each
other.'

Oh, how the girls admired this man, who said that his mother
was everything in the world to him ! It brought the tears to their
eyes. An Englishman, they thought, would not have said it,
however much it might have been the case : and Leo said it so
pleasantly, as if it were the most natural thing in the world ;
but papa, who had been so cheerful—papa kept a very serious
face.

'I hope it will be found that Watcham is not injurious to
Mrs. Swinford's health,' he said, and then there was an uncomfortable pause.

'I suppose,' cried Mrs. Plowden, rushing in to break it, 'that
you do not know any of your neighbours in the county, Mr. Swinford ? They will be eager, of course, to make your acquaintance.
There is quite a nice society in the county. We only see them
now and then, of course, in this little village.'

'Lady Wade was here on Tuesday, mamma, and the Lenthall
people the Saturday before, and Miss Twyford——'

'Yes, that is true,' said Mrs. Plowden, delighted that Emmy
had been sensible enough to remember so opportunely, and bring
in all these appropriate names. 'They do not neglect us, though
it is rather a long drive, from Lenthall especially ; but Mr. Swinford will have better opportunities of seeing a great deal of them.
When you have plenty of carriages and horses, everything is so
much easier.'

'Bobby Wade came to see us in Paris,' said Mr. Swinford, 'a
funny little man : and I have met some of the Lenthalls. One

drifts across most people one time or another. The world is such a small world.'

'Oh, then you won't feel such a stranger among them,' Mrs. Plowden said ; but she was a little disappointed. It had seemed to her that there would be a fine rôle to play in presenting this young potentate, so to speak, to the people about ; but as she reflected, with a sort of disgust, people in that position have a way of knowing each other, and are always drifting across each other in that wonderful thing called society, which is such a mystery to those that are out of it. She made a little pause of partial discomfiture, and then she said, 'Emmy, do you know where Jim is ? Is Jim in the house, my dear ? I should so like to introduce to Mr. Swinford our boy Jim.'

'Most happy, I am sure. Is that the one who has religious doubts ?' said Leo, smiling. 'Perhaps, as I am not very orthodox, the Rector may think he will not get any good from me.'

'Has Jim doubts ?' said the Rector, with his severe, precise air, transfixing the anxious mother with that regard : and then he added, 'Quite the reverse, Leo, the society of a man like you could not but be good for my boy ; I should like you to know him. I'll go and fetch him myself.'

But, alas ! Jim was not to be found. He had gone out, the maid said, immediately after Mr. Swinford came in. He had indeed seized the opportunity to escape, fearing that he would be called in, and made to form an acquaintance with this new man, for whom he had a kind of aimless dislike, as quite different from himself. The Rector came back with a serious face, which he tried to conceal with a laugh.

'We might have known,' he said, 'this was not a time to find Jim. He is reading with me to make up a little special work for his college, and as soon as his hours of work are over, he—bolts : as I suppose most young men in these circumstances would.'

'Every one of them,' said Leo. 'And do you find it answer, sir, this work at home ? Mr. Jim must be a wonderful man if he keeps hours, and all that—at home with you.'

There was not any reply made for a moment, but the father and mother exchanged a glance. Oh ! God bless the man who speaks such words ; it seemed as if there was nothing wrong, nothing but what was natural and universal in the shortcomings of their boy.

Mr. Swinford was afterwards watched by the village in his progress from one house to another of the great people of Watcham—the General's, where the family were at home, and he went in and stayed for a quarter of an hour: the Archdeacon's, where they were out, and where some close observers felt that he showed great satisfaction in leaving cards: and then he walked with his alert quick step round the village, as if to take a general view of it, and then returned towards the cottage, which all the spectators thought he was neglecting, the house of Lady William, generally the first on the list of all callers. He was not very tall, as Emmy Plowden had so regretfully allowed, but yet not short either, as she had indignantly asserted after. And it was true that he was neither dark nor fair, but brown, common brown, according to Florence's conclusion, the most well-wearing and steadygoing of all colours. His eyes, I think, were blue, which is a pleasant combination; but I don't mean by that the heroical sentimental combination of black hair and dark blue eyes which is so dear to romance, and so distinct a type of beauty. Mr. Swinford's eyes were of rather an ordinary blue, as his hair was of an ordinary brown, a little curly on his temples. And he had a pleasant colour, and, what was really the only very striking thing about him, a waxed and pointed moustache, after the fashion of his former dwelling-place. He walked briskly, but like a man not used to rough and muddy roads; stumbling sometimes, not remembering that it was necessary to look where he set his foot, and looking down now and then, with a sort of smiling dismay, upon the spots of mud upon his varnished shoes; yet he pushed on briskly all the same; and walked down to the landing-place to take a look at the river, which was looking its best, reflecting the sunshine which began to get low, and to dazzle in the eyes of the gazer. He gave a little pleased nod, as of approval to the river, and then he came back again to the village green, meeting the bands of children just dismissed, who had poured out of the school doors the minute before. He smiled upon them too, and their noise and their games, with little involuntary shrugs of his shoulders and uplifting of his eyebrows as he had to step out of their way: for they did not make room for him as they ought to have done, being rough and healthy village children, invaded by the spirit of the nineteenth century, and having passed beyond the age of curtseys and bows to the gentry. Some of the girls, indeed, stood aside with a little curiosity and pointed him out to each other, with whispers and giggles, which were less agreeable than the uproarious indifference of the rest. When he had got through the crowd, and passed the doors of the empty school, Leo suddenly stopped short at the sight of a face he knew. 'What!' he said, 'you here?' with very little pleasure in his tone.

'Yes,' said Mrs. Brown, with a slight sweep of a curtsey, 'I am here. You do not say you are glad to see me, Leo.'

'You know I am not glad to see you, and I do not pretend it. What are you doing here?'

Mrs. Brown smiled. She was a handsome woman, and looked, as all the village allowed, 'superior' to a village school-mistress. She was tall and dark, not like Leo, but there was a resemblance in her face to that of his mother which filled him with an angry impatience whenever this woman crossed his path. She smiled, and again made a scarcely perceptible obeisance as of satirical humility. 'That is my own concern,' she said.

'It is not mine, certainly: and I have no desire to know: but there is one thing I have to say,' he said sternly. 'Don't come to the Hall—I won't have you there. If I do you injustice I am sorry, but I don't want you, please, in my house.'

'And what then about your mother's house?' she said. 'Has she no house; or where are her friends to see her? It is hard if at her age she has no place of her own to receive her friends.'

'How do you venture to call yourself one of her friends?'

'Ask her,' said Mrs. Brown, with a smile. 'I am sorry you let your prejudice carry you so far. Ask your mother, Leo, and then forbid me the house if you think well. I am going to see Mrs. Swinford to-night.'

He turned away from her angrily with a wave of his hand, while she stood for a moment looking after him. There was a faint smile of triumph on her face, but it was not malicious or unkind.

'Bless us all, Mrs. Brown,' said her colleague, the master, coming up with no very amiable look, 'so it appears you know Mr. Swinford, and all the rest of the grandees?'

'I don't know anything about grandees : but I taught Leo Swinford his letters,' said Mrs. Brown.

'Oh, that's it,' said the schoolmaster, with a sort of satisfaction. It was an intelligible relationship, and seemed rather to temper than enhance the painful superiority in appearance and manners of Mrs. Brown. He added, 'It's a fine evening,' and went upon his way. He had no house attached to the school, while the mistress had : and he had wanted to get the appointment for his wife, who was not qualified, on the idea that he could help her to 'rub through somehow,' and that the house would be very convenient; but this point of view had not been taken by the authorities, and there was thus 'a little coolness' between him and his colleague, though she, of course, could not be supposed to be in fault. Now to hear that she had taught Mr. Swinford his letters partly consoled Mr. Atkinson. It showed she was no lady who had seen better days, no fallen star, but only a member of the profession all through, probably a nursery governess. He liked to be assured of this, and thought the better of her from that time.

Leo's light-hearted and amiable countenance was covered by a passing cloud. He went on quickly, as if trying to throw off the impression. He had many recollections in his life connected with this woman, who had been a member of his family in his earliest remembrance, who had taught him his letters, as she said, and who had always played a part, he did not know what, in his mother's life. She was not a servant, nor was she an equal. She had disappeared when they left the Hall in his childhood, but only to reappear again at intervals, and, he had always felt, for harm, though he could not tell what harm. The faint resemblance between her and his mother was a horror and annoyance to him more than words could say. It was, perhaps, her greatest offence, one he could not get over. And now to find her here, at their very door, as soon as they had settled in their own house, gave him a feeling of angry impatience which was intolerable. He hurried on to the only place in Watcham which was not strange to him, the little house which the village speculators thought he was neglecting, the cottage of Lady William. All the rest were curiosities to this young man of the world—the village Rectory, the retired old soldier, the decorous little establishments where everything was on so moderate a

scale, yet where the inhabitants were so calmly secure in their
position, their social elevation above the masses. The stranger
from a larger sphere is apt to smile in all circumstances at such
a little hierarchy. But to Leo Swinford it was, in addition to
all, so quaintly characteristically English, so unlike anything to be
seen elsewhere, especially so unlike France, to which he was most
accustomed, that he had felt himself walking rather through a
mild English novel—one of those he had read, amid more exciting
fare, with amusement yet tenderness for the peculiarities of his
own country—than through a real village and actual life. He
had felt that he was playing his part in this simple society, doing
his social duty, much amused and often tickled by the oddity of
all its novel ways. He had meant all along, when those duties
had been done, and when he had shown himself the amiable
young squire, friendly and accessible, to go to Lady William and
laugh with her over the humours of Watcham. She would understand all that. She knew the other point of view, and how odd
it must all seem in the eyes of the cosmopolitan, who knew
French curés better than English churchmen, and to whom the
rural parish was the quaintest thing. But in the meantime this
last encounter was not in the harmony of the rural parish;
there was another element, a tone of the more meretricious drama,
a sort of Porte St. Martin, he said to himself, thrown in. Somehow that which was so much more exciting seemed vulgar to him
in this quiet place. It was all so tranquil here and seemed so
pure, that the other tone of the fictitious and conventional came
in with a shock. Porte St. Martin, that was what this woman
was. Whereas there was nothing here that savoured of the
theatre in any way, but all pure nature and simplicity, and real,
though to him almost inconceivable life.

He went on all the same, even after this shock, to Lady
William, with a wonderful comfort in finding that here was
somebody who would understand him when he spoke. The
cottage looked more ridiculously small than ever when he reached
it. The Rectory, and the red brick mansions on the other side,
were large in comparison with this little place standing lowly in
its garden, with the trees hanging over it, and all the crop of
climbing plants with the spring sap pushing up through their
long shoots, and their new leaves forming. He almost stumbled
over the gate, and felt that to step over it would be more natural
than to open it and go in. Mab was in the garden busy about
some new flower beds, at which she was working with a child's
spade and trowel. She lifted her honest simple face flushed

with work, and laughed that she could not offer him such a dirty hand. 'I have been grubbing,' she said, 'but mother is in the drawing-room.' Her face was not only flushed, which sounds well enough, but red, and her fair hair a little in disorder from stooping over her 'grubbing.' Her plump arm was half bare, and looked very capable of work. She was a girl totally unconscious as yet of anything that was not homely and actual, not a budding woman with nerves and feelings, ready to thrill at a new presence. Whether it were Leo Swinford or any old woman that came in, it was quite the same to Mab. She laughed and pointed behind her to the tiny house, and the little open window. Even Emmy Plowden at the Rectory in all her English shyness and correctness might have made a timid effort to detain him a moment, to exchange a single word or two; but not Mab, who wanted to be rid of him simply, or even did not want that so much as to care whether he went or came. 'Mother is in the drawing-room.' She waited a moment with her trowel in her dirty hand till he should pass, then explained that she was in a hurry to get done before night, and stooped down again over her work.

'Can I help you?' he said, with the instinct of politeness, looking helplessly at her.

'Oh dear, no!' said Mab, with energy. 'I don't suppose you know anything about gardening; and then I like best to do it myself. Go in and talk to mother, Mr. Swinford. You'll find her there.'

What a change it was to go into that little drawing-room! I am not of opinion that there was more 'taste' shown in this little room than in the other houses about. There were no art stuffs, no decorative articles to speak of; one or two sketches which were not very good, and one or two prints which were better, hung on the walls; even the cheap 'pots' which country ladies prize were not to be seen here: there were no Japanese fans. But Leo felt there was something in the room which he had not found anywhere else, and which made him feel himself at home, not playing the simple drama of a country life. But I really think that he deceived himself, and that the only thing different was Lady William, who was sitting by the table at her needlework, which she laid down when he came in. She was very constant at her needle, always busy, but she knew better than to keep on sewing when a man came to see her, especially such a man as Leo Swinford, who probably would have thought it an affectation, if not in her, yet in any one else who had treated him so. A conventional man would naturally think that the woman thought herself pretty in that attitude with her eyes cast down.

'Well,' said Lady William, 'you have been parading the village, paying your visits. I have heard of your progress this hour past; and now I presume they are over, and you have come here to rest.'

'How pleasant it is,' said Leo, throwing himself into a chair, 'to be understood before one says anything! That is precisely what I have been doing, and what I have come to do.'

'There was no great insight required in either case,' said Lady William. 'And how do you like us now you have seen us, Leo? The Rectory is homely, but they're all as good as gold. Yes, they are, though they are my people. You know one doesn't often admire one's sister-in-law, and I don't pretend to admire her; but she's a good woman, and the girls are excellent.'

Leo allowed to breathe into his voice a slight, though very slight, suspicion of fatigue.

'You will not be surprised, dear lady,' he said, 'if I say that the member of the family who interested me most was your brother; and who is the son who could not be found, who is reading with his father?'

'Ah, Jim, poor boy!'

'Yes? I think I understand; there are then troubles even in this idyllic life?'

'It is so little a stranger knows. I think there is no idyllic life. We are very prosaic and poor, and our troubles are so very real—vulgar, you might call them. We look up, on the other hand, to what we call your brilliant and gay life, and think, surely there are no troubles there. Thus it is true, you see, the one half of the world never understands the other.'

'But you,' said Leo, 'know both.'

'Do I? I had a little share of the other, very short, and not, perhaps, very satisfactory. I never found it very brilliant or gay. The village life I know by heart, and its troubles, which are bad enough; small little vices and weakness, dreadfully poor and commonplace: you can't understand how pitiful they are.'

'Can't I? Well, so far as it is of any use, you must teach me. For you know from henceforth I am English, and will do my duty. My duty, perhaps, does not demand an endless seclusion here.'

'Seclusion do you call it? You will have half the people in

London pouring down soon, when your mother feels she has got established, and is ready to receive them.'

'Very likely,' he said. 'That will not change matters much. Society is the same everywhere. At all events, I shall always have you to come to.'

'It is very good of you to think that I can help you. There's metal more attractive. The village is not everything; in the county there are some pleasant people.'

'If you knew how sick I am of pleasant people! In sober fact, don't you know, I want to feel that I have something to do in the world, and if this is my sphere, to make it really so, and fill the place which you would say God had appointed for me.'

'Don't you say so, Leo?'

'I don't refuse to say so. I know so little. Religion has not held much place in my life. Between the abbé of the stage and the "clergyman" of the English, what have I ever known? I have not been instructed by any one, except'—he laughed a little. 'Do you know I remember scraps among all sorts of stuff, of the hymns you used to teach me—how long, long ago!'

'Yes, it is very long ago.' The room was rather dark; the day was waning. Mab outside was putting her tools together to leave off work. It was not possible for the two indoors to see each other's faces, but there was something tremulous in Lady William's tone. Leo Swinford put out his hand and laid it upon hers.

'You must begin again—not with the hymns, perhaps—but to teach me what is the best way.'

Evidently there was a great deal of discrimination in what Emmy Plowden said.

'Miss Grey knows, of course, everything about them. Miss Grey knows the whole story. She has been the longest here.'

'Yes,' said Miss Grey, 'I know, I suppose, all the outs and ins of it; or, if not all, a great part; all is a big word to say. I don't suppose anybody knows all—about the simplest of us—except the Almighty who made us, and understands all our curious ways.'

'That is a true speech,' said the old General, 'for curious are our ways, and strange are the devices we have to hide ourselves from ourselves.'

'Come, Stephen,' said Mrs. FitzStephen, 'let us have none of your philosophising. You like a story, or gossip, if you like to call it so, just as well as any of us; draw your chair nearer the fire, and listen to what Miss Grey has got to tell us, for I can read a whole story in her eye.'

It was General FitzStephen's drawing-room in which this conversation was taking place, in the March afternoon, when evening was falling. It had been cold and boisterous all day, with the March wind, which the farmer loves, drying and parching everything outside; the roads all gray and dusty; the fields looking as if every drop of sap in every green blade or leaf had retired to the heart of the plant. The wind had blown itself out, and fallen a little before the darkening, and Miss Grey, out, like all the rest of the world, for a little walk, had been met and apprehended by the General and his wife, and brought in for tea. How much this was on Miss Grey's account and how much for their own, I would not undertake to say. They were fond of Miss Grey, and so was everybody at Watcham: and people had a way of thinking that she was lonely and wanted cheering up—which, in most cases, only meant that they wanted cheering up themselves, and that there was nobody in the village who knew so well how to do this as the little lonely spinster. The Fitz-Stephens' house was exceedingly cosy, and though it was not large, it was much larger than Lady William's, and more pleasantly built; with cheerful irregularities in the shape of bow-windows, which gave more light, and agreeable little recesses and corners to talk in. It was not so plain in any way. It was almost richly furnished with warm Persian carpets and thick curtains, and a great deal of wadding and cushioning. The General and his wife had, indeed, reached a proficiency in the art of making each other comfortable, which only an elderly pair, without children, can attain, and which, in their hands becomes a fine art. There were no rough corners in their house; nothing that was not padded and made soft. The draughts, which Lady William could only faintly struggle against, they shut out by curtains, artistically planned, to the arrangement of which they had given their whole mind, two together, which everybody knows is better than one, and each for the other, which is better still : for not a suspicion, nor even a sensation, of selfishness can be in the man who is afraid of a chill for his wife, or the woman whose whole soul is bent on keeping her husband comfortable. The candles had not been lighted, but the firelight was shining brightly through the room, giving a brightness which no other artificial light possesses : and, through the windows, the yellow glow of a spring sunset, with a little pink in it, but none of winter's violent and frosty red, came in. Thus, between the day and the night, with the sweetness of the western light outside like a picture, and the warm domestic glow within, Mrs. FitzStephen's pretty tea-table was the most pleasant thing one could see on an evening while it was still cold. They had generally some one to share that darkening hour with them, and make it more cheerful ; and on this particular evening there were two, Miss Grey, as has been said, and the wife of the Archdeacon, Mrs. Kendal, as quiet a meek woman as ever was, not capable of doing much in the way of addition to the mirth, but quietly receptive of it, which is the next best thing.

It is a curious fact, which I don't seem to have seen commented on, how well and easily a kind old man who has fallen into quiet society along with his wife in the evening of his days, takes to the feminine element which is apt to preponderate in it. An old lady rarely makes herself at home with men in the same way, or if she does it is perhaps with the young friends of her sons who look up to her as a mother. But old soldiers as well as old parsons, to whom that might seem more natural, fall into ladies' society with a relish and satisfaction that is amazing. Pride of sex, which is rarely wanting, takes refuge, we may suppose, in the little superiority so willingly accorded, the deferences and flatteries with which he is surrounded, and which he repays with little gallantries and pretty speeches with which the ladies on their side are amused and pleased. General FitzStephen was a great hero among all the ladies at Watcham, and he took his place among them with little sense of incongruity, with a pleasant ease and simplicity, not sighing for anything better, not wasting, or so it seemed, a thought upon his club or his men. He liked Miss Grey to come in to tea as well as his wife did, and was as pleased with Mrs. Kendal as with her husband—more so, indeed, for he thought and said that the Archdeacon was an old woman, an expression which he never employed to any lady. For Lady William he had a sort of devotion, but that was not remarkable, for Lady William was of a different species, and not unlikely to secure the homage of any age or kind of man.

It was therefore a very cheerful old party that was assembled round the FitzStephen fire, none among them under fifty-five, the General within easy sight of three-score and ten, but all very well, with the exception of Mrs. Kendal, who had been more or less of an invalid all her life, but enjoyed her ill-health on the whole, and was as likely to live now as at thirty. She sat lost in the deepest of easy-chairs on the side of the fire opposite the window and where there was least light. Miss Grey was on the sofa in the full light of the fire, which sparkled in a pair of beautiful brown eyes she had, which looked none the worse for the number of years which had passed over their possessor. Miss Grey was very small, a little bit of a woman, with scarcely body enough to lodge a soul which was not little at all : at least the part of it which was heart, if there are any divisions in our spiritual being, was so big as to run over continually. She was very dark, with hair that had been black before it became iron-gray, and a gipsy complexion of olive and cherry. Her feet and hands were not so small as would have become her tiny person, but as they were feet that were always in motion for the good of her poor fellow-creatures, and hands that were noted in their service, these things are the less necessary to look into.

Mrs. FitzStephen was remarkable for little more than the neatness of her cap, and the trimness of her dress and person generally. She had been what people call a pretty little woman, and on that character she lived. She was a pretty little woman still according to the limitations of her age, and her husband was still proud of her simple and somewhat faded beauty. He had

always been pleased to hear it said what a pretty little woman
Mrs. FitzStephen was, and he was still pleased with the thought.
She had not changed for him. She was seated in front of the
low tea-table, on a low chair, making the tea. The General, who
was tall, looked taller than ever moving about in the little glowing
room between the firelight and the dark, handing to the ladies
their cake and tea.

'We are all quite new people in the place in comparison with
Miss Grey,' said Mrs. Kendal, in her little invalid voice, 'though
we used to come here, the Archdeacon and I, long ago, before he
was the Archdeacon or I was delicate : dear me, we used to go on
the water ! he was a great boating man once——'

'I remember,' said Miss Grey, 'he once took the duty for old
Mr. Plowden, before the present Rector left College. I remember
you very well—you were the bride—and there were ever so many
little parties made——'

'To be sure,' said the Archdeacon's wife, sitting up in her
chair—'dear me—it is so strange to think of the time when one
was young——'

'Emily was a little thing who was about everywhere—the
child of the parish I used to call her. A girl who has lost her
mother is so often like that, everybody's child. I don't say it's
not very nice as long as they're children. One gets more used to
them. She was always dancing about through everybody's house
—thank you, General, I couldn't take any more cake—there
wasn't a house in the parish, rich or poor, but Emily was dancing
out and in——'

'Very bad for the child,' said Mrs. FitzStephen.

'Do you think so?' said Miss Grey; 'well, I don't know,
as long as she was a child.'

'If it was bad for the child, my dear, the woman has come
handsomely out of it,' said the General, carrying the cake into the
dark corner to Mrs. Kendal. 'My dear lady, one morsel more—
to keep me company.'

'Oh ! General, on that inducement—but only a very, very
small piece——'

'It's bad when the child grows into a woman,' said little Miss
Grey, shaking her little head; 'she was as dear a girl as ever
lived—not one of them now is fit to hold the candle to what she
was. Mab?—Mab's a darling, the honestest little straightforward thing : and she would have been safer than Emily—she
would never have been taken in—as her mother was.'

'Dear Miss Grey,' said Mrs. FitzStephen, 'another cup of

tea: and you were going to tell us about the Swinfords—for we all know there was something: she was a Seymour, wasn't she, of a very good family?'

'But foreign blood in her,' said Miss Grey; 'I think her mother was a Russian; she always was fond of foreign things and foreign ways; he was a dear, good, quiet man. It never came into his head that anything could go wrong——'

'No: why should it, in a quiet neighbourhood like this——?'

'Oh! I like to hear you speak of a quiet neighbourhood. When the Hall was in full swing it was about as quiet as—as Windsor Castle in the old days, before Her Majesty knew what trouble was; always something going on, the town full of visitors; entertainments that were in *The Morning Post*, and every kind of pleasure. They used to come down in the middle of the summer, from their town house, for a few days at a time, and bring half the town with them; and in autumn in the time of the partridges——'

'There could never be much shooting,' said the General with satisfaction, as on a subject he knew.

'At the other end of the estate, the forest end—I have heard there was not very much, but it was very good; that is to say, it didn't last very long, but as long as it lasted—at all events the shooting might be only a pretence: but the house was always full, that is the only thing I know——'

'I daresay,' said Mrs. FitzStephen, 'it will be so again; a young man fond of company, like young Mr. Swinford.'

'Oh! you may be sure it will be so again. I don't know about him; but I do know about Mrs. Swinford——'

'Now, don't be spiteful, Miss Grey; when one lady does not approve of another it is the right thing to say that she is spiteful ——' the General said in an explanatory way, to take away the sting of the word which had come out unawares.

'And it is very pleasant in a country place to see a little company,' said Mrs. Kendal, 'not that I care for great parties—nor the Archdeacon; but it makes a little stir——'

'It keeps a movement in the air,' said Mrs. FitzStephen, retiring from the fire.

'Well, there will be plenty of it,' said Miss Grey.

'But, my dear lady, we must not have you cross—cross is what you never were; and society don't you know, in this paradise of Watcham is the only thing we want.'

'It would be very nice,' said Mrs. FitzStephen, with a little sigh; 'though we have all done without it nicely, with our little tea parties, and a friend from town from Saturday to Monday, and so forth.'

'I never wish for more,' said Mrs. Kendal, 'nor the Archdeacon ; it is just what we like : but dear me, when I was young —I've danced sometimes all night.'

'We've heard the chimes at midnight,' said the General, rubbing his hands; 'so I don't see any great occasion, my dear ladies, to be afraid.'

Miss Grey said nothing, but there was a little twitter and thrill in her, half visible in the firelight, as of a bird stirring on a bough ; perhaps this proceeded from a little nodding of her head, very slight, but continued like a little protest under her breath.

'And then think of the young ladies,' said General FitzStephen jauntily ; 'I have always heard that Lady William met her husband there——'

'There is not much chance for any of them to meet their husbands here : I often try to induce the General to ask a nice young man—from Saturday to Monday, you know—the only way we could ever induce a man from town to come here : but he says it isn't good enough—and asks his old fogies instead——'

'The old fogies are more agreeable to us, my dear,' said the General, 'and the young ladies must find their husbands for themselves : but when the Hall is full of fine company as our dear friend predicts——'

Upon which Miss Grey, nodding, introduced what seemed an entirely new and uncalled-for assertion.

'James Plowden,' she said, 'though he is the Rector, is not a wise man any more than his father was before him——'

'My dear lady !' cried the General.

'Miss Grey !' said Mrs. Kendal mildly, out of the dark.

'Nelly, Nelly !' cried Mrs. FitzStephen, who was the one most intimate with the culprit.

'James Plowden,' repeated Miss Grey, 'is no Solomon, as you all very well know. I am saying nothing against him—he's a very good man : but though he hasn't very much wisdom, if he thought one of his girls was to get a prince for her husband in the same way as his sister got hers, he is not the man I think him, if he ever let one of them put a foot inside that door.'

They all said 'Lady William !' with a joint cry, which, though it was very quietly uttered by each individual, rose into quite an outcry when uttered by the whole.

'Poor little Emily !' said Miss Grey, putting up her handkerchief to her eyes, 'that's how I think of her—though if she gets any pleasure out of her title, poor child, if you can call that a title——'

'Of course it is a title—she takes precedence of all of us,' said Mrs. FitzStephen.

'A courtesy title,' said the General.

'Dear, I never knew there was anything against it,' said Mrs. Kendal.

'I hope she gets some pleasure out of it, poor dear,' said Miss Grey; 'little else has she ever got. A horrible man, who never, I believe, made himself pleasant to her, never for one day : and a horrible life for I don't know how many years. If there had been a mother, or if he hadn't been——well, I won't call him names now he's in his grave—such a sacrifice would never have been made.'

'But I suppose she liked him at the time,' said one of the ladies.

'And no doubt he was in love with her,' said another; 'Lord Portcullis' son, and she a country clergyman's daughter.'

'Oh, as for that, God knows : she was perhaps dazzled with the miserable title, and her father of course, who was only a silly old man—and then she was besought and persuaded, God knows how, by those who did it for their own sake, not hers——'

'But what reason could any one have?' said Mrs. FitzStephen; 'my dear Nelly Grey, you must be making up a story in your head; what cause could any one have, unless to satisfy the man who was in love with a girl, or to help forward the girl to a match above her? These are the only two reasons possible, and there's no harm in them; we would, any of us, do it,' she said.

'Not if the man was of bad character,' said the General.

'And if the girl was not in love with him? Oh, I don't call that romantic at all,' Mrs. Kendal said.

Miss Grey shook her head again, shook it till her little bonnet, and all that could twitter and tremble about her, shook too.

'You're all good people,' she said; 'you don't know the mystery of a wicked woman's heart—or for that matter of a man's either.'

'Nelly,' said Mrs. FitzStephen, almost sharply, 'what can you know, a little single woman, about mysteries and wicked persons? A soldier's wife like me, that has been knocked about the world——'

'Or, oh, dear me, a clergyman's!' said Mrs. Kendal, 'and they are told everything——'

'Whatever you may know, you don't know Mrs. Swinford,' said Miss Grey, hastily tying her bonnet-strings—'No, I must go home, thank you; I want to be in before it's quite dark. And really there's not much to tell; nothing that I've seen with my eyes, as you may have, my dear, knocking about as a soldier's wife; or as a clergyman's wife may have heard dreadful things trickling out through her husband. No, I've no husband. I haven't knocked about the world. I may have fancied things, being always so quiet here. But good-night, for I must go; it's nearly dark, and my little maid is always frightened if I'm not in before dark——'

'The General will step round with you, Nelly dear—General, you'll put on your greatcoat——'

'Of course I am going,' said the General. It was a duty he never was negligent of, to see a lady who came by herself to tea safely home.

' I HAVE been on a tour of inspection,' said Leo Swinford. He had met on another beautiful afternoon all the villagers, that is, the gentry of the village, party by party, and he had repeated to them all the same phrase : ' A tour of inspection !' Perhaps he liked the words, for he had the love of his adopted country for significant and appropriate phrases ; and it seemed to that simplicity, which lies at the bottom of so much that is conventional on the other side of the Channel, that it was highly appropriate, and very English and business-like, to describe his prowl about the village in such words. But it was not until, after many little pauses and talks, he had come upon Lady William and her daughter, that he went further into the matter. When he saw the two figures coming along, one of which at least was like no one else in Watcham, Leo felt that he had reached the society in which he could speak freely : so, though he repeated his phrase, he did not stop there. ' I know now,' he said, nodding his head in half disgust, half satisfaction, ' what is meant in England when you speak of the slums.'

' The slums !' said Mab, who leant across her mother a little, with an ear attentive to hear what he should say ; ' but there are no slums in Watcham ; it is in London and in the East End that there are slums. We have no slums here.'

Leo was too polite to say that what he said was not intended for little girls ; but he gave that scarcely perceptible shrug of his shoulders which means the same thing, and answered with a smile :

' I did not suppose, Miss Mab, that you were ever permitted to go there.'

' Not permitted,' said Mab ; ' mother ! why shouldn't I be permitted ? I hope I know every cottage in Watcham, and about all the people, though of course they change a little. Mother, I suppose he has been down by Riverside.'

' Very likely,' said Lady William, ' where the houses do not

look attractive, we must allow. But Mab is right, Leo, though
perhaps she should not be so ready with her opinion. The houses
do not look nice, nor, in some cases, the people that are in them;
but we have nothing very bad here.'

'I don't know, then, what you call very bad; it must be something beyond my conception. I should like to clear all those
houses off the face of the earth. It is ugly; it is loathsome. How
can the children grow up with any sense of what is good in dens
like those? I have come home with the meaning to do my best
for the people who belong to me, you know. I have not very clear
ideas of what my duty is, perhaps; I only know it has been
neglected for many, many years.'

'That is true, perhaps,' said Lady William; 'but after all, you
know, the squire of the parish is not everything, and we have all
helped to keep things going. You don't know our aspect .of
poverty, Leo; perhaps it looks worse than it is. You will find
plenty to do, no doubt. If you announce your intentions, I know
several people who will be delighted to tell you just what you
must do; my brother, of course, first of all.'

'Shall I put myself, then, in the Rector's hands?'

'Oh, don't let him, mother,' said Mab (that little girl again:
how these little creatures are allowed to put themselves in the front
in England!), 'Uncle James has so many fads. He wants a new
organ (we do want it very much) and a new infant school, and he
is always, always after the drains! But I know a great many
things that it would be delightful to do.'

'Of course your advice will be the best,' said her mother.
'My dear Leo, it is so new to us to find a man delivering himself
over to be fleeced, for the good of the people.'

'Do not use such a word; I am so much in earnest; I am so
anxious to do everything I can do. All these years I have been
receiving revenues from this place and giving nothing back; and I
am lodged like a prince, while these poor people, who do their duty
to their country better than I have ever done, are in—what do you
call them, sties, stables, worse, a great deal worse, than my
horses——'

'You must not run away with that idea,' said Lady William.
'Mab, where can he have been?'

'I tell you, on Riverside, mother; there are some houses there,
old, damp, horrid places; it is quite true.'

'Dear lady,' said Mr. Swinford, laying his hand lightly on
Lady William's arm, 'you consult this child: but what can she
know of the miseries which at her age one does not understand?'

Mab kept down by an effort the reply which was breaking from her lips. Child! to a woman of seventeen! and to be told she did not understand: she that knew every soul on Riverside, and what they worked at, and how many children there were, and every domestic incident! She kept leaning across her mother to catch every word, and cast terrible looks at the accuser, though she commanded herself, and allowed Lady William to reply.

'You forget,' said Lady William gently, 'that to us there is no horror about our poor neighbours, Leo. We know most of them as well as we know our own relations, perhaps better; for on that level nothing is hid; whereas on our own, if there is trouble in a house, there is often an attempt to conceal, or perhaps even to deceive outsiders, and pretend that everything is well.'

'But, the very absence of concealment—the brutal frankness—the vice—the horror——'

'Mother, I suppose Mr. Swinford means when the men drink, and everything goes wrong?'

'Yes, Mab, that is what he means; it is not so common in France as in England. It is the root of everything here. They are not unkind generally when they can be kept from drink. Mr. Osborne, the curate, is a fanatic on that subject, and one can't wonder. He would like you to oppose the giving of licenses, Leo, and to shut up every place in Watcham where drink is to be got. I am very much with him in my heart. But I would not advise you to give yourself altogether up to his guidance either.'

'Not to the Rector's, nor to the curate's (whom I have not seen), nor to Miss Mab's? To yours, then, dear lady, which is what I shall like best of all.'

'No, not to mine. I share all of these extravagances, one now, and the other to-morrow. Sometimes I am all for Mr. Osborne's way, sometimes I sympathise with my brother. You must put yourself in nobody's hands, but examine everything, and judge for yourself what it is best to do.'

'Ah!' said Leo, throwing up his hands, 'you give me the most difficult part of all. I will pull down their evil-smelling places, and build them better; or they shall have money, money to get clothes instead of rags, to be clean. These are things I understand; but to examine and form conclusions as if I were a statesman or a philanthropist—can't it be done with money? I hear it said that anything can be done with money.'

'Oh, mother, a great deal,' said Mab eagerly; 'don't discourage him: a little money is such a help. I know people who could be

made so happy with just a little.   There are the old Lloyds, who
will have to go to the workhouse if their son does not send
them something, and he is out of work.   And there is George,
who can't go fishing any longer for his rheumatism, and poor
dear Lizzie Minns, who is so afflicted, and won't live to be a
burden on her people.   Oh, don't tell him no, mother!   Mr.
Swinford, people say it is wrong to give money,' said Mab, turning
to him, always across the figure of Lady William, who was between, with her eyes, which were not pretty eyes, swimming in
tears, 'but I don't think so; not in these kind of cases, where
a few shillings a week would make all the difference: and we
haven't got it to give them, mother and I.'

'They shall not go to the workhouse, nor die of their rheuma-
tisms,' cried Leo.   He was so moved that the water stood in his
eyes too.   'Tell me how much it needs, or take my purse, or give
me your orders.   I was a fool!   I was a fool! thinking the angels
shouldn't know.'

Mab stared a little across her mother, not in the least compre-
hending this address, or that she was the angel on behalf of whom
Leo upbraided himself.   She understood herself to be stigmatised
as a little girl, but she was not aware that the higher being had
anything to do with her.   At the same time she perceived that
his heart was touched, and that to the old Lloyd's, etc., the
best results possible might accrue.   As for Lady William, she
was half touched, half amused by the incident; pleased that her
little girl had come out so well, and pleased with Leo's enthusiasm,
yet ready to laugh at them both.   She put up a subduing hand
between.

'Don't beg in this outrageous way, Mab; and don't give in to
her in that perfectly defenceless manner, Leo.   I shall be compelled to interfere and stop both of you.   But here is somebody
coming who knows all about it, better than Mab, better than I
do, far better even than the parson of the parish.   Here is not
only the head of all the charities, but Charity herself embodied.
Look at her coming along, that you may know her again when
you see her, one of the great Christian virtues in flesh and
blood.'

Leo winked the tear out of his eye, though he was not
ashamed of it, as a man all English might have been, and
laughed in response to this new appeal, in which he did not
know that there might not be a little satire.   He said, 'I see
no white wings nor shining robes.   I see a very small woman
in the dress of a — no, I will not say that — but it's a

little droll, isn't it? scanty, to say the least, and perhaps shabby.'

'Oh, if you want an appropriate dress! It ought to be white, with blazons of gold: but it is only an old black merino, worn rusty in the service of the poor. Miss Grey, Mr. Leo Swinford wants you to remember him. He was only a little boy when you saw him last, and he wants to speak to you about the poor.'

'Of course I should not have known you again,' said Miss Grey, 'for I don't know that I ever saw you nearer than in the carriage with your mamma. But I am very glad to know you, Mr. Swinford, though not much worth the trouble—and especially to tell you anything I can about the poor.'

'He has views,' said Lady William, 'of abolishing them off the face of the earth.'

'Oh, you'll never do that,' said little Miss Grey, with a flash of her beautiful brown eyes. 'The poor ye have always with you; never, till you can make the race perfect, will you get rid of the poor.'

'He thinks money will be able to do it: and Mab rather agrees with him.'

'Money!' said Miss Grey, with a disdain which no words could express. She turned not to Lady William, who spoke, but to Leo, when she replied, 'Money is of use, no doubt: but to sow it about and give it to everybody is downright ruin.'

'Not to good honest old people, Miss Grey, like the Lloyds and old Riverside George.'

'Pensions?' said the little lady, with her head on one side like a bird. 'Well, there may be something in that. Come into my house and sit down, and we can argue it out.'

Miss Grey's cottage was a smaller cottage even than Lady William's. It was lopsided—a house with only one window beside the door; one little sitting-room with a little kitchen behind.

The little parlour looked as if it could not by any means contain the party which its little mistress ushered in. 'Step in, step in,' she said, 'don't be afraid. There is far more room than you would think. I have had ten of the mothers here at once, and not so much as a saucer broken. The ladies know where they can find places, but Mr. Swinford, as you are a stranger, you shall sit here.'

Here was a large easy-chair, the largest piece of furniture in the room, which stood almost in the centre, with a small table beside it. And there was a big old-fashioned sofa against the wall,

occupying the whole side from door to window. It was the wonder
of all the Watcham people how that sofa had been got into the
room which it blocked up. But Miss Grey's response always was
that she could not part with her furniture; and that the old
Chesterfield, which was what she called the sofa, was a cherished
relic of her dear home. But the most remarkable thing about this
little room was the manner in which it was lined and garlanded
with china. Miss Grey was poor, but the china was not poor. It
was of every kind that could be described, and it was everywhere,
on little shelves and brackets against the wall, on the mantelpiece,
on every table. There was scarcely anything in the room except
the Chesterfield which did not support a row of dishes, or vases,
or plates. Lady William and Mab, being closely acquainted with
the place, managed to seat themselves without damaging any of
these treasures : but to an unaccustomed visitor the entrance was
one full of perils. It went to Miss Grey's heart that Mr. Swinford made his entrance as gingerly as if all these riches had been
his own.

'Never mind,' she said, as something rattled down from a
corner, 'it's only a very common delft dish ; or is it the majolica?
Only the yellow majolica, it doesn't matter at all ; and besides, it
isn't broken, or chipped, or anything. Oh, that's an accident that
happens every day : but my ten mothers didn't even knock down
that plate, and some of them were big bouncing women.'

'You are a collector, Miss Grey?'

'Oh, I am not good enough for that ; they are all old things,
and I am fond of them ; most of them, Mr. Swinford, came from
my dear home ; the things that were in one's home are never like
anything else ; and a few I have picked up, but very few, not
enough to make any difference. The majolica, I daresay you
think nothing of it, you that know what is really good. And
neither do I, but not from that reason, because I only bought it
myself at a sale. It is not from my dear home.'

'And may I ask,' said Leo, with polite attention, 'what it
means, your ten mothers? You must understand that I am very
ignorant of many things.'

'Oh, that is easily explained,' said little Miss Grey; 'ten
members of my mothers' meeting, that's what they are; they
meet in the schoolroom once a week, and now and then I have
them here to tea.'

'Mothers,' said Leo, 'of children? I understand.' He was
perfectly serious in his polite attention. 'And they meet every
week, and consult, perhaps upon education?'

'Oh no,' said Miss Grey, 'poor things, they are not much up to that. They cut out things for their children, little petticoats, and so forth, and work at them; and one of us reads aloud; and they pay only a little for the material, just enough to feel that they have bought it; and the schoolroom is nice and warm and bright, and it's a little society for them.'

Leo's face was very grave; there was not even a ghost of a smile upon it. 'I should never have thought of that,' he said, 'but it is good, very good. But why not give them the material to make things for their children? I understand the women love it, and it does them good to work at it. But I will buy the stuff for you, all you want, with pleasure. Would not that be the simplest way?'

'I think so too, often,' said Mab, whose whole soul was in the question, and who understood nothing at all of the amusement with which her mother was looking on.

'Not at all,' said Miss Grey, 'for then it would look like charity; now they buy everything, it is very cheap, but it is no charity, it is their very own.'

'But charity is no bad thing; charity is to give what one has to those who have not.'

'I think so, too, often,' said Mab again. She added, nodding her head, 'It is in the Bible just like that.'

'But we must not pauperise them,' said Miss Grey; 'we must help them to keep their self-respect.'

'There is nothing about self-respect in the Bible,' said Mab quickly.

'Oh, Mab, you are only a child. I am not against giving; sometimes it is the only way; and it's a great pleasure. But it isn't good for the people; we must think first what is good for them. We must not demoralise them; we mustn't——' The little woman hurried her argument till her cheeks grew like two little dark roses, with excitement and perplexity.

'It is this,' said Leo; 'everything has been neglected by me for many years. First I was a child and did not understand, and then I was a young man, taken up by follies. I have come back. I wish now to do my duty to my people. I will put into your hands money, as much as you want, a hundred or a thousand pounds, as much as is wanted, to make happy whom you can, if they can be brought to be happy; and to make clean, and plentiful, and good. Hush! dear lady, don't laugh at me. I would like to pull down those frightful houses, and put all the poor people in pleasant, bright rooms, where they could breathe.'

'What frightful houses?'

'He means Riverside, Miss Grey.'

'He means Riverside! But they are not bad houses; the people are not unhappy there. Oh, I could show you some! But at Riverside they are only ugly. The people are not badly off; they get on well enough. One helps them a little sometimes, but they rarely come on the rates, or even apply to the Rector. Why, Mr. Swinford, you mustn't only look at the outside of things.'

'I know,' said Leo, repeating himself (but this was part of his excited state), 'that I am housed like a prince, and they—not so well as the horses in the stables.'

Little Miss Grey kept her eyes on him as he spoke, as if he were a madman, with a mixture of extreme curiosity and anxiety, to know if there was method in his madness. 'Well!' she cried, 'that is not your fault. You are not—what do you call it, Emily? for I am not clever—anything feudal to them. You are not their chief, like a Scotch clan. What makes them poor (and they're not so very poor) is their own fault. They're as independent as you are. If they drink and waste their wages they're badly off; if they don't they're comfortable enough; if they're dirty, it's because they don't mind. Bless me, Mr. Swinford, it isn't your fault. If you pulled down the houses, they would make an outcry that would be heard from here to London. Besides, I don't think they belong to you!' said Miss Grey triumphantly. 'They were all built by White, the baker. I know they don't belong to you!'

Leo Swinford sat and gazed at her with a rising perception that there was something ludicrous in the attitude he had assumed, which, at the same time, was so entirely sincere and true.

'And as for the stables being better—some stables are ridiculous—sinful luxury, as if the poor dumb brutes were not just as happy in the old way. Why, my little house,' said Miss Grey, looking round, 'is not all marble and varnish, like your stables. And you think, perhaps, it is a poor little place for me to live in, while you live in your palace like a prince, as you say?'

He did not make any reply. This little woman took away his breath. But he did cast a look round him at the minuteness of the place; a kind of wistful look, as if he could not deny the feeling she imputed to him, and would have liked nothing so much as to build her a palace, too.

'Well!' said Miss Grey, 'and I would not give it for Windsor Castle. I like it ten thousand times better than your palace; and the poor folk in Riverside are just like me.'

'Dear lady,' said Leo, in his perplexity, 'it is not the same thing; but you take away my breath.'

Here Lady William came to his aid, yet did not fail to point a moral. 'You see,' she said, 'you must not follow a hasty impulse even to do good. There are two reasons against making a desert of Riverside; first, because the people there don't find it dreadful, as you do; and next, my dear Leo, because you're not their feudal lord, as Miss Grey says, and the houses don't belong to you.'

He shrugged his shoulders, as a man discomfited has a right to do. But Miss Grey burst in before he had time to say a word: 'If that is what you want, Mr. Swinford, I can show you a place!'

WHILE Leo Swinford was making his first attempt to revolutionise, or perhaps pauperise, the parish under the irregular and unofficial guidance of Miss Grey and Mab, who had, of course, no public standing at all, though he would have been a bold Rector indeed who had disowned the abounding services and constant help of Miss Grey—other incidents were going on of still more importance to the conduct of this history. Notwithstanding the indignation with which she had received the suggestion that money was strong enough to unlock all doors and solve all problems, it was astonishing how soon that unauthorised and unofficial Providence of the parish found ways and means to disembarrass Leo of a considerable sum of money, and to produce a list of requirements for which that vulgar dross would be very useful. She adopted all Mab's suggestions as to the Lloyd couple and old George, permitting that little weekly allowances should be given them to keep them in life and comfort; and she pronounced and sealed the doom of a group of cottages which, though they were not ugly, like Riverside, rather the contrary, a picturesque group, making quite a feature in the level country, were not fit to live in, as Mr. Swinford was reluctantly brought to allow. He did not like pulling to pieces the venerable walls and high-pitched roofs, with their growths of lichen, which were a picture in themselves, and struggled long in the name of art against that dire necessity. Indeed, the case was a parable, since we are all but too willing to pull down the ugly but not uncomfortable tenements of White the baker, though it costs us a pang to do away with the unwholesome prettiness of our own. But while Leo's education in the duties of a proprietor was thus progressing, there was another young man whose training was going on in a very different way. Jim's Sophocles became more and more hard upon him as the spring days grew longer, and the east winds blew themselves out, and the sun grew warm.

H

What was the good of all that Greek? he asked himself, and there was reason in the question. If he were to be sent out to a ranch it would not help him much to know about Electra and Antigone. Less tragic heroines, and lore less elevated, would serve the purpose of the common day ; or if he went into a merchant's office, there is no commercial correspondence in Greek, even if modern Greek was the least like the classic. What, then, was the use of it? And yet the Rector would hear no reason, but kept grinding on and on. Jim had some cause for his dissatisfaction : and he could not have understood the reluctance of his father, once a scholar in his time, to resign for his son all hope of the honours which Jim neither wished for nor prized. But the Rector could not wind himself up to the point of deciding that what he fondly hoped were his boy's talents should be hidden either in a ranch or in an office. He kept hoping, as we all hope, that fate would take some turn, that some opening would come which would still permit of a happier conclusion. And nothing was settled from day to day, and nothing done except that Sophocles, that sop to anxiety, that poor expedient to occupy the lad who hated it. It is a commonplace to add that if the vexed and unhappy Rector had contrived a means to make his son's prospects worse and his life more untenable, he could scarcely have hit upon a better. To send him away had a hope in it, though it might have been destruction, but to keep him unwilling and embittered at home, held in this treadmill of forced and unprofitable labour, was the destruction made sure and without hope.

Jim was too sore and vexed with this fate from which there seemed no escape, yet too well assured that it was his own fault, and that nothing he could do was likely to restore him to the old standing-ground in which everything that was good was hoped and believed of him—to make any manly protest against it. There was no such power in him, poor boy. It was his nature to drift, and to resent the drifting, but to take no initiative of his own. When he was upbraided, as he was so often for his idleness and uselessness, he would make angry retorts now and then, that he would work fast enough if he had anything to do except that beastly Greek : but these retorts were growled out under his breath, or flung over his shoulder as he escaped, and the angry father paid no attention to them, and did not perceive the reason that lay underneath this angry folly. Even when the Rector adjured him, as he did sometimes, to say what he would do, to strike out some path of his own, poor Jim had nothing to say. He had no path of his own ; he had only an angry perception that

the one upon which he was now drifting was the worst: but if
they would only let him alone, Jim did not care otherwise much
about it.   What he proposed was to do nothing at all except a
little boating and lawn tennis, or skating in winter.   He did not
think of the future, nor ask anything of it.   If they would but let
him alone.

When a young man in the country is what he calls bullied at
home, work demanded of him which he hates, aims and purposes
insisted upon which he does not possess, it is an infinite relief to
him to escape to the society of those who will flatter and soothe,
and make him feel himself a fine fellow and a gentleman in spite
of all.   Such was the company in the 'Blue Boar' where the
Rector's son was thought much of, and his opinions greatly looked
up to, notwithstanding a conviction on the part of the honest
tradespeople who frequented the parlour that it was a thousand
pities he ever came there.   They asked themselves why didn't his
father look to it, and see that Mr. Jim had summut to do, and
friends of his own kind—in the same breath with which they
flattered him as the nicest young gentleman, and considered it a
pleasure to hear what he thought of things ; but it was a long time
before any one among them could make up his mind to utter the
words which were on all their lips, and to tell Mr. Jim that the
parlour of the 'Blue Boar,' though it was so respectable, was not
the place for a young gentleman ; and in the meantime the incense
of their admiration and pride in his companionship was balm to the
youth, notwithstanding his own knowledge that he ought not to be
there.

And there was another place which was becoming still more
agreeable to poor Jim.   Since that first visit when she called him
in, in the darkening, he had paid many visits at the schoolroom
to Mrs. Brown.   He could not go anywhere without passing the
door, and in the evening, when it was not very easy to see who
went or came, she was almost always there, looking out, breathing
the air as she said, after the day's work, and keeping a watch for
Jim.   He was flattered by this watch for him even more than by
the admiration of the shopkeepers, and yet at the same time half
ashamed.   For there was no depravity about the boy, and these
attentions on the part of a woman who was no longer young embarrassed him greatly, and gave him a sense of danger which, however,
in her presence was entirely soothed and smoothed away.   There
was a sense of danger but still more a sense of ridicule, which
seized him whenever he left her, and made him resolve with a blush
never to go near her again.   And, yet again, there was safety too.

Had Mrs. Brown had a daughter, a girl whom he might have fallen in love with, whom people might have talked about, Jim felt that the circumstances would have been quite different ; then, indeed, it would have been a duty to have stayed away : but a woman who might be his mother ! If she liked to talk to him it was ridiculous, but it couldn't be any harm. Nobody thought it anything wrong that Osborne the curate should pay long visits to Miss Grey, and take tea with her, and all that ; and why not Jim to Mrs. Brown who was much more amusing, and who had no society ? She was a capital one to talk ; she had been a great deal about the world ; she knew hundreds of people : and there was always a comfortable chair ready for him, and she had an art in manufacturing drinks which nobody Jim knew was equal to. It never occurred to him to inquire why she looked out for him in the evenings, and made those exquisite drinks for him. It was ridiculous, but it was not disagreeable, and in the evening as he prowled along, unwilling to go into the dull familiar house, where there was reproach more or less veiled in every eye, where even Florry, who stood by him the most, would rush out unexpectedly with an ' Oh, Jim ! why can't you do something and please papa ? '—there was a wonderful seduction in the sight or half-sight, for it was generally dark, of Mrs. Brown's handsome head looking out from the door. ' Good evening, Mr. Plowden ; I hope you are coming in a little to cheer me up.' It was said so low that, supposing somebody else to be passing, which was very rare, it could reach no other ear but Jim's. Sometimes he resisted the call ; sometimes when she was not at the door he went in of himself. It was all quite easy and irregular, and out of the way. The entrance to Mrs. Brown's house was close to a lane which led to the Rectory, and thus it was easy for him to dart in without being observed. Once, he felt sure, Osborne passing had turned half-back to stare, and saw where he was going. Confound that fellow ! but, what did it matter what Osborne saw ? He had never been friendly with Jim, never showed any relish for his society, which had rankled in the young man's breast, though he was too proud ever to have breathed a consciousness of the fact. But, whatever he was, the curate was not a sneak who would go off to the Rectory and betray what he had seen. Jim dived into the doorway, however, with an accelerated pace of which he was ashamed ; and the ridicule of it came over him with a keener heat and flush. A woman old enough to be his mother ! But what was the difference ? That fellow Osborne would go off all the same to little Nelly Grey.

' Oh, Mr. Jim, what a pleasure to see you ! ' cried Mrs. Brown.

'I had almost given up hope : for it is near the Rectory dinner, isn't it, and you will be wanted at home——'

'Oh, I am not such a good little boy as all that,' said Jim, with an uneasy laugh ; 'I am not so afraid of being late.'

'That's very bad, very bad,' said Mrs. Brown. 'I am sure the young ladies are always in time and punctual ; they come to see me sometimes, you know, and they always recommend punctuality. It's a great virtue. I have all the ladies to come to see me, but I sometimes think, Mr. Jim, if they were to know——'

'I don't know what, I am sure,' said Jim, growing very red, yet looking at her steadily ; 'there is nothing I could tell that would make them less respectful to you, Mrs. Brown—only that you were once in a better position, and better off than you are now ; my mother and the rest may be a little narrow, but they would never think the less of you for that.'

Mrs. Brown was not a woman who was easily disconcerted ; she could have borne the assault of all the ladies of the parish and given them as good, nay, much more than they could have given her : for though Mrs. Plowden had a good steady command of words when she was scolding the servants at the Rectory, she never could have stood for a moment before the much more nimble and fiery tongue of the schoolmistress. But before Jim's assertion of her irreproachableness and conviction that her only disadvantage was that she had seen better days, Mrs. Brown was utterly silenced ; she could not answer the boy a word ; she was a woman quite ready to laugh at the idea of innocence in a young man, but when she was thus brought face to face with it, instead of laughing she was struck dumb ; she could not make him any reply ; she pretended to be busy with the lamp, raising and then lowering the light, and then she left the room altogether without a word. Poor Jim felt that he must have offended her by this untoward allusion to better days. Did she think by any chance that he was taunting her with her poverty, or that anybody in the world, at least anybody at Watcham, could think the less of her? Perhaps he ought not even to have said that ; he ought to have made sure that it went without saying, a certainty that it was half an offence to put into words. As, however, he sat pondering this in doubt and fear, Mrs. Brown came back all smiles, bringing that familiar tall glass foaming high with the drink which nobody in Watcham could compound—nobody he had ever known before.

'Oh,' he said, 'I thought you were angry ; and here you come like—like Hebe, you know—with nectar in your hand.'

'I am rather an elderly Hebe,' she said, 'but it's a pretty comparison all the same. If I were young and blooming instead of being old and dried up, I should have made you a curtsey for your compliment; but there's this compensation, Mr. Jim, that a Hebe of seventeen, which is, I believe, the right age, would probably not know how to make up a drink like this. Taste it, and tell me if it isn't the very nicest I have made for you yet?'

'It is nectar,' said Jim fervently; 'but,' he added, 'do you know, I wish you wouldn't make me such delicious things to drink. Why should I give you all this trouble, and'—he paused, and added, embarrassed—'expense too?'

Mrs. Brown laughed and clapped her hands. 'Expense, too!' she cried; 'how good! Oh, you don't know how I get the materials, and how little they cost me; people I used to employ in—in what you call my better days, are so faithful to me. As you say, Mr. Jim, the world isn't at all such a hard place as one thinks; and even the ladies of the parish—but you do amuse me so with your stories of the parish—it's such an odd little world, isn't it? Tell me, what are they saying about Leo Swinford? Has any one made up her mind to marry him? That's what I expect to hear every day.'

'I don't know anybody that wants to marry him,' said Jim. 'I suppose he must take the first step in anything of that kind.'

'Do you think so, really?' said Mrs. Brown. 'Now, do you know, I am not at all so sure of that; the ladies will think of it first, I'll promise you. He is a nice young man, with a good estate; and he hadn't been a week in the parish, I'll answer for it, before two or three ladies had settled who was to have him—and as for the young ones themselves —— Oh, my dear Mr. Jim, you are too good-hearted; you don't think, then, of the plans and schemes that may be laid for you?'

'Me!' said Jim, with a blush; and then he shook his head. 'Nobody approves of me enough to make any plans about me.'

'Don't you be too sure of that,' she said airily; 'but Leo Swinford is a new man, and he's got a quantity of money. Now, answer me my question, for I've known him all his life, and I take an interest in him: who is going to marry him? Does your——' She paused, and the mischief in her eyes yielded to alarm for a moment. However much a youth may be in your bonds, and capable of guidance, yet it is possible that he may rebel if you question him about his mother; so she changed what she was about to say. 'Does your—aunt,' she proceeded, 'Lady William, don't you know, as everybody calls her—think of him for her little fat girl？ Oh, I beg your pardon ; I think she is a very nice little girl, but she is fat ; when she grows older she will fine down.'

Jim's delicacy was not offended by this statement. He laughed. 'Yes,' he said, 'Mab is fat ; but she is a nice little girl for all that.'

'A dear little girl,' said Mrs. Brown ; 'she comes and gives me advice about the children. You would think she was seventy instead of seventeen. Well, is she to be the bride. Have the parish ladies given their votes for her？'

'For Mab！' Jim repeated with wonder. 'Mab's not that kind of girl at all. She does not go in for—for marrying or so forth. She's too young. She thinks of her garden, and of boating, and that sort of thing. She is a very jolly girl. She has got a will of her own, just. The ladies might give their votes as much as they please, it would not matter for that.'

'Of course I may be mistaken,' said Mrs. Brown, 'I am the poor schoolmistress. I don't judge the gentry from their own point of view as you do. I have to look up from such a very, very long way down.' She laughed, and Jim laughed too, though he did not quite know why. 'But I know that he is always at Lady William's. What a little cottage she lives in to be a lady of title, Mr. Jim ; not very much bigger than mine！'

'Aunt Emily is not rich,' said Jim, with a little uneasiness, feeling that he ought not to be discussing his relation.

'Poor lady ; but if she marries her daughter to Leo Swinford？ I know he is there almost every day.'

'Yes, so I hear,' said Jim, 'but I don't believe he thinks of marrying any one. He goes to see Aunt Emily. He goes for a good talk. There are not many people to talk to here.'

'To talk to a middle-aged lady, when there are plenty of young ones？ Oh no, Mr. Jim, you must not try to persuade me of that.'

'But,' said Jim, stammering a little, 'it's quite true. What difference is there？ just as I come to see you, and Osborne—but perhaps that's not quite the same thing.'

'Osborne——' said Mrs. Brown. 'Oh, the curate, the good young curate. As you come to see me—thank you, Mr. Jim, how nice you are！—Leo goes and sits with your dear aunt. And Mr. Osborne—to whom does Mr. Osborne go？ Oh, I owe him something ; he is so nice to me about the school. Tell me where he goes to have his talk.'

'Well, perhaps it's not quite the same thing,' said Jim,

confused; 'Miss Grey, you know she is almost like another curate, she knows as much about the parish; but if he goes and has tea with her, I don't quite see, don't you know, what anybody could say—how anybody could object—or what is out of the way, don't you know, in me——'

'Going to sit a little in the evening with Mrs. Brown,' said the schoolmistress with a burst of laughter, clapping her hands. 'And quite right too; the analogy is perfect. So there are three of us,' she said, 'whom the young men prefer. You can't think how nice, and cheering, and pleasant for an old person; to think of three old ladies, Lady William, Miss Grey, and me! How much I am obliged to you, my dear Mr. Jim!'

How was she obliged to him? What had he said? Jim felt very uncomfortable, though he could not have told why.

WHEN Leo Swinford said that he was lodged like a prince there was little extravagance in the phrase. He was lodged like a prince indeed in the age of reason, not that of subdued æstheticism like this. The rooms in the Hall were spacious and lofty, and decorated with mirrors and gilding and marble, generally false marble, to an extent very rarely seen in England. And they were hung with pictures which would have been worth a king's ransom had the names upon them been genuine, which of course they were not. A Swinford of a hundred years ago, Leo's great-grandfather, had been one of those dilettanti of the eighteenth century to whom the languid Italy of those days was at once an idol and a place of plunder. He had filled his house with copies, with supposed antiques picked up here and there, with much old furniture and false statuary and bronzes. All the splendid names of art flourished on the walls ; I am not sure that there was not a fragment, so called, of Phidias, from some classic excavation, and I am certain that there were several Raphaels, and even a Michael Angelo (the day of Botticelli was not yet). The cabinets and carvings which were genuine gave an air of reality to much that was false. If it was not true art, it was at least a good representation of the age when connoisseurs were few, when the craft of the copyist was in great request, and when it was fondly hoped, with that stupidity which belongs to the cultured person in all ages, that the model of the Italian palace, designed for skies and customs so different from ours, might be made to improve the natural beauty of an English house ; the attempt was a mistake, but here and there, when carried out regardless of expense, it was not without effect, and the Hall was a good specimen of its period. A hundred years is a respectable period of time, and an example of the aims and meaning of a past century is worth preserving. But the large suites of rooms

opening from each other, with large windows and doors, and no
system of warming, were chilly and severe in a season still
scarcely genial—England in this respect, with the cheerful open
fires upon which we pride ourselves, being so much inferior to
France with its calorifères, or Germany with its endless stuffy but
effective stoves, in the art of keeping a house warm.   Our houses,
alas, are far from being warm, as many a shivering invalid
knows.

It was on a Saturday, late in the afternoon in the beginning
of April, but before the blasts were altogether over, that another
visitor who was not at all so well received as Lady William and
the Plowdens, walked briskly up the avenue and along by the
side of the lake towards the Hall.   She went quietly, looking
neither to the right nor the left, with the air of a person who
knew very well where she was going; and she was, I think,
better dressed than Lady William, with something like fashion in
the fit of her garments and the fall of her draperies, not over-
dressed either, in black with a little veil over her face, a woman
with a presence which all the poor in Watcham recognised as that
of a lady, and a person who had seen better days.   How it was
that her air and aspect which impressed all the others, even Mrs.
Plowden and most of the other ladies of the parish, failed to
impress Morris the butler I cannot tell.   There are mysteries in
all crafts, and though he was for a moment slightly flustered by
her bearing, Morris put himself straight in the middle of the
doorway and opposed Mrs. Brown's entrance with a decision
which he would not have ventured to exhibit in face of little Miss
Grey, who had the air of being dressed out of a rag-bag, or the
humblest curate's wife.   'Not at home,' Morris said with the
utmost audacity, looking the visitor full in the face.

'I know,' said Mrs. Brown, 'but I will come in till you have
sent up my name, for I know that she will see me.'

'It is quite contrary to my lady's habits to see any one at
this hour,' said Morris, who was a person of education—'if you
will state your business I will report it to Madame Julie, who
will convey it to her mistress at a fitting time, and then, if Mrs.
Swinford will receive you——'

Mrs. Brown laughed.

'Do you ask all the ladies that call to state their business?'
she said, with an air of amusement which confused Mr. Morris.

'Ladies,' he said, with a slight falter in his assurance, 'who
call at the usual hours is a different thing.'

'Why, it isn't six o'clock,' said Mrs Brown, 'and if I had not known Mrs. Swinford I should not have thought it too late. But it is precisely because it is too late that I am here; for I've no business except to see your lady, Morris, so you may as well go at once and not keep me standing here.'

Morris began to grow more and more uncertain in spite of himself. Everything was against her; her look, though how he knew that, it would be difficult to tell; her composure, not angry as a real lady should have been (in his opinion) and indisposed to bandy words. A curate's wife would have retired in high dudgeon before he had enunciated his first phrase. Little Miss Grey would have transfixed him with a look, and turned away; but this visitor was not disinclined even to chaff the butler, therefore she was no lady. Yet there was something in her patronage, in her composure, and last of all in that sudden use of his own name, which gave the man a vague sensation of alarm.

'You seem to know my name,' he said, 'but you haven't even taken the trouble, ma'am, to give me yours.'

Upon which the visitor broke into a laugh.

'Mine is not very distinguished, Morris,' she said, 'I am Mrs. Brown, but not the dressmaker from the village to ask for orders from Julie, as you seem to suppose. Come, come, there's been enough of this.' As she spoke, she passed Mr. Morris adroitly, and entered the great lofty hall which formed the vestibule of the Swinford mansion. 'There has been no change made, I see,' she said, with a rapid glance round; 'do you mean to tell me, Morris, that your lady is going to support all this and make no change?'

The hall was almost dark, the lamps as yet unlighted, and only a dim evening light in the row of long windows. Some one stirred, however, in a corner, and came forward, only half distinguishable in the twilight.

'Morris,' said this half-seen person, 'you know my mother never receives at this hour——'

'Ah, Leo,' said the visitor, with a slight quaver in the assurance of her voice, 'is it you?'

When Morris heard his master called Leo, he retired discreetly with a momentary sense that the sky, or rather the gilded roof of the hall, was falling upon him. Had it occurred to him, so assured in his duties, to make a tremendous mistake? The feeling at first gave him a sensation not to be put into words, and his impulse was to take immediate flight; but on reflection, he felt it so very unlikely that he could have made a mistake, that he subsided into the shelter of one of the pillars and waited to see what would happen. Mr. Leo Swinford was known among the servants as a most affable gentleman; but Morris was well aware that his master was not one to submit to any impertinence. It was a moment of great excitement, almost too thrilling—for a butler has the pride of his profession, like another, and it would have been dreadful to him to have to acknowledge that he had made a mistake.

'I fear I must say that you have the advantage of me,' Leo said, with a coldness that was balm to Morris's soul.

The visitor came forward with a short laugh, to one of the windows.

'You have a short memory,' she said; 'but yet if you remember we met only the other day.'

Then there was a little pause, and then Mr. Swinford said in a tone which was half rage and half contempt:

'I thought I made my sentiments clear enough that day: but I might have known——'

'Yes,' said the lady, 'I think you might have known; but I don't blame you, Leo, your views and mine don't agree, and never will; all the same you can take off your bulldog and make him understand that the house is free to your relations. I needn't trouble you otherwise; of course I have come to see your mother, and I hope I know my way.'

Morris behind his pillar beheld aghast an alert shadow glide through the gloom across the hall and up the stairs. There was now so little light that she looked like a ghost, a darkness moving through the gloom, but in no other way ghostlike, quite vigorous, full of life. The man could not move; he was humiliated in his tenderest point—a relation! and to think he should have made such a mistake; but on the whole, Morris was consoled by the fact that it was a relation; relations are not always equals, they are not always friends; sometimes the people of the house would prefer to have them shut out. If it had been a lady of a county family, perhaps, or some intimate friend, it would have been different. He gradually began to raise again his drooping spirits; he was about to start away from his post of observation when his master called him briskly, having probably heard the noise of his retiring feet. Morris did not like to be caught eavesdropping; he was a functionary of a very high ideal; he allowed a moment to elapse, during which he judiciously and stealthily edged further off, and answered, as from a distance, 'Did you call, sir?' with the air of a man who has heard imperfectly, being so far off.

'Come here, quick,' said Leo impatiently. 'Morris, I want to speak to you about that lady; you refused to let her in.'

'I am very sorry, sir, very sorry if I made a mistake; but my lady's orders are, after half-past five, no one, unless there's an exception.'

'Just so, you are quite right; but probably there will be an exception; I don't suppose my mother knew Mrs. Brown was here; she is a very old friend. Of course you must take my mother's orders on the matter; but I suppose an exception will be made.'

'Of course, sir,' said Morris politely, with a sense of giving way from his absolute right as guardian of the Swinford House; 'if it's your—or my lady's wish——'

This sacrifice made the master of the house laugh, and cleared his brow for the moment; and presently he retired into the great gilded pillared room which was the library. He was not without a little pride in the grandiose decorations which had been his ancestors' doing; but as he cast his eye round the great room, with the gilded gallery that ran round it, he thought, with a sigh, of the luxurious apartment in Paris in which he had been brought up. The one was so warm and gay, the other so glittering and cold; he believed there were a great many dummies on those huge shelves; unquestionably there were a great many worthless books; it was too big, too grand, too full of pretension to be made a home of, and everything was new and laborious and dull around him, even his own unaccustomed works of beneficence, which had been amusing at first. Had he been allowed to give up a portion of his income in order to make happy all the poor people without any trouble to himself!—but he had begun to be bored by Miss Grey and her intimate knowledge of everybody's wants, and to cease to be amused by the curate, who was all for shutting up the public-houses, those public-houses which Leo, in the toleration of his foreign training, looked upon as the only means of necessary relaxation which the poor people possessed. There was only one thing among his new surroundings that did not cease to amuse him, and that was the little, the very little drawing-room in which of an evening he found Lady William sitting in the firelight, and where he could talk of all that was in his heart. It was, perhaps, a little later than usual, for he had been detained by various matters of business, but still it was not too late, and in a few minutes more he had put on the coat with the fur lining which had made such a sensation in Watcham, and was walking very briskly down the avenue, with the gloom deepened and the vexation lightened, wondering how much he might tell her, and whether she would remember Mrs. Brown.

Now I wonder much whether the reader would rather hear what passed that evening in Lady William's drawing-room in the firelight, at the hour when people can talk more confidentially and cosily, only half seeing each other's faces, than at any other time; or whether he (or she) would prefer to be present at the interview in Mrs. Swinford's boudoir, which was going on at the same moment. I know which I prefer myself. The simple people in the world who have no mysteries about them, who have their little humours and follies, but mean no harm, and do no harm as far as human judgment can guide them, are familiar and well known. I know what they are thinking about, and what they say, and how much or how little they mean. But with the others there is a strain. I know, of course, very well what Mrs. Swinford and Mrs. Brown had to talk about and what they said, but it is a kind of artificial knowledge, and I don't like having much to do with these women of the world. There are different kinds of women of the world; but the lady who was Leo Swinford's mother was not of the good kind, neither was her old friend, or her relation, or who-ever Mrs. Brown was. They were of the kind who are enemies of the good, perhaps not absolutely meaning to. be so, but because they were intent each of them on her own way, and on pleasing herself; and looked upon every obstacle to that, only as something to be cleared away. Therefore, if the gentle reader pleases, we will put off their talk for a while, and go cheerfully down with Leo through the dark avenue, and by the side of the little wistful lake, in which the clearness of the evening sky is reflected, and along the quiet country road; till we come to the village green where the lights are beginning to shine in the windows, past the church with its low spire rising against the sky, and the Rectory behind its damp and level lawn; and at last arrive at the quarter where the best houses stand out against the west, with their trees budding and the crocuses ablow in all the borders, and a pleasant scent of wallflowers in the air. Lady William's garden was more full of wallflowers than any of the others, and the narcissus were coming out, and the primroses taking the place of the crocuses; jealous people said because, if anything, it had the finest south exposure; but chiefly because Mab was the head gardener, and had a genius for that art. General FitzStephen was in his garden when Leo passed, and called 'good evening' to him over the privet hedge, for the General knew very well where the young man was going, and thought it very natural. The old gentleman was fond of little

Mab, and hoped that it was she, though she was so ridiculously young, that was to make this great match; but he did not feel so sure as he would have liked to do, whether this was what Leo meant.

In Lady William's cottage things were a little different from the usual conditions—for Leo was late, later than he had ever been before—and he did not like them quite so well as usual. For one thing the lamp was lighted and the fire very low, the evening being, or so these ladies thought, warmer than usual; and for another thing they were very busy, Mab and her mother, over their necessary sewing. As everybody knows, the coming of summer is a much more troublesome thing, in respect to dress, than winter, when two warm nice dresses, one for common use and one for best, is as much as anybody wants. But in summer, besides the best frock on which Lady William was employed, with her daughter, when we first made her acquaintance, there are cotton dresses to be thought of, and things for the warm weather, of which a girl who is always in movement wants a great many. And indeed, at this present moment the work in hand was a white frock, which was intended for a party, to be given by the FitzStephens, which very possibly might end in a dance; and this was naturally a very interesting piece of work.

'Shall I put it away, mother?' said Mab.

'No,' said Lady William, 'a man knows nothing about it, he will think we are hemming tablecloths; and he would not be any the wiser if he did know.'

It is curious that Mab, an inexperienced little girl, should have known better in this respect than her mother, who was so much more acquainted with the world. She went on with her work, indeed, all the same, but she shook her head and felt convinced that when Leo Swinford saw what they were doing, he would perfectly well know; and, indeed, he had scarcely been ushered in by Patty, and found a chair for himself, than he said at once:

'Why, you are making a dress!'

'Why not?' said Lady William; 'we always do.'

'It is for Miss Mab, and she is going to a party,' said Leo. 'Is it a ball, and will they probably ask me?'

'Certainly, if you will go; but you are the great man, you know, here, and they may be afraid to ask you with all the little village people.'

'I love the village people,' said Leo; and then he laughed a little, remembering that there had been of late other thoughts in his mind.

'You are getting a little tired of them,' said Lady William; 'I told you so; between the time that they amuse you with their little ways, and the time that you know the real goodness of them, there comes a moment when you are bored. You must soon go to town for the season, and let Watcham rest, or yourself.'

'I have no desire to go to town for the season, or let Watcham rest. I may be a little tired of the philanthropy: I am not tired of this room,' he said, looking round upon it affectionately; 'do you know I don't think I ever saw it lighted before.'

'So brilliantly lighted, *al giorno*,' said Lady William; 'the firelight is kind and hides its little defects. But you are late to-night.'

'Yes, my mother has had a visit, which sent me out untimely; it annoys me, and of course I must come and tell you my annoyance. Do you remember a certain Mansfield woman long ago?'

'Do I remember her!'

'Of course you must; there is always mischief where she is. She has appeared again.'

'But is that a strange event? She is a relation, and your mother was much attached to her, too.'

'I suppose so; though why——? Can anybody explain these things? And there is always mischief when she comes. I don't know what may be brewing at present, nor why she comes now. Does she live here?'

'Oh no,' said Lady William; 'certainly not, she must have come from London: everybody that is uncomfortable comes from London. But you must not be superstitious. Mischief can't be created if the elements of it don't exist, and I see none that she can work upon now.'

'She might make dissension; she will make dissension, dear lady, between my mother and me.'

'Forewarned is forearmed; don't let her,' said Lady William, 'that is the only thing to say.'

'But she will be too many for me,' said Leo, shaking his head yet smiling; 'I have no confidence in myself.'

'You are too superstitious; she must not be too many for you; your mother's son is more to her than her cousin.'

'Is she her cousin? and am I——'

'Her son!' said Lady William, with a laugh; 'the wonderful question! I don't think any doubt can be entertained on that subject.'

'No, no; I meant am I more strong as son than the other as—— How can I tell what to say?'

'My dear Leo ! A son is stronger than anything in the world.'

'Except a daughter,' he said, looking at Mab.

'It is the same ; one's own child is more to one than all the world beside.'

'Do you know,' he said, 'there is one thing that I think is almost better, that clears away the clouds and brings out the sun, and makes one see him :—and that is you.' He put his hand upon hers softly, with a momentary touch.

'That is a friend,' said Lady William hastily. A little uneasy flush came over her face. She was very conscious, more conscious than was pleasant, of little Mab sewing on sedately, never lifting her eyes.

Mrs. Brown walked quickly through the darkening house. She met a footman with a lamp, who stood bewildered at the strange figure, and a housemaid in the upper corridor, who stopped her to ask what she wanted, but was soon intimidated by her look and voice. The stranger wanted no guidance, no indication, to which side to turn, as the maid perceived, who stood watching her, and saw her swift, familiar approach to Mrs. Swinford's door. 'Missis will go out of her senses,' said Mary Jane to herself, and she hurried away, to be out of it, whatever might happen. 'Nobody can say as I let her in,' the young woman said.

Madame Julie, the maid, came to the door in answer to Mrs. Brown's light knock, but not before that lady, waiting for no one, had opened it and stepped into the ante-room in which Julie sat. Mrs. Swinford's apartment was as complete as English comfort and French refinement could make it. The ante-room, in which Julie sat, was finer than any of the village drawing-rooms, kept comfortable by many carpets and thick curtains, and lighted by a large window turned to the west, by the remaining light in which she regarded with alarm and fury the bold intruder.

'What you want here?' she said in her doubtful English, unintimidated by the aspect of the lady who had overawed Mary Jane. 'Madame reçoit personne,' she added, in a less assured tone.

'Moi exceptée toujours, Julie,' said Mrs. Brown.

Upon which Julie started and clasped her hands. 'Mon Dieu!' she said, 'Madame Artémise!'

'You need not announce me, I'll find my way by myself. Has she lights, Julie? Is she alone?'

'You will startle Madame out of her life, Madame Artémise.'

'Not a bit. What is pleasant harms no one, and you know she is always happy to see me.'

Julie knew, yet did not look quite sure. 'I will say but a word, a *petit mot*. Madame will not look up, but it will prepare her. Ah, she hears us talk!' for a bell at this moment tinkled into the stillness. Julie put aside the curtain and opened a door, from which came a gleam of light, and a voice saying querulously, 'You are talking with some one; how often must I say no one must come here?'

'It is not Julie's fault: it is I, Cecile, come to welcome you home.'

Mrs. Swinford rose up from the couch upon which she had been reclining, with a cry. She made a step forward, and allowed herself to drop into the arms which the visitor held forth. It was a strange embrace, apparently altogether on one side; the other passive, receiving only the marks of affection. Yet there was something in the *abandon* with which the great lady let herself go into the stranger's arms, which showed almost a greater warmth in the receiver than giver of the embrace. She put down her head on Mrs. Brown's shoulder with a murmur of welcome and satisfaction; then raised it to wave an angry hand towards Julie, bidding her go. The maid retired without a word. She was a middle-aged Frenchwoman, very neat, and rather grim, black-haired, and dark-complexioned, with a black gown, and hair elaborately dressed. She obeyed her mistress in utter silence, closing the door noiselessly behind her, but threw her head and body, like a pendulum, to and fro as she went back to the work which she had been doing under the west window by the waning light. Evidently this stranger was no welcome apparition to Julie, any more than to more important persons in the house.

'What wind has blown you here? and where do you come from, just when I felt such enormous need of you?' Mrs. Swinford said.

'Some people would say it was an ill wind; and you know I feel always when you want me,' said Mrs. Brown.

'You must have known that when I came here, where there are so many horrible associations, I must have wanted you. It is an instinct. Listen, Artémise. Leo has forced me here against my will. He has all his father's foolish notions, with more added of his own. And he has the upper hand, which his father never had——'

'Sometimes, my dear.'

'Once, you mean,' said Mrs. Swinford. She was old, though she kept that fact at bay, and did not admit it by any outward sign: but she flushed over all her face like a girl at these words.

'Once, no more : and you know how that is brought back to me here, and every incident of the time.   That woman at my very door, bearing the name———which she never would have had but for me.'

'I never liked the expedient, Cecile.'

'Why, it was you who———and it was the only way.   But now that the whole dreadful tale is swept away into the past, and everybody, except you and me, has forgotten it, there she sits at my door, calm, with that name.   And I have to receive her ; to call her friend ; to kiss her———imagine !   I have kissed Emily Plowden, and called her by that name ! '

'I don't see what else you could do.   It was your own doing, the whole affair.   I will always stand by you, through thick and thin.   But I never approved of *that*, Cecile.   It was too heavy a responsibility.   If you like to do certain things you know you will have to pay for them.   You get nothing for nothing in this world.   But I don't like meddling with another creature's life.'

'I detest you when you preach, Artémise ; you have so fine a position for that ; hands so clean !   From whence do you come now ? from wandering to and fro upon the earth———'

'Seeking whom I may devour ?   No, I am devouring no one ; I have settled myself—at your very door, too—to do good, my dear.'

'To do———good ! '

'You are surprised.   Don't you know there comes a time when we would all like to be sisters of charity ?   But I have not gone so far as that.   I have a very nice little post in the village, gained chiefly by a recommendation you once gave me, and your poor husband———naturally that had great weight here—and other things.   I am schoolmistress of the girls' school, Watcham parish.   At your service, Madame Cecile.'

Mrs. Swinford uttered that exclamation, which means so little in French and so much in English.   She did not join in the laugh with which her visitor broke off.   She was a more tragical person altogether than Mrs. Brown.

'Mistress of the school, living in the village !   You are welcome, as you know, to live with me.   Why should you demean yourself in such a way ?   Why do you always try to compromise———'

'Not you, Mrs. Swinford.   I have never compromised you.   I don't choose to be your dependent ; to eat that bitter bread. But you have never had any trouble brought into your life by me.'

'Not that of being ignorant for years together where you are ?

of not knowing what you are doing ? whether you may be in want ? whether you may be ill ? if you may have died——'

'On some roadside, or in some hospital, nobody knowing anything about me,' said Mrs. Brown, with a harsh little laugh, 'and not a bad thing either, and probably the way it will happen at the last. But I should always, unless it was sudden, take care that you knew. It is a curious thing,' she said, laughing again, and winking her eyes rapidly, as if to shake off some moisture, 'that you and I, two such women as we are, not of the soft kind, should in a sort of a way, not caring much for anybody else, love each other, Cecile !'

'We need not be sentimental and talk of it at least,' said the other ; 'I see nothing wonderful in it. With others always contradiction and contrariety, but between you and me understanding —even when you take upon you, so much younger as you are, not to approve.'

'Oh, I must always reserve that power—if I were only four, instead of forty,' said Mrs. Brown.

'Forty and a little more.'

'If you think I am in any danger of forgetting the little more —forty-six—a sensible age. You would not imagine at that discreet period of existence that my chief friend in Watcham should be a young man.'

Mrs. Swinford shrugged her shoulders as if nothing could be more perfectly indifferent to her.

'Who keeps me informed of all that is going on,' she added, after a moment's pause.

'Ah !' Even this, however, did not awake the great lady's interest ; for what were the village news to her ?

'I hear of Leo's proceedings. He seems to mean to turn everything upside down.'

'The foolish boy ! he has got it into his head that he has neglected his duties. What are his duties ? I know not. One, that he does not regard, is to make life as pleasant as time and circumstances will admit to his mother. It is not much I ask. To reside where I can breathe. To see a few people whom I like, who understand me. To be kept from sordid calculations and cares. What he thinks more important is to come back here to look after his people, as he calls them. His people ! How are they his people ? They pay him rent, that is all. And he thinks more of them than of what is comfort and life to me !'

'I feel very much for you, Cecile, in many ways,' said Mrs. Brown, not without a hidden tone of satire, 'but do you know,

I cannot see that you are much deficient in point of comfort here.'

Mrs. Swinford looked round the pretty room with an air of disgust. It would have been difficult to imagine anything more luxurious. The old grandfather's decorations had been removed or softened with a taste more French than English, yet exquisite in its way. The curtains were of the softest rich stuffs. The walls were hung with a few bright pictures, little English water-colours, French *genre* subjects, as cheerful and smiling as could be desired. It was lighted with soft lamps carefully shaded, giving a subdued silvery light. There were books of all kinds, from those in rows of beautiful binding, which filled the low bookcases, to the French novels in yellow paper, which occupied the table at Mrs. Swinford's hand. If there was anything wanting to the beauty or comfort of this wonderful little room it was difficult to find it out. Mrs. Brown instantly compared it with the sitting-room in the school-house, and burst into a laugh.

'You should see the rooms in which I live,' she said, 'and yet I don't think they are bad rooms. I have known worse. I consider myself very well off. Oh, you are different, a great lady as you have always been, and I only a waif and stray.'

'That was at your own will, Artémise.'

'I know; I blame nobody. I have been the wilful one that have always taken my own way; you have generally succeeded in making other people take yours.'

Mrs. Swinford smiled faintly, and then she said, her face resuming its discontented expression:

'That is over; now, it is my son I have to deal with; my son, who owes me everything.'

'Be reasonable; he owes you his birth, of course, and a great deal of petting when he was a boy——'

'And the sacrifice of my life,' said Mrs. Swinford. 'Do you think I ever would have done what I did and given up all I cared for, if it had not been for Leo? Do you think I would have cared for scandal or anything but for the boy? or for what his father might say or do? The whole thing was for him. Emily may thank him for her title, as they call it—ridiculous title! When I hear that name and her rank, talked of—her rank, forsooth—and that she takes precedence of everybody—even, I suppose, she will, with a fierce laugh, 'of me——'

'Ah!' said Mrs. Brown, 'that's something, I did not think of that; but take care, Cecile, that she does not take precedence of you in other ways.'

'In what way? You mean, I suppose, that she is younger and has a sort of beauty! I cannot deny that she has a sort of beauty. She is not the common pretty girl that Emily Plowden was. It is not for nothing that I helped to plunge her into the world. She knows something of life, and though she will never make anything of the advantages she possesses, still she has them. You may imagine I looked at her with sharp eyes enough, remembering what she used to be and what she was. But her world is not my world, and what do I care for her village precedence, or for any comparison that may be made here?'

'There will be no comparison made, Cecile.'

Mrs. Brown looked with a curious pitying glance at the woman, who was old, yet had never given up the pretensions of youth. She was nearly twenty years younger, and saw the futility of these pretensions with perfect lucidity of vision ; but there was kindness as well as pity in her eyes. Did not her glass say anything to this old woman, that she should talk of comparison between her and Lady William's mature but unfaded years? Did not common sense say anything? As Mrs. Brown was much more near to Lady William's age than Mrs. Swinford's, the case was perfectly clear to her eyes.

'No, I do not suppose so,' Mrs. Swinford said ; 'and my hope is that he will tire of it presently. What attraction can he find in a country village in England? There is nothing. His philanthropy, bah! his people, ridiculous! It is ignorance that makes him talk of his people as if he were a great potentate, when he is only a country gentleman.'

'It is his breeding,' said Mrs. Brown. 'How was he to find out the difference in Paris? and you always treated him, you who are, as I tell you, a great lady by nature, as if he were a *grand seigneur*.'

'I must be patient,' said Mrs. Swinford ; 'it is difficult, but I must be patient : I gave him three months to be sick of the life, and the half of the time is not gone ; I don't think he will hold out a month more——'

'Unless there should in the meantime arise some other attraction.'

'What other attraction ?' Mrs. Swinford caught her visitor by the arm. 'An attraction—in this village? Artémise, you have heard of something! A woman? who is she? I must know, I must know !'

'Do not be frightened. But I think you are imprudent, Cecile ; you should have filled the house with company, you should

have come back in a storm of gaiety; he should have known
nothing of the village at all.'

'Who is she?' said Mrs. Swinford, tightening her grasp on
the other's arm; 'some wretched girl with a baby face.'

'It is no girl, it is nothing of that sort; it is a woman as old,
nearly as old as I am. I told you I had a young admirer too,
who comes to me for the superiority of my conversation, and my
knowledge of the world. So does Leo; to discuss the world, and
things in general, and the topics of the day.'

'You are either laughing at everything, as has been your
custom all your life, or you are announcing to me a great danger;
the loss of all my power.'

'Do not always be so high heroical. Let me tell you my own
story first. My young friend is Jim, the Rector's son. He saw
me with a gay party in Oxford, and I thought that he would betray
me. But he is as innocent as a child, and respects and admires
me as one who has seen better days. I keep him from vulgar
dangers; from the "Blue Boar"—but you don't know the perils
of the "Blue Boar"——'

'What are all these puerilities to me?' said Mrs. Swinford.
'You weary me. Do you think it is interesting to me, this story
of the Rector's son?'

'I am aware it wearies you; one sees that on your still
fine countenance, Cecile: but I am coming to what will interest
you. In the same way Leo frequents a cottage, a very genteel
cottage, far superior to the schoolmistress's house. There is a
mother and a daughter in it. He may be falling in love with the
daughter, but I think not, for the little thing is plain. But the
mother is not plain; she is a woman who has known the world.
She has been buried here, among the bucolics, for years. But
when she sees a man of manners, who also knows the world, is
there anything wonderful in it if she likes his conversation
too?'

'Artémise, who is she? Tell me her name.'

Mrs. Brown did not say a word, but looked at her companion
with wondering eyes.

NEXT day the village was roused into great excitement by the appearance of a carriage from the Hall, in unusual state, with the coachman and footman in their gala liveries—or so at least it appeared to the unsophisticated ideas of the villagers, who came out to gape at the sight. A carriage passing is nothing wonderful in Watcham, however gorgeous—but a carriage which drives about from door to door, paying visits—this was a thing that happened seldom; the great people in the neighbourhood, the Lenthalls and Lady Wade, and the rest, would come occasionally to leave a card at the FitzStephens', or to show civility to the people in the Rectory: but the sight of the prancing horses, and the footman attending his mistress from door to door, was a delight to the eyes such as seldom happened. The children were coming from school, and they ran in a little crowd to see and make their remarks with the usual frankness of a population in which the sharpness of town had crept in, modifying the bashfulness, but not the dull candour inaccessible to notions of civility, of the country. The Watcham children were, fortunately, more interested in the appearance of the servants than they were in that of the mistress, though some of the girls whispered together and indulged in pointed laughter at the lady who had to be assisted from the carriage, and who picked her steps, with such an expression in every turn of her person of impatient disgust, along the garden paths. Mrs. Swinford felt it a personal injury that the houses had all gardens and no entrance for the carriage, so that it was absolutely necessary for her, however reluctant, to walk so far before she could reach the door. But she was civil to the FitzStephens', who both met her at their drawing-room door with effusion, and handed her to the most comfortable chair —which, however, Mrs. Swinford turned from the light before she would sit down.

'My eyes will not support so much light. You seem to make really no use of curtains and blinds in this country,' she said.

'My husband likes all the light he can get,' said Mrs. Fitz-Stephen: though she had been, as the reader knows, a pretty woman, and was a fool, according to her visitor's ideas, to face the day and show her wrinkles as she did. But the General's wife had no idea that her old beauty required to be taken care of in this way.

'It is all very well for men,' said Mrs. Swinford—but she explained no further. She added: 'I do not make calls generally, and country visits are an abomination, even when one can drive up to the door.'

'We take your call as all the greater compliment,' said the General, with his finest bow; but Mrs. FitzStephen remembering that she herself was a Challoner, and certainly as good as any Swinford of them all, not to speak of the claims of the Fitz-Stephens—was not quite so complacent.

'It is a pity,' she said, 'that we have no drive, and that our garden must be crossed on foot. We feel it very much when we have company. It is impossible to put up an awning all the way.'

'Oh, you sometimes have company!' said the fine lady.

'We are even looking forward to a dance, in ten days,' said the General, 'a little ridiculous, you may think, for a quiet couple without children like my wife and me: but a dance is more pleasant to the young people than anything else.'

'And consider,' said his wife, 'there is no need to do anything to amuse them, except to provide good music and as nice a floor as possible. They do the rest themselves.'

Mrs. Swinford looked round upon the small drawing-room with an air of inquiry which she did not attempt to disguise. 'I am not much interested in amusing young people,' she said; 'where do they dance?' in a tone that showed she was quite satisfied no dancing could take place there.

Mrs. FitzStephen grew red, and the General confused. They were very fond of this pretty drawing-room. Compliments upon its furniture and arrangements were familiar to them, and they were in the habit of deprecating too much praise by a fond apology as to its diminutive size. 'Oh, it is too small for anything,' Mrs. FitzStephen was in the habit of saying, with a mild inference that she was herself accustomed to something much larger. But the great lady's seeming simple question dashed all their little

pretences.   Fortunately she left them no time to reply.   'You
have your little society in the village?' she said.

'Oh, we are not confined to the village,' said Mrs. FitzStephen
sharply, 'we have a tolerably large list—I expect the Lenthalls,
and some others.'

Mrs. Swinford again permitted her eyes to stray—with a
slight elevation of the eyebrows—round the tiny room.

'We did not venture to send an invitation to the Hall,' said
the General, with an uneasy laugh.   'We scarcely ventured to
hope—though I am happy to say that Mr. Swinford is coming,
my dear.'

'If you mean me,' said Mrs. Swinford, 'I never go out—at
least to balls—since I have ceased to dance.'

'Ah well, those days soon pass over,' said the good old soldier,
'we find other amusements at our age.'

Mrs. Swinford gave him a look—which did not reduce the
gallant General to ashes, for he was not at all aware what she
meant.

'My husband is very fond of seeing the young people enjoy
themselves,' said Mrs. FitzStephen; 'that amuses him more than
anything for himself.'

'Oh come, my dear, you must not give me too good a character,' said the General.   'I like a snug little dinner-party too, and
a good talk.'

'Do you talk here, too, as well as dance?' said Mrs. Swinford,
with an ineffable smile.

'Oh, my dear lady, I assure you we have sometimes quite
remarkable conversations.   The Rector is an exceedingly well-
informed man, and young Osborne has a great deal to say for
himself, though he is taken up with fads—too much.   And then,
above all, there is Lady William ——'

'Oh, Emily!   I had forgotten Lady William, as you call
her.'

'One can't live in Watcham and leave out Lady William, I
assure you, my dear madam,' the General said; 'besides her rank,
which of course places her in the front of all.'

'Ah, to be sure!' said Mrs. Swinford, with a little gurgling
laugh, which stopped and then ran on again, as if with a ridicule
impossible to restrain—'Her rank! I had forgotten her rank—
such rank as it is.'

'We think a good deal of it here,' said Mrs. FitzStephen.
'Lady Wade, you know, is only a baronet's wife, and of course
has to give place.   It gives quite a little distinction to our

village; everybody even in the county, at this end of it at least, must give way to Lady William. It is a great feather in our cap.'

Mrs. Swinford went on laughing, breaking into fresh little runs of merriment from time to time. 'This is really amusing,' she said. 'Poor Emily: and does she talk too?'

'She is an exceedingly cultivated woman, and one who has seen the world. I know few greater treats than to discuss either books or people with Lady William,' said the General, with great gravity, holding up his head as if he were in uniform—which indeed this fine attitude almost persuaded his admiring wife that he was. What a champion for any one to have! But Mrs. Swinford went on with her little exasperating laugh like the vibration of an electric bell. It was very disconcerting to the pair, who were a little proud of their friendship with Lady William, and liked to wave her flag in any stranger's eyes.

'You see,' said the great lady, 'Emily Plowden, poor girl, was in the bread and butter stage when I knew her best: and to hear now of her rank, and then of her accomplishments, is a new experience. I cannot convey to your minds the amusement it causes me.'

'Ah!' said General FitzStephen gravely, 'as I feel when I hear of a little ensign who came out to India at sixteen, and is now in command of my old regiment.'

Mrs. Swinford's laugh ran on like the endless irritating tinkle of that electric bell. 'More,' she said, 'for the boy would gain his promotion; but Emily!—it is more amusing than you can have any idea of to see that she takes it *au grand sérieux*, the rank and all.'

'Perhaps, General,' said Mrs. FitzStephen quickly, 'you will ring for tea, instead of standing there,' which was the most un-called-for, unjustifiable attack : for why should not he stand there, and where else could he have stood but respectfully in front of her chair, listening to their guest? He roused himself with a little start, and did what he was told, but not without a look of sur-prised appeal at his wife's face.

'No tea,' said Mrs. Swinford, rising; 'I have not acquired the habit: but I am sure the General will kindly give me his arm to my carriage. I walk so little, I stumble; I have not the use of gravel walks.'

Mrs. FitzStephen watched the lady sweep away. She had very high-heeled shoes and a long dress, too long for walking. The General's wife watched her along the gravel path, which she thought it very insolent of any one to object to. Mrs. Swinford did not sweep (except indoors) or glide, or march, majestically, as would have been consonant with her pretensions, but accoutred as she was, hobbled, not more gracefully than if she had been any old woman in the village. Her step showed she was an old woman, however she might ignore that fact, and it gave the General's wife, whom she had rubbed so persistently the wrong way, a certain characteristic feminine satisfaction to feel that it was so. Also Mrs. FitzStephen strongly disapproved of the respectful and devoted air with which her husband conducted the great lady. It was Stephen's way; he could not help it. He was an old ——, taken in by any woman that would take the trouble. But what could she mean about Lady William, and all those scoffs at her rank? Could there be any doubt about her rank? It might be a courtesy title, but what did that matter? The daughter-in-law of a marquis held precedence over quite a number of people who were Lady So-and-So. Lady Wade never disputed it, and the Wades had an old baronetcy. They were not upstart people. What did the—the—Mrs. FitzStephen paused for a word—the old hag mean?

'Oh, she meant nothing but spite,' said the General when he came back, 'feminine spite such as you all entertain towards your neighbours when they are prettier or wiser than you.'

'Perhaps you will tell me what woman I regard with feminine spite,' Mrs. FitzStephen very reasonably said.

'Oh, you, my dear, you've no occasion; you are a pretty woman still, and can hold your own : but that poor old soul,' said the General, 'as you may have perceived, I had almost to carry her down the walk; that poor old creature must be seventy if she is a day—and to see her old subaltern taking the *pas* from her : I am not subject to the same kind of feelings—but I confess I don't like it myself, if it comes to that,' the General said.

Mrs. Swinford went on to the Rectory with a curious smile upon her face. She drove past the school-room door and saw her friend standing at it, sheltered in the depth of the doorway, by no means unlike a spider standing at watch, having laid all its nets, till some silly fly buzzes in. A salutation of the eyes only passed between the two women, the schoolmistress and the great lady of the Hall. In the daylight they resembled each other, though Mrs. Brown's plain black gown was not becoming to her dark good looks, and every particular of Mrs. Swinford's attire was calculated to enhance her antiquated beauty. There was a softening in both pairs of eyes as they met. They were not good women; their aims were not fine nor the means they were disposed to use; but yet, curiously enough, they loved each other. It was a strange sight to see. The walk from the little gate of the Rectory to the door was still more trying to Mrs. Swinford than the other had been. It made her quite sure that she had no vocation to call at houses where there was no drive. Her dress was long, and she resented the fact that it must trail on the gravel and get dirty and damp. As for holding it up, it did not occur to her: that any one should think she hobbled, or was not a glass of fashion and mould of form wherever she went would have been incredible to her; but she resented much the length of that walk, and that she should be exposed to such trouble and annoyance in the act of doing what she thought her duty. Had it been only her duty, however, Mrs. Swinford would have cared very little for fulfilling it; but she had a different motive now.

There was a dreadful hurry-scurry in the Rectory drawing-room when she was seen approaching. The antimacassars, I am sorry to say, were much tumbled and untidy, and the loose covers of the chairs anything but what might be desired. Both mother and daughters flew with one impulse to the arranging of the room. Jim had been seated by the fireside all the afternoon with a bad cold, which they had been nursing; but he fled at once into his own cold room, which might, his mother thought, be very bad for him, but could not be helped in the circumstances. Florence ran, with more sense than any one would have given her credit for, to tell the parlourmaid to bring in a more elegant, less substantial tea than usual, and to give her father a hint in his study—'Mrs. Swinford, papa!' while Mrs. Plowden and Emily stood nervously awaiting the visit, anxious to go out and meet her and bring her in by the drawing-room window, which would have saved the old lady a few steps; but kept back by the fear that it might be thought indecorous, too familiar, not dignified enough. Mrs. Swinford looked round upon the Rectory drawing-room as she had done on Mrs. FitzStephen's, but with a different air. 'You have made wonderfully few changes,' she said; 'it is just the same damp little place it used to be.' She was like so many of those great ladies, not careful of people's feelings; but that was, no doubt, mainly from want of thought.

'Oh,' Mrs. Plowden said: and made a pause, that no explosion might follow, 'I assure you,' she said, 'it is not damp at all. We have proved again and again that no water ever comes in. The elevation is small, but quite sufficient; and as for the furniture and doing it up——'

'Yes, I recognise all the old things,' Mrs. Swinford said, with a careless wave of the hand (when there was not one thing, not one, except the Indian cabinet, that had not been renewed!); 'and another Emily Plowden just the same. It is only you,' she said, with a sweet but careless smile upon the Rector's wife, 'that are new——'

'New! But we have been here for fifteen years,' Mrs. Plowden said: and her visitor smiled again as if in complacent consciousness of having said the most agreeable thing in the world.

'I am glad,' she said, 'there is no other daughter, no one to disturb the harmony of what used to be. Oh, but here is the other daughter.'

'Florence, my second, Mrs. Swinford: not considered like the Plowdens, but taking more after my side of the house.'

'I see she is not like the Plowdens,' said Mrs. Swinford, with the look of indifference which was natural to her: it was of so little consequence! 'The other is a little like Emily.'

'Like her aunt, our dear Lady William.'

'You are all much delighted,' said the great lady, 'with that name.'

'My sister-in-law's name? Well, we like it, for she has no other, poor thing. We couldn't call her anything else—as long as she doesn't change it or marry again.'

'Oh, mamma!' said Emmy and Florry together.

'No,' said Mrs. Plowden, 'I don't think she will marry again—now. I did once hope she would; for, though rank is nice, a good husband who would have looked after her and her little girl would have been nicer: while the late Lord William, as I have heard——'

Mrs. Swinford made a little movement of impatience. 'Have the family,' she said, 'taken any notice of Emily—or the little girl?'

'It is very funny,' said Florence, 'to hear Mab, who has such a character of her own, spoken of as the little girl.'

'Oh, Florry, hold your tongue, you are always making remarks. The family, Mrs. Swinford?'

'Poor little thing, poor little thing,' said Mrs. Swinford, 'I think you were very wise, my dear Mrs. Plowden, in advising your sister-in-law to marry again. What a thing it would be if after all it was found that nothing could be done for the little girl!'

'They have their little annuity,' said Mrs. Plowden, startled; 'there has never been anything said of taking it away. And I could not make such a statement as that I advised her to marry, for there has really been no one that she could have married except——, and he was quite an old gentleman. Not to say that Emily ever thought of such a thing. She was not so happy the first time as to have any wish——'

Mrs. Swinford's attention had once more flagged, and here she interposed with her usual calm bearing, addressing Emmy. 'I thought you had a brother,' she said.

Emmy coloured high, being thus suddenly spoken to. 'Oh yes.'

'Yes, indeed,' cried Mrs. Plowden, recovering herself the more easily that this new subject was one on which she could be eloquent. 'He has a bad cold, poor boy, or he would have been here at once to pay his respects. Is that you, James? Mrs. Swinford is making such kind inquiries.'

The great lady held out her hand. 'You have not taken the trouble to come and see me,' she said.

The Rector had come in much against his will. He made a bow which had not his usual ease. 'I must beg your pardon,' he said very gravely. 'I am aware that I have been negligent.'

'Ah,' she said, 'you did not want to come? but I supposed when your excellent wife did me so much honour, that bygones were to be bygones; and Emily——'

'My sister acts for herself; I do not try to influence her; and my wife thinks she knows what is best for her——'

'Her family, of course; good woman. She thought it would be a wrong thing to neglect opportunities, and so did your father, as you may recollect.'

'I prefer not to recollect, any more than I can help,' said the Rector.

'Which? that Emily has come to great promotion, very high promotion, as all those ladies think—while she was in my house? There would have been no title in the case—a title such as it is! —but for my house.'

'The less that is said on that subject, I think, the better,' said the Rector, standing bolt upright before the fire.

'Oh, James,' said his wife, 'when Mrs. Swinford is so kind——'

'I gave it,' said Mrs. Swinford, bending forward, 'and, my good Rector, you will take care not to be insolent; I may also, perhaps, take it away.'

LADY WILLIAM, on this eventful afternoon, had gone out with Mab on one of her rambles. The air was full of spring, the buds bursting on every tree, the cottage gardens all blooming with those common flowers which can be got anywhere, which are the inheritance of the poorest, and are more beautiful, spontaneous, and abundant than any other: the early primroses, daffodils and Lent lilies, the rich dark wallflowers that fill the air with sweetness. Mab had a little basket with her, in which to bring home any wild thing that pleased her in the woods and slopes of Denham Hill, on the other side of the water. It was a long walk, but neither mother nor daughter was afraid of a long walk. They came back, breathing of every sweet-wildness of the spring, just as Mrs. Swinford, disappointed and angry, was leaving a card, with a message, at the cottage door; but the carriage had disappeared along the road long before they reached their own end of Watcham. It had been a lovely afternoon, warm, yet fresh with the dewy moisture of the April breezes, that germinating weather, and sparkle of showers and waters which is not damp. Several showers had fallen upon them in their ramble, but done no harm; they had taken shelter, after a laughing run against the wind and the bright falling veil of rain, under the trees, or in a cottage when one was near, and shaken the rain-drops off their dresses, and carried the freshness of the outside atmosphere, as if they had been nymphs of the air, into the little wayside houses. It would have been hard to say whether mother or daughter was youngest in these runs and shelterings. Lady William was almost more swift of foot than Mab, who more easily got out of breath, and was built on heavier lines; and though the girl's colour was higher, the delicate flush on the other's cheek spoke of almost finer health and brightness in its fluctuations and changes. They were both equally interested about the

K

plants and roots which Mab grubbed up from under the trees, but hers was the delight of superior knowledge, as she discovered a rare something here and there, a flower peculiar to one place or another. Mab was altogether absorbed in her botany and her researches, flushed with her digging, eager about her new treasures. But her mother was more free for the delights of the sweet air and sensations of the spring, the freedom of the woods, and sometimes would burst out singing, and sometimes fling bits of moss at her child, as she held the basket.

'Isn't that beautiful, Mab?'

'Yes, mother,' Mab would say, digging, her head bent over the mossy soil, nothing free of her but the ear which took in the sound of the poetry in a kind of subdued pleasure which mingled with her humbler sensations.

'You are a little grub,' said Lady William; 'you are never so happy as when you are probing among the roots and the dead leaves.'

'And you are of the kind of the birds, mother, and I like to hear you up among the branches,' said Mab. I do not mean to say that Lady William was a musician, or that you could hear the bits of songs she sang, which had been Mab's lullaby as a baby, and amusement through all her childhood — a few yards from where she stood. They were nothing but the spontaneous utterances of her fresh spirit, like breathing, or the trilling of the birds, to which Mab compared them. Mab did not herself require utterances, givings forth, of that kind. She worked away and was silent, wholly given to what she was about. But she admired the trill and movement of the lighter spirit, and thought her mother the most delightful human creature that had ever been upon this earth.

The basket was tolerably heavy when they came back, and Mab was still a little flushed with her hard work. The sky was very sweet and subdued in colour, a great band of softened gold binding the growing grayness of the afternoon, approaching night —and opening, as it were, a glimpse into the heavens, a broad shining pathway, reflected fully in the river, between the awakening greens and browns of the spring country and the soft clouds above. It was still light, but evening was in the air, and among the folds of the clouds a few mild stars were already visible. The cows were coming lowing home; the children were leaving off their games; and people coming up from the river, who found a little chill in the air after the sun had gone down. The mother and daughter met everybody on their progress home. The doctor,

another botanist, who sniffed at Mab's basket, and affected contempt at her brag of the peculiar coltsfoot she had found, which
grew nowhere but on Denham Hill. 'Common, common,' he said,
'you'll find it everywhere,' as one connoisseur says to another, upon
most new acquisitions ; but that was because he had never had
such luck himself, Mab felt convinced. And they met the tall
curate, Mr. Osborne, stalking off to a meeting, who stopped to ask
whether Lady William would not help in a temperance tea party
of his, where the ladies and gentlemen were to amuse the villagers,
and make them forget that there was such a thing on earth, or
rather, in Watcham, as the 'Why Not?' or the 'Blue Boar.' Mr.
Osborne wore his Inverness cape, as usual, and a quantity of books
and pamphlets under it; but there was something a little different
from his ordinary aspect in his looks. After he had passed he
made a step back again, and called Lady William, with a hesitating
voice.

'Do you see—young Plowden often?' he said, in the most
awkward way.

'Jim !' she said, surprised, 'my nephew?'

'Don't be vexed ; I think he goes to——places which he had
better avoid,' said the curate. Lady William looked at him,
but there was nothing further to be learned from his cloudy
face.

'That is very possible,' she said. 'Do you mean——there ?'
for she had heard something of the 'Blue Boar,' which was now
beginning to light up, and looked cheerful enough across the village
green. The curate gave a little stamp of impatience as he saw
some one else approaching, and said quickly :

'I can't say any more,' and stalked away, leaving, as such
monitors so often do, a prick of pain behind him, but nothing that
could do any good. It was the General who was coming, and he
walked a few steps with the ladies, congratulating them on their
walk.

'For I should not wonder if it rained to-morrow,' he said. And
then he told them of Mrs. Swinford's visit, and how she had gone
from door to door. 'You see you have missed something ; you
have not had that honour.'

'I am glad that we went for our long walk,' Lady William
said. And then, finally, they met Mr. Swinford, who came up joy-
fully, with his hat in his hand, and his head uncovered from the
moment he saw them.

'Ah, I have found you at last,' said Leo ; 'I have waited for
you in the cottage, sitting inside by the invitation of Miss Patty,

who is very kind to me, and observing the proceedings of my mother.'

'I hear she has been paying visits.'

'To everybody, which is not, perhaps, the way to make the visit prized; but she does not like the English climate, and she is used, you know, to do as she likes,' he said, with a smile.

'Surely, in such matters as that she has a very good right.'

'Yes, to be sure,' he said doubtfully, and then laughed. 'She came to see you, too—and I lay there, like a spider in a web, wondering if she would also come in to wait for you; but Miss Patty was not so kind to my mother as to me. I heard her answer unhesitatingly, "Not at home!" with a voice like that of a groom of the chambers. She has great capabilities, Patty.'

'And did you not go out, to say——'

'What should I have said? I was waiting, feeling that you would probably snub me for my pains, and why should I interfere with my mother? She left a card with a message pencilled on it, which I had the honourable feeling not to read. It got upon my nerves to be in the same room with it, and if I had not come out to meet you I should have yielded to the temptation.'

'That would have been as bad as opening a letter,' said Mab, who had as yet taken no part.

'Would it, do you think? It was open; there would have been no seal broken; but, at all events, I resisted temptation, so you must praise me and not censure, Miss Mab.'

'And how did you know,' said Mab, while her mother powdered, 'that we were coming this way?'

'Give me the basket and I will tell you. What is in it? Worms? But also clay and earth. Have you not mud enough already in Watcham, that you must bring in more from the woods?'

'Give me my basket again,' said Mab indignantly; 'there's a clump of wood anemones, beauties, and the famous coltsfoot that only grows at Denham. I have hunted for it for years, and I only found it to-day. Give it me back.'

'I am not worthy to carry such treasures,' said Leo, 'but the contact will do me good.'

'All the same you haven't answered,' said Mab. 'Who told you we were coming this way?'

'If you must know, it was the accomplished Patty again. She offered me tea, which I declined, and she offered me also my mother's card, which in my high sense of honour I declined too, and then she said, "My lydy was a-going to Denham Hill, and you'll meet 'em sure, if you go that way." Patty is my friend, Miss Mab; she has a higher opinion of me than you have.'

'We must hurry home now, Mab; we have been too long away,' said Lady William, with a serious face. 'It does not do for a woman of my age to go out on your long grubbings. Come, Leo, give me the basket, and let us run home.'

'I can run too,' he said. 'Are you really sorry, is that what you mean, that you missed my mother?'

'I cannot quite say that honestly. No, I am not sorry I missed your mother. Perhaps she and I have been too long apart to bridge over the difference now. How I used to admire your mother, Leo! How beautiful she was!'

'Was she, indeed?' he said, with a sort of polite attention, but surprised. Perhaps it is curious at any time for a man to realise that his mother may have been beautiful and admired. 'I should not have thought,' he said, 'with submission, that her features, for instance——'

'Women don't think of features,' said Lady William, with a little impatience. 'It was she, not her features, that was beautiful. She had so much charm—when she pleased. It must always be added, that when she did not please—but we are not going to discuss your mother. She is a wonderful creature to be imprisoned here.'

'You are not imprisoned here,' he said, almost angrily, 'who are still more wonderful: and you forget that my mother is old, and has had her day.'

'The day will not be over as long as she lives; and as for me, I am not imprisoned; I dwell among my own people.'

'How curious,' he said, 'pardon me, that the people here should be your own people! I say nothing against them, don't fear it; they are very good people, but not——'

'Thanks,' she said, with a half laugh, 'it was I who used to be the black sheep. Mrs. Plowden is not sure that she approves of me now; and if——'

'If what?'

'Nothing,' said Lady William, with the slightest tinge of angry colour in her face.

'That is just like mother,' said Mab; 'she gives you a word as if she were going to say something of importance, and then she tells you it is nothing. I have known her to do it a hundred times.'

'There is nothing like the criticism of one's children,' said Lady William, with a laugh. 'You, with your mother, Leo, and

Mab with hers, you are two iconoclasts. Now, the humble people, like my good Emmy, are very different; they do not criticise. And then you despise them as common, you two—— Ah! here we are at our own door.' She turned and held out her hand to Leo, who looked at her surprised.

'Are you not going to ask me in?' he said, holding part of the basket, for which Mab, too, had held out her hands.

They all stood looking at each other in front of the cottage door.

'It is late,' said Lady William, with some hesitation—'yes, if you wish it: but don't you think it would be better to get back to the Hall before it is dark?'

'No,' said Leo, 'why should I hurry back to the Hall? Of course I wish it; and you never told me before that I was not to come.'

'I do not say so now, but——'

'But what?'

'Nothing,' said Lady William, with a faint smile.

'I told you that was her way,' cried Mab, triumphant. '"Nothing," and one is sure that she means heaps of things more than she ever says.'

He followed her into the little drawing-room, where there was still a little bright fire, though it was no longer cold. Mrs. Swinford's card was lying upon a small table conspicuously, though there was not light enough to read its pencilled message. Lady William hesitated a little, not sitting down, giving her visitor no excuse for doing so. He followed her movements with a disturbed aspect, standing within the door, watching her figure against the light. Mab, who had seized the basket when he put it down, had gone off to put her treasures in safety. 'I perceive,' he said at last, 'that I have done something wrong. What have I done wrong? Am I troubling you coming in when you did not want me? Then tell me so, dear lady, and send me away.'

'Leo,' said Lady William, 'you should not have remained here while your mother was at the door; I do not like it; it puts me in a very uncomfortable position. Why didn't you go and tell her we were out, Mab and I?'

'I am your devoted servant, dear lady,' said Leo, 'but I am not your groom of the chambers, and Patty is. How could I have taken her duties out of her hands?'

'That is all very well for a laugh,' she said, 'but it vexes me very much; it is very uncomfortable; why should you have been in my drawing-room while your mother was sent away from the door?'

'You mean I ought not to have come in to wait.'

'That for one thing, certainly; but being in, you should certainly not have allowed——'

'What?' said the young man.

Lady William did not say 'Nothing' again, but she stood at the window looking out with her back turned to him, and as strong an expression of discomfort and vexation in her attitude and eloquent silence as if she had used many words.

'I see,' he said, 'I have been very indiscreet; I have vexed you though I did not mean it. I don't make any excuse for myself, except that I thought at first you were coming back immediately. Forgive me: and I will go away, and never at any time will I do it any more.'

She gave a little laugh, turning round. 'No, I don't think you will do it again; but, unfortunately, that does not alter the fact that you have done it, and made me very uncomfortable. Are you going away? Then good night; you will have a pleasant walk up to the Hall.'

'Not nearly so pleasant as if it had been an hour later,' he said.

'Oh, that is merely an idea. You will really like it better. Mab ought to be here to thank you for carrying her basket. Good night, Leo,' Lady William said. She stepped out into the narrow passage after him to see him away; and, at the moment, in the open doorway Mab appeared with a cry of surprise.

'Oh, are you going so soon? Are you not going to stop for tea?'

'I am sent away,' he said.

'By mother?'

'Yes. To make sure of amendment another time,' he said ruefully, and went away with so much the air of a schoolboy under punishment, that Mab came in open-mouthed to her mother.

'Oh! what have you been doing to Mr. Leo? Oh! why have you sent him away?'

Lady William made no answer, but rang the bell, as it very seldom was rung in this small house; an unusual occurrence, which brought Patty in with a rush, still rubbing a candlestick she held in her hand.

'Patty, did you ask Mr. Swinford to come in and wait till Miss Mab and I came back?'

'Yes, my lydy,' said Patty, with sharp eyes that gleamed in the light.

'And you did not ask Mrs. Swinford, when she called, to come in and wait?'

'Oh, no, my lydy,' cried Patty, aggrieved.

'Why?' said her mistress solemnly.

'Oh, my lydy!' said Patty, thunderstruck.

'Yes, why?' I want to know, why should Mr. Swinford wait for me and not Mrs. Swinford? I do not wish anybody to be asked to wait for me when I am out. If you were ever to do it again, I don't know what I might be obliged to say.'

'Oh, my lydy,' said Patty, 'I thought as Mr. Swinford was a young gentleman as perhaps made it a little cheerful for Miss Mab —— and I thought as the old lady wasn't a pleasure for nobody; and I thought——'

'If that is true of old ladies, why should you stay with me, Patty, who am an old lady, too, and not a pleasure to anybody——'

'Oh, my lydy!' said Patty, bursting into a torrent of tears.

'Go, you little goose, and think no more of it; but ask nobody to wait for me. Now remember! you are here to do what you are told, but never to think. Thinking is the destruction of little maids. Ask Anne if she ever ventured to think when she was a girl like you.'

'Yes, my lydy,' said Patty, drying her eyes.

IT is not necessary to make a room snug with curtains drawn and the draught shut out, in the month of April as it is in early March, so that it was some time even after the lamp was brought in before the wistful clearness in the east, and that gleam of yellow, 'the daffodil sky' of the other quarter, which turns to ethereal tints of green, and has so many gradations of colour all its own, was shut out. Lady William liked to see the sky when she was in a cheerful or excited, not a sad mood. Such moods came to her as to every one by times; but she was angry and active to-night. Mab was not much used to such moments of commotion, to her mother's slightly disturbed condition, and the scolding which had made Patty cry. Scolding was very infrequent in the cottage. Now and then Lady William would launch a fiery arrow; she would throw a distinct terrible light of displeasure upon dusty corners and silver badly cleaned. Sometimes even Mab would be brought to a sudden perception that her faults were quite visible and apparent, notwithstanding all her mother's love and indulgence. But a moment like this, when all was disturbed and broken without any apparent motive, was astonishing to the girl. It was not for some time that Mab felt even the courage to inquire: only after tea when Lady William's hasty ejaculations and movements of anger had almost died away.

'But, mother, now that we are cool,' said Mab——

'Cool? I have never been anything but cool.'

'Now,' continued the girl, 'that it is over, what was there so very bad in letting Mr. Leo come in to wait?'

'And not his mother?' said Lady William. 'There would have been nothing particular, though very absurd if everybody who called had been asked in to wait. Fancy coming back to find the room crowded like a dentist's waiting-room! But to bring in one and leave out another! Though I confess,' said Lady William, with an angry flush, 'that if the little goose had done so, and brought in Mrs. Swinford to find her son waiting, I should have been still more uncomfortable.'

'Then you scolded her, mother, for what it was best to do?'

'Nothing of the sort; her sin was inviting a gentleman to come in and wait for us who—— Oh, it is too horrid altogether, and if Mrs. Swinford had found him——'

'Mother, what then?' cried Mab, a little alarmed.

Her limpid gaze, so full of innocent surprise, seemed to bring back all Lady William's annoyance. 'You must take it for granted, Mab, that there are some things I know better than you do,' she said. 'By-the-bye, give me her card; let us see what message she left.'

The card did not seem to afford Lady William any more satisfaction. It was a very highly-polished card, and the pencil had cut into it, and the writing was difficult to read. She put it down with a heightened colour, throwing it from her hand. 'I wonder if she thinks I put any faith in her *câlineries*,' she said.

'What are *câlineries*, mother?' said Mab, taking up the card, which was inscribed as follows: '*Chère Petite*,—Much regret not to find you. Come to see me to-morrow; I have something important for your welfare to say.' '*Chère Petite*,' repeated Mab, 'that is a *câlinerie*, I suppose. It seems queer to call you *Petite* —but I suppose she knew you when you were quite little.'

'She knew me, certainly, when the title was more appropriate than it is now.'

'That must be the reason; and perhaps she thought you might like it. Some ladies,' said Mab, with her serious, almost childish, face, 'like to be thought young.'

'I don't think she can have thought I would like it, Mab,' said Lady William, with a little shiver. 'Close the window and draw the curtain, please. I have a sort of uncomfortable feeling of somebody looking in.'

'You are uncomfortable altogether to-night, mother.'

'Yes, I suppose it's my nerves; it's—that woman. I never thought I had any nerves before.'

'Oh, but you have,' cried Mab; 'I know better than that. Not nerves, perhaps, like Aunt Jane, but—— There *is* somebody in the garden. Shall I go and see who it is?'

Lady William started up and looked over Mab's shoulder. Whether she thought it might be Leo come again, or what other intruder at this untimely hour, I cannot tell. But she said, in a tone that was half relief and half annoyance: 'Your Aunt Jane in

person, Mab, and the girls. What can they want now?' Her
tone was a little fretful. They were in the way of wanting a great
many things from her at the Rectory, and frequently her advice on
one subject or another, which they did not generally take.

'It will be about their dresses for the FitzStephens' party,'
said Mab, to whom the ladies outside were beckoning that she
should open the door to them. But Lady William shook her head.

'Run and let them in, at all events. They have not rung the
bell,' she said, drawing the curtains with an impatient movement.
The little room looked so full that it could contain no more when
the three ladies came in ; but they knew all its accommodations,
and settled themselves in their places at as great a distance as
possible from the little bright fire. 'It is such a mild night there
is no occasion for it,' said Mrs. Plowden, 'but you always keep up
fires, Emily, later than any one.'

'Do I? It's cheerful at least.'

'And the window open ! That's rather wasteful, don't you
think ? I like to do either one thing or another ; to shut up the
house and keep all the heat in, as one does on winter nights, or
else to throw up all the windows, and get the full advantage of the
air. But I don't see the good of dispersing all the heat outside, as
if it could warm the garden. That would be a very good idea ;
but I'm afraid it would not be a success if you were to try it ever
so much.'

'I suppose,' said Lady William, 'you have come to tell me
something ; not to talk about the fire.'

'I don't know. We came over just to see you. It's such a
lovely night I thought I should like a walk. I said to Emmy,
after James had gone back to his study, I think I'd like to have a
little run ; it's so sweet to-night, not cold at all. Let's run out
and see your Aunt Emily, I said. I knew you were sure to be in.'

'Oh, yes, we are always sure to be in.'

'And, except ourselves, you are the only person of whom that
can be said ; for the FitzStephens are always dining with the
Kendals or the Kendals with the FitzStephens ; and Miss Grey,
she goes in later to tea, not to put the table out, or she is at one
of Mr. Osborne's meetings, or has some parish tea party of her own.
We are never sure to find anybody but you ; and it is such a thing
in a little place like this to know somebody you can depend upon
to be in, if you find it dull or want a little run.'

'I am afraid that Mab and I can't do much to help your
dulness.'

'Oh, yes, you can. You can always talk nicely, Emily, on

almost any subject; and I always say it is such a good thing for the girls only to hear you talk. And Mab is the most sensible little thing that ever was. I always tell the girls it's quite a treat to hear her; no nonsense, but so sensible, and taking up things so quick!'

'It is very kind of you, Jane, to have so good an opinion of my little girl.'

'Oh, it is merely the truth, Emily. I have always heard the Marquis was a very sensible man, and we all know there was once a Prime Minister in the family. Of course that's a great thing to begin with. I can't boast anything like that on my side, and I can't say I think the Plowdens are remarkable for common sense, do you? Our children have other qualities. My poor Jim complains that his father is always at him because he does not stick to his Greek, and how can you expect a young man to stick to his Greek when it is only in that interrupted broken way? James thinks he gives him his full attention. But you know what a parish is, Emily. Sometimes it's a christening, or some sick person to see, or a funeral. And then James has to tell him, "I can't hear you, Jim, to-day." Now, I ask you, Emily, honestly, do you think a boy can be expected to stick to his Greek like that?'

'I quite agree with you, Jane; it is very hard upon him.'

'Of course it is hard; everything's hard. And he doesn't know what's the good of it, or what it's for. He cannot go into the Church, and it requires so much, all the technicalities, you know, to be a schoolmaster; and if James makes up his mind at the end to put him into an office, or to send him—which is terrible to think of,' cried poor Mrs. Plowden, putting her handkerchief to her eyes—'abroad—what use would all that Greek be?'

'It is quite true,' said Lady William, 'and I wish we could persuade James to make up his mind. Do you know what friends Jim has in the parish; where he goes; who are his companions? Some one said something to me——'

'Oh, what did they say to you? Who spoke to you? Tell me what any one has to say about my boy.'

'It was nothing, after all; it was Mr. Osborne. He said Jim went to some house where it would be better he should not go.'

'Mr. Osborne!' cried the Rector's wife. 'Oh, Emily, that one who belongs to Jim should listen to that man! There is a man,' cried the troubled mother, 'who, if he liked, might have done almost anything with Jim. Not preaching to him; that's not what I mean. But he is a young man, only five years older; a University man, a man wishing to have good influence. Where does he go to exercise this good influence, Emily? To Riverside; to the men who don't care, who laugh at him behind his back— and to get the old women to give up their glass of beer, and the little children, that know nothing, to take his blue ribbon. Oh, and there was Jim in his way,' said the poor mother, 'Jim at his door, a University man, too; his Rector's son, his own kind. Did he ever try to get a good influence over Jim? to ask him of an evening, to take him for walks, to give him an interest? Never, never, never! He goes about the parish and makes the poor women promise to give up their drop of beer. What does he know about what they need, about their innocent drop of beer, him a strong young man, well fed, wanting nothing? But my Jim, that was what he wanted, a strong man of his own kind; a young man that he had no suspicion of; that didn't need to preach. That's what the boy wants, Emily; not his father, that is angry, or me that only cries, but one like himself. Is it better to gain a good influence over poor old Mrs. Lloyd than over Jim, or to hold temperance meetings when he might do a brother's part to get hold of that boy?'

'Oh, mamma, what are you saying?' said Emmy, still anxious to save appearances. 'Aunt Emily will think that dear Jim——'

Florence said nothing, but sat staring into the vacant air with wide open eyes full of trouble, while Mrs. Plowden, altogether broken down, put her head upon Lady William's shoulder and cried.

'It's mamma's nerves,' said Emmy again; 'she has been upset to-day. You are not to think, Aunt Emily, that anything dreadful has happened. Nothing is wrong with Jim; it is only that papa is angry with him, and mamma has got it on her nerves, and— mamma, this was not what you came to talk of, you know.'

Mrs. Plowden raised her head after a minute with a piteous smile. 'Thank you, Emily, you're always kind,' she said; 'and it's only my nerves, as Emmy says. I get agitated, and then every- thing looks black, as if it never would come right again. It isn't that there's anything to be frightened about, and you know what a true good heart my Jim has, and that's everything, isn't it? That's everything,' the poor lady said.

'What mamma really wanted to ask you, Aunt Emily,' said Emmy, 'was whether you had seen Mrs. Swinford. She has been to call at the Rectory.'

'Yes, yes,' said Mrs. Plowden; 'that was what we wanted, to be sure. Emily, you won't think anything more of the little fuss I've made about Mr. Osborne, will you? You would think I meant that he intended to slight my son. You know I couldn't mean that. And he is a very good curate, and James puts great confidence in him. It's my nerves that get the better of me. But Emmy always brings me up to the mark. Yes, about Mrs. Swinford, that was it ; did she come here, too ?'

'I believe so ; but before we came in. She left a card with a message——'

'My dear Emily, I don't think Mrs. Swinford is a very nice woman,' said Mrs. Plowden solemnly.

'Don't you ?' said Lady William, with a faint smile.

'You see, girls,' said the Rector's wife, 'your aunt will never say anything. Perhaps it is prudent, but it's a little confusing. One doesn't know what to say.'

'If you think you will hurt my feelings, Jane, by speaking plainly, don't let that weigh upon your mind. I know very well what Mrs. Swinford is, and I don't care to make myself her champion.'

'I don't think she's a nice woman,' repeated the Rector's wife ; 'I don't think she's a good woman. She looks to me—notwithstanding that she professes to be so fond of you, and Emily this and Emily that—as if she would like to do you a bad turn.'

Lady William took this alarming statement quite calmly. 'Indeed I should not be surprised,' she said, 'but I don't think it is in her power.'

'We must try and make sure that it is not in her power. Don't you think she could perhaps do you harm with the family? It occurred to me, and you will wonder to hear that it occurred to James. He said to me, "If that woman can injure Emily she will." Dear Emily, you have never been such very good friends with the family, and they have never seen Mab. You know I've always wanted you to do something. If you were to put yourself forward a little——'

'You are very kind, Jane, and James too. I don't think the family can do us much harm ; we have what they chose to give us, and they will not give us anything more, nor do I wish it. I have my pride, too.'

'But their countenance, Emily!'

'Their countenance!' cried Lady William, rising to her feet with a quick start of indignation. 'To me! I want none of their countenance ; I can't help bearing their name, and they cannot take it from me.'

'Oh, my dear, my dear, there can be no question of that! They can't take away your rank, nor Mrs. Swinford either, whatever she may do. My conviction,' said Mrs. Plowden, nodding her head, 'is that she can't bear the thought of your rank. If you should meet anywhere *out,* and you were to pass before her, Emily—that's the thought that she can't bear.'

A gleam of light passed over Lady William's face. 'That would be a little compensation,' she said, half to herself. 'But don't put such hopes in my head,' she added laughing; 'she and I will never meet *out,* alas!'

'If it was only for that I should like to give a dinner party at the Rectory and ask her, Emily—just to show her. Oh, I should like that! It might look strange, James giving his arm to his own sister, but I should never mind how it looked. And it would be a kind of duty, by way of welcoming them back. But you know, Emily, though Mary Jane is an excellent parlour-maid, she is not equal to a formal party. We should require to have a butler, or some one who would look like a butler. And the dinner-service is very shabby and a great many pieces broken. I am sure I would do it with the greatest pleasure, and, indeed, would think it a duty; but only——'

'No, my kindest Jane, you will do nothing of the sort for me. As for Mrs. Swinford, she will go out to no parties in the village. Don't imagine for a moment that I want to be avenged upon her in that very small way.'

'Avenged! I did not think of it in that light. And do you know James was very cool to her to-day, scarcely civil. I thought she had been very nice to you in the old times.'

'Don't let us talk of the Swinfords for ever,' said Lady William, 'we have had enough of them for one day. Let me know what the girls are going to wear at the Fitz-Stephens', and who is to be there——'

This new subject, notwithstanding that Mrs. Plowden had her head full of graver matters, was too interesting to be dropped quickly, and there ensued a long conversation, which Lady William, having set it going, left to be carried on by the others. Mrs. Plowden had naturally a great deal to say, and Emmy, whose heart was full of the consciousness that any social occasion where she could see and be seen was more important now in her life than it had ever been before, lent her attention with great earnestness to her mother's view, to Mab's remarks, and to the occasional word with which Lady William kept up the talk. Only Florence took no part in it. She had taken up a book, and so appeared to have her attention fixed; I don't know if she held it upside down, but I am very sure that she did not read a page. Her mind was occupied with affairs of her own.

THE dining-room at the Hall was gloomy but grand. The walls dark, save where they were relieved by scrolls of gilding and ornamental panels, in which were set some full-length portraits of doubtful merit, and more than doubtful antiquity. It was divided, like the drawing-room, by pillars, not of marble, though they assumed that virtue, leaving a darker strait at each end, intended, no doubt, to throw up the brilliancy of the larger central room, in which stood the dinner-table with all its lights. And this might have been the case had there been a large and brilliant party round the table, and abundance of light, with reflections of silver and crystal, as probably the builder of the house intended should be the case. But now the Swinfords, mother and son, alone at a round table of no great size, with a shaded lamp suspended over it, furnished little more than an oasis in the great desert of darkness. There was, indeed, a large fire blazing, against which Mrs. Swinford sat, shivering from time to time, notwithstanding the mild softness of the April night. And the table was adorned with a great bouquet of flowers, dazzling white azaleas, and the other brilliant children of the spring who come in such a triumph over the footsteps of winter. Mrs. Swinford was dressed, as she always was, elaborately, and like a picture, in dark velvet, just showing a little colour here and there where the light caught it—and a great deal of lace. She had a lace scarf fastened over her head, fantastically indeed, and scarcely enough to have been allowed by Mrs. Plowden to pass muster as a cap, but still softening the age of the face, and the tower of the abundant dark hair piled unnaturally upon her head. She might have been a dethroned and indignant queen. She, and the flowers, and Leo's more youthful face, gave a centre to the dark solemnity around, through which the servants moved noiseless.

'You have been in the village,' he said; 'I hear, making calls.' But this was not till the lengthened and elaborate dinner—of which both ate fastidiously, with many criticisms and remarks little complimentary to a very ambitious and highly-paid cook—was done.

'I am glad you take so much interest in my movements, Leo, as to know.'

'Of course I know. I saw the carriage for one thing; and besides——'

'You, I suppose, were paying visits, too?'

'Not much,' he said, with an embarrassed smile. 'I saw little Miss Grey about some of our schemes; but you don't give Miss Grey the light of your countenance.'

'I have never noticed any but the principal people—who, in case of an election or any public matter, might be useful.'

'I don't see what an election would be to us.'

'Nor I, Leo. But it is part of our hereditary policy to keep the matter open, should you or any one of the family be of a different opinion.'

'My dear mother,' he said, with a laugh, 'don't you think this hereditary policy is overdone a little? I am afraid I thought myself a person of much greater importance than I prove to be.'

'I don't admit it,' she said; 'but is that why you are taking so much trouble for the *canaille?*'

'No,' said the young man, growing red. 'I take trouble for the *canaille*, as you call them—our poor neighbours, Miss Grey says—because I thought I was somehow responsible for them.'

'Responsible!'

'I should have been,' he said firmly, 'had I been their *seigneur;* which I suppose in my folly was something like what I thought: now that I know they are only our poor neighbours——'

'Well: you think you may at least get the benefit in popularity,' she said, with a laugh.

'My dear mother, as we shall never think alike on these points, don't you think we had better choose another subject?'

'The subject of my calls?' said Mrs. Swinford. 'But how, Leo, about your own? You find a wonderful attraction in the village, I understand.'

'You know, I think, pretty well what attraction I find in the village,' he said coldly; 'I have made no secret of my doings there.'

'Perhaps not; but you have dwelt little upon a certain cottage. One knows how a man can be exceedingly frank in order to conceal.'

'There is no certain cottage,' he said, with indignation. 'If you mean Lady William's, I certainly go there with pleasure, and often, and will continue to do so. In such a matter I may surely be allowed to judge for myself.'

'Why do you call her by that ridiculous name? It makes me laugh—if it didn't make me furious!'

'What has she done to you?' said Leo. 'I thought you were fond of her. It has always been represented so to me. What has she done, a woman not very powerful or prosperous certainly, not coming in your way, to make you hate her so?'

'Not coming in my way!—But what do you know of my history or my feelings? She is already again coming in my way —with you.'

'That is nonsense, mother. No, I know little of your history, perhaps, except what you have told me; and as you say, excessive frankness——'

'You forget, I think, Leo, that you are speaking to your mother?'

'I never wish to do so,' he said. 'Believe me, mother, there is nothing I desire so much as to make you feel my anxiety, my strong desire, to do what will please you——'

'By bringing me to this miserable country, for example, in the middle of winter,' she cried.

Leo sprang to his feet, and began to pace about the room. 'It is my country,' he said. 'If I have duties anywhere, they must be here. But I have never wished to bind you. Why, if you hate England so, should you stay here? We have always been together; but sooner than you should suffer, leave me, mother. I will bear my loneliness as best I can.'

'Your loneliness! You would not be long lonely. You would find plenty to cheer you; whereas I am in a different position. Nay: come back with me. You have seen exactly how things are. If you want to be charitable, nothing is more easy. James Plowden, or if you prefer it, his sister,' she paused, with a harsh laugh, 'will do everything you want in that way. Come back to the life we know; come back to the surroundings you are accustomed to. You—you can't, any more than I, be happy here. Where are your *courses*, your clubs, your theatres?

There is nothing, nothing to amuse you. Leo, you know you would be more amused, you would be more happy, as well as I.'

'But this,' he said, 'is my proper sphere.'

'*Grand seigneur* again,' she cried, with a laugh; 'who takes up that view now? Your great-grandfather bought this estate; it is then four generations in the family. And you think that feudal! Ah! be kind to the *canaille* if you will; they will cheat you and hate you, but never mind. Leo, if you keep me here, and I am tempted beyond my powers, and do harm—harm, do you hear?—murder even—the guilt will not be on me, but you!'

'Mother, do you think there is any use in scaring yourself by such big words? Murder! Whom will you kill, for example? You who faint if you prick yourself and the blood runs! I am not afraid of you.'

'There are more ways of murder than one. I will take no life.'

'No, I don't suppose so,' he said, with a laugh; 'but if you think you will die of *ennui*, which, I allow, is a danger, my dear mother, your *appartement* is still open. I will make every arrangement. Pardon me if I feel it is my duty to live in my own house; but why should that affect you?'

'If I said, Leo, that I could not live without you, that you are my only child——'

'Mother,' he said, 'we both understand perfectly what that means. When I was a child you were very fond of me. I was part of your *ensemble*. You gave me everything I wanted. Now, it is not your fault nor mine that I am a man of thirty-five, not even in my first youth. If I am ever to be good for anything, I have no time to lose; but you have arrived at an age——'

'Ah!' she said, 'I have arrived at an age when I am no longer good for anything, neither the pleasures nor the duties. It is fit that it should be you who say that to me.'

'I say that you have arrived at an age when everything should be made easy to you, and pleasant, mother; and that you should live, without consideration of others, as suits you best.'

'And you?' she said with a smile; 'as suits you best? Is not that what you mean?'

'It was not what I meant; but perhaps it is true,' he said.

Then there was a silence, during which Leo stood by the
high mantelpiece, leaning upon it, looking down upon the bright
blaze of the fire, yet furtively watching his mother's face.

'I know who has done all this,' she said rapidly and very low,
as if speaking to herself. 'I know who has done it. It was a
caprice—a fancy that would have lasted a moment; a trick of his
father's blood. But I know who has done it—who has stamped
it in. I know—I know! for her own advantage as before: to
put me under her foot as before. But let her take care, let her
take care!' she cried, suddenly raising her voice, '*J'ai des griffes,
moi!*'

'Mother, for heaven's sake what do you mean? Who is to
take care?'

'A tigress, that's what men call a woman in respect to her
children, Leo. I said that a tigress has claws, that was all.'

'There is no question, surely,' he said, looking at her; at her
soft lace, her warm velvet, her carefully-dressed hair, her air of
luxury and delicacy, 'of claws or anything of the kind here.'

She burst out into a laugh, and rose, turning her face to the
fire.

'No; at the worst of little pins to prick, little pins that don't
draw blood, as you say, but still make a wound. Now, Leo,
though we quarrel, you will not refuse to give me your arm
upstairs?'

The drawing-room was also illuminated by a blazing fire, and
groups of candles placed about which made it very bright, unlike
the gloom of the room below; bright, yet with all manner of soft
shades and contrivances to temper the light. It was full of
flowers and sweetness, full of luxury. Mrs. Swinford paused and
looked round with a satirical smile. 'Charming!' she said;
'and a little more or less feudal, *grand seigneur*, as we have been
saying, with all that is novel and delightful added; but vacant,
Leo. Were we in Paris, one would come, and then another and
another, to talk, or chat round the fire; to bring the news, to
discuss everything, spiritual, gay. These words have no meaning
here.'

'I fully feel it for you, mother. It is very dull; no one
worth your trouble to talk to. I understand perfectly. But
why not, then, fill the house?'

'For what end? There is not even shooting to tempt them
at this time of the year. Nothing to amuse. It is not the time.
In the autumn, perhaps, if I survive it so long——'

'Then there is London,' said Leo; 'it is not exactly a village, though I believe it is a happy slang to call it so. Let us go there.'

'London!' Mrs. Swinford contracted her brows. 'I have forgotten all my friends, or they have forgotten me. I don't go to Court——'

'Why not, mother?'

She looked at him with a gleam of fury in her eyes, and a sort of wild laugh, which was the most unlike mirth of anything Leo had ever heard. 'Perhaps,' she said, 'Emily Plowden would present me once again—whitewashed, after all these years.'

'What do you mean by whitewashed, mother?' There was something then in the look with which he faced her, insisting with a flush on his face, and a look of determination for which she was not prepared.

'What do I mean by whitewashed? I mean'——she paused a little, looking at him with a malicious devil in her eye, as if undecided what she should say. But his look subdued her, though it was a strange thing for any look of Leo to do. It was a look of alarm yet dismay, excited and almost fierce, yet struck with sudden fear. Her eyes sank before his.

'I don't know why you should look at me so. I mean that I am forgotten—as well may be, in all these years.'

She had placed herself in the deep chair covered with brocade, which had been carefully placed for her at the exact angle from the fire and the lights which she liked. The table beside it was covered with the evening papers; the French papers, arrived by the evening post; one or two yellow novels, an English book, and all the little paraphernalia which ladies of her period affect. She sat there, lying back in her luxurious chair, looking at her son with defiance in her eyes; defiance, and yet a certain uneasiness underneath. And he looked at her, uneasily too, with a doubt, yet no wish to question her further. She broke this silence by a sudden shrill burst of laughter, clapping her delicate hands together.

'Could one give a greater pleasure to one's *protégée* of old? —to the little girl of whom one has made a lady? A lady of rank, if you please, according to all the clowns. Emily shall take me; she shall patronise me; she shall be my condescending superior. Mrs. Swinford, on her return to England, by Lady William—bah! the jest is too good.'

Her laugh rang out shrill into the silent space about them. Leo, for his part, stood before her as grave as a judge. 'I don't see anything so wonderful about it,' he said.

'What, not that Emily! Emily, the country girl, not so good as your governess, not much better than my maid! Your governess? Why, for the moment, that was Artémise.'

'Mother, I must warn you that you are speaking of a lady for whom not only I, but every one here has the most exalted esteem.'

'Ah!' she cried, still laughing, 'so Artémise tells me. The most exalted! She has thrown dust in everybody's eyes.'

'And your Artémise — I give you warning I doubt that woman.'

'Ah! perhaps you will forbid her the house.'

'You know very well that the house is free to all you please to see here. For myself I shall certainly let her know that her presence is not agreeable to me.'

'Well, Leo,' said his mother, 'that will do for a token between us. When you turn my friend, my near relation, the only creature whom I care for here, to the door—I shall understand that I have notice to quit, and that you want no more with me.'

'What folly!' he cried, 'when you know I would as soon try to interfere with the constitution of the earth as to lift a finger against any of your friends.'

'Or consort with any of my enemies, Leo.'

'Certainly, no, if I knew who they were; but I know of none here at least.'

She laughed again; then, turning to her table, took up the *Figaro* which lay there. 'Enough, enough,' she said. 'Enough, Leo; a quarrel is a fearful joy; but one wearies even of that at the last.'

Leo stood for a time in the same attitude, while she opened her paper and began to read. Then he made a turn or two round the room, stopping here and there to look at a picture, though he neither saw nor cared what it was. Finally, when this wandering had lasted for, perhaps, five minutes without any sign on the part of his mother, he went quietly out of the room and downstairs.

She did not move a finger until the sound of his steps had died away; then she put down the paper, and listened for the closing of his door. It came at last with a dull echo going through the silent house. That sound brought many memories to the mind of the lady left alone in the great room, which would have held a crowd. She remembered the times without number when his father had retired so, and gave vent to a low laugh of scorn. And then she remembered other things, and her face grew grave. The paper fell rustling at her feet. She cast a look round her upon the room with its flowers, its lights, its cosy atmosphere, which was a triumph of skill and care, just so warm, and no more. The comfort and the luxury were perfect; there was nothing that could be done to increase the beauty, the ease, the grace, and completeness of all about her; and there she sat like a queen—alone.

LADY WILLIAM was still a little disturbed next morning, her usual composure gone, her countenance clouded. She had not forgiven little Patty, who in consequence went about her work watering with tears, instead of damp tea-leaves as usual, the carpet in the drawing-room which it was her business to sweep. Patty entertained the idea which, alas! is so little general among servant-girls, that her mistress was an angel, or something even more than that; for angels to Patty's consciousness were generally little boys with wings and without any clothes, to whom it would have been profane to compare a lady. It may be imagined how hollow the world was, and how little satisfactory the routine of work when Lady William frowned; everything went badly with Patty. She broke a china bowl and received from Miss Mab— Miss Mab always so *bon camarade*, if Patty had known the qualification—a very sharp and decided scolding, not to say that Anne—old Anne, whom Patty considered almost too old to live, and whose work she was conscious of doing in great part—fell upon her and nagged till the poor girl nearly ran away. Lady William was not busy this lovely spring morning which ought to have put new heart into everything. She said very little even to Mab. She was evidently thinking of something with which even Mab had but little to do. But when the girl talked of her own afternoon's occupation, her mother interposed quickly. 'I think you had better come up with me to the Hall, Mab.'

'Then you are going, mother? in obedience to a call like that——'

'In obedience to nothing; because I hate it, and want to get it over.'

'Do you hate Mrs. Swinford, mother?'

'Oh, I hope not,' said Lady William, the tears starting to her eyes; 'don't ask me such questions. I hope not: I don't want to hate any one. I would rather not think of her. But I hate going into a house that has so many memories—into a house where I have known so much——'

'It was there you met my father,' said Mab.

'Yes;' the monosyllable dropped from Lady William's closed lips as if dropped out against her will.

'But that ought not to be altogether a painful recollection, mother.' Mab had never heard anything of her father who was so long dead; there was no portrait of him that she had ever seen. Her idea of him was not precisely a happy one. Other people talked of the husbands they had lost, especially the poor women who liked to enlarge upon the good or bad qualities of the departed—but Mab knew nothing of her father, whether he had been bad or good. And she had a great curiosity, if no more, to know something of him. It was seldom, very seldom, that an opportunity occurred even for a question.

'I cannot enter into the past,' said Lady William; 'there is a great deal that is very painful in it. I would rather not tell you the story, Mab. It would do you no good, nor any one. I had forgotten a great deal till this lady appeared again. So far as I can see now, she is determined that I shall no longer forget.'

'Is she your enemy, mother?'

'I don't believe in enemies, it is too melodramatic; and probably she means no harm; only she likes to stir up things which I prefer to forget. Do you understand the difference? Perhaps it keeps up her interest, but to me it spoils everything. Death is very dreadful to you, Mab; but it's very merciful, too. It makes you forget many things, when they are not forcibly brought back to your mind.'

Mab eyed her mother very curiously with a hundred questions on her lips: but Lady William's face was not encouraging, and with a sigh the girl gave up her intended inquiry. She added, after some time: 'The only thing, mother, is that Mrs. Swinford may want to speak to you of things that you don't wish me to know.'

'That is very possible, Mab: and it is for that I want you to go with me, to protect me. She would never bring up old stories which would be painful, before you.'

'Mother,' said Mab, and then paused.

'What is it?'

'I want to know—if I am perhaps at the mercy of a stranger like Mrs. Swinford to tell me things that would be painful—about my father—whether it would not be better for you, mother, who would do it in love and quietly, to tell me yourself and put me beyond her power?'

'Mab, you are very sensible, very reasonable.'

'I don't know if I'm that: but it seems to me the better way.'

Lady William began to speak: then hesitated, became husky, and paused a moment to steady her voice. 'There is nothing to tell about your father, Mab, that could affect you; nothing that would hurt his name in the world; only private matters between him and me, in which unfortunately Mrs. Swinford was mixed up. There is no such thing,' she went on after a pause, with a sort of painful smile, 'as trouble—without faults on both sides. I was to blame as much as any one else. You would not think the better of either of your parents if you were to be told all that there is to tell. Will you take my word for that? and that there is nothing which it is at all necessary for you to hear?'

'Certainly, I will take your word, mother. But I don't believe you were so much wrong. You are hasty sometimes, but you never keep on or nag. And sometimes you are so patient; if there were quarrels I know it was not your fault.'

The girl came to her mother's side and gave her a kiss, putting down her soft young cheek upon Lady William's, which was as soft, though no longer young. The mother took the kiss with a smile. It was not wholly a smile of pleasure at Mab's approval and vindication of her—innocent Mab that knew of nothing but a quarrel, a difference of opinion, a nagging. Mab thought it was a great pity, that perhaps her father had troubles of temper which she was conscious herself of possessing, and that no doubt Mrs. Swinford had interfered and made things worse. It brought her father even a little nearer to her to learn that he had been cross. Poor father! he had been long forgiven and his tempers forgotten, when they were not thrust back upon the memory: and poor mother, who perhaps blamed herself more than was just, and thought now how often she might have answered with a soft word! Lady William smiled, reading in the child's mind as in a book, so easy was that young interpretation, so desirable, so strange to the woman who knew all.

The afternoon was radiant: sky and air had been washed clean, as Mab said, by frequent showers, and there did not seem an atom of impurity, not even a cloudlet that was not white and shining, in the whole expanse of atmosphere. Lady William was grave, but had recovered her composure, and Mab was gay with an unusual freshness, ready to gambol about the path like the large loose-limbed puppy from the lodge who was fond of taking walks

with visitors, and who came up and offered himself as guide and
companion as soon as the two ladies had entered the gate. Mab
was acquainted with the puppy's family for several generations,
and knew his mother upon intimate terms, so that there was no
need of ceremony. He and she had gone up the avenue to the
point at which the house becomes visible, rising high above the
little lake and among the trees, when Lady William called her
daughter back. 'You have had enough of the puppy,' she
said; 'now you must turn into a young lady, Mab.'

'It is not half so amusing, mother; but, oh, look at the violets,
how thick they are under the trees!'

'About the ashen roots the violets blow,' said Lady William.

'I never knew any one have so many bits of poetry ready for
all occasions,' said Mab admiringly. 'It's a pity they're only dog-
violets, and not sweet at all; but they are pretty like that all
the same.'

'Why, I wonder, should one speak of dog-violets, and dog-
roses, and dog-daisies?' said Lady William. 'I suppose it is in
contempt of things that grow wild.'

'A dog is the wisest thing that lives,' said Mab; 'there's no
contempt in such a name. Puppy! puppy! where are you going?
I must run after him, mother, and keep him from frightening
those ducks.'

'There's contempt, if you please! The famous Swinford wild
fowl!'

'Oh, I can't bear them, the stupid things. Puppy! puppy!
oh, don't be a fool, they are not worth your while.'

'Nor yours either, puppy mine. You will be as red as a
peony next, and what will Mrs. Swinford say?'

'I hate Mrs. Swinford,' said Mab; but she walked soberly
the rest of the way. Mrs. Swinford was in the same room and
chair as she had occupied on the previous night: with flowers
piled in the jardinières, on the tables, everywhere; a wood fire
blazing very bright, but more bright than warm, and the mistress
of the house arrayed, as always, in dark velvet, with a crimson
tone in the lights, but without the lace which had softened at once
her features and her age. Her hair, in which there was not a
thread of white, was dressed high on her head; her back was, as
usual, to the light.

'Oh, you have brought your little girl,' she said, in a tone
almost of displeasure. 'You are very perverse and contradictory,
my dear, as you always were. I had something to say to you,
alone.'

'Oh, as for that,' said Mab, angry, 'I can go away.'

Her mother gave her a restraining look. 'There is so little,'
she said, 'in my life that requires to be talked about *en tête-à-tête*,
and Mab goes wherever I go.'

'That is to say, you bring her with you as young women sometimes bring their babies, in defence.' Mrs. Swinford laughed, and,
holding out her hand, added, 'Come here and let me see you, little
girl.'

'I am not a little girl,' said Mab, still angry; but another
glance from her mother to the lady of the house restored that
reasonableness in which the girl was so strong. 'And I am not
much to look at,' she added steadily, 'but, as it does not much
matter, here I am.'

Mrs. Swinford took her by the hand, and, drawing her forward,
looked at her closely. Then she dropped the girl's hand and
laughed. 'She proves her parentage, at least,' she said; 'no
doubt upon that subject; she is a Pakenham all over. And she
is like them, Emily, in temper and intellect, too.'

Mab, unfortunately, did not understand the whole weight of
the insinuation in this remark, and she did not see her mother's
face behind her. She answered quickly for herself. 'I have not
a very good temper, Mrs. Swinford. When people say nasty
things to me, I can be nasty too.'

So I presume,' said the lady of the house.

Or to my mother,' said Mab; 'she is too patient and too much
a lady; but I'm not.'

'Mab!' said her mother's warning voice behind.

'It is that I think this lady wants to provoke me,' said Mab,
'and I don't see——'

'My dear, you will show your superiority best by not suffering
yourself to be provoked.'

Mab went off to one of the jardinières with a little toss of
her head, and it was at this moment that Leo came in, a little
hurried and not without agitation. He came in saying quickly,
'I have just heard that you had visitors, mother.'

'Leo,' said Mrs. Swinford, 'I have something to say to Emily
here. I did not expect her to bring her daughter, and I did not
desire my son's company. You can go and show the young lady
the pictures; it is a young man's business; and you ought to thank
me for giving you the opportunity. Now, Emily, *à nous deux*.'

'I was not aware,' said Lady William, pale but steadfast,
'that what you wanted to say to me was of particular importance.'

'You thought I only sent for you to say I love you,' said Mrs. Swinford. 'Well, you knew that already; but I had something much more serious to say. And I am glad, after all, you brought your little girl, Emily; for she is the strongest argument I can bring forward to make you do what I want you to do.'

'And what is that?' said Lady William. 'I must warn you that I am not very open to advice.'

'As if I did not know you were not open to advice! except, my dear, you will recollect, when you wished to take a certain course which was advised.'

'Did I wish to take it?' said Lady William; 'that is what has never been clear.'

'Oh, did you wish it?' cried Mrs. Swinford, with a laugh. 'However, that is old ground; but if I have any responsibility for that first step, Emily, I have the more right to speak now. For that child's sake you must make overtures to the family. Whatever they may do or say, it is for you to put your pride in your pocket, and make friends with them, if they like it or not. Your claims must be fully established.'

'My claims?' said Lady William; 'there has never been any question made of my claims.'

'Probably not, so long as you live; but look at that child. You must make everything certain for her; I must press it upon you with all my might, Emily. Life is uncertain, and you have nothing of your own.'

'Not much, that is true.'

'And what would she have to depend upon if you died? You don't even know what questions might arise. They might ask her what her proofs were, what evidence she had.'

'Of what?' said Lady William, wondering. 'What evidence does Mab require to prove that she is my daughter? But all the parish could prove that, with the Rector at their head.'

'Oh, so far as that goes; but it does not suffice to be proved to be her mother's daughter when the money is on the father's side.'

'What do you mean, Mrs. Swinford?' Lady William had grown red and a little angry. She fixed her eyes upon her adviser. 'There is something in what you say that I do not understand.'

'Nevertheless it is very true,' said Mrs. Swinford; 'the money is, you know, on the father's side, and the father's family have a right to know everything about it. It should be put quite out of their power to say afterwards that they never had any proof.'

'Of what? You mean something that has not been suggested to me before. I have been told I ought to make overtures; but what is this? Please to tell me,' she said, almost sharply, 'what you mean.'

'You must surely have thought of it yourself. Here you are, a widow, not very young, with an only child. They call you Lady William, and you enjoy the rank. Oh, you need not wave your hand as if to say no; I know you better than you know yourself; you enjoy your rank.'

'For the sake of argument it may be allowed that I enjoy my rank, such as it is.'

'Well, you do, I know, whether you choose to allow it or refuse. Emily Plowden, it is your first business to prove your claim to it, and your child's to her name.'

'I am not Emily Plowden,' said Lady William; 'you mistake that, to begin with; and I can only repeat that my claim, which I have never required to prove, has been doubted by no one, nor my child's right. Is it for pure insult you say this? My movements have always been open as the day.'

'What! when you left this house in the dark, in the middle of the night! I have never questioned your claims till now. My motive is not to insult you, but to help you. Where were you married, Emily Plowden? Who married you? Have you your certificates all in order? You disappeared, and then you came back, and I never asked, but took it all for granted. It is only when I see your little girl that I begin to ask myself, Emily, have you got your papers, whatever they may be? Emily Plowden, are you sure that you have any right to another name?'

In Miss Grey's drawing-room, which was as small as Miss Grey herself, there were three persons assembled. Miss Grey, seated at the writing-table—much too large for the place, like the rest of the furniture ; Florence Plowden on the big 'Chesterfield' sofa ; and a large and tall individual standing in the middle of the floor. He was large in comparison with the ladies, and with the limited space in which he stood. But otherwise, though tall, he was a spare man ; his length of limb and scantness of flesh made particularly apparent by his long clerical coat. Needless to say that he was the curate, and that it was parish business that formed the staple of the conversation. Florence had come in with her district visitor's book ; and other books of a similar description were on the table. They were talking in that curious jargon of business and gossip which makes up the talk of the workers in a parish or ecclesiastical organisation of any kind.

'In whose district is Mead Lane ?' said Mr. Osborne. 'A man came to me last night from No. 3, to ask me to go and see his wife. She had been in bed for about six weeks— very ill now. There is a baby, of course, and I don't know how many children ; man occasionally out of work—though not now. Everything in disorder, as you may imagine. Nobody had called to see them for weeks. A lady had come once or twice before the woman fell ill ; never since.'

He made this report very drily, in staccato sentences, as if he were abridging from a book.

Miss Grey turned round, twisting on her chair to give Florence a look. 'I knew it would be so,' she said ; 'they are a couple of old maids wrapped up in themselves. She says : "Do you think you should go out, my dear, such a cold day ?" and he says : "The parish can surely wait ; but you mustn't go out, with your delicate throat, in the rain."'

'This is very interesting as a social sketch,' said the curate, 'but it does not answer my question.'

Florence was far from being in high spirits, but her native genius was too much for her. She turned upon him with a little mincing air, and deprecatory friction of her hands. 'Oh, don't you really think so, Mr. Osborne?' she said.

He laughed, though with a certain look of disapproval, as if amused against his will. 'I see,' he said. 'Mrs. Kendal; what is to be done with her? If she will not do what she undertakes, some one else must be got to do it.'

At which both Miss Grey and Florence shook their heads. 'It would be such a slap in the face,' said the little lady of the house. 'They are good people in their way, and liberal enough. We must just manage it a little. Florence and I will go and see this poor woman, and if Mrs. Kendal hears of it we can say—— Oh, some excuse will be found easily enough.'

'Excuse! When she has let the woman die nearly——'

'A miss is as good as a mile. I'll go over at once, and send in the nurse if she wants it. What did you say was the name? Brownjohn! Oh,' said Miss Grey, with a sudden diminution of energy, 'I'm afraid, Florry, we know the illnesses of Mrs. Brownjohn. She has a great many, and whatever district she is in, the visitor always neglects her. We know her case very well.'

'The woman is very ill now, and the house in a dreadful state; and the man, of course, as if things were not bad enough, taking refuge in the public-house.'

'Ah, that I can understand——'

'The filthy place, Miss Grey, or the public-house?' the curate said, with a little severity.

'Oh, both, both! You must be a little human. The public-house is the natural consequence of a crowded little room, and no comfort—even without the dirt.'

'But surely you don't think that ought to be so? Surely you don't suppose that it isn't the man's duty to rectify things instead of making them worse? If the wife's unable to do her part, instead of abandoning her brutally, and letting everything go to destruction, oughtn't he to stand in, to do what he can, to make life possible? That's how I read a man's duty, at least.'

'Oh, my dear Mr. Osborne,' said little Miss Grey, 'it's a man's duty to be a good Christian and a perfect man. And so it is everybody's duty; we all acknowledge that.'

Mr. Osborne snorted slightly, with the impatience of a fiery horse suddenly pulled up. 'I hope I demand less than perfection, though I know that I ought not to be content with less,' he said. 'But in the meantime,' he added, pausing a minute to expel that hot breath of impatience, 'I don't suppose you will think it right because of Mrs. Kendal's feelings, or even her own imperfections, that this poor creature should be left to die ?'

Miss Grey and Florry exchanged glances behind the curate's back, with a slight shaking of heads. Oh, these arbitrary young men, wanting everything their own way, and thinking you have no feeling if you don't go so far as they do ! This was the sentiment in the older lady's mind ; but Florence was naturally more fierce.

'We are not in the habit of leaving poor people to die—when there is any truth in it,' she said.

He gave her a look half fierce, half tender, full of the natural animosity of a man checked in his certainties of opinion, yet with a longing that she at least should understand and know what he meant.

'Oh yes,' said Miss Grey, 'I'll go ; and have a little order put in the place, at least. That little girl—the eldest, Florry, don't you remember ?—who was sent to the seaside after her fever, she ought to be good for something now.'

'There is a little girl,' said the curate.

Miss Grey turned round upon him with a laugh that made him furious. 'As if we didn't know !' she said. Then, turning to Florence again, 'You might go in, as you pass, my dear, to Mrs. Gould, and see if the nurse is engaged. Tell her, if she can, to run round to Mead Lane about two o'clock. She'll probably find me there, and if it is anything really serious we'll get the doctor to see her. Come now, let's see if there is anything else we want to consult Mr. Osborne about.'

'I want to ask you, at least,' he said, 'if you will help me with my meeting, to give them an evening's entertainment. I recognise,' with a little severity, 'as well as you do, that they must be amused as well as looked after.'

'Well,' said Miss Grey, 'if it's children I am quite ready to play any number of games with them. But I'm not a great one for providing amusement, Mr. Osborne. In the first place I can't sing to them, or dance to them, or play the fiddle ; in the next, I think they like their own amusements best.'

'The public-house, Miss Grey ?'

The little lady had tears in her eyes. 'I am not in favour of the public-house, God knows—but I am not so sure that your

meetings will do away with that. It's just as likely to make them
thirsty coming out at nine, after you've sung to them and fiddled
to them, and seeing the red light in the window that looks so
cheerful to them. But never mind me—Florry and Emmy will
sing, and the London young ladies in the new villa will play the
piano, and you can get a quartette of fiddles, you know, quite
easily from Winwich. And Jim—Jim might recite ; he used to
be very good at it.'

'Oh—Mr. Plowden ?' said the curate, with a slight hesitation.

'Jim I mean : he used to read very well when he was a boy.'

'I asked Lady William,' Mr. Osborne said hurriedly, as if to
change the subject, 'but she said like you, Miss Grey, that she
neither sang nor—I am not aware I suggested that any one should
dance.'

'They would like that ! but the thing is not so much what they
would like to see, but what all the ladies and gentlemen would like
to do. And by-the-bye there is that dark-eyed woman at the
school—whom I have a strong feeling I have seen before—and who
looks no more like a schoolmistress than—any one does. I feel
quite sure she could act or recite or something—or perhaps sing.
I would ask her if I were you.'

'I am unfortunate in not being of your opinion, Miss Grey ; I
should not think of asking that person to help in any case.'

'Oh, you're too particular,' Miss Grey said.

And then Florence got up to go.

'The old Lloyds,' she said, 'want to have a week of their
pension in advance—may I say you will give it to them, Miss
Grey ?'

'Oh dear, don't say anything of the kind ; if they get a
week in advance how are they to live the next week when they
have none ?'

'I said so—but then she cried, poor old body, and said they
were worse off now than before—for if they wanted something very
bad out of the usual way, some kind person used to give it to
them—whereas now when they have a regular pension they have to
stick to it, and nobody minds.'

'There's a sermon,' cried Miss Grey, 'on the uses of beneficence
in a small parish. You have only to tell Mr. Swinford, Florry,
and he'll give them the advance and the week's money too, and
next time they'll want a fortnight's advance—it's what I've always
said. He's a nice young fellow and a warm heart, but to sow
money about is no good.'

'You said yourself, Miss Grey, that so much a week——'

'Oh yes, I said it myself—I'd like to give them the advance and the week's money too, just as well as Mr. Swinford does—though Mr. Osborne thinks on the other hand that I am ready, because I've little faith in her, to leave a poor creature to die. Oh, don't say anything—I know of course you didn't exactly mean that. Are you going too? Good-bye; I'll get my bonnet and I'll be in Mead Lane before you've got to the Rectory gate.'

It did not appear, however, that there was any intention in the mind of these two young people to take the road which led to the Rectory gate. There was a momentary pause when they got outside, and Florence hurriedly, in view of the fact that the curate's way to his lodging did lie in that direction, held out her hand to him. 'Good morning, I am going up to Mrs. Gould's to see about the nurse,' she said, somewhat breathless and eager to escape.

'I am going that way, too,' said the young man, but not without a blush. Curates are, after all, like other men, and do not hesitate to change their route and to assert that they always meant to go that way; but there is so much consistency in the young Anglican that he blushes when he announces that innocent fallacy. He was going that way: where, then, was he going to? The part of the parish in which Mrs. Gould lived was not in the curate's district, and he could not surely have any impertinent intention of interfering with what was in the Rector's hands? These ideas flashed through the mind of Florence, but naturally she did not put them into words. She was very angry with Mr. Osborne, full of indignation, and yet she did not wish him to turn back and leave her at Miss Grey's door. The blush which had surprised him as he told that fib reflected itself on her countenance, but in both their hearts there was a thrill of pleasure as they turned thus into the wrong way—the way that Florry had chosen to elude him, without in the least wanting to go to Mrs. Gould's (for she knew all the time where the parish nurse was); the way that he falsely asserted to be his, though he knew it was nothing of the kind. It was a guilty pleasure, which neither of them would have owned to, but yet there was not much guilt in it after all.

'Miss Grey is a very good woman,' said the curate, 'and excellent for the parish—but she has very old-fashioned ways of looking at things.'

'I don't see that,' said Florence lightly, 'at all.'

'You would, I am sure,' said Mr. Osborne, 'if you would allow yourself to take a larger view. You won't, I am afraid, adopt my standing-point, for you think that I am opposed to her and that I don't appreciate her.'

'You can't of course know her as we do,' said Florence, 'for all our lives she has been an example before our eyes.'

'That is again entirely the individual view of the question,' said the curate gently, 'and in that I grant you—but don't you think we might take a more extended range when the question is a public one? I don't in the least object to that, far from it. I know there is nothing so good as the way of working by individualities, of getting hold of Tom, and Will, and Peter, one by one, the door-to-door system, as I may call it; but when you have a great public evil like that of intemperance, don't you think, Miss Florence, it is well, while not leaving the other undone, to try what some large public method will do——'

'Like Father Matthew's?' said Florence.

'Father Matthew was too sensational,' said Mr. Osborne; 'and it is impossible to tell how much fiction there was in such a movement. Indeed, I rather think the one by one system is the best; but to interest them *en masse*, to make them see what a thing it would be for all their families, and themselves, of course, and how much purer and more rational pleasure they would get out of their lives——'

'Do you think they learn in that way?'

'If they don't, I do not know how they are to learn.'

'But they all know beforehand how dreadful a thing it is—they know it's destruction. Oh, don't you think they know far better than we do, since they see it before them every day, and all day long?'

'What would you do, then,' said the curate, 'to bring this home to them? I've got all the statistics. Of course they know, for misfortune brings it home; but if we could fully convince them what a prodigious evil it is over all the country, how many better things they could do with the money. I remember proving to a man once, that if he only put by every penny he had been accustomed to spend in drink, he could buy his cottage, he could have a little garden of his own, and a pig, and I don't know how many things which every man prizes——'

'And did he do it?' said Florence.

'Do it!' said the curate. 'Of course that meant a course of years. One could not tell whether he did it or not, till a long time was passed. Well, no,' he added, with a sigh, 'I am trying to deceive you, not to admit my failure; he did not do it. He went on just in his old way, and almost killed his wife, and starved his children, till he died.'

'Is it true, Mr. Osborne,' said Florence, 'that you said to old

Mrs. Lloyd, if she would give up her beer, and take the pledge, you would do so too?'

A flush came over the curate's face, of ingenuous pleasure and satisfaction. He liked her to know that he was capable of any sacrifice to save his flock. 'It is quite true,' he said. 'I was quite ready, and had made up my mind to do it; for how can I ask my people to give up what I don't give up myself?'

'But why did you choose poor old Mrs. Lloyd? It did her no harm, her little drop of beer.'

'Every drop of beer does harm, in a community like this, scourged by that vice——'

'Mr. Osborne,' said Florence timidly.

'Yes,' he said, bending towards her, 'you were going to say something.'

'I want to say something; but, oh, I don't know whether I ought, I don't know whether I may.'

The curate trembled, too, as much as she did. They were in a quiet road, with nobody in sight. He put his hand suddenly upon hers with a hurried, tremulous pressure. 'There is nothing you ought not to say to me,' he said. 'Nothing, nothing that I will not gladly hear. If you should reprove me, even, it would be as a precious balm—whatever, whatever you will say!'

There was a little pause, and it was very still all about, a bird or two trilling in the half-clothed trees, not a harsher sound to disturb the two young creatures, there standing at the crisis of their lives. 'But first,' he said, 'first let me say something to you——'

'No,' said Florence, 'no, that was not what I meant, not now —I had something to say. Mr. Osborne, listen. If, instead of an old woman, and her a good old woman that did no harm, it were a man, a boy, a gentleman, that you could have held out your hand to—oh, not to make him take pledges and things! and perhaps, you, hearing of him, thought him no company for you. But if you could have turned him away from harm to go with you; if you had suffered his society, not approving of it, because your society might have saved him; if you had thought to yourself that to be your companion might have been everything for him, and that to make him do things with you, and almost live with you, though you might not like it, would have made life another thing to him. Oh, Mr. Osborne, would not that have been a better way?' Her eyes were so full of tears that she could not see him, but when he spoke she heard a sound in his voice which made her start and turn hastily to where the man who was almost her accepted lover, who had the words on his lips that were to bind them for ever, stood. The music and the softness had altogether gone out of these staccato tones.

'Miss Plowden,' he said, as if a sudden gulf had come between them over which his voice sounded far away, 'I will not even ask what you mean. I should feel myself a most presumptuous intruder, and impertinent—— Good morning. I find I have not so much time as I thought for this roundabout way.'

FLORENCE went faithfully to Mrs. Gould's to ask for the nurse, though she knew the nurse was not there. A man, perhaps, would have departed from that position when it was no longer necessary, but she considered it needful, as a proof of good faith, to carry out her announced intention. It was a long way round, and then she had to make another tour to get to the place where the nurse really was, so that her walk altogether occupied some three-quarters of an hour more than it need have done, and the time was long, although, on the other hand, she was glad to have it to herself, and to get over the pang of that abrupt separation. She knew very well what it was that the curate had to say to her. It had been on his lips for many days, and she had dreaded it, not because she did not want to hear it, but because of a girl's natural evasion of the moment she wishes for most, the shy, half mischievous, half visionary putting off of the sweet cup from the lips. The expectation of it was sweet ; all the pleasures of imagination lay in that moment which would bring an entire change in her life, a remodelling of all its circumstances. Florence had taken a pleasure in stealing away, in postponing till to-morrow. But it cannot be said that she experienced that pleasure to-day. She felt that she had received a blow when the curate turned with that hasty leave-taking and left her. To run away is one thing, and hold off a joy which is on the way ; but to be thus abandoned is another. It gave her a dull shock like that of an unexpected, uncomprehended blow. She had wondered how he would take her remonstrance, her statement of what she thought his duty, which had been on her lips so long ; but she had never expected him to take it with instant offence, with a resentment which drove all other thoughts out of his mind. What did he resent ? To have this duty which he did not wish to recognise pointed out to him, or that she should venture to point it out—she only a girl, and the girl who, by loving him, he perhaps thought was bound to see no flaw in him? Florence was not one of those who can see nothing but excellence in those they love, but she felt, with a momentary gleam of insight sharpened by pain, that perhaps Mr. Osborne was of the kind which requires that in a woman. She had not thought of the possibility before, that this might not be merely a momentary offence, but a wound from which he would not recover, which he would not forgive. A love-quarrel ever seems thus even when of the most trivial origin. It appears at once tragic, a thing never to be got over: an end of all the romance. Florence's heart went down, down to the very depths. She said to herself that it was all over: that the last step would never now be taken, that there would be no more all her life but only an aching void, not even the recollection of words said that never could be forgotten. Had she let him speak she would at least have had that to cheer her; but as it was she would have nothing, not even the gloomy importance of an engagement to break off, a farewell that would have a whole tragedy in it: not even that: only a mere drifting asunder, a vacancy where there had been so much hope: a life blighted before it had come to bloom.

This thought occupied her mind sadly as she made that unnecessary round. He had gone off like a racehorse, scarcely touching the ground in the heat of his vexation and offence, but she went along very slowly, with the depression of the one who is in fault; whose interference and perhaps unreasonable censure had made the breach. Who, after all, was she that she should tell him of his duty, or that something else than the course he had adopted was a better way? she, only a girl with no education in particular, dictating not only to a man trained to discriminate what was the best, but a priest with the highest of vows upon him, and a special consecration to God's service? Her presumption overwhelmed her when she thought of it in this light. But perhaps to be a member of a clerical family, used to see gentlemen of that profession too closely, and amid all the little trials of life, takes away to a certain extent the visionary reverence which it would be perhaps better to keep like an aureole about them. Florence could not surrender her natural judgment to this extent, nor convince herself that she had done wrong. She had taken perhaps an inopportune moment, but she had not said anything that was not true. She had managed badly for herself, and she would have to bear the result: but it was not wrong what she had said, nor was it wrong to say it; for perhaps, who could tell, he had never thought of that side of the question before? Very likely he had never thought of it. Some people are so happy that they never have in all their lives to encounter misery in their family, and how can they know, unless somebody who does know it, somebody who has been forced to understand it, tells them? And perhaps—she thought with a forlorn consolation—what she had said would bear fruit, though he might never have anything to do with her again. He was too much offended, wounded, hurt, to think of her any more; that was a thing to be received as certain once for all; but perhaps what she had said would come back to him, and he might feel that it was true.

Then if she had let it alone for the present, if she had allowed him to say what was on his lips, and had answered what was on hers, and had become his, and had pledged herself to him—why, then one time or other she must have spoken, not as now in the general, but plainly of Jim? And what if the righteous young man's high disapproval and disgust with the unrighteous had gone even further, to the length of putting poor Jim, whom his sister loved, out of the charities of life altogether and casting him off as some good people do? Florence felt that no tie, not even marriage itself, would have made her bear that, and so concluded at last, mournfully, that what she had done was, perhaps, after all the best, so as to warn him off in time, and show him that her views were very different from his. Oh, what mistakes men can make even when they are the most highly instructed, the most high-minded and nobly purposed of their kind! Edward Osborne was all that; yet he thought that it was a more pious thing to make poor old Mrs. Lloyd and such harmless old bodies give up their little harmless indulgences than to risk a little trouble or company that, perhaps, might be distasteful to him, in order to save Jim.

Florence got home at last just in time for the family luncheon, which was a good thing for her, as it kept her from exposure to the close personal observation of her mother and sister, who were too well acquainted with every change of her countenance not to perceive at once when anything was wrong with Florry. But the family meal occupied Mrs. Plowden, and Emmy was fortunately so full of her own morning's occupations that her sister escaped notice.

'You are not eating anything, child, and you have no colour,' her mother said, 'after your long walk.'

'It is the long walk that has done it, she has over-tired herself; you shouldn't permit those long walks,' said the Rector. This was his favourite way of treating any annoyance—with that consolatory conviction that it must be his wife's fault, which supports many men through the smaller miseries of life. Mrs. Plowden took an equal pleasure in the pleas of self-defence. 'How am I to prevent long walks when there is always so much to do in the parish?' she said. 'I am constantly telling you you should have more district visitors, or a mission woman, or something. Those girls have never a moment to themselves.'

'Oh, it is nothing, mamma,' said Florence. 'I had to make a long round to get the parish nurse: for I went to Mrs. Gould's to find her, and, of course, she wasn't there.'

'You ought to have known that, Florry, so it is your own fault. Why, you sent her off yourself to the little Heaths.'

'I know, mamma: I can't think how I could be so stupid,' Florence said.

'And who wants her now?' said the Rector curtly.

'It is that woman in Mead Lane, who is always in trouble. Mr. Osborne,' said Florence, so anxious to keep her voice firm that she gave the name an emphasis and importance she had no intention of giving, 'had been sent for to see her last night.'

'Osborne! he's always finding a mare's nest somewhere—do you mean that woman that always is in trouble, as you say? —trouble, indeed! drink you mean, and all that follows. If he could get her to take the pledge it might do some good: that's if she would keep it—which I don't believe for a moment.'

'Then why should he take the trouble, papa, if it is to do no good?'

'That's what I tell him for ever: but he believes in himself, the young prig: I wish he would keep to his own business, and not mix himself up with things he cannot possibly understand.'

'My dear James,' said Mrs. Plowden, 'Mr. Osborne is an excellent young man. There has not been a curate in the parish I have liked so much since Mr. Sinclair's time. And he is very well connected and well-off, I believe, and altogether a creditable person to have about—an Oxford man and all that.'

'That's why he gives himself so many airs,' the Rector said— which was not to say that the Rector did not really approve of Mr. Osborne, but only that it was his rôle to take the critical side. Mrs. Plowden, for her part, knew very well what was going on, and though she had burst forth in the fulness of her heart to her sister-in-law upon his shortcomings, she was on ordinary occasions very careful to keep up Mr. Osborne's reputation, and to impress Florence with a due sense of all his qualities.

Now there arose a testimony in Mr. Osborne's favour which was totally unexpected. 'He wasn't at all a bad lot at Oxford, said Jim. 'Fellows that knew him liked him there: he played racquets for the University, and won. I wonder if he ever gets a game now.'

'You astonish me, Jim,' said Mrs. Plowden. 'I never should have thought he was a man for games. What is racquets? is it a kind of tennis? for of course tennis is played with racquets. Perhaps we could get up a game for him here.'

At this Jim laughed loudly, and his father, who did not often join in his jokes, such as they were, backed him up faintly with a smile.

'No, I don't think we could get up a game for him here. It's a tremendous game; not like anything so simple as lawn tennis. It is the old *jeu de paume*, isn't it?' said the Rector, 'the beginning of them all.'

A conversation between the Rector and his son, on a general subject, on a question, something they were both interested in, without reproof on one side, or defence on the other: what a thing that was! Mrs. Plowden's eyes grew lambent with the light of unusual happiness; after a moment she said: 'I suppose you play it, Jim?'

'I!' said the young man. 'Oh, I'm not half enough of a swell for that, mother.'

'I don't see,' said the mother, half happy, half indignant, 'why you shouldn't be swell enough, Jim, to do anything Mr. Osborne does.'

'You don't remember,' said the Rector sharply, 'that it takes application to play a game well, as well as to study well, and that Jim never thought it good enough, either for one thing or another.'

Alas! how short the moment of happiness is!

'Oh, girls,' said Mrs. Plowden, when lunch was over, and the three ladies were in the drawing-room again, 'if Mr. Osborne would only take up Jim! He is the only man in the parish who could do it; and now that I hear he plays games and things I feel a little hopeful. For whatever your father may say, I know that Jim is good at all games. We might get up this racquets, whatever it is, and get them to play together. We might ask the General, Florry, what it is. Army men always know everything of that kind. Or, Emmy, you might remember to ask your aunt; and there's Mr Swinford; perhaps he plays it too.'

'I suppose it is a gentleman's game,' said Emmy, with perhaps not so strong an enthusiasm.

'Do you think I might speak to Mr. Osborne about it?' said the mother, pondering. When she asked advice of her girls it was in fact a sort of thinking aloud, a putting of the question to her own mind. A thing often seems quite different put out in audible words from what it does when only turned over and over in the recesses of your own heart. 'I might tell him that Jim was very fond of it, and that hearing he was good I thought I would consult him how we should get it up.'

'But Jim never said he was fond of it, mamma.'

'Oh, how matter-of-fact you are, Emmy! Jim would be fond of anything that was a game. He would be glad of any break; and to get him surrounded with nice companions like himself, and taking his pleasure with them, wouldn't that be better for him than Sophocles, or any old Pagan of them all? Your father doesn't think so, perhaps, but I do; and, if you look at it reasonably, so will you too.'

'I would not trust to Mr. Osborne if I were you,' said Florence. She was standing in the corner beyond the window at the big old-fashioned round table, which had been dismissed from its old-fashioned place in the centre of the room, but was retained in the corner because it was so useful. Florence had her back to her mother and sister, and was very busy cutting out clothes for her girls' class, which, like Miss Grey's mothers' meeting, met weekly for needlework. 'I would not speak to him about it. He sometimes takes offence when you suggest a thing, and then goes away and does it. I would not say a word if I were you.'

'But it never has been suggested to him, Florry! Why, you know I never heard of this even, till to-day. Here is your aunt Emily coming. We can ask her what she thinks. She has been more in the world than any of us, and probably she can tell us what racquets is.'

A considerable time elapsed, but no visitors appeared; and then Mrs. Plowden, from wondering what Emily would say, at last came to wonder where Emily could be, or if her eyes had deceived her, and Lady William had not crossed the lawn at all. 'I declare,' she said, 'I shall feel quite unhappy if your aunt does not appear: for I saw her as plainly as I see you. I saw her black gown, and the feather in her hat, which really ought to be renewed if she will go on wearing black for ever—and that umbrella of hers with the long handle.'

'But, mamma dear,' said Emmy, 'you must have known at

once whether it was Aunt Emily or not, without thinking what she had on.'

'Well, so I should have supposed,' said Mrs. Plowden, bewildered, 'but then where is she, and what has become of her? She should have been here ten minutes ago. Oh, who is that? Mab! Why, child, where have you come from? And where is your mother? I am sure I saw her cross the lawn ten minutes ago or more.'

'And we think it must have been her wraith, Mab.'

'Mother has gone to talk to Uncle James,' said Mab. 'She says it's about business, but I think it is some worry, she looks so serious. So I came on after to wait for her. Oh, are you cutting out, Florry? Shall I help you, or do you want any help?'

'Some worry?' said Mrs. Plowden, with a sorrowful brow. 'I hope it is not anything new about your uncle Reginald, girls.'

Reginald was the brother to whom Lady William had given her money, and who had never come back.

'Hadn't we better wait till we hear what it is, mamma? I thought Uncle Reginald had not been heard of for years.'

'That is quite true, and it was my opinion we should never hear from him any more; but what worry can your aunt Emily have if it is not about him? For I am sure otherwise she is a happy woman, and never has the shadow of a trouble. Was it after getting a foreign letter that she grew so serious, Mab?'

'She has had no letter at all,' said Mab, 'and she did not say it was anything but business. The worry was only my own fancy; and I daresay I was wrong.'

'What else could it be?' said Mrs. Plowden. 'She may have heard he is coming home. And I am sure, if he is coming home, I don't know what I shall do. He shall not come here. I could not have him in this house. Our own burdens we must bear; but Reginald Plowden—oh, Reginald Plowden is too much! If he comes here I shall run away.'

'Dear mamma, don't you think we had better wait a little? Aunt Emily is sure to come here when she leaves papa, and then you will know.'

'Oh, it is all very well to tell me to wait—when Reginald Plowden would just put the crown upon everything,' the poor lady said.

LADY WILLIAM had gone across the lawn, not to the usual door which admitted into what may be called the private part of the Rectory, but to the little parish door where people came who wanted the Rector on parish business. This was always open, always accessible, though I don't know that the parishioners used it very much. It was at least an excellent thing for them to have their clergyman always within reach, and suited the Rector's theory of his duty, which was a great matter, even if it were not of very much practical use. Miss Grey trotted in by it with her parish books, and the curate came, when something occurred about which it was necessary to consult his chief. He did not, Mr. Plowden thought, consult his chief nearly as much as would have been appropriate and desirable—being a young man who liked his own way, and considered that the elder generation did not always understand.

The Rector, however, was much surprised when the door sounded with the familiar little click which he knew so well, and his sister presently appeared in his study. He had expected one or other of the two functionaries above named, or perhaps the churchwarden, or the treasurer of the schools, who was a troublesome person with nothing to do, and consequently an endless number of things to suggest. When he saw Lady William his heart—which you may say ought to have been sufficiently experienced to take things quietly—gave a jump. Experience does not make us indifferent in certain cases, and the Rector was as easily disturbed on one subject as if he had no experience at all. It flashed into his mind that his sister, who was not much in the habit of consulting him, must have something to say about Jim.

'Emily!' he said, with great surprise: and then, with a little attempt at a lighter tone, which was not very successful, 'What, have you fallen into parish business, too?'

'No,' she replied, with a quickly drawn breath, which the Rector, as a man accustomed to have to do with people in trouble, knew must mean excitement, or anxiety, or distress. 'No,' she said, 'I want to consult you, James: but it is entirely about my own private business.'

The Rector drew a long breath. He was not glad—oh no !—to think that his sister was in trouble : but nothing that affected her could be so serious, he felt, as if it had been something about Jim. He drew forward a chair near himself for her. He had always been both fond and proud of Emily. Perhaps the fact that she was Lady William (though he knew the marriage had not been a success) added a little to the feeling that she was a being by herself, not to be compared with any one else. But still, a great deal of it was very genuine, and meant a conviction that he knew nobody comparable to Emily. He was pleased that she should consult him on her own affairs, of which, generally, she said very little. She had thrown away almost all her own money upon Reginald—provided only that she did not mean to tell him that scapegrace was coming back to trouble his respectable connections again ! Thus the same idea that had disturbed his wife occurred to the Rector, both terrors, no doubt, arising from the fact that neither could imagine what Lady William could wish to consult the Rector about.

'My affairs,' she said, with a faint smile, as she got her breath, 'haven't for a long time been very troublesome to my family, James. I hope they are not entering now into a new stage.'

'A new stage?' he said, and the Rector's middle-aged heart actually took a jump again. What could it all mean ? Good heavens !—Emily's affairs in a new stage ! What could she be going to do ? It could not be about any change in her life that she was going to consult him. Change in her life ! That was what people said when somebody was going to marry. He looked at his sister with sudden alarm. Emily marry ! Vague things he had heard said of Leo Swinford and jests about Lady William's attractions, started up in his mind. It rarely happens, I think, that a man likes his sister (if she is not dependent upon him) to compromise her dignity by a second marriage. He did not like to think that Emily might intend to come down from her pedestal and show herself a mere common person, like the rest.

'What do you mean by a new stage?' he said, with a pucker in his brow. 'You are very well as you are, and occupy a very good position, and all that. I don't see what need there is for a new stage.'

'Nor I,' she said; 'and I hope you will continue of the same opinion when I tell you. I knew,' she continued, with a little hot colour flushing across her face, 'that the coming of the Swinfords would upset all our tranquillity. I was sure of it. She is a woman of evil omen wherever she appears.'

'Yet you were once very fond of her, if I remember right.'

'When I was a girl, and she petted me, and made much of me—I was going to say for her own ends; but I hope it was not for her own ends from the beginning—that would be too diabolical.'

'What ends could she have had that were to be promoted by you?' said the Rector, with a smile. He was sufficiently used to these preposterous notions women so often have of their own importance, prompting them to think the attention of other people, who probably never thought of them, is fixed upon them, and that intentions of various kinds are formed respecting them, without the least foundation in fact. Thus his own wife was in the habit of thinking that her girls were watched and followed; that their movements and their dresses were the subject of constant remark, when in all probability nobody even knew that they were there. He was surprised, however, that his sister Emily should share this view.

'We need not discuss that,' she said. 'James, I want to ask you—do you think it is my duty by Mab to seek further acquaintance with her father's family? We are exceedingly well as we are. The allowance they make is not large, but it is enough, and there is something settled on Mab when I die. They have done their duty, if not very liberally, yet they have done it. And I don't want any more from them. Mab is quite contented, she likes her home better than anything; and though she is a very dear girl, and my hope and comfort, I don't know if she is fitted to shine in—what people call the great world. I might get them, of course, to bring her out in a way more fitting, perhaps—to take her to Court, and all that——'

'I don't see,' said the Rector, 'that that would do her much good.' Men ought not, to be sure, to be touched by any of those motives, which are entirely feminine; but it did certainly flash across the Rector's mind that his own girls had none of these advantages, had never gone to Court or anything of the kind, and yet could not be said to be any the worse.

'No, that is just what I think. She is quite satisfied as she is: to go out with her Pakenham cousins, probably to their annoyance and against their will, and to be taken to places where she

knew nobody, would be no pleasure to my little girl. She is such
a thoroughly reasonable, sensible, understanding child. I am so
glad that you agree with me on that point, James.'

While she was speaking the Rector began to think that
perhaps all was not said in that hasty opinion of his, and that a
man consulted by his nearest relation should not be moved by any
little trifling feeling—like that which might be legitimate enough
in a mother, about his own girls. And he said, 'Stop a little,
Emily. You're still quite a young woman, but life is uncertain.
Perhaps, you know, if anything were to happen to you :—as long
as you are there, that is all right, of course—but she would be
very forlorn, poor little thing, if she were left——'

'There would be you and Jane, James. You would both be
very kind to her.' But Lady William was a little startled by
what he said. It is startling to all, however little objection we
may have to that catastrophe, even however desirable it may be,
to be spoken to abruptly of our own death.

'Both my wife and I are older than you are, and we could
introduce her to nobody in—well, in her father's rank of life. If
she married it would probably be a curate—the Marquis of Portcullis's niece !'

'Oh, if it were no worse than a curate!' said Lady William,
with a laugh. The laugh was a little strained, and under her
eyes there was a hot, red colour which did not consort with
laughter. She grew suddenly very grave, and added hurriedly,
'That was not exactly all. James, in case of the—risk of which
you were speaking, do you think as Mrs. Swinford does——'

'What, Emily ?' He was frightened when he saw the excitement that seemed to come over her.

'Well ! That the family would have a right to—examine
into—and have all the papers about—my marriage, and her birth,
and all that.'

It was of Lady William's marriage alone that Mrs. Swinford
had spoken, but it made it a little easier to state it so.

'Oh !' said the Rector, startled. 'Well,' he added, 'I suppose
it's a very good thing to have your papers all in order, and saves
trouble afterwards. It is so seldom that people take the trouble
to do it. I am sure I don't know anything about my own
marriage certificate, though I furnish them to other people. Have
you got them all ?'

Lady William's face blanched out of its momentarily high
colour. 'I have got none of them,' she said, in a faint voice.

'Well, there is no particular harm in that. I don't know who

N

has—not me, I am sure. What does your friend want you to do
—send these things to the Marquis? What does the Marquis
want with Mab's baptismal certificate? My dear Emily, I suppose
that woman, being partly French, thinks that you should always
have your *papiers* in order? There could not be greater nonsense.'

'Do you really think so? I did myself. Why should there
ever be any question? Nobody asks you, as you say, for your
marriage certificate, James.'

'No,' said the Rector; but he added, looking at the question
from a purely professional point of view, 'of course, you can get
that sort of thing, when it's wanted, at a moment's, at least, at a
day's notice. Where were you married, Emily?'

She was evidently not prepared for this question, and came to
herself with a little start. The colour forsook her cheeks. She
clasped her hands together nervously. 'Oh James, that is what
gives it its sting. I don't know.'

'You don't know?'

'Is that dreadful? Is it dangerous? Might it throw a doubt?
My father went with me, that is the only thing—to London somewhere.'

'I knew you were not married at home,' said Mr. Plowden,
rising up and placing himself in front of the fireplace. 'I knew
there was something queer about it. In the name of wonder,
Emily, why, if my father went with you, didn't he have you
married at home? He can't, in that case, have disapproved.'

'I don't think he disapproved.'

'Then why, *why* weren't you married at home? My father
went with you, and you don't know? What a very queer
business! And who went with you beside my father?'

'Old Meredith, do you remember, who used to be my nurse—
and a lady. But Meredith is dead, and papa is dead—and the
other——'

'This grows rather funny,' said the Rector. 'I mean it isn't
funny at all. So there is nobody living who was there, and you
don't know where it was? Does your friend, Mrs. Swinford, know
these circumstances, Emily, and does she want to frighten you?
It would be like her amiable temper.'

'James, tell me, is there any real reason to fear?'

'Oh, dear, no. Of course not; the only thing is to find the
place. Of course, it must be on the register. What a queer
thing not to know the church you were married in! I thought
a woman always remembered that, whatever she forgot.'

'I was a frightened girl,' said Lady William. 'I didn't know

what they were going to do with me. I was sent down from the
Hall at midnight, as I thought in disgrace—though I could not
tell for what. There was a great tumult in the house. Mr.
Swinford, who was so quiet, in the midst of it all; and then my
husband came down here with me, and my father was called up
to speak to him; and then it was all like a flash of lightning. I
was taken up to London two days after, and there I was married.
It was a little old church, in a district which I didn't know.'

'How is it I never heard anything of this before?'

'How can I tell?' she said. 'I was taken away, frightened,
not knowing what had happened. Oh, I suppose that I was not
unwilling: I did not understand it: but my father was there—
and he liked it, James. He said it was a great match for me, and,
though it was so hurried, I was not to mind. After, I understood
better—but at the time not at all.'

'It must have been by special license,' said the Rector; 'but
why in the name of wonder didn't my father have it here?—Why
——— But I suppose it's no use saying why and why. There
must have been reasons———' He looked at his sister fixedly,
yet avoiding her eye.

But Lady William neither met nor avoided his look. She sat
before him, pale, with an air of deep and melancholy recollection.
'Oh, there were reasons,' she said, shaking her head sadly. 'It
was years before I found them out. I would rather not enter
into them even now—reasons which for a time made life odious
to me. It had not been very happy before. Don't let us speak
of that.'

'They were reasons—which Mrs. Swinford knew!'

'Don't speak of her to me,' said Lady William. 'I was a
fool to go near her, to see her again. Knew! ah, indeed she
knew—indeed she knew! She was my patroness, my kind friend.
My father thought it such a fine thing for me to be at the Hall.
Oh, James, why should a girl be allowed to live when she has no
mother? She ought to be put away in her mother's coffin, and
not enter helpless into the world.'

'In my opinion fathers are some good,' said the Rector, with
severity.

And then a few hot tears fell from his sister's eyes. 'Poor
papa!' she said. Mr. Plowden added nothing to this phrase.
They remained silent, both thinking of the parent who had not
indeed been very wise, but always kind. After a while Lady
William resumed: 'He approved: if he had not approved—I
should never——— But what could I do against my father? And

Miss Mansfield told me I should be ungrateful to the friend who had made such a match for me.'

'Who was Miss Mansfield, Emily?'

'The lady I told you of—a cousin of Mrs. Swinford's, who was with me that day.'

'And is she dead, too?'

'I think not. No; Leo Swinford said something of her the other day—that she had been here.'

'Then she must be found, Emily.'

Lady William gave him a startled look. 'Do you think, then, James, after all, it is necessary to go into all that again—to rake up everything? Oh! when I think of it—the hurry, the strangers, the unknown place, which looked as if there was shame in it——'

'My dear Emily, it is only the hurry and the unknown place that make it important. As soon as you know where to write to find the marriage in the register it does not matter, you can let it rest. But now that I know—even if Mrs. Swinford had never said a word—I shall not rest till I find it out.'

'Then I wish,' she said, with returning spirit, 'that I had said nothing to you on the subject, James.'

'Don't say that. To whom should you go but to your brother? And be sure I'll find it out, Emily. I don't like to say a word that will hurt you. I am afraid you have been the victim of some plot or other, my poor girl.'

She did not answer for a moment, then she said: 'I cannot have been without blame myself. I was pleased with the promotion, I suppose, and with the romance, and all that. Romance! it seemed so strange to be carried away, to be married almost in spite of myself; and I suppose the name—— It is all very vague and dreadful, though at the time I was dazzled, and it sounded like something in a story. I wonder, rather, that you do not despise your sister, James.'

'Poor Emily!' he said, patting her shoulder with his hand.

Mrs. Plowden awaited with some anxiety the appearance of her sister-in-law in the drawing-room, which was an ordeal which Lady William would have liked much to escape. But as this was not possible, she submitted to it with as good a grace as might be. The Rector kindly led the way, saying on the threshold : 'Here is Emily, Jane,' as if that had been at all necessary ; as if they had not all been on the outlook for her appearance for the last half-hour. Mrs. Plowden took her by the hand, and led her to a comfortable sofa in the corner, which was where she took her friends when they had something to say to her, or she something to say to them. 'My dear Emily,' she said, 'I hear you have been sadly worried about something, and, of course, you know I have been trying to guess. You have heard from Reginald again ?'

'From Reginald ?' said Lady William. 'Poor fellow ! Ah, no. I wish I had. And who said I had been sadly worried ? I had only some business I wanted to talk over with James.'

'Not Reginald—really ?' said Mrs. Plowden. She was much relieved ; but there sprang up in her a fresh curiosity, very lively and warm, to think, if it was not Reginald, what it could be ? Of course she said to herself she would hear all about it from James ; but she did not like to wait till the uncertain moment, never to be calculated on during the day, when she should find her husband alone.

And then it occurred to Lady William that to tell a half truth frankly as if it were the whole is sometimes a wise thing to do.

'To tell the truth,' she said, 'I was asking James's serious advice on that matter which you have so often spoken to me about, Jane—whether I should attempt to improve my acquaintance with the Pakenhams, and get Mab, now that she is almost old enough, introduced to the world in their way.'

'Oh!' cried Mrs. Plowden, making a very large mouthful of that word; astonishment, and satisfaction, and pride, and yet a little drawback of another feeling was in her tone. 'So you are thinking at last, Emily, that there may be something in what I said.'

'I always knew,' said Lady William, 'that there was a great deal of sense in what you said. But, I was very unwilling to do it, it must be allowed. And now Mrs. Swinford says the same thing; and though I am very doubtful whether it would be to Mab's advantage, still—I am thinking it over once more.'

'And what advice did you get from James? James is too like yourself in many ways, Emily, to be your best adviser.'

'Do you think he is like myself?' The Rector had gone back to his study after, as it were, introducing his sister into the feminine part of the house. 'Well, perhaps,' said Lady William, with a smile, 'there may be a family resemblance. There is so far as this—that he is by no means certain, I think, of the advantage to Mab.'

'Oh, what nonsense,' said the Rector's wife, 'and what does he know about such things? Advantage! of course it would be an advantage. Dear me, to go to Court with the Ladies Paken-ham, to be taken out into society by the Marchioness, to see the best of company at her uncle's house! My dear Emily, you might just as well say, to confuse small things with great, that it would not be an advantage in the parish of Watcham to belong to the Rectory—and that is what nobody would say.'

The comparison was one which made Lady William smile, though she was not much inclined to smiling. 'There are differences,' she said, 'however; for you could not but be kind to a girl thrown on your care. Whereas, I doubt very much if the Marchioness would be at all kind to a poor relation; and I don't care to have my Mab thought of as a poor relation in any case.'

'You are so proud,' said the Rector's wife; and then she said, with a laugh, 'Fancy little Mab to be the one of us all that will see the great world, and make her curtsey to the Queen!'

If the Rector himself had thought of this, it would have been wonderful indeed that his wife should not think of it. She laughed continuously for a minute with an odd little trill in her laugh, looking at her own girls, who she could not help thinking were more worthy than Mab of such a distinction. It was a thing she had urged upon Mab's mother since her child was ten. But now that it seemed an actual possibility, nay more than that

—for Mrs. Plowden's mind leaped forward to the ceremony, and already wondered what Mab would wear, and if feathers would really be wanted upon her little head—the ridicule of the thought that Mab, little Mab, would be the one to go to Court, an honour which was quite beyond the hopes of Emmy and Florry, gave their mother a shock of half-irritated feeling. That their cousin should have this glory would not hurt them—but still—if honours went by merit in this world how different things would be!

'I wonder,' said Lady William, as they walked home, 'what your opinion, Mab, may be in the matter which everybody has been discussing. It was your little fortunes that Mrs. Swinford wanted to talk to me about yesterday, and that I have been advising about with Uncle James to-day.'

'My little fortunes?' said Mab. 'I never knew I had any.'

'Your future, perhaps, it would be better to say.'

'My future! is that to be detached and put separate from other people's like an odd piece in a puzzle? I don't know still what you mean, mother!'

'And yet it is plain enough,' said Lady William, with a sigh. 'The other girls here are all in their natural sphere. But you, Mab, are a bird of another species in a sparrow's nest.'

'I hope you don't compare me to a cuckoo, mother.'

'Something very different, my dear; the others are plain brown homely birds. Emmy and Florry will twitter under the eaves in some parsonage or other, probably all their lives; but you are a Pakenham.'

'What's a Pakenham?' said Mab; 'you speak as if it were a Plantagenet.'

'Well, not so grand, perhaps—but still it is different. And I have brought you up only like what I was myself: a little country girl.'

'Only like what you were yourself! You know very well, mother, and it's unkind to remind me of it, that if I were to live a hundred years I should never get to be like you. It's Emmy that's like you. I'm not envious; but to think that your daughter should be a little—just a—Pakenham, as you say; and Emmy like you!'

'She is not very like me—if I'm any judge myself,' Lady William said.

'She is not half nor a quarter so pretty as you are, mammy dear.'

'You little flatterer! Emmy is a much better girl than I

ever was, Mab, and perhaps that's pretty much the same thing. She is a much better girl to tell the truth than my own little girl is.'

'I know; my own opinion is that Emmy is too good. She is never out of temper, always puts up with everything, is bored by nobody. That, I understand, is one reason why—as you say, mother. For I think, to tell the truth, that to look really nice, and be like a human woman, you must not be quite so good.'

'That is a dangerous doctrine, Mab. And it is not the question; which is, what do you think? The Pakenhams are more or less fashionable, and of course they have a fine position. With them you would see a little of the world. You would meet people very different from any you ever see here in the village. I am told that I ought to make advances to them; to tell them of my child who is growing up, and ought to be introduced properly into the world.'

'Oh, is that what it means?' said Mab. 'Tell me more about them, that I may be able to judge. I don't know anything at all about them, and how can I say?'

Lady William's heart sank a little at this calm and judicial tone on the part of her child. She, too, jumped, as Mrs. Plowden had done, to the spectacle of Mab's presentation under the wing of the Marchioness, and at all that might follow.

'I have never seen Lady Pakenham or the girls. Your uncle I have seen, and he was—not unkind. No, I am sure he was not in the least unkind; he did what he could for me. He took a little notice of you as a baby, and so did the other brother—your uncle John. They were not clever, nor distinguished in any way; but they were by no means without feeling.'

'That was when my father died.'

Lady William, who had rarely to Mab said anything about her father, nodded her head. Her eyes had a dreamy look, fixed far away. Mab never was sure whether it was for grief that her mother was so reticent, or from some other cause.

'And do you mean to say, mother,' said Mab, 'that my aunt —if she is my aunt—never came near you when you were in such trouble?'

'She is just exactly as much your aunt as your uncle James's wife is—neither less nor more. No, she never came near me. But I was not surprised. It happened in Paris, and then I came away as soon as I could to this little place. I neither expected her to come to Paris, which would have been absurd: nor to come after me here, where she knew I would be among my own people.'

'Why,' said Mab, 'you would have gone! You would not have minded if it had been in Paris, or at the end of the world.'

'I do a great many foolish things,' said Lady William, with a smile, 'that wise people don't do; besides they hadn't approved much, as was natural. Substantially kind is what you may call them, practically kind; your uncles were that, and have been——'

'And yet I am seventeen and I have never seen them.'

'If you had been a boy,' said Lady William, they would have felt their duty more; a girl is supposed to be best with her mother. You must not be surprised at that, my dear child. Your uncle Pakenham has always supplied all your wants.'

'You never showed me any of his letters——'

'His letters! oh, he is not a man who writes letters. His lawyer does all that; but substantially, he has been very kind.'

'Mother,' said Mab, 'instead of wishing to know these people, to visit them, and all that, I'll tell you what I should like to do. I should like to be able to work for you, and throw their money in their face—which is what you mean, I suppose, when you say they are substantially kind.'

'That would be very foolish, Mab; the money is your right, and for that matter mine too.'

'It may be right, but I should like to fling it in their faces all the same. Had my father nothing to leave us, to give us to live on, that you should have to accept it from them?'

Lady William made no answer for some time. Then she said in a low tone: 'Your father had many things to do. I cannot enter into such questions, Mab; you are not old enough. No; we were destitute but for them.'

'You had money of your own, mother?'

'Fortunately,' said Lady William, 'that did not come to me till after.' And then she stopped short and bit her lip with annoyance. 'I didn't do much with it when it did come,' she said. 'I gave it to your poor uncle Reginald. He was to make his fortune, poor fellow, and ours.'

'Perhaps he may yet, mother.'

'Thank you for the suggestion, Mab; perhaps he may. Alas! I am afraid it is not very likely——'

'If he were to do so, mother, you would take this dirty money and fling it back in their faces?'

'I don't know that I should, Mab. I doubt if it would be kind or just—and still more, whether it would be wise.'

'Oh, you may be sure they wouldn't mind, people like that! They would only be glad to have it back, whether you flung it at them or not, provided they had it.'

'My dear, you are very hot-headed. In that respect you are, I fear, of my side of the house.'

'And Emmy, who is like you, isn't. She would eat any amount of dirt; she thinks it her duty not to resent anything. That's not my way of thinking,' cried Mab. 'I resent it, and I should like to fling it in their face.'

The two ladies went on after this in silence for a little while, Mab pondering many things in her heart. Some she knew about, and some she did not know. Of her father she had very little idea, scarcely any at all. She had never seen any one belonging to him. He was dead; that was all she knew; and she had never missed him, or any one, having her mother. Vague ideas that he had not been good to her mother had floated through her mind, and yet she never was sure that it was not out of great love that Lady William spoke of him so little. She had known in the parish people who grieved like that, who could not mention the names of those who were gone. It might be for that reason. She walked on pondering, saying nothing till they had nearly reached the cottage door. Then she suddenly turned on her mother, having forgotten till this moment what was the question that had been given her to answer.

'And you want me,' she said, 'to say that I would like to go to those people—to leave you?'

'Not to leave me, Mab, except for a little time.'

'Then I won't, mother, short time or long time! What! to a woman that knew you were in trouble, and never went to you— whom you don't even know! If I am allowed to have any say in it, I would not for anything in the world. And what is it for? To go to parties with them, to be taken out, to enjoy myself? Mother, mother, do you think I am like that—to enjoy myself with people who don't know you, who leave you, who are insolent to you?'

'No; they are not insolent—they ignore me; but, then, I have always wished to be ignored. To tell the truth, Mab, I doubt very much whether you would enjoy yourself. It is possible that you might, but I fear it is more likely that you would not. That is why I am against it.'

'Then you are against it, mother?'

' For that reason—that I could not bear my Mab to be treated like a nobody, to be taken out, perhaps, because they could not help it, or left alone and snubbed——'

' Snubbed ! They should not snub me twice, mother ! '

' No, you little hothead ! But everybody here thinks it would be so much to your advantage to go to Court—that is something—to be introduced as you ought to be.'

' Introduced to whom ?—to the Queen ? Yes, that would be nice. But then I don't suppose the Queen would take the least notice of me, would she ? I would just be another little girl among so many. No, mother, people here—Aunt Jane, or whoever it is—may say what they like. I will have nothing to say to those people who took no notice of you.'

' Your uncle James is of the same opinion — and Mrs. Swinford.'

' Odious old woman ! ' said Mab.

' My dear child, how do you know that she is an odious old woman ? She was a very fascinating woman once. When I was like you I would have laid down my life for her.' Lady William breathed forth a long, soft sigh involuntarily, unable to restrain herself. ' I think I did,' she said under her breath.

Mab did not hear these words, but she said somewhat loudly, ' Odious old woman ! ' again.

' Who is that you are describing so succinctly ? ' cried a voice behind them. ' Miss Mab has an energy and conciseness of expression which I admire.'

' She has a pitch of voice occasionally which is not at all admirable,' said Lady William, turning round. Mab, as may be supposed, turned a bright scarlet up to her hat, her very hair warming in the quick suffusion of colour. But her mother was skilled in such emergencies and betrayed nothing.

' It is always admirable to know what you think, and to express it clearly,' said Swinford. ' I was on my way,' he added, putting his hands together with a supplicating movement, ' to inquire whether I might consider myself forgiven. You know you turned me out the other day. May I come back with you now ? You take so much from me when you shut your door. Miss Mab will intercede for me. She was as much shocked as I was when you sent me away.'

' There was no sending away,' said Lady William. ' We have been having an argument—my daughter and I. You shall be the impartial umpire and set us right.'

' With all the pleasure in the world,' he said.

'It is a very good thing to have somebody impartial to refer to,' said Lady William; 'all our advisers take a side strongly. Now, Leo, you are of no faction; you can give us fair advice.'

'I am of your faction always,' he said.

'Ah, but I am of no faction. I am the seeker of advice. We want to be well advised, Mab and I. By the way, she does take a side strongly, but I will not tell you which it is.'

'Expound the case, Miss Mab; I must know before I can say.'

'So you shall know; but Mab must not tell you, for she has a bias. The case is this: Mab you see is grown up——'

He gave a glance at her in her (still) short frock, with her (still) large waist, and round, artless, almost childish look.

'I see,' he said, with a smile.

'And must presently be introduced into society. The question is, must it be the society of Watcham, and is the dance at the FitzStephens' to be her *début?* or is she to enter the world in a different way, and be taken to town for a season with all that follows? What is your opinion?'

'Can there be two opinions?' he said, opening his eyes wide. 'This is not treating me well. I hoped it was to be a difficult and delicate question, but it is no question at all.'

'You see,' said Lady William to her daughter.

'If you put it to him in that way, mother: but that is not the way. Imagine, Mr. Leo, what they all want!—that mother, who is, I know, better than the whole of them, every one, whoever they may be—should go and—and—petition my uncle and his wife, who have never taken any notice of us—to take me by the hand and introduce me, as people say, into society: to introduce me—me, Mab, do you understand, to the Queen and all the rest; to get me asked to parties with them—me, Mab, do you understand?' said

the girl, beating upon her breast, 'only me ; and that is what everybody wants, and mother hesitates and wonders whether she ought
to do it : and I,' cried the girl, her dull eyes growing bright, 'I
will obey mother. I have never gone against her yet except in the
way of reason, and if she were to tell me to jump into the river I
would do it (hoping to scramble out somewhere lower down) ; and
I'll do this of course if I must, and perhaps escape alive—but never,
never of my own free will. Now say what you think, Mr. Leo.
Isn't it I that am in the right ?'

'The question has a very different aspect, certainly,' said Leo,
'from Miss Mab's side.'

'Hasn't it ?' said the girl triumphantly. 'Now I should be
proud, mother, if he who is of your faction should pronounce for me.'

'But there is a great deal more to be said on both sides,' said
Leo ; 'we have not come to a decision yet. And just tell me why
you should not go to town yourself as everybody does, and introduce
your daughter in your own person, and show yourself in the
world ? That would seem so much the most natural way.'

'Ah !' cried Mab, with something like a shout of triumph.
'That is something like advice ! I did not think much, I tell you
true, of consulting Mr. Leo—but now I see he is a Daniel come to
judgment. And to think that none of us ever thought of that
before !'

Lady William grew red and she grew pale. It had not occurred
to her, strangely enough, that any one would suggest this simple
alternative. The other advisers, indeed, knew her position too
well to think of it. She said with a laugh : 'You speak very
much at your ease, you young people. Where am I to get the
money for a campaign in town ? I might squeeze out a few dresses
for Mab—that is all I could do. You forget that I am not a
wealthy person like you, Leo. And then I know nobody. We
might as well stay here for anything I could do for her. Yes, the
Lenthalls might invite us, or Lady Wade, who belongs to this
neighbourhood ; but nobody else. And we should be ruined !
No, no ; that is more impossible than anything else. It must,
I fear, be Lady Portcullis, or nobody. Her aunt is her only
hope.'

'If I am to be sent off to Lady Portcullis like a brown-
paper parcel,' said Mab, 'I will do what I'm told, mother ; but
I won't discuss it any more. Mr. Leo, I would ask you to
stand up for me, if I thought you could ever stand up against
mother.'

'It's hard, isn't it ?' said Leo ; 'but I will try as much as

I can.' He got up to open the door for her (for by this time they had reached the cottage), which was a thing Mab hated, feeling the attention very right for her mother, but a sort of mockery in the case of a little girl like herself. She submitted with her head bent; and then bolted like a young colt, which she still was. It must be allowed that the young man, who, according to all laws, ought to have preferred her company, was relieved when she was gone. He came quickly back to where Lady William sat, her head bowed upon her hand in much thought, and drew a low chair, Mab's little baby-chair, to her feet.

'I have a counter proposition to make,' he said, lightly touching her hand to draw her attention.

She smiled, and said, 'What is that?' with a friendly indifference which made him frown. It was very clear that his proposition, whatever it might be, awakened no excitement, scarcely even curiosity, in Lady William's breast. He made a very long pause indeed, but she took no notice until there had been time for various tumults and revolutions of thought in his mind. Then she looked up, with a little start, to see him in an attitude which was strangely like supplication, though he was in reality only seated in the low chair. 'Well,' she said, in her easy tone, 'what is it? You keep me a long time in suspense.'

'It was—nothing,' he said.

'Ah,' said Lady William, with a laugh, 'you pay me back in my own coin.'

'Rather,' he said in a changed tone, 'let us say that it was this. We must, I suppose, go to London next month—though my mother does not seem to care for it now as I thought she would. However, we shall go; and why should not you come too? Come with us; take Miss Mab where you please, and come back when you please. It would obviate all the difficulties you were speaking of, and secure all the—— What! You will not listen to such a simple suggestion as that?'

There had been a great many exclamations on Lady William's lips as he went on, but she had smothered them one by one till it was impossible to keep silence longer. 'With your mother?' she said, almost under her breath.

'Well: I should like it, oh, a great deal better, if it were with me; but you think of me as if I were a cabbage, and my mother was your friend—was she not your friend?—and I am your servant—to mount behind your carriage, if you like.'

'Do not speak nonsense, Leo; you are my very kind friend, and the greatest acquisition, and if you had been going to town with your wife instead of your mother—— It is not indispensable, don't you know, that old friends should continue friends for ever. Your mother was very good to me once—that is, I believe, for a time : but it would do no good to go into those old questions. She would not suffer me with her, nor would I—— No, no ; forgive me. That does not mean necessarily any harm, does it ? that we do not now—see things—exactly in the same light——'

'Then that is settled,' he said gloomily, 'so far as my mother is concerned ; as for me, though, you call me a friend and all that——'

'My dear boy,' said Lady William, 'you don't imagine for a moment, I hope, that I would let you pay my expenses—for the benefit of Mab ?'

He paused again, gazing at her, saying nothing ; then threw up his hands with an impatient sigh.

'And yet friendship is supposed to be something more than words,' he said.

'There is one thing that friendship is not,' said Lady William ; 'at least, in England, Leo. It is not money. When that comes in it is supposed to spoil all.'

'What an absurd, false, conventional, inhuman, ridiculous view !'

'Perhaps. Oh ! I don't know that it need tell between two young men. There is an allowance to be made in that way for *bons camarades*. But I think it is a just rule on the whole. My poor little experience is that it is best not to be very much obliged to one's neighbours. No, no ! I don't say so for you, Leo. I believe you might give everything you have to a friend, and never remind him of it—never recollect it even yourself, as long as you lived.'

'Is that much to say ?'

'In the way of the world, it is something extraordinary to say ; but this is a totally different question from my little problem, which is urged upon me by your mother, Leo, as well as by my innocent people—my brother and sister here.'

'You think my mother is not innocent—that she had some other motive ?'

'I did not say so ; why should she have another motive? Whatever there may have been between her and me, I, at least, have done her no harm.'

'Then it must be she who has harmed you ?'

'No ; what can any one do to you, outside of yourself? All

our troubles come from our own faults or mistakes. We say
faults when we speak of others, mistakes when it is ourselves.
You told me once that Miss Mansfield—Artémise—had appeared
again ? '

'Ah ! I should like to know what she had to do with it,' he
cried.

'Nothing,' said Lady William ; 'but it would be important
to me to know where to find her. Will you find out for me ?
There is something which she only knows which I am anxious to
make sure of.'

'Something important to you ? '

'They tell me so. I was not aware of it, and yet—if you
could bring me to speech of her, Leo, for five minutes. She was
never unkind to me.'

'She is a bird of evil omen !' cried Leo ; 'wherever she appears
some harm follows.'

'Ah !' said Lady William, 'and you said she was here the
other day ! '

'There is something which has happened between you and
my mother—something she has done to you which you will not
tell me ? '

'What could she have done to me ?' Lady William made a
movement as though shaking off some annoyance. 'No ; all she
has done is to persuade me to this—about Lady Portcullis and the
introduction of Mab into society. What could be more innocent ?'
she said, with a laugh.

'There is one thing,' he said, 'that one ought to do before
giving an opinion. Has Lady Portcullis ever shown any interest ?
I have met her ; she is very commonplace—one of the rigid
English. Oh ! very English. You do not know her ? she has not
sought your acquaintance ? Would she ?—has she ever ?—do you
think it is likely——? '

Lady William laughed again, but uneasily, painfully. 'You
are a sorcerer, Leo—this is the doubt I have never mentioned to
any one—not to Mab herself, not to my brother. Do I think it is
likely——? Since you ask me, I must answer no ; my pride
prevented me from saying it—not even to your mother did I say it
—but she—ah ! ' Lady William broke off again, still laughing—
and the evening was beginning to fade, but Leo thought he could
see the hot flush on her cheek.

'I am not my mother's champion,' he said ; 'she has her
peculiarities. She may have thought it would embroil you with
the family.'

'That,' said Lady William, 'was the least of what she thought !'

'Dear lady,' he said, 'here is some mystery. You know that I am of your faction whatever happens. But you must tell me before I can do any good.'

Lady William did not make any immediate reply. She said at last: 'Artémise: if you can bring me to speech of Artémise, I shall want nothing more.' Then with a change of tone—'Here is Mab coming back; no more of it—no more of it! there has been too much already. Mab, Leo is waiting till you give him some tea.'

'Give it me strong and sweet,' said Leo, who had jumped up from his low chair with perhaps a touch of embarrassment—but Lady William felt none—'sweet and strong; for my head is a little confused, and I want it clear.'

'Is it all about me and my father's people? That is very good of you, Mr. Leo,' said Mab, 'to take so much interest—and have you converted mother to my way of thinking?—which is the thing I want most.'

'I have been doing my best,' he said, standing up beside her against the waning light in the window. And then it was for the first time that it occurred to Lady William—— Well, she was no more a matchmaking mother than you or I; but to see two young people together—one of them your own child, and the other a very good match—very well off, and kind, and true, and good, *par-dessus le marché*—this is a thing which will make the most unworldly woman think. To be sure, Leo was twice or nearly twice the age of Mab—but at their respective ages that was of no consequence. It was true also that Leo gave unmistakable signs at this present moment of much preferring Emily, the mother, to any seventeen-year-old; but that Lady William in her wisdom thought less important still. That would blow over quickly enough; it was scarcely even worth a thought; but they were smiling at each other in a very happy, pleasant way, she appealing, he answering the appeal. It was nothing, but yet it was a suggestion—and how many pleasant things it would involve! It was far too distant, too misty and vague to suggest to the mother how she should feel in her cottage if her Mab was spirited away. But it was a suggestion—and gave a new and agreeable direction to her thoughts.

Leo remained until the lamp was brought in by little Patty, whose eyes shone at the sight of him, partly because it pleased her to see 'a gentleman' again in the house (for Patty was a match-maker, if you please, and never looked upon a 'gentleman' without an immediate calculation whether or not he would 'do' for Miss

Mab), and partly because she felt that she must now be wholly forgiven for any wrong thing she had done in respect to him, seeing he was allowed to come back. Patty had never been sure what it was that she had done which was wrong ; but none the less was it evident to her that she herself must have shared the pardon of the worst offender. And in the meantime there had been a pleasant little hour over the tea-table ; as if to encourage her mother's imagination, Mab had for once been seized with an impulse to talk, which was a thing that happened to her now and then. And it was beyond doubt that Leo was amused by her chatter, and responded gaily. They discussed Lord and Lady Portcullis with great mutual satisfaction, and the Ladies Pakenham, whom Leo had met in Paris ; and he gave Mab a great deal of information as to her family, which the girl received with a mixture of amusement and offence, proving to her mother that there had been more things even in little Mab's thoughts than were dreamt of in her philosophy. And then the young man went away, and they were left alone to resume the controversy or not, as fate might decide. Lady William, who had been brought into very close observation of her daughter, left the subject in Mab's hands—but Mab did not enter into it again. She changed the subject to the FitzStephens' dance, which was now so near, and led her mother to a discussion of the dresses they were to wear, which had the air of absorbing all Mab's thoughts. 'Do you think I will look very fat in white, mother ? and my arms so red and healthy,' she said. And this sort of conversation was carried on until Mab fairly put her mother, with all her anxieties and questions, to bed. The little girl was not without questions in her own mind, questions about her father, about the life she could not remember, or scarcely could remember, in Paris ; about the family and relations she had never seen. By dint of much reflection it appeared to her that she could recollect a stiff gentleman with a fat face, who must have been Lord Portcullis himself. Why was it she knew nothing of her uncle ? Why did he take no notice ? Was there any reason for it ? or was it her mother's fault ? If so, Mab was as strongly determined that she was of her mother's faction as ever Leo Swinford could be ; but more still than Leo Swinford she wanted to know from the beginning, and find out how and why it all was.

THE night of the FitzStephens' dance was a great one in Watcham. It was not precisely a dance, to tell the truth, as, to temper the pretensions belonging to the name of a ball, there was to be a little musical performance to begin with—a duet from Emily and Florry Plowden, a few pieces for violin and piano, and so on— which was sufficient to give something of the air of an impromptu and accidental performance to the dance, which, of course, was the real meaning of the whole. Some of the people were so unkind as not to arrive till the music was over, which was thought exceedingly bad taste by the performers and their families, and gave the General and his wife a moment of dread lest the party they had got up so carefully might not be a success after all. But by ten o'clock the music was over, the piano rolled into its appointed corner, and the music stands, which had been prepared for the violinists, put away. The musicians who were engaged for the dance did not want any music stands, and the assembled party required every scrap of room that was available. The excellent FitzStephens had done wonders to enlarge the space. They had taken away everything—almost the fixtures of the house : doors were unhung, carpets lifted : I cannot really calculate the trouble that had been taken. Even after the party assembled, the removal of the chairs on which they had been seated to hear the music was a matter of labour, for they were not all light chairs like those which people in Watcham borrow by the dozen from Simpkinson of the 'Blue Boar,' but included a number of comfortable easy-chairs for the ladies who did not dance, of whom there were a considerable number. The FitzStephens did not see the necessity of leaving the elder people out. They were old themselves, and though they delighted in seeing the young ones enjoy themselves, as they said, yet they liked also to have their own playfellows, with whom to have a comfortable talk, while they looked on. What

Mrs. FitzStephen would have liked best would have been to keep the elder ladies apart in the room which was called the General's study, which had a door (removed) into the dancing room, by the opening of which (had it not been crowded by the elder gentlemen) the matrons could have seen enough of their children's performances, as well as have been out of the way. This, however, was the one point which was not successful in the arrangements, for the mothers preferred to cling to the walls in the dancing room itself, at the risk of being swept away by flying skirts, or trodden upon by nimble feet ; and the fathers occupied the doorway in a solemn block, so that nobody could see anything through them. Even Lady William, who generally was so great a help in getting people to stay where they were wanted, herself got into a corner in the dancing room, taking up, it must be admitted, very little room, as she stood up against the wall to watch how Mab got on among the dancers ; and Miss Grey, in a costume in which she had gone to all the parties in the neighbourhood for the last twenty years, flitted about like an aged butterfly, getting the puffs of super-annuated tulle about her into everybody's way, in order to see not only how Mab got on, but how everybody got on in whom she was interested, and that meant every girl in the room. Thus Mrs. FitzStephen had one little point of vexation amid the perfect success of everything else. But it was so natural. The General declared that he himself liked to see the dancing, and was not at all satisfied to be sent away into another room.

The reader, perhaps, would like to know at once how Mab, who was the *débutante* of the evening, got on. Her white frock was very simple, being, as has been said, the manufacture of her mother and herself ; but Lady William was universally allowed to have great taste, and it is saying a great deal to say that she herself was satisfied with the effort. As a matter of fact, the finest dress-maker in the world could not have disguised the fact that Mab's figure was too solid, and her well-formed, round arms a little too rosy with health, for perfect grace. But that solid form and rosy tint agreed very well with the childish roundness of the face, under the dimpled and infantile softness of which Mab hid so much good sense and independent judgment of her own: She looked as she was, like a little girl just escaped from the trammels of childhood, enjoying the dance with all her might, without thinking for a moment whether anybody admired her, or what people thought of her dancing or demeanour, and without the slightest thrill of consciousness in mind or person. Mab was so popular that she was a little bored at first by her own success, for many of the most dignified persons present, men quite old enough to be her father, considered it a right thing to show their interest in her by 'coming forward' and performing a solemn dance with her—General Fitz-Stephen himself (who might have been her grandfather) taking her out for a quadrille as he might have taken Mrs. Swinford had she been there. There passed through Mab's mind a devout thanksgiving that Uncle James was a clergyman, or perhaps he might have asked her too. The Archdeacon, indeed, who was also prevented by his cloth from any such escapades, insisted on taking her to have an ice, which she did not want, and which almost lost her one waltz. It will be seen from this that the dance was all that a first dance ought to be to Mab. Her card was filled before she had been two minutes in the room, the gentlemen crowding round her, so that before the end of the evening she, who accepted everybody at first with smiles and pleasure, became critical, and actually threw over young Mr. Wade, one of the county people, whom most girls delighted to dance with, in order to career over the floor with Jim for the third time in succession, to the astonishment of everybody. Jim, with whom she was on terms of easy family intimacy, finding fault with him all the time, was, on the whole, the dancer she preferred—though there was much to be said for Leo, who was making himself extremely agreeable, and whose 'style' most of the ladies admired greatly as something quite out of the common, and not in the least like the careless romping of Bobby Wade, who had been supposed to be the representative of the fashionable world, and to bring the last graces of the *beau monde* to astonish the villagers. That Mr. Swinford, on the contrary, should be so quiet, so far from any ideas of romping, filled the ladies with surprise, who had been watching Bobby as the glass of fashion and the mould of form. But Mab thought, and did not hesitate to say so, that Leo was a little stiff. She said whatever came into her head, that daring little girl—she was not afraid of offending anybody, especially not Mr. Leo, as she called him, to the admiration and wonder of all the other girls.

Mab, in short, enjoyed herself so much, and was so frankly delighted with the progress of events, that the questions that were poured upon her by all the old ladies became superfluous.

'Well, Mab, are you getting partners?' Mrs. Plowden said, whose attention had been riveted upon her own children, and who, in sincerity, had scarcely noticed Mab until she danced with Jim.

'Partners! she has never once sat down the whole evening,' cried Miss Grey.

Mrs. Plowden was aware that Emmy had not danced the two last dances, and she felt the humiliation; but she smiled. 'Everybody is anxious that a girl should enjoy her first ball,' she said. 'Jim wanted you so much to enjoy yourself to-night.'

'Well, she paid him back for it,' said Miss Grey; 'she threw over Bobby Wade for him.'

'Bobby Wade!' cried Mrs. Plowden.

Bobby Wade had not asked either of the Rectory girls. This little heartburning ran on along all the line of mothers who sat or stood by the wall. Mr. Wade and Mr. Swinford were the two men whose approach made every heart beat. Those who had not been asked by them—or, rather, whose daughters had not been asked by them—felt the vanity of the whole affair, and that the apples which were so bright outside were but ashes within. Leo, for his part, worked very hard that nobody might be left out; but young Wade did not care in the least, dancing up with his arm extended to the young lady he fancied, when he pleased, and carrying her off sometimes under the very nose of her partner.

'He had better not try that on with me,' said Jim.

'What would you do? You couldn't knock him down in Mrs. Fitz-Stephen's room?'

'No, I don't suppose I could do that,' said Jim, 'for their sakes; but I should certainly give him to understand——'

'How could you give him to understand?' said Mab, pursuing her cousin with pitiless practicality. But, as it happened, the proof of what Jim could do occurred at once, for Mr. Wade made a long step up to her—her very self—and held out that insolent arm.

'Our da-ance, I think,' he said.

'Indeed, it is nothing of the kind!' said Mab; 'I am not engaged to you at all——'

Wade opened his eyes very wide, and looked as if he could not believe his ears. 'I assure you this is ours—booked first thing in the evening. Come!' he said.

'We are losing half the waltz,' said Mab to her partner, and they dashed off, brushing against Mr. Wade's extended arm. It was very rude, and Lady William took her daughter very much to task for her want of politeness.

'But it wasn't the least his dance—he had nothing to do with it, mother.'

'That may be,' said Lady William, 'but it is one thing to refuse a partner and another nearly to knock him down.'

'Oh, did we knock him down?' said Mab, delighted, and

softly clapping her hands. She was disappointed to hear that he
had not been knocked down at all, but was standing in a corner
of the room very sulky, and vowing vengeance upon the little
fat thing who had rejected his condescending offer. When, however, the Rectory girls and some others surrounded her open-
mouthed, to hear what it all meant, Mab took higher ground.
'If I hadn't snubbed him,' she said, 'Jim would have punched
his head, or something. He told me he would not stand it, so
I thought it better a girl should do it than a boy. He may sulk,
but he cannot do anything to me. And what do I care for his
sulking? He cannot dance a bit,' said this high-handed young
lady, who had not a dance, not even an extra, to give to any one ;
others who were not so deeply engaged did not, perhaps, feel
themselves so free. They surrounded her, however, with a certain
wondering admiration, and those girls who were not acquainted
with Bobby Wade, and who had hitherto been a little ashamed
of the fact, now proclaimed it as a superiority. ·

'He is such bad form,' they all said.

It need scarcely be said that there were other things in
Lady William's mind than even her child's success, as she stood
up in her corner watching the dancers. It would be to do great
injustice to Mrs. FitzStephen, a woman of very good connections, and who had taken so much trouble to make her party
everything that a party in a village, out of London, out of the
great world, could be, to say that it was in any sense of the
word common or inferior. They were all very nice people, some
even, as has been seen, from the county, for Bobby Wade had
brought his sisters with him, who really gave themselves no airs
at all among the village folk, though they did what they could
to appropriate Leo, and gave him to understand that he was
the only man in the least degree of their own set. But Lady
William, as she looked round the room, was haunted by an
altogether unreasonable regret and discomfort, which she was
indignant with herself for feeling, but which came into her mind
in spite of her. This was not the scene, she said to herself, in
which Mab should be making her first acquaintance with the
world. Then, why not? her self said to her, hotly. It would
have been far better for Mab's mother if she had never known
any other ; if she had looked forward to an innocent dance in the
village as her greatest pleasure, and never stepped out of that
simple circle. Ah, but she had done so, the other visionary party
in the argument said. She had stepped out of that circle, and
her daughter was Lord William Pakenham's daughter as well as

hers : and was it not a wrong to Mab that she should be here
where everybody looked up to the Wades, people who were of
no particular importance, whose origin could not be compared to
hers ? These things Lady William was pondering with a grave
face, when General FitzStephen came up to her, dodging between
the dancers, to take her to supper.

'I know you never take supper,' the General said, 'but none
of the ladies can move till you do, and I should think you would
at least be glad to sit down a little.'

None of the ladies could move till she did. That was true
enough ; she had the benefit, such as it was, of her rank. Lady
Wade it was well known would not come to the village festivities
because she was unseated from her usual priority by the superior
claims of Lady William. She had the advantage, such as it was ;
but the child——

'Mab is having a thoroughly "good time,"' said the General.
'You need not concern yourself with her any more. She is as
happy as the night is long, and I hope the young ones will make
it long and keep it up. They all seem to be enjoying themselves
tremendously now.'

'Yes ; they all seem very happy. It is so kind of you——'

'To give ourselves the pleasure of seeing them so ?' said the
old General. 'I don't call that kindness but selfishness on our
parts. My wife was always fond of young people—which made
it more a regret to us in former times that we had no children of
our own.'

'Yes, indeed ; how strange it is—you who would have done
them so much justice—who would have been such perfect
parents ! and they seem to be sown broadcast about the streets at
everybody's door.'

'We must not say that, for, of course, Providence arranges
for the best,' said the General, 'and I don't regret it now—I
don't regret it now. The worst troubles that people have come
through their children—either they have not enough for them ;
or they spend everything their parents have got ; or they are ill-
behaved ; or they are unhappy. And there is scarcely a moment
of their lives that fathers and mothers are not at their children's
mercy, to be struck to the ground by one thing or another—
perhaps misfortune perhaps death. Oh no, my dear lady, I do
not regret it. I am very glad to be ending my life with my dear
wife without anxiety—now.'

'And yet I can't contemplate life at all without my Mab,'
Lady William said.

'Ah, my dear lady, that is exactly what I say. You are entirely in her power. You can't call your soul your own. If she were to take a perverse line, or if she were to fall ill——'

'For Heaven's sake, General, don't be such an evil prophet,' she said, with a shiver, and then laughing, 'I had meant to distinguish myself at supper, and you have taken all my appetite away.'

'I don't believe in your appetite,' said the fatherly old gentleman; 'I have never seen it yet. But seriously, even you must be pleased with Mab's little success; and I hear she snubbed Bobby Wade. Do him all the good in the world to be well snubbed by a little girl. The little fool thinks he has all the girls at his feet. But Mab will never be of that mind.'

'She is independent enough. I wonder what you will think of my puzzle, General. They say that I ought not to keep her here in the village—that she ought to come out under her aunt, Lady Portcullis', auspices, instead of living so quietly here with me.'

'They talk nonsense, my dear lady,' said the General; 'a girl is always best, and I think she always looks her nicest, by her mother's side.'

'Thank you for that kind opinion, General.'

'But I can't see any reason,' said the old gentleman, 'why her mother, a lady whom we all admire and honour, should not herself abandon the quiet corner a little (though we should miss her dreadfully), and bring out her daughter, which would be better than any Lady Portcullis in the world.'

'Ah, but that is impossible,' Lady William said quickly. She was moved a little out of her place by the rush of the procession from the drawing-room, all the elder ladies going in; but presently she went back and addressed herself to doing her duty by Mrs. FitzStephen in guiding these elder ladies as they returned into the smaller room. 'We may as well make ourselves comfortable here,' she said, 'since all the children are happy and in full swing.' It was always Lady William who settled these things—and so quietly. The ladies were very glad of comfortable seats after standing half the evening against the wall, and the General managed to get up the quiet rubber he loved, while still one waltz followed another, and the whirling figures went round and round.

'Tell me,' said Leo Swinford, coming in behind her a little out of breath, 'why Miss Wade tells me I am the only one of her set. I am not of her set, or any set; is it intended to be civil, or what does she mean?'

'She means that the rest of us are of the village, and she and you are of the county, which is a very different thing.'

'It is a distinction I do not understand. Nobility and gentry!—yes, I know what that means: but we are not noblesse at all, neither she nor I. We are more or less rich—no two of us the same—but is that the only distinction here?'

'Oh no; there are a great many grades of distinction. The county means the aristocracy——'

'Permit me; you and Miss Mab are the only persons noble here—is that not so? Ah, you will have to give me many lessons to bring me to a proper understanding.'

'And yet I condemn Mab to be nobody,' said Lady William. 'Yes, that is what I am doing. Her old friends are very good to her. She has her little triumph to-night. But it will not always be her first ball. And it is I who keep her in obscurity. I think I am learning my lesson more quickly than you do yours.'

THERE is nothing that happens more frequently in human experience than that, after long doubting what to do, and hesitation over a new step, the whole matter is suddenly taken out of our hands, and the question solved for us in a moment, and in the most summary way. Lady William had found many reasons for resisting the advice, whether given in love or enmity, of her friends. Her husband's family had not been hostile to her, but it had been bitterly indifferent, taking no notice, making no inquiry into her condition or that of her child, and she had but small inducement to endeavour to draw closer that very loose and artificial tie which united her to the great people. It seemed to herself a sort of accidental tie, meaning so little to any body except to herself—and to herself whose whole life it had shaped, it was no pleasure to recur to the few years of marriage in which she had been taken so entirely out of her sphere without attaining anything else that was of pleasure or advantage to her. Sometimes she had been tempted to ask herself whether that was more than a terrible dream, a sort of fever through which she had passed, and at the end of which she had found herself back again in her native place, among the quiet scenes of her childhood, but with a different name, a changed personality, and Mab—the greatest sign of all that things were not as they had been. The Rector and his wife, however, did not take into consideration the great indifference of the family to Lady William and her child. They knew but little about the details. Mrs. Plowden for one could scarcely have got into her head that to be Lady William, to have lived in France, as well as in the great world, and to have grown familiar with many things that appeared very grand and delightful to a country lady who had never moved out of her parish, was perhaps to be rather humiliated than elevated both in one's own opinion and in that of the world. Such an idea

could have found no place in her intelligence. And she had not
the slightest doubt that Lord and Lady Portcullis, if it were
properly represented to them, would do their duty by their niece
if not by their sister-in-law. She thought it was Emily's pride
which alone stood in the way. And though her husband knew
the world better, yet he, too, was of opinion that it was chiefly
Emily's pride. Mrs. Swinford's thoughts on the subject were of
a very different complexion, even before she had thrown that
horrible uncertainty into Lady William's mind, that feeling that
even her position, so modest as it was, might be assailed and
turned into shame. If she had held back hitherto it was not
from pride nor from fear of inquiry, but from a doubt whether it
would be of the least advantage to her child to make any overtures or petition. Petition, that was the right word—and a
petition which was more or less likely to be rejected, as she
felt sure.

She was seated in her little drawing-room full of these doubts
and questions one morning very soon after the FitzStephens' ball.
It seemed impossible now that things could go on as they were.
The mere fact of all that had been said on the subject shook the
foundations of life. And Mab's age made a change in everything.
So long as she was a child, the obscurity of her position was of no
consequence. All that was needed for her was her mother's care,
and to be with her mother wherever she might happen to be; but
with every day the position changed. Lord William Pakenham's
child was one thing, and Emily Plowden's another. Was it her
duty to let Mab grow up in the humbler region, perhaps fix her
own fate in that, and settle for ever as a poor man's wife in the
village, while another world might be open to her? Had she any
right to bind her child to her own limited fortunes, to keep her all
her life a mere pensioner on the bounty of those who ought to
recognise and care for her in a very different way? But if she
made any attempt to alter the position, might she not make it
worse instead of better? Might she not subject herself only, and
Mab, who was of more consequence, to a repulse which would be
much worse than neglect, to perhaps a question even of the humble
rights which had been already recognised, the right of the widow
and child to a subsistence, however doled out? The thought of
having to fight for those rights, to open up the secrets of her life,
and prove that she had a right to her name, was an idea intolerable
to Lady William. She said to herself with a sick heart that she
would rather die—she would rather die! Oh, that would be an
easy way out of it; but that she should die and leave Mab behind

her to fight it out, to prove her own lawful birth, her mother's honour, that was impossible. If she were to die she must climb out of her grave, she felt, to prevent that, to take the brunt upon herself, to save from such a horrible struggle the child, the little girl who did not know what dishonour was—Mab, of all creatures in the world, to have any stain upon her of any kind! Then Lady William tried to brace herself up to think that she must no longer hesitate, that for Mab's happiness she must venture everything, and prove at last, beyond any question, that whatever her fate might be there could never be in it any doubt or possibility of shame.

She was seated thinking of all this, her needlework going mechanically through her hands, her head bent, and every faculty occupied with this debate within herself, when she heard the little click of the gate which announced a visitor, and then the rap of Patty's knuckles upon the door. 'If you please, my lydy, it is Mr. Swinford and a strange gentleman. Am I to say as your lydyship's at home?'

'Did I ever tell you to say I was not at home, Patty?'

'I don't know, my lydy. You wouldn't speak to me not for two days, 'cause I let Mr. Leo come in.'

'You are a little nuisance,' said Lady William, which was enough to make Patty's heart dance as she rushed along the narrow passage to answer—what was not yet, however, a knock at the door.

For the two gentlemen had met Mab in the garden. Mab was very busy in the garden in the end of April. She had a hundred things to do. She had a large apron with pockets heavy with all kinds of necessities covering her dress, and a very homely hat upon her head—one of those broad articles plaited of brown rushes, which are called reed hats, and may be bought for sixpence anywhere. It was not unbecoming, though it was entirely without decoration. Mab's hair was slightly untidy from much stooping over the flower-beds, and her cheeks were flushed by the same cause. She had fortunately large gardening gloves on, which kept her hands from the soil and pricks which were too familiar to them. Mab met the two young men as they came in. She was hurrying past with a box full of roots in one arm. But she was not in the least embarrassed by the encounter. She put the trowel which she carried in the other hand, among the roots, and stopped to speak. 'I am very busy,' she said. 'It is beautiful this morning, isn't it? but we shall have rain before night. So it is just the very opportunity to put in my carnations. They are a little late, but I was waiting for some good kinds.'

Of course, while she spoke to Leo her eyes had wandered to the other man with him, who was of quite a different kind—younger than Leo, still in the twenties, Mab thought, and not handsome; but surely she had seen him somewhere before. He was fair, like herself, with blunt features, and eyes that were blue, but not bright. In every way his appearance was quite different to that of Leo Swinford—no foreign air about him—clothes that looked much less thought of and cared for, more carelessly worn, but somehow giving, Mab could not tell how, a more perfect effect. She gave him a friendly glance, though she did not know him. But, indeed, she did not feel at all as if she did not know him. She was confident that the face was quite familiar to her, and that she must have seen him before.

'I have brought a friend to introduce to you, Miss Mab: and I expect you to be friends at once, although you have never seen each other before.'

'Have I never seen him before?' said Mab. 'Perhaps you are mistaken, Mr. Leo. I am sure I know his face, though I don't know his name.'

And then the young men both laughed. 'I will tell you where you have seen his face—in your own glass when you dress in the morning—I am sure you never look at it afterwards. This is Lord Will Pakenham, Miss Mab, and to be sure you ought to have known each other all your lives.'

'Lord Will——' Mab grew very red from the tip of her chin to the untidy locks on her forehead. 'Does that mean Lord William—my father's name?'

'And I am your cousin Will,' said the young man.

Mab paused a few moments longer before she held out to him her big gardening glove. 'I do not remember my father,' she said, 'so you cannot remind me of him. Did we ever—perhaps when we were little children—see each other before?'

'Every time,' said Leo, 'did I not tell you, that you have looked in the glass.'

I do not know what was the effect at that moment upon Lord Will, but the impression on Mab's mind was one full of pleasure. These other people, with their clean-cut features, Leo himself, her cousin Emmy, who had the impertinence to be like Mab's own mother, who belonged to her—were a sort of reproach to the girl. But here was somebody who had a blunt nose, and eyes which were rather dull in colour, like her own, and who looked friendly, homely, as if he did not mind—who also smiled upon her in a very natural way, as if he too felt that he had known her all his life.

'Stop,' said Mab, suddenly drawing off her glove with her white, strong, small teeth. 'This time my hand is cleaner than my glove.' She caught the glove in her other hand as it fell. If she had been a year older, of course she would not have done it : and her frock was short and her manner entirely at ease. Though she had been at a dance, and might be supposed to have come out, she was still Lady William's little girl.

'Come in to mother ; she will be glad to see you,' she added immediately. 'I can't go into the drawing-room, can I, with all this ? and I must get these put in before I do anything. Mr. Leo, please go in to mother ; you know the way.'

Next minute Leo was presenting Lord Will to Lady William. It was a very curious scene. She rose up in the midst of her thoughts, wondering, questioning with herself what she was to do, and heard in a moment her husband's name pronounced in her ears. The effect was so great that as she rose hastily from her chair the blood forsook her face altogether. She held by the table before her, letting her work fall out of her hand.

'Dear lady,' said Leo, 'we have startled you. I ought to have known.'

'Whom did you say ? '

'I am William Pakenham,' said the young man. 'I beg you ten thousand pardons. Swinford has brought me to make acquaintance with—my relations.'

She sank back into her chair, and for a moment covered her eyes with her hand. 'You must forgive me,' she said, 'I am very foolish ; but the sound of your name so suddenly in the midst of all I was thinking——' She paused a little, and then looked up at him. A smile came upon her face. She felt like one who has looked up and, expecting to see some painful apparition, sees instead a smiling face. 'You are like my Mab,' she said, tears coming with a rush to her eyes.

'So Swinford tells me ; but I am not like my uncle.'

Lady William did not say anything, but something in her eyes, something in the momentary tremor of her lips, seemed to say, 'Thank God.'

It was an exceedingly awkward, stupid, uncalled-for remark upon the part of Will Pakenham, who knew that his uncle had been a scamp, but did not know whether or not his wife might have cherished his memory all the same. There are some wives who deify a blackguard after he is gone. But the visitor was young, and this possibility did not occur to him.

'You have been living here,' he said, 'a long time.'

It may be supposed that Lady William was very much shaken
out of her usual self-command before she would allow the stranger
to take the conversation thus into his own hands, and to begin an
interrogatory examination.   It was not so much the suddenness of
his introduction that had this effect upon her, as the bewilderment
of thoughts in which she was involved when these intricacies were
thus cut as by a knife, by the appearance of such an astonishing
and unexpected figure upon the scene.   She began now, however,
to recover herself, and to realise that these questions were not at
all of the manner in which she chose to permit herself to be
addressed.   Accordingly, though she smiled in reply, she gave no
other answer, but turned to Leo, who stood by watching her, and
by no means at his ease.

'You were telling us the other day of the ladies of the family,'
she said, with a half-reproachful smile; 'but you did not tell us of
Lord Will——'

How quick she was, seizing the diminutive which made the name
less dreadful to her—though she had never heard it before!

'We are old friends,' said Leo; 'but I did not think—in short,
it is years since we saw each other.   He has come on purpose to
make your acquaintance, and his cousin's.'

'He is very good,' Lady William said, with a little bow towards
him.   'I have been here for many years open to a visit.   And you,
are you adopting any profession or service? or are you merely a
gentleman at large?'

She smiled upon the young man with her usual gracious
reserve; and he began clearly to perceive that questions to her
were practicable no more.   He answered, 'Oh, Coldstreams,' a
little awkwardly, feeling somehow that this lady in the little
cottage, whose daughter did her own gardening, and who had a
little charity girl for a servant, had put him back in his own place.

'That is a great deal better than doing nothing,' said Lady
William; 'but it is not very hard work.   I thought you were all
adopting professions, to work hard, you young men about town.
Has your father come to town yet?'

'My father?' said Lord Will vaguely.   'Oh, he's——somewhere fishing.   My mother comes up after Easter.   The governor's
not very fond of town,'

'And your uncle John?——'

'Oh——' said the young man, colouring a little, 'we thought
you would be sure to see it in the papers—everybody is supposed
to see everything in the papers: he died about a fortnight ago.'

'Died!'

' Well, he was rather an old fellow, don't you know,' said Will in an apologetic tone, 'and lived hard. I don't think it was ever expected he'd have dragged on so long.'

' In France,' said Lady William, 'there is such a thing as a *faire part*. They don't exist in England, I suppose ?'

' They are hideous things in France,' said Leo, with a shiver, ' when you get a letter black to your elbow with a long string of names which you don't know, till you come to one little one at the end——'

' They are better, however, than no information at all.'

' Oh, I hope you will not think there was any incivility meant. I myself heard my mother say that you must be informed. There was a search through all the address books, but we could not find at first where you lived. And then I volunteered——'

' To come here, of all places in the world—next door to my cottage ! How extraordinarily acute your *flair* must be, my dear Lord Will !'

' It's not that,' said the young man, very red. 'I knew that Swinford knew you. He wrote to one of the girls, saying what a stun—I mean that you were in his neighbourhood, and about your daughter, and all that——'

' Perhaps it was the first intimation you had of our existence,' she said.

' Oh, no—no ; don't think so. Besides, you are in the peerage; there can be no mistake about that.'

' That is an honour I didn't think of. And so your uncle John is dead ? He was a very strange man—not like any of the family——'

' Not at all like the rest of us. None of the others had ever two sixpences to rub against each other. He has died leaving a great fortune.'

' A great fortune !' said Lady William, startled.

The young man looked as if he had said more than he intended. ' A—a good deal of money,' he said. 'I don't mean a great fortune as people think of fortunes nowadays. A good bit of money.' He paused a little as if unwilling to go further, then quickly throwing the words from him like a stone, ' And no will,' he said.

'So,' said Mrs. Swinford, 'you have seen your dear aunt.'

Lord Will had arrived in the afternoon, and she had scarcely seen him until dinner. After that meal—in the moment always anxiously awaited when there is any subject to talk of, when the servants had left the room—she entered into conversation. It was not by her invitation that he had come to the Hall—neither, of course, were any of the circumstances of her arranging. Sometimes, strangely enough, when there is an evil deed to be done, Providence will seem to arrange all the circumstances for it with special care—to give the intending sinner a clearer light for the resistance of temptation, or to commit him to his evil choice and inevitable doom. Thus Mrs. Swinford's whole soul was set upon the ruin of Lady William—if she could fathom it—and the chain of possibilities seemed woven for that end.

'Yes,' said Lord Will, though a little embarrassed by this description, 'I have seen Lady William : and being a dear aunt whom I never saw before, and whom I did not expect to be proud of, she is the greatest piece of luck I ever came upon. You know her, I suppose?'

'Know her!' said Mrs. Swinford, with that little continuous laugh which was like the tingling of an electric bell. 'Indeed, I know her—to my cost.'

'Ah ! there's mischief in her, then?'

'There are always old sores in a friendship of twenty years. Isn't that true, mother? But whatever they are, they must be of very old date, and there can be no reason for bringing them forward now.'

Thus Leo, who was evidently very uneasy, and had showed symptoms of rising from the table though his mother had as yet given no sign.

'Leo,' said Mrs. Swinford, 'has fallen under the fascination

which a woman of that age often exercises—too old to be
dangerous, but old enough to know how to make herself very
agreeable.'

'Oh, she's very agreeable,' said Lord Will; 'as for fascination,
one doesn't associate it somehow with the name of an aunt, don't
you know.'

'That is true, but you see she is not everybody's aunt. To
some people she is——'

'I should say to everybody a charming woman. Do you take
your coffee downstairs to-night, mother?'

'I know what you mean, Leo: but coffee or no coffee, you
must understand that I have a great deal to say to Lord Will.
It may be now, or it may be later—but I have a great deal to
say——'

'I need not tell you I am entirely at your disposition, Mrs.
Swinford.'

'You know,' said Leo, almost angrily, 'it is bad for your health
to stay up late: and Will wants a glass of wine, or perhaps to knock
about the balls a little——'

'I hope I don't look like a fellow to knock about balls—when
I have so much better within reach——'

'It's always well,' said Mrs. Swinford, 'to know how to turn a
compliment. Will you now give me your arm upstairs like a
Frenchman, or wait like a Britisher till you have had your glass of
wine?'

'Perish the glass of wine!' said Lord Will with a laugh,
'though I hear ladies say nowadays that they like the British
fashion best.'

'These are strong-minded ladies, who are, I believe, the fashion,
too—whom the men don't care for, and who, consequently, pretend
not to care for the men.'

'Well, that's very flattering to us, at least,' said Lord Will.
He was perhaps a little too much in the movement of his time to
accept it as the gospel it has always been supposed to be, and was
even a little disposed to laugh in his sleeve at the antiquated
charmer who held by that old doctrine. Mrs. Swinford's air of the
ancient seductrice and devourer of men was not a new thing to this
experienced youth.

'It comes to much the same thing,' said Leo, 'for the Frenchmen adjourn for their cigarette after they have reconducted the
ladies. Come, mother, let him be English for to-night. I have
something to say to him, too.'

'My son,' said Mrs. Swinford, with the blandest smile, 'Lord

Will shall choose between us.   I am not going to exercise any
pressure, or pull against you.'

The natural result, of course, was that in a minute or two more
Mrs. Swinford was established in the great drawing-room in her
favourite chair, just within reach of the influence of the blazing,
cheerful fire, amid the banks of flowers and pleasant twinkling of
the lights, with Lord Will before her, at her feet.

' We need not detain you, Leo,' she said, with a nod and a smile ;
' I know your liking for this hour by yourself.'

' I have no choice of one hour more than another by myself,'
said Leo, ' and I, too, prefer the company of my guest to my
own.'

' Go, dear boy,' she said, kissing the tips of her fingers.   ' I
prefer that you should not remain : I have a great deal to say, and
it is grave.   You can say your say afterwards.   At present, I
don't want to be contradicted.   It puts me out.'

Leo looked at her with an earnest remonstrance in his eyes,
but she continued to nod and smile at him, waving him away with
that action of her arm which had once been so graceful and playful.
Leo had been brought up to think all his mother's movements
graceful, and herself the most distinguished of women.   But there
was a painful sense of unwilling ridicule in his mind as he looked
back at her waving him away, placed in the most careful pose in
the great chair, and with the young man, much perplexed between
curiosity and embarrassment, and a sense of ridicule, too, in the low
chair at her feet.   He withdrew into the shade beyond the pillars,
but he did not go away.   His mother could still see him moving
in the partial dark, standing staring at a half-seen picture, or
taking up and throwing down again book after book.

' We are not to be left quite alone,' she said, shrugging her
shoulders ; ' Leo acts sheep-dog.   It is a new rôle for him.   But
whether it is in my interest or yours, Lord Will, I cannot tell.'

' There can be only one of us who is in any danger,' said the
young man.

' I might say that was enigmatical still : but I will receive it
as I am sure it is meant, and I congratulate you upon a very pretty
turn of speech.   Few young Englishmen deserve that.   My Leo I
used to think--but he is getting heavy in England, as most young
men do.'

To this Lord Will, who was much intent upon the revelations
to be made to him, was prepared with no reply ; and serious as
this old woman's meaning was, and fatal in intent, she was nevertheless half disappointed that he did not continue a little the

badinage with which she would have been pleased to preface what she had to say. She had an eye to serious interest even in desiring to prolong this moment. For no man likes to see his old mother imitating the coquette, and it might have resulted in sending Leo away.

'I think I heard you say — and you must pardon me for interfering with your family affairs — that there was a question of money involved in your coming here to see after these unknown relations?'

'Yes,' said Lord Will, straightening himself up with relief; 'there is money. My uncle John died the other day, rich, and without a will. There were only two other brothers, my father and my Uncle William. In that case, Uncle William's heirs would come in for half the estate.' He stopped with a little embarrassment. 'And my father was of opinion—my mother thought—— It seemed a little hard perhaps that people we know nothing of— and then, for his rank, and with all he has to keep up, my father is a poor man.'

'So you came to see——?'

Whatever her own motives might be, Mrs. Swinford had no thought of letting off a culprit of another kind. The young man grew red under her searching eye. 'You thought it a pity,' she went on, 'that the money you could spend so much better should be wasted upon a couple of insignificant women—who perhaps had never heard, never knew that they had any claim to it, so would have been none the worse?'

'You take me up too sharply,' answered Lord Will. 'I don't think I meant anything like that. I meant that it was best to see something of them—to know something. My father has given Lady William an allowance all along. I don't know that he was compelled to do it. He has not abandoned his brother's widow. We thought that perhaps——'

'I will not ask what you find so much difficulty in putting into words. What would your father say to any one who gave him a chance of proving—that Emily Plowden was not William Pakenham's widow at all?'

She had lowered her voice, but yet spoke with such a keenness of meaning that she was heard further than she intended. Leo came striding out of the dark where he was, calling out in a voice of indignation, 'Mother!' She turned to him and waved her hand quickly, threateningly, without any of the former consciousness of a gracious pose.

'Go away!' she cried, 'go away, go away! What I am saying

is not for you. Go away, Leo Swinford, or you may hear something you will like still less—go away, go away!'

'Swinford,' said Lord Will, standing up, 'this you see is too serious to be suppressed. Whether it's fact or not, don't you see I must hear out what your mother has got to say?'

Leo did not make any reply. He retired again to the darker part of the room, but instead of lounging about drew forward a chair almost ostentatiously, and placed himself therein.

'I see,' said Mrs. Swinford, with a laugh, 'the Devil's Advocate—on the part of his client. That will not make any difference. Would you like me to tell you how these two came together? I can do so in every detail.'

'The question for me is,' said Lord Will, after a pause: for to tell the truth, being a young man with a clear view of his own interests, but no wickedness in him, nor desire to harm his neighbours—at least no more than was essential to benefit himself—he was a little frightened by the gleam of devilry in Mrs. Swinford's eyes; and he was well enough aware—as people in society are aware of everything of the kind—that there was something about Mrs. Swinford herself which had kept her out of England for so long. 'The question for me is simply about the marriage. If there is scandal there is no use in raking up old scandals; besides, whatever happened before, if she is his wife and the girl his child, nothing else matters to us. I am sure it would be all very interesting—but you see——'

'I am not going to rake up old scandals,' Mrs. Swinford said, 'but as it all happened within my knowledge—— She was here—a pretty little country girl, nothing more. She has immensely improved—quite, quite a different creature. A girl I had taken a fancy to. I am not sure that she did not teach Leo a little. That was her standing, the daughter of the parish clergyman.'

'That I am sure she did not,' said Leo from behind; 'you forget that I had a governess, mother.'

'Oh, you are there still, old Truepenny! You seem practising for the ghost in *Hamlet*, Leo. No, decidedly I cannot go on while he is there. It shall be for another time. To-morrow you will come to me in my boudoir before you go away.'

Lord Will looked round to his friend with an appealing air. Then going up to him, 'Swinford,' he said, 'like a good fellow, let me hear it all now. I must know it.'

'In order, if you can, to keep what is theirs from two helpless women?'

'I want to keep nothing that is theirs from any one,' said the young man, with an angry flush.

'And yet it appears this is what you came here for. But forewarned is forearmed. Yes, you shall hear it all now; I will not interfere.'

'Is he gone?' said Mrs. Swinford, 'really gone? Leo is the most scrupulous and delicate of men. He hates your talk of the clubs, gossip and scandal, as he calls it. If I had brought him up in England would it have been so? Shut the door, and draw the curtain, Lord Will. I have the temperature kept up as well as I can, but there are always cold winds about.' She shivered a little and drew round her a film of a white shawl that had been hanging over her chair. 'Now come back and put yourself there. Now I may speak my mind.'

'You must know,' she went on after all had been done as she ordered, 'that your uncle William was a great deal here in this house—a very great deal—it was a kind of home to him. I cannot say that I myself remarked that he had been attracted by Emily Plowden, but I have told you that she had a certain bread-and-butter-prettiness. I do not say *beauté de diable*, for it was neither *beauté*, nor had she enough in her for the devil to have anything to do with it. Youth alone sometimes attracts a man. *Enfin*, I never saw anything of it: but one evening, nay, it was pretty late—he came to me '—she paused a little and drew a long breath—'to tell me—it was a confused story—something about having committed himself. Mr. Swinford, Leo's father, was a little like Leo, but more English, more rigid. He burst in while this was being explained to me, took up a false idea, got what you call the wrong end of the stick——' She spoke not with her usual ease, but with strange breaks of breathlessness. ' 'Enough, he got it all wrong, completely wrong from beginning to end, and stormed and made a scene. And when he understood that it was Emily who was concerned — Emily had always been a great favourite,' with the electrical tinkle running through her words, 'he insisted that a marriage should take place at once. She left our house late that night, escorted by your uncle: and what happened I cannot tell. I never met her again except in Paris, where she was called Lady William, but saw no society, except the sort of men among whom your poor uncle, by that time heartbroken and misunderstood——'

'But why heartbroken—if he had been in love with her?'

'You are an innocent young man,' said Mrs. Swinford, tapping him on the shoulder with her fan. 'Oh, a very innocent dear boy! You don't think what a man like that would feel with a creature like her—a country girl tied to him, and no doubt leading him a life! She kept him—from saying a word to me, watching over him like a cat over a mouse. He was burning to tell me— something; I know not what. My husband also was much pre- judiced, and would not let us meet. So that I never heard his secret, if there was a secret, as I suppose there must have been. I have never seen her again till I saw her last month, shining as Lady Wil- liam, and believed in by all the country folk—taking precedence,' Mrs. Swinford cried with her little laugh, throwing up her fine hands, with all her rings flashing, 'upon next to nothing a year.'

'But she was acknowledged by my uncle as his wife.'

'She was called Lady William among the sort of *demi-monde* they lived in. But what happened between the time she left my house and the time I saw her there——'

'Do you mean to say that my uncle eloped with this young lady, Mrs. Swinford?'

'My dear Lord Will, you are young, but you know the world. They left the house together, late at night. I tell you, quite late, after midnight. He, a man who was known to be—well, not the safest for women: and she a country girl of nineteen—oh, very well able to take care of herself, but as silly and ignorant as they usually are: and—I know no more.'

Mrs. Swinford threw up her hands again, with the dazzling rings. There was a thrill and tremble in her whole frame with the excitement of the story, which was so elaborately false yet so nearly true. The young man had not seated himself a second time. He stood leaning upon the mantelpiece, his head bent, looking down upon the blazing fire.

'And you?' he said, 'you allowed a girl to go out of your house like that—a girl, unprotected?'

'What could I do?' said Mrs. Swinford. 'I was not her keeper, neither was I in command of affairs. I tell you that my husband insisted——'

'For the marriage, you said, for a marriage—that was very different.'

'Ah, you are *difficile!* And she, a hot-headed girl full of her own attractions, do you think she would be restrained——'

'From leaving home with her lover in the dead of night?'

'Her lover!' cried Mrs. Swinford, with the tingling laugh; 'her lover!'

'Was he not her lover? For heaven's sake say what you mean.'

XXVIII LADY WILLIAM

There was a little pause again, through which her laugh ran on, as if she could not stop it when once it had begun. Lord Will was the first to speak. He said: 'All this is very curious and dramatic and strange; but the one question of my uncle's marriage is, after all, the chief thing. I don't think my father ever entertained any doubt. It is in the peerage——'

'That is no proof,' said Mrs. Swinford sharply.

'I know; but still—my father was sent for at his death. There was no suspicion. I have heard that it was a *mésalliance*, but that is all I have ever heard.'

'Your father arrived when he was dying, had no communication with him, nor had any of his true friends. She kept them away. Lord Will, perhaps we have talked on this question long enough; it is no matter to me, it is only you who are affected. If there is money involved it is of the more consequence. You will require proof of the marriage before you do anything further. That is all you have to do. Ask her to send in her certificates, child's birth, and all that. Women of that class are very wary; they generally see after their papers. I have thought it over; I thought it all over before I made up my mind to speak to you. I felt that I could not allow what might be a great wrong to be done to the family of one who was once a dear friend——'

Mrs. Swinford put her handkerchief lightly to her eyes; it was scarcely substantial enough to have imbibed one tear. And there were perhaps other reasons why tears would have been out of place; but, had they existed at all, they would have been not dew, but fire.

XXIX

Lord Will was greatly impressed, as may be supposed, by that interview with Mrs. Swinford. When he joined Leo downstairs he had very little to say. He had not the heart to play a game at billiards, but knocked the balls a little vaguely, and took the refreshment which was given to him while he puffed at his cigar. 'I say, Swinford, your mother and this aunt of mine don't seem to hit it off,' he said.

'Don't they?' said Leo. 'I don't know, indeed; they were great friends once.'

'Which makes women hate each other all the more when they fall out.'

'Does it?' said Leo. 'You seem to know so much. I am older, but my knowledge is much less.'

'By Jove!' said Lord Will. 'You ought to have learnt a thing or two,' and then he became suddenly silent, thinking it would be very difficult if he were called upon to explain himself. Leo did not ask any questions, but he was not indifferent to what his friend said.

'I think you should not take anybody's opinion,' he said. 'If you want to know about your aunt, go and see her for yourself.'

'I've done that, thanks to you, Swinford; and I thought her stunning—that's the truth. But you see there's money in it, and we're not to call rich at Pakenham. It would be a deal pleasanter for my father to keep all Uncle John's money than to divide with a lady who perhaps has no real right. Don't jump up in that way —I think her stunning. But still you know that's a very queer story of Mrs. Swinford's. Uncle Will was no end of a bad old man, I've always heard. Why mightn't he do that as well as the rest?'

'I do not know,' said Leo, who had grown pale, 'what your

respected uncle is supposed to have done. He may have been the greatest reprobate that ever lived; but I do not see how that furthers your case. I presume there must have been two of them before it would do you any good; and the man who will endeavour to cast a blemish upon that lady—well, I may say he will have to do with me first.'

'Swinford! for goodness' sake don't take up that tone. Why, what have you to do with it? Do you mean to challenge me? These are your French ways—you know as well as I do they're no go here.'

'The more's the pity, when it is a question of injuring a woman!' said Leo, whose moustache had taken a warlike twist, and every nerve in his person seemed strung.

'I don't want to injure her; but if you think fifty thousand pounds or so—that's a nice bit of money to hand over for no motive but sheer love of justice — if it should turn out perhaps—'

'If what should turn out?'

'Well—that perhaps they had no real right. I don't mean that it would be their fault. She might have been taken in, and never known. I've always heard he was a horrible old scamp, up to everything—and would have cheated you as soon as look at you. It would be nothing wonderful if he had cheated a girl who, I suppose, was fond of him. A woman will be fond of anything that notices her, I believe. And fifty thousand pounds is a big bit of money to throw away.'

'Well, my friend,' said Leo, 'I am quite well aware that fighting is, as you say in England, no go; but I am bound also to allow that it is a farce in France, and that if it were ever so serious and real it is not a way to decide a question like this. However, let us try, if not to decide it at least to throw some light upon it.'

'Oh, that's easy enough done, old man,' said Lord Will. 'You needn't trouble yourself. She has a solicitor, I suppose, and he will have to send in all the papers to our man, and they'll manage it between them. Of course, if our fellow has a hint that there is anything irregular he will be more particular. That's more or less what I came for, don't you know: to see what she had heard about old John, and so forth, and what she expected and——'

'What you say,' said Leo, 'sounds as if you meant—that you were to try whether she could be made to be content with less than her rights—with anything that it was thought well to give. I don't suppose that is what you mean.'

'It's kind of you to add that much,' said Lord Will, who had stopped in his amusement of knocking about the balls, which he had been doing savagely, to stare in a threatening way at his friend. Then he threw down the cue and began to walk up and down the hall. 'Swinford,' he said after a while, coming back to the table, 'do you know that is, I believe, exactly what I was intended to do? I knew it in a kind of a way, but I never put it into words. I believe they thought she might have been put off with a thousand pounds or two, as if it had been a legacy.'

'But your lawyers—I suppose they have a character to lose— would not have consented.'

'Oh! there's no saying what lawyers will consent to when they're on your side. I note what you say, about having characters to lose. I suppose you think that we—haven't much, perhaps.'

'I did not mean that,' said Leo briefly.

'Well, perhaps you will now—but that would be a mistake. We're none of us lawyers. Don't you know that people sometimes take up an idea that looks quite allowable until you put it into words? Here's a woman living quite by herself in a corner, wanting very little money. And the governor, you know, has been making her an allowance all this time. What can she want with a lot of money like that? It would only worry her, make her think, perhaps, she could set up in a different way of living, and bring her to grief in the end. And she as good as owes the family her allowance all these years, which my father wasn't any way compelled to give. D'ye see? Well, it doesn't sound very high-minded, I allow, but it's very plausible. It would be no end of use to us—fifty thousand pounds, or say forty-five with five thousand or so off to her——'

'Oh! you mean to be so liberal as that!'

'By Jove! don't drive me to it, or I may—— Look here, don't let's quarrel, Swinford. It's so caddish. I never thought of the business, I tell you, from your point of view. It sounds very plausible. It's quite possible the lawyers wouldn't have stood it; I don't know. They never thought of the law, nor that she had any natural right, don't you see, to old John's money. They knew very well he would never have left it to her, when he knew how heavily the governor was dipped and all that. I fail to see even now what harm there was in it. The allowance, of course, would be continued, and five thousand pounds is as much to a woman living like that, as fifty is at home. It would have been an enormous windfall; that is what my mo—I mean what my people thought.'

Leo Swinford had a mind which was very tolerant, and he wanted of course, now he had calmed down a little, to make the best of it. He nodded his head, and said : 'I allow that perhaps it was plausible ; but I presume it would be felony all the same.'

'Felony,' said the other with a stare of astonishment—the word seemed to puzzle him. 'The governor is the head of the family,' he said vaguely, which somehow seemed a reason.

'It would be defrauding one of the heirs of an intestate person of her just share. The heir would be Mab, I suppose, not her mother.'

'Oh,' said Lord Will, quite confused ; what between the transference of the heirship, the inattention of his friend to his plea that his father was the head of the family, which to himself seemed to be a condition of importance, and the extremely big word that Leo had used, this young man, who was not clever, but who was not at all a bad fellow notwithstanding the mission in which his dull intelligence had not seen any harm, was quite bewildered, and did not know what to think.

'Yes,' said Leo, 'I don't know much about English law, but Mab no doubt would be the heir ; and any reasoning brought to bear upon her to make her accept a portion of her natural right in place of the whole, would be the same, I presume, as if you had stolen so much from her.'

'Oh, stolen ! rubbish !' cried Lord Will ; then he explained ingenuously, 'there was to be no reasoning brought to bear ; I was to inform them simply that Uncle John had left—a legacy.'

'That would have been what I believe is called in English—lying.'

'Swinford ! you mean, I think, to make me forget that I am your guest, in your house.'

'In French,' said Leo, taking no notice, 'it is called *mensonge*, and has sometimes interpretations more or less favourable. When you save your mother's reputation or your father's honour, as it is called, *mensonge* is the word, and you are not judged too severely ; but I have always heard that in England to lie was the worst offence.'

Lord Will was a little stupid, and therefore very placable. But this stung him to the quick. He knew what a lie meant, and though he felt a resistance and profound objection in himself to accept that dreadful word as representing his action, still, he felt there was a horrible resemblance between his intentions and that theory. Certainly the legacy would have been a lie. He did not see that though he had come to say this, he had already in the frankness which was far deeper down in his nature than any intention of guilt, committed himself to the actual truth. No consciousness of that fact softened his sensations. What Leo said was true. He had come not only to say but to act a lie.

'You're tremendously severe,' he said. 'I should knock you down by rights for hinting at such a thing.'

'Yes, you might,' said Leo, 'and you could if you liked. You are bigger than I am; but I don't see what difference that would make.'

'I don't either,' said Lord Will. And then there was a pause; he was not clear enough in his mind to stop there. 'But if this,' he said, 'that Mrs. Swinford tells me is true——'

'What did my mother tell you?'

'Well! you ought to care more about what she says than about any other woman's pretences. She says that it's very uncertain whether they were ever married at all. Look here, don't you know, it isn't me, it's your mother. She says they went off from her house together, eloping, as far as I could make out, in the middle of the night: and that the next time she saw them, she—this lady—was with my uncle in Paris and called Lady William. That's all. Of course, if it was a marriage she'll be able to prove everything about it; but if not, it does seem a little hard, dosen't it, that those fifty thousand pounds of old John's money should be lost? And you must remember, Swinford, it is your mother who says so; it is not I.'

Leo was silenced by this speech. He had not been prepared for so bold a statement, nor that Mrs. Swinford would interfere in such a way as this. Whence had she derived this hate against her old friend? His mind went back easily to the period when Emily Plowden was the pet of the house. He had only been a child, indeed, but a child remembers every detail which older people forget. And he remembered more vaguely, yet well enough, to have heard his father speak of Lady William after their establishment in Paris. Leo had not known very much of his father, who was a reserved man, and not demonstrative to the boy, who was his mother's toy and darling, a little drawing-room puppet, everything that an English father would most dislike in his son. Leo was aware of all this now, and exaggerated it, as was natural, his own later conduct in life having been revolutionised more or less by compunctions and repentances in respect to his father. He could not tell how it was that in a moment the image of that father leaped into his mind. It seemed to him that he could almost see the little scene—the ornate suite of rooms in Paris, his mother lying back scornful and splendid in a great chair, his father walking up and down in high indignation and something about Lady William on his lips. What it was he did not remember, but that his father had spoken in respect, he was sure. The recollection came to his mind like an assurance and pledge that all was well.

'You must take care,' he said, taking the cue which Lord Will had thrown down, and beginning in his turn to torture the balls, 'that the wish is not father to the thought. When it is for one's interest that a thing should be, it is so easy to persuade oneself that it is.'

'That is not my case, Swinford. I did hope I might have made something of the business; but to have it settled for good and all in this way was never in my thoughts. The governor himself never knew, nor any one. I don't believe he ever suspected——'

'And yet you are certain, all at once?'

'Well, not certain,' said Lord Will; 'but when a lady, a friend of the woman, with nothing in her mind but justice, I suppose——'

'My mother,' said Leo, 'has told you nothing from her own knowledge. She informs you of a possibility of wrong. Your own father was on the spot; he went over when his brother died, but he suspected nothing; and my father, a man of the highest honour, though I did not know him as I ought, suspected nothing. Take care how you let a mere insinuation—a doubt——'

'It was your mother who made it, Swinford.'

Leo was very pale, and an angry cloud came over his countenance. He turned round with an impulse of indignation towards the young man who forced this upon him. 'My mother,' he said, 'may be mistaken; she is human, like the rest of us. In the meantime, I think you are showing little knowledge of human nature, Pakenham. Do you think that lady whom you saw to-day could have lived as she has done for all these years under a burden of shame? and could look as she does if she knew that she might be found out any day?'

'Women are dreadful hypocrites,' said Lord Will. 'They can face things out in a way no man could do. Why, I've seen at home how things can be faced out—and no doubt so have you, too.'

'She is not of the kind to face things out.'

'Oh, I quite acknowledge she's a stunner, and all that. Reason the more why she should hold her own, and refuse to understand if a fellow dared to put a question—oh, not that I should ever dare to do that. I'm no more a coward than most other people, but say to a woman like that that I believed she wasn't rightly married, I'd sooner jump into the river any day with a bullet at my heel.'

'Which means simply that your inner man—the better part of you—is aware of the fact, which, for your interest, you would like to deny: that is all about it. I advise you to drop the idea, like a hot potato, as they say here. It is not true.'

'Prove that it isn't true, and I'll not say another word.'

'I prove it by simply pointing to the lady in question,' said Leo hotly.

'Oh, that! but even if I were to take that view, she mightn't know, herself. She might be deceived as well as the rest.'

A look of sudden alarm came upon Leo's face. Lady William was a person of high intelligence, but she was not a woman of the world. In the quick look he gave upward, in his way of returning to his aimless play, and the impatience with which he struck again the innocent balls, sending them coursing to every corner, the trouble of his mind might be guessed. This gave his visitor fresh courage.

'You needn't fear, Swinford,' he said, 'that I'll bully a—person like that. Whatever her position may be, there's nothing common about her, that's clear. I'll give our man a hint. Get it all clear about marriage and all that, and the proof of the child's birth and so forth—all in the way of business. You may trust me for that: not a word to her, but just what's necessary between the two solicitors, don't you know. I think now I'm going to bed.'

'I advise you,' said Leo, taking care not to see his companion's hand stretched out to him, 'to be careful how you discount your hopes. Do not count your eggs, as they say here, till they are hatched.'

'You mean the chickens: and I should not dream of putting the fifty thousand pounds in my own pocket. Why, man alive, it's not for me! I shan't get twenty thousand farthings of it, nor anything like that.'

'Ah, then you are hopeless, for you will feel yourself disinterested,' said Leo, so busy with the balls that once more he missed seeing Lord Will's hand stretched out.

'I say, Swinford, there's no ill-feeling, I hope.'

' Why should there be any ill-feeling?' said Leo, raising his
eyes for a moment with a benign but too radiant smile. He
turned to the balls again the next moment as he said lightly with
a wave of his cue, ' Good night.'

It is confusing, it must be allowed, to a plain intelligence, to
have one member of a family force information of the most serious
kind upon you, while another avoids shaking hands with you because you believe it. Such things happen, no doubt, in the world,
but they are rare, and Lord Will went upstairs to his room in a
very uncomfortable state of mind, not knowing which he should
depend on of those two conflicting powers. Leo remained for
some time after, still knocking about the balls. Morris, with
whom his master in the dearth of other companions had sometimes
played an occasional game, hung about in prospect of a call. But
Morris was disappointed, though it was perhaps an hour later
before Mr Swinford left that uninviting occupation. He went on
with the gravest face in the world, but very devious strokes, evidently as indifferent to what he was doing as he was overwhelm-
ingly serious in doing it. The click of the balls and of his steps
round the table gave a curious sound in the midst of the silence of
the great house. Such sounds say more of solitude than the most
complete stillness, and Leo's countenance was as grave as if he had
been playing, like a man in an old legend, with some unseen being
for his own soul.

It is not to be supposed that during this period the visits of Mrs. Brown, the schoolmistress, to her friend at the Hall, who was so like yet so unlike her—so unlike in personal importance—so superior in position, and yet so strangely resembling—should have ceased. There were no other two persons in all the precincts of Watcham so evidently belonging to the same world and species, and yet there were no two more separate in all those externals that distinguish life. Mrs. Brown's visits were almost all paid in the evening, sometimes very late, sometimes at that hour before dinner when Mrs. Swinford was known to receive no one. But there was no bar at any time against the entrance of this privileged visitor. On the evening which Lord Will spent at the Hall Mrs. Brown came late, while dinner was going on. She had an entrance of her own by which she preferred to come in, a door which gave admittance to the servants' quarters, but which was always open, and spared the schoolmistress the intervention of Morris, whom she did not dislike to see now and then, and meta-phorically put her foot upon with the pride of a superior knowledge which he could not understand. But this malicious gratification, though she enjoyed it occasionally, was not enough to make up for the disadvantage of having her movements known and chron-icled, and it suited her character and habits better to have a mode of access absolutely free and beyond control. She was so swift and subtle in her movements, and so fortunate, as the clan-destine often are, in finding her passage free, that on many occasions she had glided through the great house, mounted the great stairs, and appeared noiseless in the ante-room occupied by Julie, the maid, without an individual in the house being aware that she was there. It had so happened on this particular night when even Julie was out of the way. Mrs. Brown came in noiseless, slightly breathless, having hurried upstairs, and just escaped meeting a strange young

man, whose wide shirt-front indicated him in the partial darkness of the corridor as if he had carried a light, but whom to her
surprise she did not know. A woman with her wits so much
about her, knew by sight by this time everybody in the neighbourhood who was likely to dine with Leo. She avoided him by a
rapid step aside, and consequently she was a little out of breath
when she arrived in Julie's room, where there was no one, a
dereliction of duty that might have cost Julie her place had it been
known. Mrs. Brown looked round her with a nod of satisfaction
as she put off the heavy veil in which she was accustomed to wrap
herself on these visits. She went into the inner room, and
looked round with an even more vivid look of satisfaction. Mrs.
Swinford's luxurious room was as she had left it in the perfection
of silent repose and comfort—soft light, soft warmth, everything
that the most refined suggestion of luxury and ease could command. Mrs. Brown gave a sigh, and then a laugh. She said to
herself, ' How little a difference would have made me like this ! '
and then she said, ' What a bore it would have been ! ' The laugh
suited her better than the sigh. It called forth a twinkle of
mischief and lurking vagabondism in her eyes. She then lay
down on Mrs. Swinford's sofa, put back her head upon the cushions,
took up first one book, then another, and read a page or two.
Then she threw them down one after another, and looked round
the room again. How pretty it was ! Her eyes lingered for a
moment here and there on the pictures, the little graceful bronzes,
the prevailing ornament, the lights, carefully planned to the advantage of the decorations. And then a strange shadow came
over her face. Good heavens, to lie here, and remember! she said.
Perhaps in her energy of feeling, these words were said aloud. At
least, they brought in Julie, who had in the meantime returned to
her room, not suspecting the presence of this visitor, and who
peeped in suspicious, half-terrified, with her hand on her breast.
' C'est vous, Madame ? ' she said, with a look of mingled terror and
relief.

' Who else should it be, unless a thief ? ' said Mrs Brown.
' But as it might have been a thief and not me, you know, you
ought not to be absent, *ma chère.*'

Julie clasped her hands and entreated that Madame would
not say anything. ' This is not the house for thiefs,' she said.

' On the contrary, it is just the house. Don't you know all
the robberies of jewels are done when the family are at dinner ? '
Mrs. Brown rose from the sofa and took a low chair beside
the fire, where she continued to sit when she had dismissed

Julie much alarmed by the admonition. Many thoughts went through her mind while she waited, and she had a long time to wait. She compared her own vagabond lot, now up, now down, which she had led after her own wild fancy—the life rather of a man than of a woman—with this beauty and luxury, with a shudder of pity going over her. The pity was not for herself, but for the other woman shut in, in this gilded cage to —— remember! The pictures on the walls, the carefully arranged lights, the unchangeable surroundings, all luxury and brightness, affected her like a spell. Good heavens! to sit there day after day, evening after evening, and remember! Mrs. Brown thought of her own little rooms which it had given her pleasure to arrange and decorate in a manner which she felt to be fictitious and out of character, but which amused her all the same, and which she laughed at, having done it, with a full consciousness that it was trumpery, and that the trumpery was out of place, as a woman who knew better could not fail to see. 'Ah, well!' she said to herself, 'I'd rather have my trumpery that I can throw away any day, and probably shall some day, and that I can run away from when I like, when it gets too absurd.' And then there were the books : French novels, going over and over with fantastic variations the one story—the story of (so-called) love—that is, the complicated ways by which two people, generally old enough to know better, are brought into the relations of intrigue or passion with each other—which ends badly, either in the death of one or the disgust of both : and so *da capo*, always beginning over again. 'Good heavens!' said Mrs. Brown to herself again, 'how can she go on day after day, day after day, reading *that*—and remembering!' The schoolmistress had no objection to a French novel of this class herself now and then ; and reading only now and then—being within reach of such indulgences only now and then—naturally she got only the best, the ones that had wit and genius in them. But the unhappy woman who lived upon that food for ever! What garbage, what insipidity of nastiness must go through her hands! The poor Bohemian whose life was a continual scuffle (chiefly of her own choosing) looked upon this unvarying luxury, ease, and wealth, with a horror and wonder which it would be difficult to describe. 'Good heavens!' she repeated to herself; 'why doesn't she take a little chloral and be done?'

Mrs. Swinford gave a start of pleasure when, sweeping into her room in those long and splendid robes which were more fit for a Court than for a country house of so little distinction as the Hall at Watcham, she perceived Mrs. Brown sitting by the fire.

It was, perhaps, the only event which could have lighted up her
face with pleasure. She was cross, excited, full of the impatience and exasperation of effort which she felt to be at least only
half successful; and Julie had perceived by her first glance at
the lines on her lady's brow that her evening's task to undress,
and soothe, and persuade into calm and sleep this agitated and
disturbed old woman would be no easy one. 'You come at the
best time. You always know when I have need of you,' Mrs.
Swinford said, letting herself drop, as was her wont, into Mrs.
Brown's arms. The very passiveness of the embrace was a habit
—a habit of reliance and expected help which had never failed.
If such a thing as affection had ever been in Mrs. Swinford's heart
it was this other woman, so like her, and so unlike, who was its
object.

'I see you are got up for conquest,' Mrs. Brown said.

'Conquest! I am dressed as usual. There was one guest
at dinner—an insignificant boy. You can leave us, Julie, till I
ring. A boy, but with such a name! What do you think? A
nephew—Lord Will they call him fortunately, or it would have
been too much.'

'A nephew—— ! of——'

'Do you need to inquire? Then you are growing dull, dull
as your surroundings. You who used to understand everything *à
demi-mot* !'

'I understand. I almost met him on the stairs. I thought
there was something familiar in his face. And what does he
want here?'

'Is it necessary to ask? Might he not come to see me, or
Leo, whom he knows? But no, no, Artémise, I will not deceive
you. He has come to find out about that woman—her rights to
his name—which she has none, having stolen it, as you know;
and to some money that has fallen in, do I care how! He
could not have come to a better quarter. I gave him some
information.'

'What information?' said Mrs. Brown, sitting up in her chair.

'I told him all that I knew. You will please to remember
it is all I know: that she left the Hall hastily at midnight, that
I met her after in Paris bearing his name.' Mrs. Swinford, too,
sat upright, with a colour in her cheeks and a fire in her eyes
that recalled something of the beauty of old to her worn face.
'What do I know more? Nothing,' she said, with a movement of
her hands, which made the rings upon them flash and send out
rays like sparks of light.

'Ah! you told him that?'

'There is money in the question,' said Mrs. Swinford, leaning forward and speaking low, 'and their object is to find out that she has no rights. He took my hints like milk; they were balm to him. Fancy so many thousand pounds—I know no details—and if not to her they will go to him. Is not that worth the trouble?'

'To the man, perhaps, Cecile—but why to you?'

'To me much more than to him,' she said, with flashing eyes.

'Why?'

'You are stupid to-night,' said Mrs. Swinford coldly; 'not for a long time, for many years, have I found you so before.'

'Because,' said Mrs. Brown, 'this that you have said is, as you are aware, not——'

'Your scruples are engaging, they are beautiful, they are something to put in a story-book,' said the lady. 'You to stand for that! You, who——'

'It is better not to go too far. I have done a great many reckless things. I am a reckless woman altogether, and have not cared what became of me for many a long day: but I have never done anything like that. Ah yes, I have scruples; every one has, you even, if one knew where to look for them.'

'It was you,' said Mrs. Swinford, 'who made the suggestion at the first.'

'To save you, Cecile, to save you.'

'I should have found some other way to get out of it. There was never a difficulty yet but I found a way of getting out of it. I should have done so then, had you not come forward to say it was Emily—Emily, a child, a nobody—whom he loved, and that I was his confidante. I can see it all now. He had no escape. Artémise, I have loved you better than any woman all your life, and you repaid me by taking away from me—handing over to that girl——'

Her eyes were ablaze in her flushed yet withered face. Her whole frame was trembling with angry emotion. Mrs. Brown rose quickly and went to her, taking her hands, holding her fast. 'It is twenty years ago,' she said, 'and it was to save your honour, your position, everything, Cecile—your child, your wealth, everything you had in the world.'

'I can see the scene now as if it was yesterday—my husband there, blazing like white light. He never looked like that in his life but once. And he—confused, afraid—on the other side of me, trembling for me.'

'And a little for himself, Cecile.'

'Silence! If you say so, I will strike you. And you, with your smooth tongue—always with your smooth tongue. How many lies it must have told first to be capable of that!'

'For your sake; you know it was for your sake. If you remember all that, remember, too, how the storm died down in a moment, and all was well.'

'Well!' said the other. She leant back her head upon the breast of the woman whom she was accusing. 'If it had raged itself out, and done its worst, would not that have been better than all that has followed—the bitterness and the hate, and the horror, and that girl living at my very door, to make me mad?'

'Why did you see her, Cecile? You might have ignored her altogether, forgotten her existence.'

'You forget,' cried Mrs. Swinford. 'She is the great lady of the village—takes precedence'—she laughed out with a hysterical violence which shook her from head to foot—'precedence of me, if we were in the world together! Don't you know that? But it will soon come to an end,' she added, laughing again with that electric tinkle which wore out the nerves of all who heard her. 'What a good thing they are so sordid a family, those Pakenhams, loving money as other people love their children, whatever is dearest to them! She will be called on to prove every step, and she will not be able to prove one. And then!— we shall see what the village will think of her title and her precedence then.'

'You have been agitating yourself in the most imprudent, in the most foolish way. Where are your drops? Her precedence, poor thing, will not hurt you, but a long faint will hurt you. Cecile, must I call your maid to see you in this state, or will you be quiet and listen to me?'

'Give me my drops. I must not, I must not, have another attack. The doctor says so. Artémise, don't leave me, don't leave me!'

'I will, if you do not turn from this subject at once. Throw it away from you. What on earth is Emily Plowden, or Paken- ham, or whatever her name is, to you? Cecile, I begin to think a woman like you never learns, and that you are no better than a fool.'

While she said these words, however, Mrs. Brown was busy with the most affectionate cares, soothing the excited woman, bathing her forehead, rubbing her hands, administering the specific, loosening the elaborate dress, which made the heaving of the shrunken figure, and the strain of the emaciated throat, so much the more dreadful. The passion calmed down by degrees, and then Julie was summoned, and the robes of state replaced by a quilted dressing-gown, scarcely less fine, but more appropriate. After this the conversation was resumed in a less exciting vein. Mrs. Swinford was perhaps a little ashamed to have betrayed the fury of her feelings even to so trustworthy a confidante.

'It is fine to see a family like that,' she said, 'not carried away by passion, Artémise, like you and me. Love or revenge are not in their way, nor hatred; but money, money. To secure a few thousands, they will be my instruments, or any one's, to punish a traitor. And what you are horrified to think I should want to do, for such good reason as you know, they will do for nothing at all—for money, as I say.'

'Many people think money a much more sufficient reason than what you call passion,' said Mrs. Brown. 'And it will be well to keep your Lord —— whatever you call him, from knowledge of me, for I can spoil his little transaction.'

'Ah, you—you were there !'

The two women looked at each other, and Mrs. Swinford, notwithstanding her age and her knowledge of the world, was sensible of a sudden heat rising to the edge of her hair; not the blush that comes to more innocent faces, but that burning colour of shame at a self-betrayal which she ought to have been too strong to fall into. Mrs. Brown nodded her head gravely. 'You said you had no means of knowing, but you perceive that you have: and for me, I can make an end of any such pretension. He had better not come across my path.'

'You would not balk me, Artémise ?'

'I would balk him, as soon as look at him, and the family, bless them; and I would not bring the innocent to shame, not even for you.'

'Artémise ! after all we know of each other, such a pretension——'

'My dear Cecile, what I know of you is one thing, what you know of me is another. I have broken every law, especially of society; but to harm the innocent is what I have never done—at least,' she added after a moment, 'not in that way. And though I'd give my head for you, which is, of course, a figure of speech, I will not ruin Emily Plowden for you, and that's flat, whatever you may say.'

'Don't interfere, Artémise,' said Mrs. Swinford, with a sound of tears in her voice, 'don't, don't interfere. Go away, and let things take their chance. No doubt she must have other evidence; I was a fool not to think of that. But don't you, who are my nearest and dearest, go against me; don't interfere. It is not, it has never been, a fit position for you, wherever you are; go to London, where I will find a home for you, Artémise.'

'Do you think after standing out so long, I will consent to be dependent on you now—for a reason?' Then she laughed, changing her tone. 'If you can imagine a better place to hide myself in than the Girls' National School at Watcham,' she resumed, 'you have very much the advantage of me.'

IT was not very often the Rector found time to visit his sister. They saw each other constantly at the Rectory, at church, in the village street, in all sorts of places, almost every day; but his visits were few, especially such a visit as the present. He paused at the further end of the garden and called over the hedge to Mab, to know if her mother was alone. 'I have got some business to talk over,' Mr. Plowden said. 'Take the trouble, will you, Mab, to see that no one comes in to disturb us.'

Mab thought it curious that, thus for two days within a week, her mother should have private business with Uncle James; but she said nothing except a ready assent to what he asked of her. 'I'll come towards the gate,' she said; 'I've got some things to put in on that border, and if any one comes that I can't send away, you will hear me talking with them, Uncle James.' She walked through the garden with him, so to speak, she on one side of the hedge, he on the other. 'Fancy who turned up yesterday,' she said; 'a cousin whom, of course, I never saw before—a Lord William like my father; but fortunately they called him Lord Will.'

'Lord William!' cried the Rector, 'a Pakenham—a son of the Marquis! Did he come to see you, or—for—for anything special?'

'I don't know what he wanted,' said Mab. 'To see us, I suppose. The funny thing is, he is like me. From this you may imagine he is not a beautiful young man, Uncle James.'

'I don't know why I should imagine that; I like your looks very well, my dear.'

'Thank you, Uncle James,' said Mab, with a laugh. 'He is staying at the Hall, and I think he said that he would come back this morning, so, of course, if he comes I cannot send him away.'

'I understand,' said the Rector, with a countenance somewhat troubled. And he went into the little drawing-room, where Lady William rose up to meet him looking a little anxious. 'You, James!' she said. 'I did not expect, especially at this hour, to see you.'

'I can't see why you should not have expected me, Emily; our last interview was serious enough,' he said, shutting the door carefully behind him : and then he went across the room to the window, which was open. Being so nearly on a level with the garden it would, of course, have been easy enough for any one to hear from outside whatever conversation was going on within.

'You frighten me with these precautions, James.'

'There is nothing to be frightened about. You may imagine I have been thinking a great deal of what you told me the other day.'

'Yes : and I heard Mab tell you the new incident.'

'The appearance of the cousin? What is the signification of that, I wonder? But let us take the other, which is more important, first. Did you know my father kept a diary, Emily?'

'I have seen him making little notes in various little books : but it is so long ago.'

'And you were not here, of course, when we came into the Rectory. I found a quantity of these little books in the study, little calendars and almanacs, and so forth. I didn't pay much attention to them—that is, I looked into one or two and they didn't seem interesting. Queer, when people might really make such a record important, and they put in the merest trifles instead.'

'"Chronicle small beer,"' she said, with a faint smile ; but she was pale with an interest much deeper than any record of public events could have commanded.

'Eh?' said the Rector, who was not literary ; 'but I thought it might be just possible—so I have been making a hunt through them, and I came upon something that might—that must help us.'

'Thank God!' she said, clasping her hands instinctively together.

'We must not be too sanguine : and yet, of course, a dead man's diary is evidence itself in a way.'

'Tell me,' she cried, with excitement, 'tell me what papa said.'

'Nearly twenty years ago,' said the Rector, with a little emotion. 'It's like hearing the old man talk—with abrupt sentences, don't you know—just as he spoke.'

'What does he say? What does he say, James?'

'This is the one, I think; no, it's the next—no. I hope I haven't brought the wrong ones after all.'

Lady William sat very quietly with her hands on her knee, only her fingers, which clasped and unclasped each other, showing a little the excitement of the suspense in which she was, as he drew forth one little book after another from the ample pockets of his coat. At last the right one was found, and then a minute or two elapsed before the Rector with his spectacles could find the entry of which he was in search. Lady William made no attempt to snatch it from his hand. She sat quite still with a self-enforced patience which was belied by the glitter in her eyes.

'Here it is at last—October 23rd. Would that be the date?'

She bowed her head quickly, and her brother began to divine that she could not speak. He gave her a keen look, and then returned to the book.

'"October 23rd.—Very agitating and extraordinary night. Em. came home after midnight accompanied by woman M., and Lord W. Extraordinary explanations. Marriage immediately or not at all. Leaving England. Gave consent." Is that right?'

Lady William moved impatiently in her chair. 'If you find it in the book, it must be right.'

'Ah, well, that is true, no doubt. Then comes another— "25th.—Emily married. Old Gepps. Gave her away. They left train, Paris."'

'Is that all?'

'It is all. I suppose old Gepps is the man who performed the ceremony. Did you ever hear my father speak of any one of that name? Do you remember the man?'

'I recollect an old man with a white beard. I think I have a vague recollection even of the name.'

'It is most extraordinary,' cried the Rector, getting up from his chair, 'that on an occasion of such importance you should not have remembered both place and name!'

'Ah! it was just because it was an occasion of such importance, and everything so dreadful and so strange.'

'Emily, I have hesitated to ask you: why in heaven's name were you married like that? What was the cause?'

She pointed towards the book with a hand that trembled. 'Papa has put it down there.'

'He has put down the fact, but no explanation. The explanation apparently was given to him, but not recorded. But you— why should you not tell me? A sudden marriage like that, in such headlong haste—why was it? What did it mean?'

Lady William was silent for some time, clasping her fingers and unclasping them, gazing into the vacant air. At last she said : 'James, you will think me too great a fool if I say that I did not know, at the time.'

'Emily,' he said, with a tone so sharp and keen that it went through her like a knife, 'it is a long time since, and I have a right to know. Was it—was it through any fault of yours ?'

She turned her eyes to him with a look of the utmost amazement. 'Fault of mine !' she said. 'What could that have had to do with it—any fault of mine ?'

She was a mature woman, and was supposed to know the world ; but Mab herself could not have given him a more limpid look, could not have received his questions with more surprise. The Rector, quite confused, stepped back a pace, and said, 'I beg your pardon,' with a humility which was entirely out of his habits. He had grown quite pale, and glanced at her with a sort of fright, terrified lest perhaps it might dawn upon her what he meant.

'I was bewildered,' she said. 'I was taken altogether by surprise. It was the romance that dazzled me—what seemed the romance—and all that they told me : that he had to leave England, must go, would be in danger of I know not what, yet would not go without me. And poor papa thought of—oh the folly, the pettiness of it !—the title, perhaps, and what he thought the connection. My poor father thought a great deal of connection.' She smiled a little sadly, looking back with a sort of tenderness upon the weakness and folly of a time so long past. Then she drew herself up unconsciously, holding her head high. 'I discovered the real meaning, but not till after. It was very bitter and terrible ; but after all it is Mab's father of whom we are speaking. James, let us return to the question of most importance. What is gained by this I don't see. I don't understand things of that kind.'

It was very conciliating and satisfactory to Mr. Plowden that she did not understand. 'It gives a clue,' he said. 'We must look up Gepps. He must have been a friend of my father's, and he must, of course, be in the "Clergy List." I have been looking up what old ones I have, but I cannot find him. I have not got that year, but it can be got, it can be got. He was an old man, you say, and he must have died, I suppose, but he cannot have taken his church and his registers with him. We must ascertain what was his church.'

'It was a little old-fashioned place, very dingy, with heavy pews ; a small place with an old-fashioned pulpit and canopy. I remember the look of it—and the clergyman, an old man, with a white beard.'

'In the City, most likely?'

Lady William shook her head. 'I knew nothing of the City —nor anywhere except the parks and the streets round about that in which the Swinfords had a house. We went seldom, very seldom, to town in those days; I never, except with them.'

'It must have been in the City,' said Mr. Plowden. 'What you describe settles the question. Well, then, I think now, Emily, there need be very little difficulty. Gepps must be in the "Clergy List." If he is living, so much the better; he may have retired somewhere. But at all events the register must exist. I will go up to town to-morrow, and find the list for 'sixty-five, and after that it will be plain sailing. All the same, how my father and you, but especially my father, could be such a fool!'

Lady William made no reply. To have her mind so thrown back upon that wonderful tragic moment of her life: to think of herself, the bewildered romantic girl, with all the wonderful tales poured into her ear by the flatterer by her side—that flatterer who was not the silent, disturbed bridegroom who himself said so little to explain the hot haste, the desperation of the strange wedding—was of itself painful enough and exciting. She had herself broached the subject to her brother when the question opened up by Mrs. Swinford had burst upon her, but she had not then entered into it so fully as now, and her mind was shaken by all those recollections. She seemed to see the shabby old church already, even so long ago, an anachronism among churches, with its heavy pulpit and pews and small round-headed windows, and the old clergyman with his white beard, and the complete absence of all those prettinesses with which a girl's imagination surrounds her bridal—prettinesses, however, made up for by the thrilling romance which, when the moment came, had begun to yield a little to the natural pain of the position. She remembered with what a start of alarm she had found herself consigned to the husband of whom she knew so little, who was so little like the romantic hero of such a marriage, and who—as she only began to see when the step was irrevocable—showed so little of any sentiment for her which could justify the impetuous impatience of the proceedings. She remembered the awful sensation in her mind when she looked back from the window of the railway carriage upon her father's smiling, complacent old face, enchanted by the consciousness that his daughter was now Lady William, sister-in-law to the Marquis of Portcullis, and on the mocking smile and exaggerated courtesies of Artémise: and felt everything she loved sliding from her, and nothing left to her but the saturnine countenance opposite—the almost strange man, who if he loved her hotly had, as yet at least, shown no signs of it to herself. She did not hear her brother's voice speaking to her in the heat and hurry of her thoughts. Oh, what recollections were these! So much more real than anything that occurred to her now, so much more potent in their terror and excitement than anything that could happen. She had known nothing in all her experience, read nothing, so tragical and terrible as the feelings of that poor little bride of nineteen, as she woke up from her romantic dream, and saw her father's foolish old face so fresh and ruddy, so innocent and unconscious, just before it finally dropped out of sight to be seen no more. Perhaps it was her brother's question, though she was scarcely aware that she heard it, how could my father be such a fool? that gave the impression of foolishness, of strange, cheerful imbecility to her last view of that rosy old face.

'I repeat, Emily,' said the Rector, with a little heat, 'how could my father be such a fool? A girl of your age, of course, could not be expected to think of such things—but my father!—And I suppose he knew that the man you married was not—a model of every virtue.'

'He was Mab's father, James, and he was at least quite honourable, so far as I was concerned; he took no advantage—in respect to me.'

'He could scarcely have been such a brute as that,' the Rector said. 'Well, I'll go, Emily. To-morrow I'll go to town and see if I can bring back all the papers square. Hush, what is that? Who is Mab talking to? We've done our talk, however, and it's no matter being interrupted now.'

'Good morning, Lord William,' Mab's voice was heard saying, perhaps a little louder than was necessary, to give her uncle the warning she had promised.

Lady William started violently at the sound of the name. She put her hand upon her breast where her heart had begun to beat loudly. 'All those old recollections have upset my nerves,' she said, with a little piteous smile. 'Forgive me, James; it is the young man that Mab told you of, the cousin with the same name.'

'Poor Emily!' he said, taking her hand in both of his. 'You have, I fear, no pleasant memories connected with it: but why, then, in the name of heaven, or the other place perhaps——'

'The other place,' she said, bursting into a faint hysterical laugh. 'But wait a moment, the boy is coming in.'

'I thought you were going away this morning,' said Mab, evidently leading the way into the house. 'You need not think of shaking hands, for I am always muddy when I am working in the garden. Yes, I do a great deal of work in the garden—indeed, I'm the gardener. Patty's father gives me a hand for the heavier things, but do you imagine I would trust any one else with my flowers? Ah, it's a little too early, but if you came here in June, then you should see! It's not very big, to be sure. Mr. Leo has a great deal more space at the Hall, and I don't know how many men, but——' Mab said, ending abruptly with a little grimace (which, of course, could not be seen indoors) which said more than words.

'I daresay it's great fun working in the garden,' said Lord Will, with a very serious face.

'A garden is no fun at all when you don't work in it,' said Mab, 'and, so far as I've seen, most other things are just the same. They become fun if you take an interest in them, and not in any other way.'

'But then Miss Mab was always a philosopher,' said Leo's voice, with the faint sound in it that was not English.

'Oh, Swinford's there, too,' said the Rector to his sister inside. 'Don't you think, Emily, you have him a little too often here?'

'The other is staying with him,' Lady William said, which was no doubt a subterfuge: but then it was very evident that she had no time to say any more.

It was Leo who led the way, but the Rector was quite uninterested in Leo. His eyes followed to the other young man behind, who came in with something like diffidence, though that is not a common aspect for a young man of fashion to bear. He came in, indeed, with the air of a most unwilling visitor. He would have greatly preferred to go away without repeating his visit in the changed circumstances in which he found himself, but Leo had insisted that the visit should be paid. He shook hands with Lady William, and was presented to her brother, with the air of a man who wished himself a hundred miles away.

'I've just come, don't you know, to take my leave,' said Lord Will. 'I'm summoned to town. I thought that you would understand; but Swinford here said I ought to come—that is to say, I was glad to take the opportunity of saying good-bye.'

'Yes,' said Lady William, looking from one to another; 'I should have understood, I think. It is a pity, Leo, that you gave your friend the trouble.'

'Oh! delighted, of course,' said Lord Will.

'I have been telling my brother,' said Lady William, 'about your visit: and to see one of Mab's relations is a pleasure—so unlooked-for.'

'I will not say unlooked-for. I have always looked forward,' said the Rector, 'to making the acquaintance of the family. How do you do? And, of course, at once I perceive the likeness you spoke of, Emily. You are here on a very brief visit, it appears, Lord ——.' It seemed to Mr. Plowden that to say Will would be too familiar, and to say William would affect his sister's nerves; therefore he stopped short there, and said no name at all. 'You have scarcely had time to make your cousin's acquaintance,' he said.

Lord Will had been quite unprepared for a man and a brother

R

taking the part of the poor lady about whom he had been holding
so many discussions.   He was a little taken aback.   'As a point
of fact, a fellow has so little time,' he said, hesitating a little.
'I came down to see Swinford—dine and sleep, don't you know—
that sort of thing.   Swinford's such a capital fellow to know in
Paris—takes you everywhere—shows you all the swells, and that
sort of thing.'

Mr. Plowden had not, perhaps, very much acquaintance with
the highest order of society, at least in its young and fashionable
branches.   To hear Lord Will Pakenham talk of swells took
away his breath.   He smiled, however, paternally upon the
young man who was Mab's cousin and Lord Portcullis's son.   He
was unwilling to believe that a young man of such a family could
make any pretext or tell any fibs about the plain duty of paying
his respects to his near relations.   'I hope,' he said, 'that we
shall have other opportunities of seeing a little more of you.   My
sister, Lady William, has been for a long time established here,
and all the neighbourhood would receive with pleasure any—any
relation—any connection—I mean any member of such a family
as yours.'

Lord Will stared a little, as is the manner of his kind, but
made no reply.   What reply could the poor young man make?
It was so bewildering to be offered an enthusiastic welcome from
the society of a village because of being related to the little
gardening girl in the muddy gloves outside, that all his self-
possession, which was sufficient for ordinary uses, was taken away.
He gave a glance at Lady William, and espied a gleam in her
eye which gave him a little comfort.   There was agitation in her
face, yet she saw the absurdity as well as he did.   Decidedly,
under other circumstances, this widow, real or fictitious, of his
disreputable uncle would have been a woman not to be despised.

'But I hear,' said the Rector, 'that you are the bearer of bad-
news.   Another relation, my sister tells me, has joined the
majority.   I had once the pleasure, many years ago, of meeting
Lord John—before there was any connection between the families.
And he is gone!   Well, we must all follow—we have here no
abiding city.   It is almost fortunate for Mab that, not having
known her uncle, the shock of his loss will affect her less than it
would otherwise have done.'

'My dear James,' said Lady William, 'Lord Will will excuse
you from all condolence, I am sure.   There can be no shock to
Mab, who has scarcely heard her uncle's name: and to the other
members of the family the shock is also softened by, I believe,

the joys of inheritance. For he has not carried his money with him, which is always a good thing.'

'I did not think to hear, Emily, any such cynical speech from you.'

'But it is true,' said Leo Swinford, 'and my friend has come for the reason of communicating this intelligence, *n'est-ce pas*, Will?—which Lady William did not understand, I am sure, yesterday. Lord John has died without any will: his fortune, which is all personal, is therefore divided—is not that so?—between the nearest relations: therefore, Miss Mab, on account of her father, will become——'

'Bless me!' said the Rector. He had seated himself in order to do justice to the new acquaintance who was at the same time a connection, but now he sprang to his feet. 'Bless me!' he said, 'an heiress! I must congratulate Mab. Emily, my dear——'

'An heiress is a big word,' said Lord Will, who had sucked his cane with anything but a countenance of delight while Leo was speaking. 'There's money,' said the young man, 'but it would be a pity to make the mistake of thinking it's a big fortune. I told you,' he said, turning to Lady William, 'last night. I said there was no will.'

Lady William had grown very pale. 'I did not understand,' she said faintly. 'I was not aware—and that my Mab would come in——' The news had rather a painful than exhilarating effect upon her. She gave her brother an anxious look, then turned to the young man whose explanations were so disjointed. 'It was kind, very kind,' she said, with a troublous smile, 'to come and hunt us up—strangers to you—to tell us this.'

'Oh! as for that——' said Lord Will.

'You have no idea, dear lady,' said Leo, 'how disinterested, how high-minded are the golden youth in England. They will go any distance to make such an announcement, never thinking that what is given to another diminishes their own share.'

'Shut up, Swinford,' growled Lord Will over his cane.

'I hope,' said the Rector, smiling, 'that Mr. Swinford does not think this is any information to us, Emily? I hope I know what the instinct of an English gentleman is. To a lady in my sister's position, living out of the world, who might never have heard even of the death, let alone the inheritance, that feeling is the best protection—as I hope we both know.'

'Oh, sh——,' murmured Lord Will. He could not say 'shut up' to the Rector, but a more crestfallen and abashed young man did not exist. He sat with the head of his cane to his lips, but

evidently deriving no consolation from it, when Mab, who had
taken off her gardening apron and washed her hands, came in.
Mab had her curiosities like other girls. She wanted to know
what they were all talking of, and what was being done in the
room where there were so many interesting people met together.
She was by no means sure that it was not her own fate that was
being decided. After all that had been said about her father's
family, the sudden appearance of her cousin was too curiously well-
timed to be a mere accident, and she could not help fearing that
while she was busy over her carnations they might be settling the
course of her future life. Mab had no idea that this should be
done without her own concurrence, or the utterance of her opinion,
and accordingly, after turning it over in her mind for a few
minutes, she left her flowers and hurried upstairs to make herself
presentable. Such a conjunction as that of her uncle, so rare a
visitor, her new unknown cousin, and Leo Swinford, her mother's
counsellor, could not, she thought, have happened for nothing.
But when Mab went into the room the first thing she saw was
Lord Will—in whom she took a natural interest as resembling
herself, and as being a relation, and a new-comer—seated in the
middle of the group with a depressed and sullen countenance, his
eyes cast down, and his lips resting upon the head of his cane.

'Mother,' said Mab, 'what have you been doing to Lord
Will ?'

No one had thought of Mab's appearance at this particular
crisis of fate, and the mere sight of her as she opened the door
sent a little thrill through the party, who were all aware of troublous circumstances involving Mab, of which she herself was entirely
unconscious, and of prospects utterly strange to her, which were
opening before her feet. They all turned to look at her as she
stood there with the fresh morning air about her, not beautiful,
certainly, but honest and fresh as the morning, and so free from
all embarrassment, so unaware either of troubles or hopes which
could affect her beyond the wholesome round of every day, that
even the Rector, the most ignorant of the party, felt something
like a conspirator. Mab came forward quite unconscious of breaking into the middle of a strained situation. 'What,' she repeated,
'have you been doing to Lord Will ? Has he done anything
wrong that you are all round about him, sitting on him like this ?
I'm glad I've come to see fair play.'

'My dear,' said the Rector, who was the only one who could
speak, 'you are quite mistaken. Your cousin is receiving on the
contrary all our thanks for bringing some news which will be of the

greatest importance to you, I hope, and will make your future more suitable, my child, to your rank.'

'Oh, I thought that was how it must be!' cried Mab, in a tone of disgust. 'Rank! I have no rank; and if it is this idea of recommending me to Lady Portcullis, and getting her to take me to Court and all that, which has brought Lord Will here——Mother, let me speak; I am not a little child. I want to judge for myself. I don't wish it, you must all know. I care not the least in the world for going to Court. I am quite happy as I am—a country girl. Lord Will is very kind if he came about that. I shall always remember it of him, that he is the only one of my father's family that has been kind; though why you should sit upon him for it—for you were all sitting upon him—I'm sure I don't know.'

'I think I'd better go,' said Lord Will, rising from his chair. 'It's true they have been sitting upon me, though what for I can't tell—any more than I can tell why this'—he paused a little with the impulse to say little girl, but thought better of it—'this young lady should be grateful to me; for I have done neither good nor harm that I know of. But now I think I'd better go.'

'Have I said anything wrong? Is it I that have broken up the talk?' cried Mab in consternation, coming to her mother's side.

'Well,' said the Rector cheerfully, 'perhaps we can scarcely go on with a business matter just now; but if Lord William Pakenham will do me the pleasure to come to the Rectory, which is close by——'

'I'm not a business man,' said Lord Will. 'Swinford, you brought me into it, can't you get me out of it?—and be hanged to you,' he said in an undertone.

'I am afraid you have broken up the consultation, Mab: but perhaps it is as well.' Lady William held out her hand to the young man, who stood dangling his cane, and eager to get away. 'I think we must have something to thank you for,' she said, with a smile. 'Of course, a piece of business is not settled by a friendly visit. I shall hear, no doubt, from the lawyers about what you have told me, or my brother will communicate with them for me. Thank you for the information, and for bringing it yourself. Good-bye.'

He had been standing ready to tell her, as he took his leave, with a tone that might convey some of the suspicions that were in his mind, that the lawyers would communicate with her further. But in taking the words out of his mouth, Lady William took all

the courage out of his mind. He stared at her for a moment with
those heavy blue eyes, which she did not now think were so like
Mab's, and touched the hand she held out with a cold momentary
touch, as if he were afraid it might sting him. Mab stood by
looking on with an astonishment which slowly grew into consternation, and which burst forth as her cousin made her a stiff and
slight bow.

'What is the matter?' she said, following him out. 'Are
you not my cousin after all? Why, you were very nice last
night, and I was delighted to know somebody that belonged to
me on my father's side. And they all said we were so like
each other. What has gone wrong? Are you not my cousin
after all?'

She went out after him as she spoke into the garden, where a
little while before she had greeted him so heartily, filled with astonishment and dismay, yet with a sense of absurdity also. And
the young man, who had made so abrupt an exit, was in fact rather
sore in heart, feeling that he had not done himself any credit, and
that he had been snubbed and 'sat upon,' as Mab said. Her frank
surprise and regret gave him a little consolation. He turned round
when they both came out into the garden from the narrow doorway.
'I am just the same,' he said, still somewhat sullenly, but melting,
'as I was last night.'

'But then,' cried Mab, 'why did you call me "this young
lady"? and why did you look at mother so, and let her hand drop
as if it had been a frog, and do like this to me?' Mab was not a
mimic, like her cousin Florence, but the imitation she made of his
stiff and angry bow was so ludicrous that he could not but laugh
—stiffly. And Mab, who did not know what it was to be stiff,
laughed out with all her heart, with a half childish cordial crow,
which sounded into the fresh air with the most genuine tone of
innocent mirth. 'You had better shake hands with me after that,
Cousin Will,' she said.

'You are making peace, Miss Mab,' said Leo Swinford, who had
followed them out.

'No, I am not making peace, for we never made war,' said
Mab, who had given her cousin a warm grasp of the hand. And
she stood at the gate looking after them with some regret. For
Lord Will was young, and they were of the same blood, and he was
a great novelty, something far more new than even Leo Swinford.
She was unfeignedly sorry that he was going away. And she could
not understand why, nor how it was that the young man who was
so cordial yesterday should be so cold again now.

Lady William stood as she had done when young Pakenham dropped her hand until Leo Swinford, following his friend, had closed the door of the little drawing-room. I think she heard through the open window all that Mab said—at all events, the laugh so full of merriment and spontaneity bursting out into the pleasant air. Then she suddenly sank into the chair, and covering her face with her hands fell into a sudden burst of silent weeping. There was no sound, but her shoulder heaved with the effort to control and subdue the sudden emotion. Mr. Plowden had been standing, too, perplexed and disappointed by the stranger's sudden withdrawal, but a little consoled by the laugh which seemed to prove that there was at all events a good understanding between Mab and her cousin. He did not perceive for a moment the effect upon his sister, and it was only after the young man had gone out of the garden gate, that, turning to speak to her, he perceived the attitude of abandonment, the restrained but almost irrestrainable passion by which she had been seized. He was not so much afraid of seeing women cry as men less experienced are. But Emily had never been of the weeping kind, and the Rector was startled and touched by the sight of the paroxysm with which she was struggling, to keep it down.

'Emily,' he cried, 'Emily, my dear, what is it? You're not breaking down?'

'James,' she cried, but very low, suddenly lifting to him a face full of anguish and exceedingly pale, 'if we should not be able to prove it; if we can't get the evidence! Oh James, my Mab, my child!'

'Why shouldn't we be able to prove it?' he said, with half-angry calm. 'Where is the difficulty of proving it? and what has that to do with it? Why, Emily, I never knew your good sense fail you before.'

'My good sense!' she said, with a miserable smile.

'To be sure! Why, what is there to cry about? Such an unexpected windfall to Mab—a fortune, no doubt, though he did not tell us how much. You cut the young man short, Emily. I can't see why. He seemed a very civil young man.'

Lady William raised herself up and dried her wet eyes.

'You are quite right,' she said, 'it is my common sense that is failing me, James.'

'Failed you for a moment,' he said, indulgently patting her on the shoulder. For to be a man with a wife and daughters of his own he was very fond of his sister; and he was also agreeably excited by the sight of the second Lord William, actually one of

the Portcullis family, Mab's own cousin, about whom the ladies of
the Rectory, when they heard, would be so deeply excited. Mr.
Plowden was anxious to convey that wonderful intelligence to them
as quickly as was possible. 'Well, my dear Emily,' he said, 'I
must go. I have no doubt you've been a good deal excited this
morning, and I should advise you to lie down and rest a little.
And to-morrow — well, no, perhaps not to-morrow, for now I remember, I have some churchings and various other things to
attend to, but the very first free day I have——'

She put her hands together beseechingly. 'Oh, go at once—
don't keep me in this suspense.'

'My dear girl! you are frightening yourself in the most absurd
way. After to-morrow, the very earliest minute that I can get
away.'

Lady William did not lie down and rest when her brother left
her, but she went upstairs and took refuge in her own room, very
thankful that Mab had returned to her gardening. That Mab was
an heiress and that 'the family' were seeking her acquaintance
was the news Mr. Plowden longed to tell. But Mab's mother was
filled with another thought. If it could be that the search should
fail! She believed more in failure than success with her experience.
If it should fail, if there should fall upon Mab any cloud, any
shadow of possible shame! She wrung her hands till they hurt
her, but her heart was wrung more sorely still. It was a view she
had not thought of before. Shame for herself would be bad enough.
But for Mab! And even the possibility that Mab should turn
astonished eyes upon her, should ask even with those eyes alone a
question—should have such a thought suggested even for a moment,
to her mind! Lady William had borne many miseries in her
not yet very long life, but in that there would be the crown
of all.

It will be recollected that Mr. Osborne, the curate, ended very suddenly, and with no small amount of heat and displeasure, that walk with Florence Plowden which had so nearly decided the whole colour of his life. He had fallen in love (as people say—and, indeed, it is as good a phrase as any, for it is often by no means a voluntary action) with the Rector's daughter in spite of himself. It was so perfectly *banal* and commonplace a thing to do; the sort of thing looked for by everybody; so suitable, that bugbear of youth; so exactly what might—except by his own ambitious relations, who thought him worthy of a loftier fate—have been expected, that the young man had resisted almost fiercely the tide of being which led him to that commonplace conclusion. But yet, when there is fate in it, what is the use of struggling? Florence Plowden was, Mr. Osborne thought, the prettiest, the most delightful and attractive of all the girls in Watcham—more than that, of all the girls he had ever seen. I do not know that this idea was justified by universal consent. Many people gave the palm in respect to good looks to Emmy, and, indeed, neither of them was at all up to the level of many of the girls from London who came down during the boating season, or of Dora Wade, for example, who was the belle of the county. However, the fact that this opinion was by no means universal did not affect the certainty of the curate, who had a very high idea of his own judgment, and, in fact, was better pleased that it should not chime in with other people's, which was the last thing in the world he wished to do. He was a young man who was very well connected, and to lift his eyes even to Dora Wade would scarcely have been beyond his pretensions. But the mere fact that she was the acknowledged beauty was enough to make that pursuit unlikely to Edward Osborne. The *banalité* of falling in love with his Rector's daughter was bad enough, but it would have been nothing in comparison with the

downright vulgarity of falling in love with the beauty who had, as
it were, signposts put up all round her to indicate her position as the
Queen of Hearts.   Edward Osborne would have died rather than
follow these indications.   They convinced him instead that she was
not fair at all, but a most matter-of-fact and commonplace Blowsi-
bella, whose radiant complexion was of the mere dairymaid order,
and meant nothing but high health and good digestion—good
enough things in their way, but altogether devoid of romance, and
of any attraction which could dominate a highly trained and fastidious spirit like himself.   At first, when he came to Watcham, he
would have also said that the attributes of a Rector's daughter,
the delightful good young woman of the parish, acquainted with
all the poor people and their wants, and occupied with clothing
clubs, penny banks, sewing classes, and mothers' meetings, were
also the very last things that would attract a young philanthropist
of the higher order like himself, who proposed to get at the people
in a loftier way, to convince them by reason and argument of their
foolish ways of living, and to inaugurate some large movement
among them which would have little to do with the petty methods
of feminine supervision.   Florence Plowden, by universal consent,
was made to be a clergyman's wife, which was almost as strong an
argument against her as if she had been an acknowledged beauty.
But, as a matter of fact, there is no rule which tells in those
mysterious ways of mutual attraction which draw the most unlikely
or, which is worse, the most likely people together.   And it had
grown a certainty with Mr. Osborne that he had never met any
one like Florence before her attention had been directed to him at
all, and before even it had occurred to himself as possible that he
could ever get over the dreadful obstacle of all that there was in
her favour, and think of her as in possible relationship to himself.
He represented it to himself as a thing that could affect him in no
possible way, but yet a certain thing—that Florence Plowden was
as a swan among the ducklings about her, that there was no one
at all equal to her far and near, and that it was one of the mysteries
of humanity how such a creature could spring and blossom from
such a root, and among such surroundings.   But I will not attempt
to follow the matter from that first germ—obstinately held against
all the force of the general idea that Florence was a nice girl and
a very good girl (praises both calculated to drive an idealist mad),
but nothing very particular—just like other girls, in fact, and a
little like her mother.   'When she is Mrs. Plowden's age, Florence,
indeed, will, I think, be very much like her mother,' the General
had once said, without the slightest idea that the curate, who was

an athletic young person, would have liked to knock him down for saying it. And why shouldn't Florence Plowden resemble her mother? But it was blasphemy to Mr. Osborne's ears.

I will not, I repeat, attempt to follow all that happened from that first impression to the moment when he had made up his mind that without the companionship of Florence life would be, if not unworthy living, yet so diminished in everything that was fair and sweet that all its glory and hope would be over. Many notions about life had been in this young man's head. He had once thought that there was no institution in the world so great as that of a celibate clergy, and that it would be his highest duty to tread that austere and lofty path. I don't know whether Florence could be justly chargeable with the destruction of that ideal. He had come to see at last that it could not be made a general rule of, or universally enforced, before he arrived at the sudden conviction that he was not himself adapted for that form of self-abnegation. I am obliged to confess that all the different steps in Mr. Osborne's progress had been made suddenly, as with a bound, surprising himself as much as any one else. And perhaps he had no certain idea upon that morning when he found himself engaged in a discussion with his fast friend, Miss Grey, and opposed by the object of his affections—that these affections were to burst all the restraints with which he had bound them, and pour themselves forth in a burst of enthusiasm at Florry's feet. And then, to think that when the flood could scarcely be restrained—when despite her opposition, despite all her naughty ways, he was about to tell her that there was nobody like her in the world (a statement which would have been as astounding and incredible to Florry as any miracle)—that she should have stopped him by contradicting all his theories, by finding fault with what he felt to be, in its way, a small martyrdom, and by suggesting something quite different—she a girl, a nobody —to him, a priest and consecrated person set apart to instruct and lead mankind, as the better way!

Edward Osborne would not pause to refute, to reprove, to pour down the thunders of his wrath upon the girl whom in another moment he would have asked to be his wife. He did what was the only thing possible in the circumstances, turned and left her, flinging her image and her counsel behind him in the fury of his indignation. He walked from that spot to his lodgings, which was about a mile off, in three minutes or thereabouts, his long steps skimming over the soil, his mind in a turmoil scarcely to be described, boiling with anger, with indignation, with resentment against this interference with his superior rights of manhood and

of priesthood, as well as with the strong revulsion of thoughts
thrown back upon himself and disappointed feeling. It would
scarcely be too much to say that for the moment he would have
liked something dreadful to happen to Florence, and if there had
been a thunderbolt handy, which happily is not a missile within
ready reach, he would probably have blackened the face of the
whole country in order to dumb and to frighten (for I don't think
he would have gone so far as to blind) the girl he loved. When
he got home he shut himself into his sitting-room, giving a stern
order that no one was to be admitted, and betook himself to the
writing of a sermon, which seemed the best way to *sfogarsi*, as the
Italians say, to blow off the pernicious excitement which made his
veins throb and his heart beat. But he soon threw that aside,
finding it quite inadequate to the occasion, and wrote a letter to
the newspapers, which was so fierce that it frightened the editor to
whom it was addressed. I need scarcely say that it was on the
subject of temperance.

After the vehemence of the first shock was over, which, however, took some time, Mr. Osborne made a distinct but insufficient
effort to cure himself altogether of Florence. He never entered
the Rectory, contriving to settle any question he might have with
the Rector either when they met in church or by letter. He
refused all invitations lest perhaps she might be there—for where,
indeed, could a man go in the parish, to dinner or tea or evening
solemnity, without the chance of encountering the family of the
Rector? Of course Mr. Osborne was unaware that for a somewhat
similar reason Florence refused the same invitations at this crisis,
and, indeed, awakened the curiosity of her mother and Emmy—to
whom, even to Emmy, she had said nothing—by her disinclination
to go 'out.' 'I'd rather stay and keep Jim company,' she was
forced to say on several occasions—though, alas! with very little
hope that the temptation of her company would have much effect
in keeping Jim indoors. It did, however, once or twice, and that
was both reward and justification.

But it is not to be supposed that this curious incident passed
over the head of the Rev. Edward Osborne without a certain
effect. His heart began to long after Florry long before the smart
of the wound she had given him was healed. And what she had
said rankled in his mind even before that. Was there any truth
in what she had said? Was it, perhaps, a better way, to win a
young man who was his equal—*i.e.*, whom no missionary effort was
likely to be brought to bear upon, a man quite beyond the blandish-
ments of district visitors, Bible readers, temperance lecturers, or

even, in a general way, of the curate—to the paths of virtue, than
to persuade an old lady to relinquish her poor little glass of beer
by the sacrifice of his own very moderate glass of wine? The
latter sacrifice had been mentioned in one or two papers, and held
up as an example to other men.   He had been applauded, but with
reproof which was another kind of praise, by his own people and
others.   'Remember,' his mother had written, 'that Timothy was
bidden by St. Paul to take a little wine for his stomach's sake: and
I am sure you are not such a giant of strength that you can afford
to do without the little you take : though I quite appreciate the
sacrifices you think it your duty to make, my dear boy.'   Sacrifice!
It was no sacrifice.   Osborne did not care in the least for the beer,
which he took as a matter of habit, or the wine which was served
to him at other people's tables when he dined out.   He rather
liked, if truth must be told, to gently, tacitly snub his hosts by
taking nothing.   And it seemed to him, on the whole, an achieve-
ment which partook of the nature of the sublime to get old Mrs.
Lloyd to give up her beer—not that it did her a great deal of
harm, poor soul!   But if she took none herself she would be
strengthened to refuse it to her husband, and it would be an
example to her sons and to the rest of the world—that small, dingy
unenlightened world which it was so difficult to teach, which had
so little to brighten or cheer it, and which pays so dearly for its
indulgences in that sordid, dreadful way.

But Jim Plowden ! that was a very different thing from Mrs.
Lloyd.   I do not for a moment believe that Mr. Osborne would
have hesitated to take the pledge for and with Jim : but that was
not at all what Florence had suggested.   She had suggested that
he should admit him to his society, take him for a companion,
induce him to share in his pursuits—that last above all.   She did
not know, of course, that among the drawbacks to herself, of all of
which Mr. Osborne was so conscious, her brother and her family
took the first place.   He would need to be friendly, or even more
than friendly, with all the Plowdens.   Nothing but the fact that
Florence was unique in the world, that there was none like her,
none, could make up for that.   And now she demanded of him
that he should take her brother into his bosom, so to speak, not as
a consequence of being accepted by her, but as a matter of duty in
his capacity as a priest, as a better way than that of taking the
pledge along with old Mrs. Lloyd.   That lout ! he repeated to
himself : that fellow to whom had been given all the same
advantages as other people, even as Mr. Edward Osborne, and who
had thrown, or was throwing, them away : the brother, who

frequented the 'Blue Boar,' who was the friend of the school-mistress, who shunned all the ordinary assemblages of his kind ; and yet it was suggested to him that to take up this rowdy under-graduate, sent down from Oxford, would be the better way !

Is it to be wondered at if Mr. Osborne was angry ?—if, when-ever it came into his head, for as long a time as a fortnight after, he flung down whatever he was doing and turned aside to something else that would be more exciting, to forget the exasperations to which he had been exposed ?   But this did not effectually chase the suggestion, it appeared, out of his mind.   It recurred to him at times when he could not chase it away ; in the middle of the night, for instance, when he could not jump out of bed and write a letter to a temperance newspaper, and when it bored in quietly to his brain, like some fine, delicate instrument used by a cunning, persistent hand.   It was not the hand of Florence, it was that of some demon, or some angel, or his own.

Had he, after all, perhaps as much responsibility for Jim Plowden as for Mrs. Lloyd ?   Was Jim Plowden, perhaps, in his youth, and with certain faculties that might be of use in the world, of as much, nay, even of more importance, than the old washer-woman ?   Strange questions for a young idealist, a young man deeply compassionate of the poor, deeply indignant as concerns those who throw their own advantages, their own education, and other good gifts away.

These wonderful convolutions of thought—returns upon itself of the disturbed mind, bubblings up of a suggestion not to be got rid of, however trampled upon and thrown aside—brought Osborne to the day on which the Rector had gone up to town, and Jim was left free of that controlling influence of his father's presence which kept him within certain limits.   But the curate knew nothing of this incident of the day ; indeed, save in so far as concerned the church and 'duty' he had known nothing of the movements of his chief since the day when Florence stopped the words on his lips which might have made him a son of her father's house.

Mr. Plowden went up to town by a morning train, 'and it was Jim's duty, of course, to go to his Sophocles, however unwillingly, as on other days.   He was always unwilling, but his father being present, went grumbling to his work, as a tired horse goes into the shafts, knowing there is nothing else to be done.   The morning, however, was bright, and when he got into the little room which was called his study—vain title !—the sunshine came in and called him, almost as if it had been a comrade at his door.   The window was open, and the air could not have been more fresh and sweet

(as far as we can tell) had it blown out of heaven. The breath of
the first lilacs was upon it, and other celestial things of spring.
The leaves waved above in all the first new greenness of spring
leaves. The book lay open on a table before the window. It was
not green nor bright, nor did it smell of the spring. A great
lexicon was open beside it, and other books with prodigious notes
to them, and notebooks lying ready to the hand. He was expected
to construe into such halting English as he could manage that
great page, and search into its difficulties by the help of the notes
of a dreadful German worker (who no doubt liked that sort of
thing), and some English ones. Unfortunate Jim — and the
sunshine outside ! and the soft air blowing in through the window !
and the green leaves fluttering ! and the silvery river flowing !
And the Rector out of reach in London, after some private business
of his own.

He made a little fight, be it said to his credit ; but what
virtue faintly said in favour of the Sophocles was boldly contradicted by something else, not virtue, and yet not vice either, which
asked, 'What good is there in Sophocles ? I am not to go back to
Oxford ; I am to go to a ranche in America, or else I am to go to
a merchant's office in town. What good will Greek, or all the
finest poetry in the world, do me there ? If I were learning book-
keeping by double entry (whatever that may be), it might do me
some good—or something about cows ; but Sophocles !' One note
of admiration was not half enough to express Jim's indignant
sense of a folly which could not be defended from any point of
view. Sophocles ! Slaughter, the butcher, who had greasy books
to keep, could have shown him a mystery more worth knowing, if
he went to an office ; and the vet., with all his experience of
animals, was a professor worth (to Jim if he went to a ranche)
more than Sophocles, Eschylus, and the rest, with the German
notes and the English dons all thrown into one. Fancy construing
a hard chorus when you should be out after the cows ! Fancy
spending your time over a disputed passage when you have a batch
of letters to write for the mail—much good Sophocles would do a
man in either of these circumstances ! And to fancy that father,
who had such sense in an ordinary way (the day was so bright that
Jim felt quite just and amiable even towards his father), should be
so bigoted, so ridiculous in this !

It may be imagined that after such a self-argument, the sunshine, calling him exactly as one of his comrades used to do,
drumming on his window, soon had the best of it. Jim—poor
Jim—learned in clandestine movements by the very fact of the

anxiety of all about him, listened a little to make sure that the coast was clear. He heard his mother go upstairs, and the voices of the girls in a room they had for their work at the back of the house. All the exits of the house were therefore open to him— not a jealous eye about, not an anxious ear. He strolled out whistling softly, with his hands in his pockets—whistling, thereby convincing himself that he was afraid of nobody; that there was nothing clandestine, or stealthy, or wrong in the whole proceeding, but only that natural inclination towards the fresh air which every- body feels on such a day. When he had got beyond the bounds of the Rectory, and was quite free and at his ease on the public road, with nobody to make him afraid, and Sophocles as much out of the question as if he had never existed, Jim strolled on for a little, enjoying the air, and then paused to think what he should do. That, after all, was not so easy a question to decide. Every- body about was busy with something. No possibility of dropping in upon Mrs. Brown at this hour. There was the river, to be sure: but to go and get a boat, and then to toil up-stream by himself, which either coming or going he would have been obliged to do, seemed too much trouble on this sweet, indolent morning. It occurred to him that if he dropped in at the 'Blue Boar' to see the papers he might very probably meet the vet., and acquire from him some useful information; or something else might turn up; so he turned his steps that way with a delightful sense of freedom. There was nobody about, and he was responsible to nobody. For this once he would take his own way.

But Jim met Mr. Osborne before he reached the 'Blue Boar.'

JIM was not in any way afraid of Osborne, the curate—that is, he was not afraid of being stopped by him, or interrupted in any way in his career. He could not, indeed, go into the 'Blue Boar' while the curate was about; that would be giving an occasion to the adversary to blaspheme. But Jim did not dislike Osborne. He was quite willing to walk along with him so long as their ways ran together, turning back when the curate turned the first corner. It would always be something to do; and whether he arrived at that undesirable destination half an hour earlier or later was of importance to nobody. He did not notice that the curate's salutation was anything more than usual, or that he came up to him with a distinct purpose, instead of the usual cool nod with which the two young men passed each other by on ordinary occasions.

'Oh, Plowden,' Mr. Osborne said, 'have you got work over early, or are you taking holiday?'

Few people in Watcham took Jim's work seriously. Most of them, having the advantage over him of having known him all his life, were disposed to be a little admonitory, and shook their heads when they met him out. 'No work to-day, Jim?' the General would say: and most people shared the same feeling. But Osborne, probably because he also was young, never took a mean advantage. He spoke as if it were quite natural that Jim should have a holiday now and then.

'Well, yes,' said Jim, moved to confidence, and to take the matter easily, too. 'The Rector has gone to town, and I have half a day to myself. If I had been wise no doubt I should have taken it in the afternoon,' he added, with ingratiating frankness; 'but then, who knows, it may rain this afternoon, and it's too fine this morning to work.'

'Then you'd better come with me,' said Osborne quickly. 'I'm going to walk into Winwick to see if I can pick up some musicians

s

for my entertainment. There never was a finer morning for a
walk. It is not too hot, and what with the shower this morning
there will be no dust. Will you come? We can look in upon
Ormerod for a bit of bread and cheese if we're kept late for
lunch.'

Jim hesitated a moment, but all the same there mounted up
into his cheek a pleasant colour and into his heart a certain
warmth of gratification. He had always entertained a certain
admiration for Osborne, a fellow who had played for the University!
On the other hand, it was agreeable to lounge into the 'Blue
Boar,' where everybody was so very civil to him, and where he
anticipated meeting the vet. Thus it was with a mixture of
pleasure and reluctance that he received the unlooked-for invitation.
To look in upon Ormerod, who was another parson in Winwick,
was not without its temptations too, for that gentleman was a fine
cricketer, known over all the county. Jim was not often led into
such society—his usual cronies admired Mr. Ormerod at a distance,
talking big of having seen him do this and that feat. A fear of
being *de trop*, of being looked down upon by these men, of having
to act the part of an undesired third, checked, however, his
pleasure in that thought. Poor Jim was proud, though he had
not very much reason for it, and his pride had received some severe
blows, and was always on the watch for more. For a moment its
whisper that he would be nobody between these two, and that he
was always somebody at the 'Blue Boar,' had almost turned him
back. But then 'Come along,' said Osborne, 'come along, don't
let us lose the best of the day!'

If Jim had known that Florry was at the bottom of it all—
Florry, only a girl, one of the home police who kept that insufferable watch upon him, his sister! But, fortunately, no such idea
could by any chance have crossed his mind. Florry! what could
she have had to do with it? And he was moved by the cheerful
call of the curate, who was not in general a very cheerful man, and
who rather preferred in an ordinary way to tramp through the
slush and cold than to take advantage of a beautiful morning for a
walk. He said, 'I suppose you will not be very late,' hesitating
at the corner.

'Late! You know how far it is to Winwick,' said Mr.
Osborne, 'a matter of three miles—not much that to you and me.'

'No, it's not much,' said Jim. 'I think I'll risk it,' he added,
when the turn was actually taken, and the Winwick Road stretched
before them. 'I'm on an easy bit to-day. I'll have time to get
it all up when we get back.'

'A good walk always clears a man's head,' said Osborne; and he resumed after a pause, 'What are you reading now?'

'Oh, it's Sophocles. Seven against Thebes, don't you know, with all those hard choruses.'

'Oh, for Greats?'

'I wish I only knew what it was for,' cried Jim. 'You know I haven't been lucky, Osborne. I got into a scrape, don't you know. I suppose everybody knows: though we think at the Rectory that if we make-believe strong enough nobody need know.'

'A great many men get into scrapes,' said the curate oracularly.

'Don't they, now?' cried Jim, with eagerness; 'that's what my people won't see.'

'The only thing is to get out of them as fast as possible,' added Mr. Osborne.

'Ah,' said Jim, a little crestfallen. He went on after a pause: 'If you knew what your governor meant, don't you know. He wants me to read, and yet he says I'm to go out to a ranche or into an office in the city. Why doesn't he make up his mind? And what good will Greek do me on a ranche? Morris the vet. could teach me what would be more use for that than all the Sophocles in the world.'

'But then you see,' said the curate, 'Morris is not just the kind of tutor for a gentleman.'

'Oh,' said Jim again. His pride was of the kind that could not bear to desert his friends, however undesirable. 'He's a decent fellow enough.'

'In his own sphere—I suppose so,' said Osborne; 'and clever, they tell me, in his way; but not our kind.' He added: 'I believe, from what I've heard, if you are going to a ranche, the best way of learning is just—to go.'

'If any one he minds would only tell my father that,' said Jim, gratified by the pronoun, and that Osborne had said 'our' instead of 'your.' He was aware that Osborne's 'kind' was different from his own, and that his kind would not have been, perhaps, very desirable for one of the curate's cloth. Thank God, there was no question of Jim going into the Church, though it had been his mother's desire. 'That's the chief thing I complain of,' he said; 'let them tell me straight out what I'm to do. Whether it's one thing or the other I don't mind. If it's to be Oxford over again, well, then the Greek's good for something; but if it's the ranche——'

'That is reasonable,' said the curate, 'and if you put it to the Rector like that, surely——'

'Poor father!' said Jim, moved to unusual sympathy, 'I don't believe he knows himself. First he thinks one thing and then he thinks another. And chiefly, I suppose, he thinks that I am not good for very much, any way.'

'That's an idea that you must get him out of, Plowden.'

'It's easy to say so, but how am I to do it? When people lose their confidence in you——' said Jim. And then he hesitated and drew back. 'What did you say you were going to Winwick for?' he added hastily. 'Musicians for your——what did you say?'

'Musicians for my entertainment—to amuse my temperance people. Your sisters are going to sing: and I hear you recite, Plowden.'

'No, I don't—not good enough for you. I used sometimes to do things at penny readings; but that was before I went to Oxford,' said Jim, with a sudden flush, which seemed to envelop him from head to foot—a flush half of unexpected pleasure, half of overwhelming shame.

'Well,' said the curate, 'you had better begin again: unless you disapprove of my temperance meetings, like'—he paused a little and said fiercely—'your sister.'

'My sister!' cried Jim with amazement; and then he laughed. 'I don't suppose you mind very much. Which was it? Emmy? She's dreadfully serious about everything that God has given us being meant for use. I think that myself, you know,' he said.

'But perhaps you haven't seen, as I have, the terrible misery it has brought,' said the curate, watching secretly with great interest to see what the result would be.

Now Jim knew a great deal about himself, more than anybody else knew: but he did not accuse himself in this respect. He had not realised the danger here. In other ways he was aware that there was danger; but in this, for himself, no.

'I'm not such a novice as you think,' he said. 'I've known fellows at Oxford—Good God! if one was to think of it, it's enough to make your brain go round—nice fellows, men that there was no harm in, and yet——'

Jim walked on very soberly for a few minutes, thinking of tragic scenes he had seen. Even though he was so young, Heaven help him, he had seen tragic scenes. He had beheld with his own eyes the tribute of youth, which the infernal powers demand and receive wherever youth abounds. He knew it well enough. But for himself there was no question of that; for himself there was only a little escape from paternal coercion—a place to lounge in when he had nothing to do, a set of people obsequious, admiring him whenever he opened his mouth. Danger in the 'Blue Boar!' He could have laughed at the thought; and so had the nice fellows by whose example he was not warned. He did not say anything at all for a few minutes, being deeply moved by things he remembered, though not by any trouble for himself.

'Plowden,' said the curate, 'that's one thing I wanted to speak to you about. I don't know how you feel, but to think upon those men makes me so sick at heart that I don't know what to do. They're so often nice fellows : and how are we to get hold of them? How are we to stop them? You're freshly out of it, you're of the present generation. What is a man that wants to stop them to do?'

Jim gave him a frightened half-glance, then lowered his eyes. 'Good Heavens,' he said, 'what a question to ask! How am I to know?'

'How is one to get at them? How is one to get hold of them?' said the curate. 'There's always some way of getting at the young fellows in the slums. You may not do any good, but yet you can say out what you've got to say. There's the river men, the boatmen, and all those. I don't say that usually they pay a bit of attention, but now and then there's a chance of getting hold of them and speaking one's mind. They can't help listening to you, and they know what you say is true. But the gentlemen are different. You can't get at them, and they wouldn't believe it if you did; they don't know the result. They think they can stop when they please, and there will always be some one who will stick to them. How are we to get hold of them, Plowden?—our own very brothers, men of our own kind. They're all our brothers, every one, to be sure; but think, Plowden, those fellows at Oxford, in London, everywhere. God help us! all the harm isn't in the slums. There must be some way of getting at them too!'

Jim Plowden looked at the curate with an interest he had never felt before. He was moved by this earnestness, almost passion, that was in him. 'The poor beggar must have a brother that's gone to the bad,' he said to himself. That it should be he himself about whom the curate was concerned, or that there was any reason why anybody should be so concerned for him, never entered into Jim's head.

'I see what you mean,' he said, 'but I couldn't answer your question if you were to give me a fortune for it. They know fast

enough. They see other men going to the dogs every day. I
suppose that ought to be better than sermons or any other kind of
missionary work, or what a parson could do. I'm sure I can't tell
you, or how you're to get hold of them. It won't be with any
teetotal stuff, if I must say what I think.'

A shade of anger crossed the curate's face, and he looked at
Jim with a wondering gaze, which awoke that young man's surprise
in return. 'What do you look at me like that for?' he said, half
irritated in his turn.

'Like what? I beg your pardon. I didn't mean anything—
particular. I suppose I thought I saw the others, the men I want
to get hold of, through you, or behind you,' he said. This was
not a speech which was very agreeable to Jim, who did not see any
reason why he should be chosen as a type of the young man of
whom the curate wanted to get hold. But Mr. Osborne here made
a diversion by another reference to Jim's suspended power of recitation or reading, and by entering with him into a discussion of what
would be suitable for the occasion, which distracted Jim's attention. Before they got to Winwick Jim had proposed to read something—unwillingly, yet not without a little gratification too.

When they had accomplished their business, and secured the
aid of two or three amateurs all very willing to exhibit themselves
and their accomplishments, the two young men made their way to
the lodgings of Mr. Ormerod, who was one of the curates of the
place, and who produced for them the bread and cheese demanded
in the shape of a beef-steak, round which they were all mildly
merry as befitted the character of the party, and talked cricket and
music, and other matters in which Jim felt himself quite able to
take his share, and did so, to the surprise of his host, who had
heard the usual derogatory murmurs which breathe into the air
concerning every such young defaulter—and of his companion, who
had given poor Jim the credit of being a fool as well as other
troublesome things. The entertainment took solid shape in the
hands of the two curates, and poor Jim felt a certain elation in
feeling himself one of them—taking a part with those who were
of 'one's own kind,' as Osborne had said. A passing reflection
even glanced through his mind that it would not have been nearly
so comfortable had he been leaving the 'Blue Boar,' a little heated
by the refreshment which it was necessary to take there, after an
hour or two's talk with Morris the vet., and the landlord, even on
a subject so instructive as cows. He knew exactly what would
have happened in that case. He would have been very late for
lunch, for which meal the ladies would have waited till he

came in; and his feeling that his morning had not been very profitably employed, as well as the refreshment that had been necessary, would have made him irritable. He would have answered his mother (who of course would have said something brutal to him) insolently, and then there would have followed a hush at table, no one saying anything, since all were angry, for the sake of the servant who waited. And his sisters would have looked as if they would like to cry, and his mother would have been red with wrath, and as soon as the meal was over he would have strolled off—to his study in the first place, where he would have opened his books, and then sat down to think how hard it was upon a fellow never to be left to himself, never to have funds for anything, to get angry words and tearful looks whatever he did. And then, after half an hour's indignant musing, he would have strolled out again. Now how different everything was, as he walked through the hilly street of Winwick, keeping up with his companion's long strides, fresh and good-humoured, feeling that he had done himself credit, with Mr. Ormerod's wholesome beer, light upon both mind and stomach, and the three miles' stretch of leafy road before him. To be sure there would be a little rush at the Rectory to meet him, a cry of 'Jim, where have you been?' But he was not afraid of that cry. If there were tearful looks they would be looks of pleasure. If his mother met him red with anxiety, she would soon be bubbling a hundred questions full of satisfaction. 'Walked into Winwick with Osborne. I know I ought not to have done it, but don't be frightened, I've time to do the Sophocles before father comes back. And we lunched with Ormerod at Winwick, who gave us a capital beef-steak.' What a secret thrill of pleasure would run through the faded drawing-room at this explanation! There was no virtue in having gone off to Winwick instead of doing his work. To tell the truth, it was not a whit more virtuous than strolling into the 'Blue Boar.' But oh, the difference! the difference! The difference to himself, walking home with a calm conscience and a light heart! And the difference to them, whose trembling would all at once in a moment be turned into joy, though he did not doubt that for the moment they were unhappy enough now!

'Come over, will you, in the evening, and try over that "Ride from Ghent,"' said Mr. Osborne, when they parted.

'I will, with pleasure,' said Jim. They parted, though neither was aware of it, in sight of Florry, who had come out very wretched to see whether in her perambulations about the village she could catch a glimpse of Jim, and who came up to him a few

moments after he had left the curate, in a state of curious commotion which Jim found it very difficult to understand.

'Oh, Jim,' she cried, 'where have you been?'—the usual
phrase. But then she added, 'Have you been somewhere with
Mr. Osborne?' in a voice that fluttered like a bird.

'I have been to Winwick with Osborne, and we lunched with
Ormerod off an excellent beef-steak,' said the complacent Jim.

But Florence answered not a word. She put down her veil,
which was unnecessary, and struggled with it a little to draw it
over her face, turning away her head.

JIM was very busy about the book-shelves that evening, taking out and putting back various books, until, at last, his movements called forth the observations of his anxious family. The Rector, who had come home moody and troubled, and who had made no inquiry into Sophocles, neither had shown the interest that was expected in Jim's expedition to Winwick with the curate, looked up fretfully and begged his son to have a little respect for other people's occupations if he had none of his own. Mr. Plowden was doing nothing more serious than reading the evening paper, so that the gravity of this address was a little uncalled-for; but he was put out about something, as all the family was aware.

'What are you looking for?' said his mother, who had boundless patience with Jim.

'I want to take two or three things over to Osborne,' said Jim, 'to let him choose. I'm to read something for him at his entertainment.'

'What?' said the Rector, looking over the top of his paper with angry eyes.

Upon which Jim repeated his announcement a little louder and with a slight air of defiance; or, at least, the air of a man ready to be defiant, as—when there is nothing but virtue in his mind, a man feels that he has a right to be.

'His entertainment! His teetotal entertainment! Stuff and nonsense—cramming the fellows' heads with pride and folly, as if they were better than their neighbours.'

'Oh, James!' said his wife, 'let them be as silly as they like. What does that matter in comparison with ruining their families by drink?'

'They'll ruin their families by something else,' said the Rector; 'if not in one way they'll get it out in another—politics, most likely, and socialism, and that sort of thing. What Osborne will

do is to make them all a set of insufferable, narrow - minded
prigs.'

'Even that, James——' began Mrs. Plowden.

'Don't tell me,' said the Rector, 'that you'll make men
Christians by teaching them that there's a curse on one of the
gifts of God. You may abuse any and all of the gifts of God;
but to make a young ass think he is superior to his honest father,
because he abstains, forsooth, and the old man likes his honest
glass of beer!'

'Mr. Osborne doesn't teach them that, papa,' said Florry from
the further corner of the room, in which, her eyes, she said, being
a little weak, she had established herself. Mr. Plowden turned
upon her like a tempest.

'Who are you?' he said; 'a little chit of a girl, to tell me
what Osborne teaches them or doesn't teach them! I should hope
I am still able to judge for myself—at least, in such a question
as this.'

'Hush, Florry!' said her mother, with a little nod at Florence.
They were all aware that in certain conjunctures it was inexpedient
to contradict the Rector. As for Jim, he held up two books to
his mother behind backs over Mr. Plowden's head and disappeared
with them, shutting the door softly behind him. He was too
much in the habit of closing doors softly and stealing out; but
Mrs. Plowden's mind being otherwise occupied, she did not think
of this to-night.

If there had been anything wanted to throw Jim into the arms
of the curate, that tirade did it. Had his father sent him forth to
Mr. Osborne's company with a blessing, it would have spoiled all;
but to escape for all the world as if he were going to spend the
evening with Mrs. Brown, put things at once on a right footing.
Jim walked through the village, not in his usual lounging way, but
with a long stride and head high. He glanced at the 'Blue Boar,'
with the cheerful light shining through its red curtains, and
thought with a little contempt of the fellows who were seated, he
knew, in a cloud of smoke within, and with talk as smoky as the
air, he thought to himself lightly. It was a place where a man
might go to pass the time when he had nothing else to do; but he
had never entertained any illusion on the subject of its dulness,
Jim said to himself.

It is doubtful whether Mr. Osborne heard Jim's step coming
through the little garden of the cottage in which he lodged with
the same exhilaration. The curate, indeed, had been of opinion that
Jim was not at all likely to come, and had settled himself to his

evening's occupation with that view. He had not found much
pleasure iu the young man's companionship during their long walk.
He had caught the look of surprise, the lifting of the eyebrows,
with which the people of Winwick testified their amazement to see
such a superior person as Mr. Osborne accompanied by that unlucky
Jim—and Mr. Osborne had not liked it. The fact that he did
not like it, however, was the one good thing in the matter, for it
gave him the conviction that since he did not like it, it must be
the right thing. He had liked that little glorification of taking
the pledge to induce old Mrs. Lloyd to do it; and this sensation
had made him much less strong than he might have been as to the
absolute virtue of the act. Mr. Osborne, as will be perceived, was
really a very superior young man. When Mr. Ormerod had taken
him aside, with again a lifting of the eyebrows, and asked him
whether that young cub of Plowden's had turned over a new leaf
as he (Osborne) had taken him in tow, the curate of Watcham had
been angry. 'Don't you think it might be perhaps my duty to
help him to turn over a new leaf?' he had said, with some
asperity, at which the Winwick curate had lifted his eyebrows
more and more. They had all thought that to consort with Jim
was rather a token that Mr. Osborne himself was acquiring a relish
for indifferent society, than that it was his duty to endeavour to
reclaim that species of lost sheep. This naturally and beneficially
excited the temper of Edward Osborne, which was a fine, animated,
vigorous sort of temper, capable of doing a great deal to encourage
him in an unpopular way. If it had been a young boatman ou
Riverside there would have been no lifting of eyebrows. So much
the more was it evident that this particular thing was his duty,
and that he was bound to pursue what these asses took upon them
to disapprove of. A man may be a very good man, and yet feel
his virtuous determination strengthened by the consciousness that
those who are against him are asses. And just as Jim was encouraged by his father's angry opposition, so was Mr. Osborne by
the surprise, whether put in words or not, of his Winwick friends.
They had all been greatly complimentary and touched to the heart
by the episode of old Mrs. Llyod.
     But he had thought that his reformatory effort was over for
the day. The invitation he had given Jim for the evening had been
a sudden and passing impulse, and he had never suspected that
it would be accepted. Even when it was accepted iu word, he
still thought nothing more would come of it. The young fellow
would not be able to pass the 'Blue Boar,' or he would be
caught at the schoolhouse by Mrs. Brown. Having done his duty

amply, as he felt he had done, it was almost with relief that the curate concluded that Jim would never manage to pass the ' Blue Boar.' When he heard, on the contrary, a footstep ring upon the little line of pavement which divided in two the cottage garden where his lodgings were, Mr. Osborne was much startled, and it cannot be said that his start was one of pleasure. ' Oh ! here's this confounded fellow again.'   I am afraid that was the thought that passed through his mind : and he pushed away his work with impatience, clearing away several books which he had been consulting.   He wanted to make a conquest, a convert of Jim.   He had a hundred reasons for wishing it. First, the conviction that on the whole it was a far more difficult task than administering the pledge to Mrs. Lloyd : second, that Jim Plowden, after all, would be a more considerable prize than the old woman, that he was at least worth as much trouble as a young waterman on Riverside ; third, that perhaps it might be allowed that an Oxford man and a gentleman has a peculiar duty towards another Oxford man and gentleman who is going astray, even though that duty is very little acknowledged. Fourthly——   No ! there was nothing at all about Florence Plowden in the matter, nothing but an undying resentment against the girl who had presumed to teach him his duty !   She might be right.   I presume he felt in his heart that she was right, or he would not have taken the measures he had done.   But he also felt in his heart that he could never forgive her for her temerity, for departing from the woman's part so much as to venture to suggest to one of the priests of her parish what he should do.   No, Florence Plowden told for nothing in the effort he was making.   When her name floated up it awakened nothing but feelings of anger in his breast.

Poor Florry !   She sat half in the dark with her knitting, pretending she felt her eyes weak, in order that she might not betray the melting mist of happiness that was in her face, the soft dew that kept coming into her eyes.   If anybody had seen how near she was to crying, they would have thought her unhappy : whereas she was almost too happy to think, certainly too glad— except in a momentary impulse like that which had called upon her the reproof of both parents—to speak.

Jim put his books before Osborne, who grinned at the sight. It was intended for a smile, but it was a poor version of a smile. ' Oh, yes,' he said, ' Browning, the " Ride to Aix."   Isn't it just a little hackneyed ?   Oh, no, not the poem itself.   I don't mean that : but everybody does it.   What's the other ?   Ingoldsby.   O—

oh. I don't know, if you ask me my opinion, that I care so very much for Ingoldsby, myself.'

'Perhaps not,' said Jim, who for this once was wiser than his leader, ' but *they* do, you know. He's always the most popular of all.'

'Eh—oh—ah,' said Mr. Osborne, putting his head on one side as though to see in that way the virtues which were visible to the people in general. 'Now, I should have thought,' he said, 'that this sort of stuff was too—too conventional, too fictitious, in the wrong sense of the word, to please these sort of rough intelli- gences; that they would like something more—more straightfor- ward, don't you know.'

'Like the "Ride to Aix"? But then they're awfully anxious to know,' said Jim, 'what it was for, what the news was, and when it was, and all that; and I've never found yet any one that knew.'

Mr. Osborne discreetly turned that question aside, for on this point he had no more information than other people. 'Suppose you read it and let me hear,' he said. It was very good-humoured and kind of him. He expected nothing, if truth must be told, and he was really very full of occupation and had a great many things to do. But Jim, as it turned out, did not read badly at all. And there came a note of emotion in his voice as the gallop rang on; that sort of sympathy with the excitement of the strain, and climbing passion in the throat, which only a few readers are moved by. The curate listened in amaze while this high note of poetic sympathy thrilled through the lines, which Jim read with a pause or two and strain of breath to overcome himself. He could not understand what it meant to feel thus, and yet to drift into the parlour of the 'Blue Boar'; to tremble and flush with the poetry, and then listen to Slaughter and White maundering about politics, or sit with the schoolmistress. There came over the curate for the first time in a great many years a sense of humility, a sudden con- viction that there were more things in heaven and earth than were dreamt of in his philosophy.

'By Jove,' said Jim, 'I got through it pretty well this time. The worst is my voice always breaks at that line: "And into the square Roland staggered and stood." One gets wound up so, don't you know. After that I can always manage the rest.'

'Give me the book,' said Osborne; and he, too, read the last verses, but his voice did not break at all, the water did not come into his eyes. He read it all as if it were one of his own sermons. Decidedly there were things in heaven and earth—perhaps he acknowledged it a little grudgingly : 'Evidently, Plowden, you have the knack of it much better than I.'

'Nonsense,' said Jim, with a good-humoured laugh. 'You read so well. I've got no knack. It is only that a few of these things get over me somehow. Because—because they are mere stories and of no consequence.'

'Plowden,' said the curate.

'Yes ?'

'I wonder if you'd be dreadfully offended if I asked you one thing ?'

'I am not very peppery,' said Jim ; 'fire away ?'

'Well,' he said, 'I will, but you will be angry, I fear. It is just this. When you feel these things so, more than most people —more,' he added, with a naïve surprise, 'than I do myself; how is it, you know—that—I don't want to offend you—how is it that——'

Jim's countenance grew deeply red, a cloud came over it for a moment ; then he shook his head as if to shake off any con- sideration of such questions. 'I say, don't ask me that kind of conundrum. I'm not good at guessing things,' he said. 'Will the "Ride" do ?'

'The "Ride" will do capitally,' said the curate. He too shook off with a flush the questions which had risen involuntarily to his lips. He was grateful to Jim for passing it over, for neither taking offence in words nor jumping up and breaking off the con- ference. 'What sort of people do you think will come,' he said, 'since you seem to have experience of these things ?'

'Oh !' said Jim, 'a number of the village people will come —the daughters of the tradespeople, and those shifting folks that live in Pleasant Place, and a number of the "gentry"—the General——'

Mr. Osborne made a sign of impatience and dissatisfaction.

'Don't you want the gentry to come ? But the others like it. I assure you they do. Mrs. White and Mrs. Slaughter will not come, they are too grand. They're able to pay for their pleasure when they make up their minds to go out.'

Jim said this with a gleam of Florry's mimicry, which dis- composed the curate more than he could say. 'You seem to know all about it,' he cried, a little sharply. 'But I want the men from Riverside, the fellows from the boats. I don't want ladies and gentlemen. What I want is to keep the men from the public- house. Do you mean to say the same sort of thing has been done here before ?'

'Oh, yes,' said Jim, 'we have done it before; but I don't think we got any of the Riverside men. The people who come generally are—well, just the village people, Osborne, the people you know, particularly the women and the Sunday School lads, those that my sisters teach carving to, and so forth; and the ones that come to the night-school.'

'Ah!' said the curate, 'that is always something,' with a sigh of relief.

'And all that my mother calls the nice, respectable people,' said Jim, with a laugh, destroying the momentary good effect he had produced.

The curate put his face in his hands, and was silent for a minute. 'So that I have been taking all this trouble,' he said, 'and getting people to come over from Winwick, and laying myself under obligations—to amuse the old women—and the gentry, as you call them.'

'Well, yes; there will be old Mrs. Lloyd, and some more of her kind,' Jim said.

Mr. Osborne looked at his visitor for a moment, with as deep a colour as that which Jim had shown when he was being questioned—as much heat of embarrassment, and an air of offence much more marked. Mrs. Lloyd! The curate felt that the name of this old woman was a missile that any one was now at liberty to fling at him, to turn him into ridicule. Strange! when a very short time ago it appeared to him the finest feather in his cap.

'We must do something about this, Plowden,' he said. 'We must lay hold on some of these fellows, and get them to come. I've pledged myself it's for them. I've meant it all along for them. What can we do to get hold of them? You've been here all your life; you must have known half of them as boys. Can't we do something? can't we find some way of attracting them? Think for yourself. Do you want to read that "Ride," which you do so well, to——Mrs. Lloyd?' It would be impossible to express the tone of disgust with which Mr. Osborne said this name.

'I don't suppose she would understand much of it, poor old body. But she will like to hear the girls sing,' said Jim, more charitable, after all, to the old lady than was the instrument of her conversion from beer. 'About the men, I don't know; they're very hard to fetch. Yes, I used to know a lot of the young ones as boys; but I haven't seen anything of them for a long time.'

'I tell you what, Plowden,' said the curate, 'we'll go down

there some evening when the fellows are about. You can talk to
them, for old acquaintance' sake, while I—— Put your shoulder
to the wheel! Of course, you could do a great deal if you chose.
Don't, for the credit of the parish, let those fellows say we bring
them over here to play to the old women. I can't stand it. I
may have been a fool,' Mr. Osborne said. He said it with a force
and bitterness which Jim could not understand—not to Jim, that
was clear, but to some unknown adversary. 'But stand by me,'
he said, putting his hand on Jim's shoulder, 'and we'll tell another
tale.'

'Stand by me!' Was it the curate that spoke, and was this
Jim to whom he appealed?

XXXVI

JIM was hurrying home to the Rectory full of the plans that had been settled between him and his new friend, full of the unusual excitement of something to do which was novel at least, and might be amusing, and was voluntary, exacted from him by no one. It was the loveliest spring night, the first of May, but full of a softness which is little to be depended upon at that season, the stars shining sweetly in a sky which was fresh and luminous, with nothing of the sparkle of frost in it, but a prophecy, almost a realisation, of summer. The village was quiet, as it usually was at that hour; the window of the 'Blue Boar' still shining with light, for it was not yet the closing hour: but all except the *habitués* of that respectable place, where general drinking was not encouraged, had left. Jim did not feel the drawing to-night of those invisible links which drew him to the 'Blue Boar,' and he was hurrying along towards home, when he encountered a wrapped-up figure which paused as he approached, but which he did not at first recognise. Indeed, to tell the truth, he thought for a moment with a quick movement of anger, that it was one of his own belongings, mother or sister, who had taken the liberty of coming out thus, veiled and covered up, to look for him, which was a thing that the young man in his greatness of superiority would not very readily have forgiven. But it was not anything so innocent as poor Mrs. Plowden with her shawl over her head, strolling forth, as she would have explained, because it was such a beautiful night, just to breathe the air; not anything nearly so innocent. The dark figure stopped as Jim came up, and with a little cough to call his attention, said: 'Is this Mr. Jim?'

'Oh!' he said, coming to a sudden pause, 'Mrs. Brown!' but not with any delight in his tone.

'I fear,' said Mrs. Brown, 'there is not much pleasure in seeing me in that exclamation; but then, of course, you can't see

T

me, which takes from it all the uncomplimentary meaning. And where are you coming from at this hour—some of your smart parties?'

'You know as well as I do,' he said, aggrieved, 'that there are no smart parties here.'

'What do you call Mrs. FitzStephen's ball?' she said, with her laugh of mockery. 'I have heard that it was very smart— the young ladies' dresses beautiful, and diamonds upon some of the old ones. I call that very smart. Unfortunately, I hear, there were no Royal Highnesses—unless it was yourself, Mr. Jim.'

'How fond you are of laughing at people!' said Jim.

'I—the most innocent woman in the world! I will be very civil, now, if you will walk as far as my house with me. I don't mind the road up to the Hall, but here in the village, where a tipsy man might run up against me——'

'Oh, I don't think you need be afraid,' said Jim; but he could not refuse so small a request, though he did not like it— neither the interruption nor the fact, indeed, of escorting the schoolmistress, who was exceedingly amusing, and knew how to make herself agreeable in her own place; but here, outside, where he might be recognised by any one! Jim was half disgusted with himself for this feeling, yet felt it all the same, and turned back with a little reluctance, which he concealed, indeed, but which, from his companion's quick eyes, was not altogether to be concealed.

'You have been somewhere to-night where you ought to have been,' said Mrs. Brown. 'One soon gets to know the ways of young men. Sometimes you are not proud of the place in which you have been spending your evening, but to-night it's different. You are going home in a hurry to tell them all about it before they go to bed. What a pity that I should have met you just to-night!'

'It can never be a pity that I should have met you,' said Jim, a little sulkily, 'if I can be of any use.'

'Poor boy,' she said, with a half laugh, and then she added: 'I have been among naughty people to-night, who have been putting naughty schemes in my head. Tell me what nice, good society you have been having, to put it out of my mind.'

'Where are those naughty people to be found?' said Jim.

'Ah, you would rather know that than tell me your news! But they are not naughty people of your kind; they wouldn't amuse you at all. There is no fun in their naughtiness, but rather the reverse: envy and malice and all uncharitableness, not the folly that pleases you poor boys. Poor boys! for the one often leads to the other, don't you know, when you outgrow the fun and yet love the naughtiness, and get out of the way of all that's good——'

'You are in a very serious humour to-night.'

'No,' she said, 'not more than usual. I'm a very serious woman, though you may not have found it out. You have not found it out, have you?' she said, with a sudden laugh, apparently overcome by the absurdity of the situation, which, however, Jim did not feel at all. He saw no fun in it: all that he was afraid of was that with her laugh, though it was very soft, she might attract the observation of some one whom they met.

'No,' he said, 'I—I haven't thought about the subject, I never tried to——'

'Understand, did you?' she said quickly; 'took me as you found me? Of course you did. And you were quite right. Don't be afraid that any one will find you with me. In the first place, there is nobody to be seen, and in the second place——'

'I am not at all afraid of any one seeing me. I am not responsible to any one. I hope I am of an age to choose my own friends.'

'Well spoken, Mr. Jim, and very manly of you; and I am glad you would stand by me like that, as one of your own friends. Now, there is something I would like you to do for me. It is a great secret, and you must tell nobody of the request I am going to make.'

'Well,' he said, with a laugh, 'I hope I don't want much cautioning on that subject. The moment one is told that a matter is private, it is sacred—at least, to a man.'

'Ah! you think more sacred to a man than a woman, Mr. Jim? I don't agree with you; but still, I'm glad that it's your view. If you should find out—— You know of all that is going on in the family, don't you?'

'In the family,' cried Jim, astonished; 'in what family?'

'You may well be surprised. What should I have to do with your respectable family?' cried Mrs. Brown, laughing again. It was not like other people's laughter; it was a thin little sound, which, if it conveyed mockery of other people, seemed in some indescribable way to mock herself too. 'But yet,' she added, 'it is really your respectable family I mean. If your aunt should be hard pressed by those people, and felt as if she might be crushed altogether—now, mind what I say—felt as if she might be crushed altogether——'

'Do you mean my aunt Emily, Lady William? Why, who in the name of wonder wants to crush her altogether? You have got some joke in your mind that I don't understand.'

'Felt,' repeated Mrs. Brown with emphasis, 'as if she might be crushed altogether. I will make you say it after me to impress it on your memory, if you don't mind. Felt as if she might be crushed altogether—you understand?'

'I understand the words: but what they mean, or what you mean——'

'That is quite enough, so long as you know the words. Keep them fast, and in such a case let me know; not until you see there is very grave trouble, mind—not if you hear that she sees her way out of it.'

'You are speaking Hebrew, I think,' said Jim.

'No, I am speaking English. You will see, even if they don't tell you, by your people's looks, or you will get it out of one of your sisters. Mind! if you find that they are all in the dumps, and she feels herself beaten—you'll see it in their looks—let me know. If I should not be here I will let you know where I am.'

'Are you going away?' said Jim.

She did not make him any immediate answer, but turned round upon him, in the light of a lamp which they were approaching, putting back her veil a little, with a mischievous look. 'Should you be very sorry? No, I'm afraid you would not be very sorry,' she said.

'Yes, I should,' said Jim, with an impetuosity which alarmed him next moment, as he suddenly realised that somebody passing (but there was no one passing), or somebody unseen at a door or window, might hear what he said. 'I should be very sorry indeed to think I should not see you any more,' he added, in a lower tone.

'But that dreadful fate need not come, even if I were to leave Watcham,' she said, in her mocking tone. 'We met before I came here, which is the origin of all our acquaintance, and we may meet after I leave here. The world is a wide place. I shall let you know, somehow, where I am: and in the case I have so impressed upon you——'

'The case in which Aunt Emily (of all people in the world!) should find herself crushed altogether.'

'You are a good scholar. You have learned your lesson. In that case you will take care—but only when there is no other hope—to let me know. Now I'll release you, Mr. Jim. I won't exact that you should come to my very door. No harm can happen to me between this and my door.'

'It is the only part of the way where anything could happen,' said Jim. 'It's the middle of the town.'

'A wonderful town, and a wonderful middle,' she said, laughing. 'No, nothing will happen. Good night, and I am more obliged to you than I can say.'

Jim stood irresolute, and watched her as she drew down her veil over her face, and hurried along to the door of the schoolhouse. He was, on the whole, well pleased to get rid of her, but he did not like the idea of being thus dismissed at the moment it occurred to her to do so—a sensation which roused his pride and kept him, accordingly, standing where she left him until he saw that she had reached her own door. She turned round there and made a slight gesture of farewell, or dismissal. It was just at that moment that the *convives* at the 'Blue Boar' began to stream out, with a little noise of voices and feet, the last jokes of the little convivial club. Jim turned and hurried homeward, not without an uncomfortable feeling that his return would correspond unpleasingly with the dispersion of that assembly. But yet it was not his fault.

His mother was in the drawing-room still, waiting for him, or at least pretending not to wait for him, but to be very busy with something she had to do. And Jim had by this time remembered again the great news he had been carrying home so eagerly when he met Mrs. Brown. Though Jim detested the 'parish' in the official sense of the word, he was not without a natural feeling for his own side; and it pleased him almost as much as if he had been a Rector's son of the more orthodox description to find that the new curate, with his immense commotion as of a new broom, found it necessary after all to have recourse to the old rulers and their ways for help. He had, I need not say, not the faintest idea of the curate's benevolent intentions towards himself; but Mr. Osborne had been a little superior in the morning—it was his nature to be a little superior—and his final appeal for help to Jim, who of all the Rectory family was the only one whom nobody else would have thought of appealing to, was a triumph which Jim could not but be sensible of. His mother looked up at him from her sewing with those curves about her eyes which he had grown accustomed to, and did not at this present moment take any notice of, notwithstanding the keen inspection of him which she made instantly, an inspection so keen that it seemed to cut

below the surface and see what never can be seen. Jim was
more or less aware of this inspection when he had anything to
conceal, but on this occasion, having nothing to conceal, it did
not occur to him. 'Have the girls gone to bed?' he said, in a
disappointed tone. He had brought in with him no heavy odour
of tobacco or other scent inharmonious with the place, but a whole
atmosphere of fresh air, cool and pure, to which the haste of his
arrival gave an impetus, and which seemed to fill and refresh the
whole room, which was half dark, with only Mrs. Plowden's
solitary lamp shining on the round table. 'They've gone upstairs,' she said, rising to meet him with that sudden sweetness
of relief which fills an anxious heart when its anxiety is found
unnecessary. 'Do you want them? Shall I call them? Oh,
Jim, they will be too happy to come.'

'I'll call them myself,' he said, then paused—'unless it will
disturb my father! He looked a little worried at dinner.'

'It is like you to think of your father.' Mrs. Plowden could
not but caress her son's shoulder as she passed him. 'You can
always see farther than any one—with your heart, my dear.
Yes, he was worried. But never mind that; I'll call the girls.'

They came at the call like two birds flitting noiselessly down
the staircase, and came into the room with a faint rustle as of wings.

'Jim has something he wants to tell you, ' the mother said,
and there went a quick glance round the three like an electrical
flash; oh! of such ease, joy, consolation to themselves; of such
admiration, enthusiasm for him! That there should be nothing
to lament over, nothing to find fault with, meant whole litanies of
honour and praise to Jim.

He told them his story with a pleasure which found an
immediate echo and reflection from his mother and Emmy.
Florence, of whose sympathy he had felt most sure, had turned a
little away.

'He seemed struck all of a heap,' said Jim, not pausing to
choose his language, 'when he heard we'd had those sort of things
before. He thinks he's the first to do everything; and when I
told him it was the respectable folks that came and the Fitz-
Stephens and so forth, and the old women—Mrs. Lloyd and the
rest——'

'Jim,' cried Florence, seizing his arm, 'it was ungenerous to
mention Mrs. Lloyd.'

'Why?' cried Jim, opening his eyes; and Florry made no reply.
'Well,' he continued, 'Osborne was taken all aback, as I tell you.
He says it is the men he wants to catch—the fellows down by the

river, that sort. When I told him he might as soon look for the Prince of Wales, I never saw a man so broken down. He said, "How are we to catch hold of 'em, Plowden? What are we to do to fetch 'em? Come down with me," he said. "You must have known some of them from boys. Come down, you and me together, and let's see what we can do." I said to myself, "Oho, my fine fellow! for all so grand as you think yourself, you can't get on without the oldest inhabitant after all."'

'But, Jim, you'll help him,' cried Emmy; 'so will I, I am sure, with all my heart. We have always wanted to get hold of them; and you could do something, Jim, if you were working with him.'

'Oh yes, I shall help him,' said Jim in a magisterial way, 'fast enough. He isn't a bad sort of fellow when you know him. I said I'd go down with him when the fellows were at home in the evening whenever he liked. Of course, as he said, I know them all; half of them I've licked or they've licked me. He has sense to see the advantage of that, and, of course, now he's asked me I'll do whatever I can for him; and see if I don't have them up to hear all the tootle-te-tooting and you girls singing and all the rest.'

'If your father approves, Jim,' said Mrs. Plowden. 'We cannot make quite sure that your father approves.'

'Oh, papa will approve,' cried Emmy. 'I am sure he really knows how much good there is in Mr. Osborne. He only does not like his little—— Well, I don't like to call it conceit.'

'Excellent opinion of himself; but that's so common with young men,' said the Rector's wife.

And Florence—Florence who was the lively one, who on any ordinary occasion would have been in the heat of the discussion, talking now in the tones of Mr. Osborne, now like old Mrs. Lloyd, now like all the 'fellows' at Riverside—Florence said nothing at all! That is, nothing to speak of—nothing for her. She kept her face away from the light, and threw in a monosyllable now and then; and when Mr. Osborne's conceit was spoken of, threw up her head with an indignation which happily nobody perceived. To think they should discuss him so, who was doing all this, giving up his pride in his superior management, for their sake—appealing to Jim! It seemed to Florry that the force of noble self-abnegation could not further go.

THE Rector, when he came home upon that day, when Jim's alliance with Mr. Osborne began, did not show any such pleasure in the circumstances as his wife expected. He mumbled and coughed, and with a lowering brow said that anything was an excuse that kept the boy from his work, and that if Jim picked up Osborne's fads in addition to his own faults they would make a pretty hash of it altogether. Mrs. Plowden, however, made the less of this that the Rector was evidently in but an indifferent state of temper and spirits generally. 'He has been put out about something,' his interpreter said to the girls; 'something has gone wrong with him in town; he has not got his business done as he wished.' But what that business was, his wife was obliged to allow that she did not know. 'I can't help thinking,' she said, 'that it's something about your uncle Reginald. What else could Emily have come over in such hot haste about? And then your father going up to town in this wild way without giving any reason. I can't imagine what can be the cause unless it was something about Reginald. They are dreadful for sticking to each other, the Plowdens; they would think, perhaps, that I would make a remark, and I am sure that there are plenty of remarks I might make, for if ever there was a man who was utterly unbearable in a house it was Reginald Plowden, and nothing in the world would make me consent to have him here again, nothing! Your father has had something on his mind for some time back. Don't you remember he burst in one day as if he were full of something to tell us, and then stopped short all at once?'

'But that looked as if it was good news, mamma. He had met Mr. Swinford and he was just going to tell us.'

'What good news could come to us through Leo Swinford?' cried Mrs. Plowden scornfully: which was to poor Emmy as if somebody had given her a blow in the face. She fell back quite suddenly behind her sister, and attempted no reply.

'It did look at first as if it was something good,' Mrs. Plowden allowed ; 'but when I tried to draw it out of him he only got into a fuss you know, as he does so often, and told me I'd hear it all in good time. I am sure ever since he has had something on his mind ; and when he came back from town last night he could have torn us all in pieces. If it is not about Reginald I am sure I can't imagine what it can be.'

'It may be something about Aunt Emily, mamma.'

'What could there be about Emily ? No, she has heard from Reginald, that is what it is, and he has told her he was sending back her money, or something of that sort, and your father has gone up to town to see if it was true. And he has found out, of course, that it was not true, as I could have told him before he went a step on such an errand. And now he can't contain himself for rage and disappointment, and if I'm not mistaken, he has gone over to tell your aunt Emily that she is not to think of it any more.'

'He did walk over to the cottage,' one of the girls said ; and the other added :

'How do you find out things, mamma ? Now I am sure I never should have thought of anything of that kind.'

'My dears,' said Mrs. Plowden with a certain complaisance, 'you never knew Reginald Plowden. And I do. You cannot gather grapes off thorns, or figs off thistles ; and if there ever was thorns and thistles in flesh and blood, Reginald Plowden is the man. That your Aunt Emily should still expect to get her money back from him, just shows what a thing family affection is ; but she might as well expect it to drop down from those lilac-trees.'

The girls did not say anything in reply ; but Emmy, for her part, thought of quite a different explanation. She believed that Leo Swinford, whose proceedings had been so great an object of interest, and of whom she knew both by her own observation and by common report that he was 'always at the cottage,' had offered himself and his fortune to Lady William. Proposed to Aunt Emily !—that was how poor Emmy put it. A girl cannot but think such a proposal wholly ridiculous, if not an absolute infatuation. Her respect for her aunt made her still believe and hope that the proposal had been rejected ; but this wonderful event would quite account for the 'something on his mind,' which it was very clear the Rector had. What he had gone to town about,

however, and whether his mission could have any bearing upon
this disquieting question, Emmy could not say.   Florence was
so preoccupied with other matters that upon this, even though
it cost her sister so much disquietude, she expressed no opinion
at all.

The Rector, as had been perceived, had gone towards the
cottage when he went out with care upon his brow.   He had not,
after all, as the reader will understand, proclaimed the wonderful
news about Mab when he went home after his meeting with Lord
Will.   He reflected to himself that it might be some time before
he could set his sister's position quite straight, and that in the
meantime the report of Mab's heiress-ship would flash all over the
parish, and that any question, any hesitation, any delay, on the
subject would attract the curiosity and interest of the village folks.
Mab an heiress !   It would go from one end of the county to the
other, and questions as to when she would come into her fortune
would come from all sides ; very likely that last horror of
impertinent gossip which reveals what everybody leaves behind
him to the admiration of the public, would communicate the news
in spite of all precautions.   Lord John's death intestate and the
amount of his fortune would be in all the papers, with a list of the
kindred concerned.   But at all events, the Rector said to himself,
he would say nothing till the matter was more assured.   It was
not an easy thing to do.   He felt it bursting from his lips during
the first day when he allowed himself to mention Lord Will simply
to relieve his mind, but by main force kept the other communication back.   And to say that it was not with the most dreadful
difficulty that he kept his mouth shut on those many occasions when
it is so natural to let slip to your wife the secret that is in your
heart, would be to do Mr. Plowden great injustice.   He was not in
the habit of keeping things to himself.   Even the secrets of the
parish, it must be allowed, sometimes slipped—things that ought
to have been kept rigorously inviolate.   He had not, perhaps, the
most exalted opinion of his wife's discretion, and yet she was his
other self—a being indivisible, inseparable, with whom he could
not be on his guard.   But she had shown great discrimination when
she said that the Plowdens stuck to each other.   Nothing would
have made him confess to his wife that there was any insecurity in
the position of his sister.   Emily was a thing beyond remark, a
creature not to be criticised.   He would have nothing said about
her—not a word of compassion.   There are a great many men who
deliver over their sisters and mothers without hesitation to be cut
in small pieces by their wives, but here and there occurs an excep-

tion. Emily was James Plowden's ideal and the impersonation of the family honour and credit. He could not have a word on that subject, and thus he was strengthened in his resolution to say nothing of Mab's prospects—until, at least, they were established beyond any kind of doubt.

This did not by any means look like the position in which they were now. Mr. Plowden went into the cottage almost with a little secrecy—looking round him before he opened the little garden gate —for the gossips in the parish were quite capable of reporting that there was something odd and unusual in the Rector's constant visits to his sister, and that certainly something must be ' up.' To be sure it was only his second business visit—but even so much as that was unlike his usual habits, and he was extremely anxious that no question should be raised on the subject. He found her in the drawing-room, at her usual sewing. Mab was out, which was a thing of which the Rector was glad. She looked up hastily at the sight of him, reading his face, as women do with their eyes, before he had time to say a word.

' You have not succeeded, James ? '

' How do you know I have not succeeded ? ' he asked crossly. ' I have not, perhaps, done all that I hoped to do—but Rome was not built in a day. It was absurd to expect that I had only to go up to London—an hour in the train—and walk into old Gepps' parsonage and find him still there.'

' You did not find him at all ? '

' No, I didn't find him at all. I never expected to find him, considering that he was an older man than my father, and that my father has been dead for sixteen years.'

' To be sure,' said Lady William faintly.

' I found his name, however, all right, and the place—not quite in the City, as I thought — St. Alban's proprietary chapel, Marylebone.'

' Ah ! '

' Do you remember the name ? '

' No,' said Lady William ; ' I'm afraid I don't remember even the name.'

' Well, never mind ; Gepps was incumbent then. And a very good place, too, for anything that was to be kept quiet — hidden away in a labyrinth of little streets ; not so noticeable as the City, where an old church in the midst of warehouses is often something to see. Lady Somebody or other's proprietary chapel ; incumbent, the Rev. T. I. Gepps. No doubt that was the one.'

'Was it like my description? But, to be sure, it may have been changed, or restored, or something.'

'I can tell nothing about that. It has been changed with a vengeance. Emily, the chapel has been burned down——'

She gave a little scream of annoyance, but more because of the face he had put on, than from any perception in her own mind of the significance of the words.

'A few of the things were saved—the books, I mean—but not all, not all, by any means : and all those between 1860 and 1870 perished.'

'What do you say, James?'

She began to awaken to a little consciousness that this concerned her, which she had not at first understood. 'The books?'—she took it up but vaguely now—'the books? What—what does that mean, James?'

'It means that of the period of your marriage there is no record at all. Do you understand me, Emily? No record, no certificate possible—nothing. It is as if you had planned it all. A clergyman who is dead ; a chapel which is burned down ; a registry which is destroyed. That is what it might be made to look by skilful hands—as if you had invented the whole.'

She sat half stupefied looking at him, the work still in her hands, her needle in her fingers, looking up at him more astonished than was compatible with speech. 'The clergyman dead, the chapel burnt down, the registry destroyed !' She said these words in a kind of half-conscious tone—repeating them after him, yet not knowing what she had said.

'That is about the state of the case ; if you had meant to deceive, you couldn't have done better all round.'

Lady William looked at him with a curious half smile, yet wistful wonder in her eyes. 'But,' she said, 'I did not want to deceive.' There was a sort of startled amusement in her tone, mingling with something of reality, a question half rising, a faint feeling of the possibility, and that even, perhaps, her brother —— 'James,' she cried, 'you do not imagine that I—I——'

The words failed her ; the colour forsook her face, and she sat looking up at him dismayed ; her work fallen into her lap, but the needle still in her hand.

'Of course I do not imagine that you—nor, did I doubt that, could I doubt for a moment when there's my father's hand and date upon it. And I suppose that would be evidence in a court of justice,' the Rector said, knitting his brows—'I'm rather ignorant on such subjects, and I don't know. But I suppose it would be

evidence. 1 could prove my father's handwriting, and that I
found his notebooks, and produce the rest of them, and so
forth. But it's touch and go to rely upon a thing so close as
that.'

'The books destroyed!' she said, repeating the words, 'the
church burned down, the clergyman dead. Do such things happen?
all to overcome a poor woman? If it was in a book one would say
how impossible—how absurd——'

'Emily,' said the Rector, 'you must forgive me for saying it,
but that's just what your whole story is—impossible and absurd.
It has been so from the beginning; people have no right to launch
themselves on such a career. You had it always in your power
not to take the first step. I blame my father almost more than
you—he ought not to have allowed you to do it: but I blame you
too. For even a girl of nineteen is old enough to know what's
possible and what's impossible. You ought not to have allowed
yourself to be launched upon such a bad way. After your ridiculous
marriage you might have expected everything else that was ridiculous to follow. It is all of a piece. Nobody would believe one
word of it from the beginning to the end—if it was, as you say, in
a book.'

Lady William listened to this tirade with a curious piteous
look, almost like a child's; a look that was on the verge of
tears and yet had a faint appealing smile in it, an appeal against
judgment. Oh what a foolish girl that had been, that girl of
nineteen, that ought to have known better! and what a good
thing for her if she had known better; if she had been able by
her own good sense and judgment to overcome those about her:
the foolish old father, the false friend who led her into the net.
Listening to her brother's voice so long, long after the event, and
looking back upon the thing that was so impossible, the thing
which between them these foolish people had done—she could see
very well how preposterous it was, and how it could have been resisted. Mab (all these thoughts flew through her mind while the
Rector was speaking) would not have done it. But Mab's mother
had done it, and could not even now see what else she could have
done among these three people surrounding her, arranging everything for her. And there was a sort of whimsical, ridiculous
humour in the idea that all these complications must have followed
from that foolish beginning. What could she expect but that the
clergyman should die, the church be burned down, and the books
destroyed? To the disturbed and disappointed Rector, thoroughly
put out, touched in mind and in temper by a *contretemps* so painful

and disconcerting, there was nothing whatever ludicrous in the thought. But to her, whose whole life hung upon it, her child's fortune, her own good name, everything that was worth thinking of in the world, there was an absurdity which had almost made her laugh in the midst of her despair.

'I am very sensible of the folly of it now,' she said, commanding her voice, 'and I know all the misery that has been involved better than any one can tell me—but it is too late now to think of that. We must think in these dreadful circumstances what is now to be done.'

'You see, Emily,' said Mr. Plowden, 'I never knew the rights of it till the other day. I knew there was something queer and hasty about it, a sort of running away; but you know that till you came back here a widow with your little girl I had heard actually nothing—and, indeed, not very much until you came to the Rectory the other day.'

'That is quite true; and I am very sorry, James.'

'I don't say it to upbraid you, my dear. My father was much more to blame than you were. I would not like to have any of my daughters exposed to such a temptation, even at their age. And Florence is twenty-three. And you were always a spoiled child, getting everything your own way.' The Rector had gradually worked out his impatience and had gone round the circle to tenderness and indulgence again. He put his hand on her shoulder, and patted it as he might have done a child. 'My poor girl,' he said, 'my poor Emily!' with the voice of one who brings tidings of death, and a face as long as a day without bread, as the French say.

She looked up at him with a gaze of alarm.

'James!' she cried, 'do you think it is all over with us? Don't say so, for Heaven's sake! I'll find Artémise if I seek her through all the country; I'll find evidence somehow. Don't condemn us with that dreadful tone.'

'Condemn you!' said Mr. Plowden, 'never will I condemn you, Emily. Even if you had done something wrong instead of only something very foolish, you may be sure I should have stood by you through thick and thin. No, my poor dear, you shall get no condemnation from me; and Jane, I am sure, has far too much sense and too good a heart——'

Here the Rector's voice broke a little. The idea that his wife would have to be made the judge of his sister, and might almost, indeed, hold Emily's reputation in her hands, was more than he could bear.

'Jane!' said Lady William, with a ring in her voice as sharp and keen as that of her brother's was lachrymose; but, happily, she had sufficient command of herself not to express the exasperation which this suggestion of being at Jane's mercy caused her. She said, however, with a painful smile, 'You are throwing down your arms too soon; I don't intend to be discouraged so easily. Now I know that the fight will be desperate I can rouse myself to it. It is evident that the one thing that is indispensable is to find Artémise.'

'Who is Artémise? Some French maid or other?' said the Rector, with a tinge of disdain.

'Artémise is Miss Mansfield, who was with us—a cousin, or some people thought a half-sister, of Mrs. Swinford. Their father was a strange man, more French than English, and that is the reason of their names, and—many other odd things. She is a strange woman, and has a strange history. She was at the Hall, a sort of governess—when—— And she was sent with me that night. And without her I don't think—but we need not enter into those old stories now. One thing I know is that she is living, and that Leo Swinford has seen her—not very long ago.'

'A disreputable witness,' said Mr. Plowden, shaking his head, 'is not much better than no witness at all.'

He was in a despondent mood, and ready to throw discouragement upon every hope.

'I don't know that she is disreputable; and at all events she was present,' said Lady William. 'That must always tell—in a court of justice, as you say: though God grant that it may never come there.'

'I suppose you can lay your hand upon her without any difficulty, through Mr. Swinford,' the Rector said, suddenly adopting an indifferent tone as if with the rest of the business he had nothing to do.

'That is, perhaps, too much to say; but at least she may be found—or I hope so,' Lady William replied.

'And now I must go,' said Mr. Plowden. 'Of course, anything and everything I can do, Emily—when you have tried what is to be accomplished in your own way——' He turned towards the door, and then returned again, with a still more cloudy face. 'My dear sister,' he said, in a tone of solemnity and tenderness adapted to the words, 'you may have to seek his help for this; but for all our sakes do not, any more than you can help, have young Mr. Swinford here.'

Lady William looked up quickly with a half‑defiant glance.

'Above all,' said the Rector impressively, 'while there is any sort of doubt, any sort of cloud, and when every step you take will be remarked—— Don't make me enter into explanations, but, for all our sakes, don't have Mr. Swinford always here.'

It is almost needless to say that the Rector left his sister in a
state of mind in which exasperation healthily and beneficially con-
tended with despair. She might have been crushed altogether by
his discovery; but he had managed to mingle with that so many
other sentiments that Lady William felt herself no broken-down
and miserable woman, but a creature all full of fight and resistance—tingling, indeed, with pain, and scorched with a fire of injury, feeling insulted and outraged to the depths of her being, but
all the same full of angry strength and force, determined that nothing
as yet was lost, and that sooner than yield herself to the tolerance
of her sister-in-law and indulgent interpretations of her friends,
who would pity and assure each other that whatever dreadful thing
had really happened, poor Emily, a mere child at the time, was
innocent—there was nothing she was not capable of doing. To
change from Lady William—in a sort, the head of the little community—to poor Emily, was a thought which fired her blood. For
that, as well as for her child, the small motive thrusting in in the
immediate present into the foreground—there was nothing she
would not do. To find Artémise was a trifle to her roused and
indignant soul. If she went out herself on foot with a lanthorn,
she said to herself with a vehemence which soon turned into an
angry laugh, she would find her. The lanthorn and the search on
foot turned it all into stormy ridicule, as the Rector's suggestion
that the little, dingy, dark private chapel had been burned and the
books destroyed as a natural consequence of her folly in being
married there, had done. Lady William felt the laughter burst
out in the middle of the bitter pain. For the pain was bitter
enough down in the breast from which that stormy humour burst,
so sharp that she could not sit still, but went raging about like—
as she said to herself—a wild beast, pushing the crowded furniture
aside, holding her hands together as if to keep down the anguish

U

by physical torture.   A thumbscrew or a deadly boot to crush her
flesh would have been something of a relief to her in the active
anguish of her soul.   Mab to hear that her mother was——   Oh
no ; never that her mother was—— but only that there was a
doubt, a horrible peradventure, a failure of proof.

Lady William paused in her movement to and fro and tried to
look at it for a moment through Mab's eyes.   That is often a very
good thing to do, but a difficult.   We forget nature when the
question is one so all-important as this, what a child will think of
its mother.   Often we believe in an opinion too favourable, without inquiry, forgetting what a formidable criticism is that which
our children make of us from their cradles, learning our habitual
ways so much better than we know them ourselves.   But there
are some ways in which the natural judgment of candid and clear-
sighted youth may give any who is unjustly accused comfort.   In
the light of Mab's eyes (though they were neither bright nor
beautiful) Lady William felt for a moment that her trouble melted
away.   Mab might not see the fun—that she should see fun at
such a crisis of her life !—of James's suggestion of the connection
between the burning of the church and the folly of the marriage :
but she would be utterly stolid like a block of stone to any idea
of shame.   No one could cast suspicion upon her mother's honour
to Mab.   Lady William thought she could see the girl's look of
utter disdain on any one who could suggest such a suspicion even
by a glance.   There was once a lady known to fame who, moved
by a hot fit of jealous pain and misery, left the house in which
she was being entertained, and walked home alone at night up
the long length of Piccadilly.   A man who met her, moved, I
suppose, by her solitude and the unusual sight, followed, and at
last addressed her.   When her attention was attracted she turned
round upon him, looked at him, and uttering the one word
' Idiot ! ' walked on, as secure as if she had been surrounded by
a bodyguard of chivalry.   Somehow that incident floated into
Lady William's memory.   That was what Mab would do.   She
would think, if she did not say ' Idiot ! ' and pass by, too con-
temptuous almost to be angry, feeling it unnecessary to answer
a word to the depth of imbecility which was capable of such a
thought.

Yes ; it made her quieter, it calmed her down, it delivered her
from that worst and deepest horror, to look at it through Mab's
sensible, quiet eyes.   But when Lady William remembered that
James would tolerate her, and be kind, and that everybody else
would say, ' Poor Emily ! ' the intolerableness of the catastrophe

caught her once more—and the advantage which even her brother
even James, who loved her in his way, who would spare no trouble
for her, had taken of it already.   While there was a shade, while
there was a shadow of a doubt upon her, she must not admit Leo
Swinford 'for all our sakes.'   Women do not habitually swear,
or I think Lady William would have used bad words, had she
known any, when this intolerable recollection came into her mind,
just as, if she had not been bound by the inevitable bonds of
education and natural self-control, she might have broken the china
or the furniture to relieve herself. A gentlewoman cannot do either
of these things, fortunately, or unfortunately, for her, and they are
outlets which must sometimes be of use.   But the quick movement
with which she dashed her hands together when that last thought
came into her mind, upset a little table upon which was a plant,
one of Mab's especial nurslings just shaping for flower, as well as
various other nicknacks of less importance.   The sense of guilt and
shame with which she saw what she had done, the compunction
with which she stooped over the broken flower-pot, and gathered
up the fortunately uninjured plant, and the specially prepared
soil in which it had been placed, and which was but dirt to Patty,
who came dashing in at the sound of the crash to set matters
right—did Lady William as much good as smashing a window or
two might have done to a poor woman out of Society.   She was
very penitent and much ashamed of herself, and horribly amused
all the same.   To express her rage, her injured feelings, her pride
and desperation, by breaking a flower-pot, was again where bathos
and ridicule came in.

    'I'll sweep it all up, my lady,' cried Patty, 'and there won't
be no harm.'

    'Miss Mab's leaf-mould?   No, you shan't do anything of the
kind.   Find me another flower-pot, and let us gather it all up carefully, and put it back.'

    'Miss Mab's full of fads,' said Patty, under her breath.

    But Lady William did not allow herself such freedom of criti-
cism, and she had scarcely gathered up the mould and built it
securely round the plant in the new pot before Mab came in.
'Oh, are you filling it up with fresh mould, mother?   My poor
auricula!   It will never produce a prize bloom now, and I had
such hopes.'

    'You ungrateful child! when I have gathered up every scrap
of your famous mould with my own dirty hands!'

    'Poor mother,' cried Mab, 'that can never bear to dirty her
hands! let me see them.'

Mab kissed the fingers which Lady William held out, smiling. 'After all it is clean dirt, nice mould carefully made, and with everything nice in it both for the colour and the health. Mother, your hands are a little like the auriculas, velvety and soft.'

'And brown, and purple,' said Lady William, laughing. Who is it that says that if we would not cry we must laugh? Heaven knows how true it is.

'It must have been Patty that did it,' said Mab. 'That child will never learn to take care. And, oh! the little Dresden shoe is broken that I got off the Christmas tree, and the silver things all scattered. I wish Patty might get a whipping; it is the only thing that would make her take care.'

'Whip me, then, Mab, for it was I. I was vexed and angry——'

'You! angry, mother?'

'It is not a thing that never happens, Mab.'

'No,' said Mab judicially; 'it is not a thing that never happens: but it only happens when you are put out. And I should like to know what had put you out.'

'Nothing,' said Lady William, with a smile.

'Oh! mother; you may say that to other people—but to me! Of course, I shall find out.'

'It was something your uncle James said to me, Mab.'

'Oh!' said Mab, satisfied; 'I am not surprised if he was in it. He does say such strange things. But he means well enough. Come out, then, mother, for a walk. That always does you more good than anything.'

'It is too early; it is not noon yet. It is dissipated going away from one's work at this time of the day.'

But the conclusion was that the two ladies did go out, and went to the river-side, where Lady William sat down on a bench by the landing-place, while Mab made certain investigations in respect to the boats. It was a fine morning, but not over bright—one of those gray days in the beginning of May, when Nature seems to veil herself capriciously by way of making the after-glory more glorious. The day was gray, with breaks of quiet light, not bright enough to be called sunshine, through the clouds, and all the new foliage tempered and softened in its fresh greenness of spring by the neutral tints that enveloped everything. The river flowed quietly upon its way, stopping for nothing, indifferent whether overhead there was sunshine or clouds, working away at the tall growing reeds on the edge, and sweeping round them, pushing them back out of its way, sapping the camp-shedding on the other side,

hollowing out the bank that intruded into the current. The soft,
strong flowing carries one's thoughts with it, whatever they may
be, and Lady William gradually gave way to that silent coercion,
and let her more painful reflections escape her, and the thoughts
she could not get rid of swell round and round her mind like the
circles of the stream. The scenery was not remarkable at that
point. From the river, indeed, the pretty little landing-place, with
its bit of green bank, its marshalled boats, and the old red-and-
white houses behind, made a delightful touch of life and colour :
but to the spectators on the bank there was nothing exciting to
be seen, only the grassy shore opposite, the trees, a brown cow or
two coming down to the river, or a passing boat full of travellers,
or of merrymakers, as the chance might be. How softening,
pacifying, composing it was ! Mab's voice talking to the boatman
on the river's edge came softly through the harmonious air. Who
can think, in the mild calm of such a day, of confusion, or trouble,
or shame ?

'I am in much luck,' said Leo Swinford's voice behind her,
'to find you here ; you are not usually to be found out in the
morning.'

'No,' said Lady William, telling him the reason with a burst
of assumed cheerfulness. 'It is possible that all Mab's hopes of
her auricula are spoiled by my fault ; yet she forgives me,' she
said. Then suddenly she put forth her hand and gripped his arm,
with a change on her face—'Leo, where is Artémise ? Find me
Artémise !'

'What is the matter, dear lady ?' he said.

'Ah ! it is of no importance what is the matter. I will tell
you afterwards. It is only this, that I must find Artémise—if I
take a lanthorn myself and go out and search for her.'

'Ah ! you laugh,' he said, 'and I am relieved. It is Mrs.
Mansfield you mean—is she Mansfield now ?—I think not, nor
can I tell what her name is. Certainly I can find her. I saw her
once, as I told you—twice—here in this village, as if she were
living here ; and then she came to see my mother. I am sure
she has been with my mother since ; but I have not seen her
again.'

'With your mother is not the question. Your mother, I fear,
Leo, would rather I did not see her. She likes no one to meddle
with those she cares for.'

'Does she really care for this woman ?'

'Can you ask me ? They are near relations, and dear friends,
and love each other.'

'Are you sure of all that?' he said; 'from my mother I have never heard——'

'But it is true.'

'The last I suppose is true,' said Leo reluctantly. 'My mother is fond of her—though why——'

Lady William gave him a look, as if there might be two sides to the question; then she said: 'It is of the utmost importance to me to see her, Leo—and soon. Will you give me your attention, and remember it is no mere wish—for an old friend.'

'An old friend! I cannot conceive that she should ever have been a friend of yours.'

'Yet, more than that; I desire to see her more than the dearest friend I have in the world.'

'Your bidding shall be done, dear lady: should I go myself and take the lanthorn—as you say. But that will not be necessary. I shall find her, I hope, more easily—or whatever else you are pleased to wish for,' he added in a lower tone. 'That is too easy. Set me some task that will prove what I can do.'

Lady William cast at him a keen look from under her eyelids. She remembered her brother's adjuration, 'for all our sakes.' 'A romantic task,' she said, 'that would prove what you could do is quite different. I ask my friend to help me in a way I really want; but no one ever wanted a white cat that would go through a ring—or was it a shawl? I forget.'

'I never thought,' he said, with an uneasy laugh, 'that you would send me off in search of a white cat.'

'I might, though,' she said, 'if the white cat would turn out an enchanted princess and make you happy all your life after—which I hope is what will happen one of these days. And my gracious nephew, Leo, did he leave you as he said?'

Leo replied with another question: 'How does Miss Mab like it that she is to be an heiress? I have not seen her to ask her.'

'You can see her at once. She is there, you see, with her friends the boatmen; but you must not ask her, please, for she knows nothing of heiress-ship as yet.'

'Ah!' he said, 'you are afraid to turn her head.'

'I am not at all afraid of her head, but I am afraid of other things. Tell me, why did he come here? The Pakenhams are not generous people, and they are not rich, and I should have known nothing of Lord John's fortune. Was it out of kindness to his cousin, whom he did not know, that he came here?'

'Ah, who can tell?' said Leo. 'He thought, perhaps, that you were sure to see it in the papers.'

'But even then I should not have known that Mab had any right.'

'Who can tell?' said Leo again, shaking his head, 'what are the motives of these people who are above rule, who do not require to behave like ordinary mortals? He thought, perhaps, yes, of his little cousin—he thought, perhaps, most likely of himself. He might have thought with all that fortune that it might be well if Miss Mab, perhaps, should—what do you call it?—take a fancy to him, and return it all to his pocket, which is not too full. How can you tell what any one's motives are, not to speak of a Lord Will?'

'It is true,' said Lady William, with a sigh ; ' but I suppose my best course now is to wait—to take no steps till I hear from the lawyers.'

'Perhaps, instead, your own lawyer——'

'Ah, I have had so little need of one—of course there is a man of business who used to manage my father's affairs. One does not seem to care,' she said, with a faint laugh, 'we poor people, who have nothing but our poverty—to confide all our affairs even to such a man.'

'Ah, but they are not men—they are like priests. There is a seal as of the confessional upon their lips. I should not have thought you, who are so transparent, so open, would have had such a scruple.'

This was a little duel, though neither suspected the object of the other. Lady William was eager to find out from Leo what ' the family' had intended to do by sending that messenger, and Leo was eager to persuade Lady William to confide in him, to show him what her difficulty was, and how far the broken revelations of his mother's attack upon her were true. But neither ventured to unravel the motive which was foremost in their minds. Both endeavoured to extract the information which the other had no intention of revealing. But to the spectators who were looking on, the two people on the bench, who were in reality thus resisting and eluding each other, had an air of great and tender intimacy as they sat together, each turned towards the other, pursuing their mutual investigations by the study, not only of what was said, but what was looked, by the betrayals of the eyes as well as of the tongue. Even Mab, returning from her long talk with old George the boatman, was a little struck by the absorbed attention of Leo to her mother, and of her mother to Leo. With what interest they were talking; seeing no one else that was near; paying no attention to anything that passed! Lady William was not wont to lose herself thus in conversation. She had always an eye for what was going on; for the passing boats on the river, or even for the clouds and brightness of the sky—and much more for her little girl who was hanging about anxious to join her, yet daunted a little by this too animated, too eager talk. Mab had heard a stray word here and there on the subject of Leo Swinford and his visits, to which she had paid no attention, but such words will sometimes linger without any desire of hers in a little girl's ear.

'I ASKED old George to go to your fandango, Jim, and he said he would, and take another man or two. He said he'd like to hear the young ladies sing, if they'd sing something as an old man could understand; and he wouldn't mind hearing Mr. Jim if he said somethin' as was funny and would make a man laugh. Lord, you didn't want to cry when you went out for something as pretended to be pleasuring. The old woman can do that fast enough at home. And as for Mr. Osborne, old George said as he draw'd the line at him.'

'What a horrid old man!' said Florence.

'No, he's not at all a horrid old man. He is a great friend of mine; but he doesn't like, as he says, and I agree with him, to have some one always a-nagging at him. When one's mother does it, it's horrid: and the curate would be worse. Jim, do you really like Mr. Osborne that you have grown such friends?'

'Well,' said Jim, with much innocence and a touch of complaisance besides, 'it's him that looks as if he liked me.'

'What excellent grammar, and what still more excellent humility!' cried Florence. Florence was, it must be allowed, a little bitter. Jim's acquaintance with the curate had gone on increasing daily. It had done him a great deal of good—in one way. The doors of the 'Blue Boar' were closed to him: he went there no longer. He thought of the vet. and Simpkinson, the landlord, with a sort of horror, asking himself whether it was true that he had actually sought their society. It had been in pure vacancy he knew now, and because there was no other to be had. But yet he had persuaded himself that they were very good fellows, and that to make acquaintance with their ways of thinking was a good thing, and expanded his knowledge of life and the world. He had all the fervour now of a new convert in respect to the superiority of his present surroundings, but still

was pleased with the thought that it was Mr. Osborne who had
sought him, and not he who had sought Mr. Osborne. The
curate had thus fulfilled towards him all, and more than all, that
Florence had ventured to suggest. In making Jim believe that
it was pure liking that attracted him, Mr. Osborne had bettered
the prayer that had been made to him. Had he done it for her
sake?—who could tell? If it was so, it was a transfer complete
and thorough, for he had never approached Florence, never
spoken to her when he could avoid it, never looked at her since
that day. He said, 'How do you do, Miss Plowden?' as if he
had never known more of them than from a chance meeting in the
village street, when he met the sisters. Not even his anxiety
about his entertainment broke down the barrier he had raised
between himself and the girl to whom he had all but offered his
heart and life. 'What is the matter with Mr. Osborne?' Emmy
had asked of her sister, in consternation, for it is needless to say
that Florry's sister and constant companion had been well enough
aware of the previous state of affairs. Florence had not answered
the question, but she had preserved her composure, which was a
great thing, and had thus led her sister to believe that, whatever
the matter was, it was a temporary one. Mrs. Plowden, too,
had put a similar question, but had herself answered it in the
most satisfactory way. 'What has become of Mr. Osborne?'
she said, and then replied to herself, 'I suppose since he sees so
much of Jim at his own place, he doesn't think it worth his
while to come here. It isn't perhaps very civil to the rest of us;
but what does it matter to any of us? and it is quite an advantage
to Jim. I am sure he may be as rude to me as he likes; if he
is nice to Jim, what do I care?'

This did not perhaps make Florence feel less sore. She could
not help feeling that all her own prospects might come to nothing,
and so long as it was well for Jim her mother would not care
or any one. To tell the truth, Mrs. Plowden was of opinion that
the curate's apparent admiration of Florence had been only a cover
for his desire to secure the friendship of her son, so wonderfully
had her mind changed since the evening when she had bemoaned
the use that Mr. Osborne might, but would not, be to Jim, and
when Florence had formed the heroic resolution of setting that
duty before her lover, if he should ever become her lover. The
poor girl had carried out that vow, and had achieved that purpose.
She said to herself that she had nothing to regret. It was far
more important that he should tide Jim over this dangerous
period, that he should restore him to better aims and hopes, than

that he should 'pay attention,' as the gossips said, to herself. Florry said to herself proudly that she wanted no 'attentions,' from Mr. Osborne. If he had loved her, as she once thought, that would have been a very different matter. But it was apparent enough now that this had never been the case; and what did she want with him and his attentions? He had been angry, furious with her for the suggestion she had made to him. Evidently he was one of the men who think that women should never open their mouths, should see only what they are told to see. But he was a man with a conscience, and even the suggestion of a despised girl had borne fruit. He had been able to put her out of his mind, but not to put the thing she had said out of his mind. So much the better! He had held out a rescuing hand to Jim. He was doing the work of a Christian knight towards her brother. And as for any little delusion of hers, what did it matter? It was far better so, so long as nobody suspected—as nobody should suspect, did it cost her her life!—the pang that was in poor Florry's heart.

It had been suspected, however—nay, more, divined—by one person, who was one of the group, coming down the street of Watcham together from the practice which had been held in the schoolroom on the morning of Mr. Osborne's entertainment. Emmy and Florence had gone through their song, with some applause from the other performers, but not a word from the curate, who seemed not to make even a pretence of listening, and whose indifferent aspect was actually rudeness to the two young ladies, his Rector's daughters, who had the greatest call upon his attention. He made himself, on the other hand, very agreeable to the two young London ladies who abode in one of the villas at Riverbank, and whose performance upon the piano was not remarkable. Miss Grey, who was present in her capacity of lay or feminine curate, the official best known and most fully recognised in the parish, could not help but see this; and, indeed, there were plenty of other people who remarked it, wondering whether Mr. Osborne had quarrelled with the Rectory family, a supposition, however, which was untenable in sight of his intimacy with Jim. Jim's reading had the curate's warmest applause. He referred to Jim on everything, sent him off to arrange matters, consulted him about the programme, and the succession of the performances; in short, conducted himself as if Jim Plowden were his other self and as much the giver of the entertainment as he was. The last thing he did after the practice was over, was to call to Jim that he should expect him at five to look up the fellows at Riverside.

In the meantime Mr. Osborne had to entertain the Winwick contingent. But all this was so strange, so marked, so unlike Mr. Osborne's former behaviour, that little Miss Grey, between consternation and amusement, did not know what to think. She was an experienced little woman, and she saw very well what was coming when Florence and the curate left her house together, three weeks before. She had expected that very day to have another visit from one or both of them to tell her the great news. And, instead, there was to all appearance a total disruption between them ; and not only so, but Jim—Jim !—received into the curate's heart as closest friend and first favourite apparently, in his sister's place.

Miss Grey felt that there must be an explanation of this, though she could not make it out as yet ; and, above all, she was very sure that Mr. Osborne's rudeness to the Plowdens did not come from nothing. There must be a reason for it. Whatever it meant, indifference was certainly the last thing it could mean. And Jim's complaisance in respect to his new friendship with the curate made the whole question still more complicated. 'It's him that looks as if he liked me.' Looks as if he liked Jim, and looks as if he disliked Florence ! But that was more than Miss Grey, with all her knowledge of man, and even of curate-kind, could understand. And the slight sharpness in the tone of Florence threw an additional cloud upon the whole matter. Nobody but must feel that it was good for Jim to be engaged in the curate's schemes instead of talking second-hand politics at the 'Blue Boar.' But Florence's voice had a sharp tone in it, and in Florence's self there was a sort of thrill of offended dignity, which Miss Grey was quick to see. The girl was wounded, and not much wonder. Her part of the performance was precisely the one in which Mr. Osborne seemed to take no interest. To be sure, Miss Grey was not aware that since that fated morning Florence and he had not exchanged one word that was not indispensable to the preservation of appearances. And yet she had not refused Mr. Osborne, which would have explained everything —at least, there was no reason to suppose that she had refused him. Had she done so it would somehow have oozed out. Birds of the air carry these matters. It shows upon the aspect of the rejected more surely than does the delight of acceptance. And besides, Florence Plowden had not intended to reject—there was no appearance of that purpose in her. The matter became more and more mysterious the longer Miss Grey thought it over. She could get no light upon this mysterious question.

They were all walking along together—a bevy of young people with Miss Grey in the midst, with a little excitement consequent upon the performances past and the performance to come, making a good deal of cheerful noise in the cheerful road. Two or three were always talking at the same time, and nobody was listening, though Jim found it possible to hear what Mab was saying to him, and Florence could not help but remark upon every word that concerned Mr. Osborne. The rest were discussing their own share in the performance and what the violinists from Winwick and the rest of the people were going to do. 'Fiddlers are thought everything of nowadays,' said the pianists, 'and yet where would they be without an accompanist?' They thought the same thing of the singers more or less, and the singers, who were aware that they were themselves the most popular part of the entertainment, returned that feeling. As for those who were merely to read, the musical part of the performers had a sort of impartial and indifferent contempt for them, as for people who were merely making a little exhibition of themselves—not rivals at all. Shakespeare or Ingoldsby, the young ladies from Riverbank did not think it mattered a bit which it was. And even Mab asked, more from civility than with interest, what Jim was going to do.

'The "Ride to Ghent"? We have had the "Ride to Ghent" so often. If you had wanted a ride, you might have taken that other one from Browning, where the man thought "Perhaps the world will end to-night."'

'Do you think the boatmen would care about that?' said Florence. 'Oh no, you don't know it, Jim. It is a man who is going to have a last ride with a girl who does not care for him. At all events, he thinks this is their last ride. And then perhaps he thinks the world may come to an end.'

'I don't see much meaning in that,' said Jim. 'I suppose there will always be plenty other girls in the world. Browning is always so far-fetched, except——'

'When he isn't,' said Mab, laughing. 'The "Ride to Ghent," is not far-fetched.'

'But what is it about?' said Jim. 'I've been asking Osborne, who did something tremendous in history, in Greats—and he can't tell me. Now, if I could say before I begin, "This was after a great fight between the—what? the Spanish and the Dutch, or something——"'

'You can say,' said Mab, 'that it was a starving time, and if they didn't hear the good news they would have to give in—after

holding out till they were nearly dead: though I can't make
out,' added that young lady, 'if the country was so free as that,
and Loris and the other two could ride a whole day without any
one disturbing them, why the town should be starving? But you
are not called upon to explain. They would like the "Pied Piper"
still better, you know,' she continued reflectively. 'It's easier to
understand. They want a story, and they want it to go quick,
without reflections—like this,' said the experienced little woman
of the parish, striking her hands together, which startled them all.

'There are nothing but vulgar stories that do that—claptrap
things, things that ladies and gentlemen could not listen to,'
said Emmy Plowden.

'Oh, what does it matter about the ladies and gentlemen? I
should not care a bit for them. There is that new Indian man,
that writes the stories—a man with a curious name; but, then,
they are not *good* stories at all. The soldiers drink and
swear, and that would never do. Is it necessary to drink and
swear in order to have "go" in you?' said Mab. 'As for your
old Ingoldsby, they see it's meant to be fun, and they laugh. But
they don't care.'

'I fear,' said Florence, always with that little sharp tone in
her voice, 'that Jim will have to take what he has got, instead of
waiting till the right thing comes.'

'Is the new schoolmistress going to do something?' said Miss
Grey. 'I heard a report—— I don't like the looks of that
woman, but she is as clever as ever she can be. She could do
Lady Macbeth, or—anything she likes. And she knows—
quantities of things, far too much for a village schoolmistress. I have seen her somewhere before, I am certain, and
she is quite out of her place here. But why doesn't Mr. Osborne
get hold of her, and see what she could do? She'd make them
attend, I'll warrant you! There wouldn't be much wandering
attention if she were there.'

'It's a pity,' said Jim stiffly, 'that she could not hear you,
Miss Grey: for she said the ladies would not like it if she
appeared.'

'She thinks she could throw us all into the shade,' said
Florence—'we should be jealous of her, I suppose.'

'Yes,' said Jim, 'of course she would; she would throw everybody here into the shade.'

He spoke with a little fervour, forgetting, unhappy boy! that
he had no right to know anything whatever of Mrs. Brown.

'Jim, how should you know?' said Emmy, mildly; and then,

to make bad worse, Jim stumbled into an explanation how he had gone to her from Mr. Osborne, and how she had laughed, and 'said' something to him, 'a piece of poetry,' Jim called it, which made his hair stand upright on his head; but after that, she had refused, saying, 'No, no; the ladies would not have it, the ladies would not like it.'

'As if we should care!' said Florence, with a little sneer. 'You can go and tell her if you like, that the ladies have no objection. We are not jealous, are we—of Mrs. Brown?'

This was not poor Florry's natural tone, and the sharpness of it went to one heart at least—that of Miss Grey, who discovered what it meant: and startled the rest, who did not understand any meaning in it at all.

'Don't send Jim,' said Mab, 'let me go. I'll tell her we should all like her to do—Lady Macbeth or whatever she pleases —and that none of the ladies would mind—not you, Miss Grey, I may tell her—for perhaps she thinks the young ones don't count.'

'Don't bother, Mab,' said Jim hastily, 'It is too late; even if she were willing we cannot change the programme now.'

'Oh, but I am going! I have a fancy for Mrs. Brown,' said Mab, waving her hand.

MAB left the others separating on every side towards their homes, and ran back to the schoolhouse, from which the children had all dispersed a little while before. She was full of her errand, in which there was a little sense of mischief as well as of pleasure, the one giving piquancy to the other. No doubt it was quite true that the ladies were not jealous of Mrs. Brown. It was to Mab the most amusing thing in the world that anybody should think so. Florence and Emmy, for instance, jealous—of a woman twice as old as they were, if she were the most beautiful and attractive woman in the world! How absurd it was! Youth has confidence in youth, in a manner as astonishing to the rest of the world as is the futility of that confidence in so many cases. And to a girl of seventeen a woman of forty is so entirely out of any sort of competition with herself that the suggestion is too ridiculous to be taken into the mind at all. Mrs. FitzStephen, perhaps, or Aunt Jane might be jealous of Mrs. Brown, but then they had nothing to do with it: and it was still more absurd to think that these good ladies could have anything in hand that would make it possible for jealousy to come in. All this ran through Mab's cheerful mind as she went back, not noting the half-alarmed, half-displeased look which Jim threw after her, and his hesitating step in advance, as if he would have gone too. It was an exceedingly good joke to Mab, for though, of course, the ladies were not jealous, they would no doubt be much surprised to see Mrs. Brown appear—surprised, and perhaps not quite pleased. It was not that they habitually looked down upon the schoolmistress —even Mab in her short memory knew of some who had been much petted by the gentry in Watcham. There was one girl, who was delicate, and who was as much thought of as if she had been a princess in disguise, all ' the best people' uniting to spoil her, Mab thought, who, being more on this young woman's level, saw things with a clear eye. But Mrs. Brown was not a favourite though nobody could tell why. She had seen better days, which was nothing against her; but then she had none of that genteel decay about her, which ought to be characteristic of those who had seen better days. She appeared, indeed, to make a joke of it all, rather than to lament her fallen estate. There was always a twinkle in those eyes, which were so bright, so bold, and so all-seeing. Mab had felt, like all the rest, an instinctive revulsion against her. But this had died off in that appreciation of cheerfulness and courage, which was deep in Mab's nature. To be less well off than you used to be, and yet take it, not with a moan, but with a jest, or even a gibe, laughing at yourself, seemed to Mab a much more attractive thing than the melancholy of decayed gentility; but this was not the aspect in which the other ladies regarded it. They would all have been sorry for Mrs. Brown had she taken her humiliation sadly. What they did not understand was the joke she made of it, which, to them, seemed impudence and defiance. Perhaps, Mab thought to herself in the abundance of her thoughts as she ran along, this feeling on the part of the ladies was what the gentlemen called jealousy. It was not so bad a guess for a little girl.

It may be added here that Lady William had not made acquaintance with the schoolmistress from the fact that Lady William, probably by right of having been herself the Rector's daughter and born to that work, refused determinedly to have anything to do with the parish. She did not keep Mab back from that inevitable work, but she would not herself take any part. District visiting, schools, mothers' or girls' meetings, penny banks, clothing clubs, all the machinery of the parish, Lady William kept religiously apart from them all. She had a recipe for beef tea which was known far and near, the strongest and the most quickly made, everybody knew, that had ever been heard of, and would go to the kitchen and make it herself, if old Anne, who was the sovereign there, was out of the way or out of temper: and puddings came from her house for the sick people which would have tempted an anchorite to eat: and if warm things were wanted for the winter there was no end to the flannel petticoats, the children's frocks, and the knitted comforters and stockings which Lady William could turn out. But that was all. She said lightly that there were plenty of people to manage the parish, and that it was not her rôle. She took no responsibility, and had not entered the schools since she was Emily Plowden aiding and abetting all manner of little rebellions in a way not at all becoming for the

Rector's daughter. This was one reason she gave for taking no supervision of the schools now. 'I should always be on the children's side,' she said, and thus it happened, which was so strange, that she had never even seen Mrs. Brown.

But Mab knew her very well, and burst into her little house at this hour which was Mrs. Brown's own hour, in which the parish had no right to interfere with her, with an absence of regard which the girl did not realise, and which no doubt was an unthought-of result of the inferior position in which the schoolmistress was, though quite unintentional on the part of the young intruder. She gave the lightest little tap at the door of Mrs. Brown's sitting-room, and burst in without waiting for any reply. Mab was, how-ever, a little taken aback when she found Mrs. Brown seated at a little meal, which was not only very agreeable to the smell, but extremely dainty in appearance, much more so, Mab felt instinct-ively, than any table she was herself accustomed to. Perhaps it was the sight of this, so very different from the usual slovenly repast of the schoolmistresses, which brought Mab up suddenly with a little start, and cry : 'Oh, I beg your pardon !' which she gave forth in spite of herself.

'Why should you beg my pardon?' said Mrs. Brown. She had what seemed a little silver dish before her—some dainty little twists and loaves of French bread—a cover on her table of exquisite linen, white and fresh. Mab knew how it feels when the table-cloth is not in its first freshness when any one comes, and how frequently that little domestic incident happens ; but Mrs. Brown's table-cloth shone like white satin, and was fresh in all its folds. 'Why should you beg my pardon?' she said. 'Do you think I do not know, Miss Pakenham, that I belong to the parish, body and soul? I must eat, to be sure, in order to live, but I ought to know better than to expect that I am to eat undisturbed.'

'Oh, I beg your pardon,' said Mab again, crimson with shame ; 'it was so silly of me not to think : but as it is so early——'

'I must take my food when the children do so,' said the schoolmistress ; 'pray sit down. I am not much of a sight when I feed, but still——'

'I hope you don't think I came on purpose to disturb you at your—lunch,' said Mab. To the schoolmistress of the old *régime* she would have said dinner. 'I came—to ask you if you wouldn't say something—I mean recite something, or act something, at the entertainment to-night. We all think you would do it much better than any one here.'

'Do what? How kind of you—almost as if I were on an

equality : though perhaps it is because of some one having failed that the schoolmistress may come in ? Who has failed, Miss Pakenham, at the eleventh hour ? I see, of course, that in these circumstances to apply to a dependent was the only way.'

'Mrs. Brown,' said Mab, 'I have always thought you were a lady ; but if you are so ready to think that we are not ladies, I shan't think so any more.'

'Well said !' said the schoolmistress, laying down her fork. 'Will you have a little of my ragout ? I have taught my little maid to make it, and I think it's very successful. I am fond of good cooking—that is one of the remnants, though, perhaps, at your age you will not think it a very romantic one—of my better days.'

'I should have thought,' said Mab, 'if you were like most of the people who have seen better days, that you would not have cared what you eat.'

'Ah, yes !' said Mrs. Brown, 'that is very true : but I am not like most of those people. I am not so sure that I regret my better days — or that if I liked I might not have them back.'

'Then in the name of wonder,' said Mab, 'why do you stay here ?—don't they often drive you half-mad, those little things that never will learn to spell, and that can't remember anything if you were to say it to them twenty times in an hour ? I would not be a schoolmistress a moment longer than I could help it, if it were me.'

'Then let us hope it will never be you,' said Mrs. Brown. 'The little girls are not alone in driving one half-mad, as you say. There are hundreds of things in the world that would drive you much madder if you knew them as I do.'

'I suppose you have known—all kinds of things ?' said Mab, looking with curiosity at her companion, whose eyes were full of knowledge too strange for the little girl. Mab had forgotten all about her object in coming, in the interest with which she looked at this curious human creature, who was like an undiscovered country, a world unrealised to her young imagination. She felt like an explorer coasting about in a little skiff to discover unknown headlands and bays of some quaint island far at sea.

'Yes, I have known a good many kinds of things,' said Mrs. Brown, 'things that would make the hair of the ladies in Watcham stand on end. I have been in a great many places—and, I am sorry to say, in a great many wrong places. I am not, to tell the truth. a sort of a woman for you to associate with, my dear young lady. You ought to draw your petticoats close round you in case they should touch anything of mine.'

'I don't understand you,' said Mab, greatly startled.

'No; I did not suppose you would. You would be a capital confessor, for that reason; for I might pour all my sins into an innocent little ear like yours, and you would never understand them. Will you really refuse my ragout? It is very good, I assure you. Then have one of those *pommes au sucre;* I rather pride myself on them.'

'They are like apples of gold,' said Mab, who was so young that a sweetmeat was a great temptation to her.

'I wish they were in a dish of silver—for your sake; but here is a little Dresden plate, which is quite as pretty. And there is a little pot of cream. This is friendly, now, and gives me pleasure. Your cousin, Mr. Jim——'

'Do you know Jim?' cried Mab, looking up from her apple, which was very good, with great surprise.

'Ah, I have known a great many people,' said Mrs. Brown, 'your father among others, and old Lord John, who died the other day. You never saw your uncle John? Well, you had no great loss; but his money will do you just as much good as if he had been the greatest hero in the world.'

'I do not know what you mean about my uncle John and money. Do you mean to say that you knew my father?'

'Ah!' said Mrs. Brown, 'they have not told you—and I don't doubt that was wise enough until all is settled. It was the right thing not to do.'

'Did you know my father, Mrs. Brown?'

'My dear, I told you I have known all sorts of people. I knew them all, more or less, in Paris. There was always plenty going on; and I love to be where a great many things are going on. I will tell you how I know your cousin Jim. I am in a very frank humour to-day—in a coming on mood like Rosalind. I had met him in Oxford, when I was not as I am now, at a very gay, noisy party indeed, where I was with some people—whom I would not name in your hearing. I spoke to him here out of prudence, thinking he might say to his father, the Rector, or his mother, the Rectoress—I have seen that woman before, and she is not fit to have charge of your school. So for a selfish motive I made friends with him. It took away his breath at first; but he is a lamb, poor innocent, like yourself, and was very sorry to think I should have so come down in the world.'

'Mrs. Brown!' cried Mab. She was put at a dreadful dis-

advantage by that apple, which was very good, especially with
the little pot of cream poured over it in the most lavish hospitable
way. When you have once accepted such a thing, and are in the
middle of it with the spoon in your hand, and the sweetness melting in your mouth, it is very difficult to express your consternation, or indignation, or dismay.

'And my opinion is,' said the schoolmistress, 'that he can be
stopped and brought back, if anybody will take the trouble—
judiciously—not in the driving and nagging way. I'm glad to
see the curate has stepped in, though he is no friend of mine.
Well! but you would like to hear a little more of my history.
Do you know what a Bohemian is? You must have seen the
word in books. Well, then, I was a Bohemian born. We were
both so ; but the other, who was the great lady, settled, as great
ladies do, and had her irregularities about her, in her own kingdom, don't you know ; but I went out to seek mine. I never did
very much harm, however, or I would not talk to a little girl like
you about it. I looked on at other people's fun, and that was fun
enough for me. There is always mud about it in the end, and it
sticks. I like best to look on——'

Mab had finished her apple by dint of taking large mouthfuls.
She had felt that it would be something dreadful, ungrateful,
uncivil beyond description to put it down and run away. So,
though she was much troubled, she only hurried the more over the
consumption of what was on her plate. When it was finished
she put down the plate, thankful to have it over, yet feeling that
even now she could not be so beggarly as to jump up at once and
go away. 'I wish,' she said, faltering, 'please, Mrs. Brown—
that you would not tell me any more——'

'Oh, don't be afraid,' cried Mrs. Brown, with a laugh ; 'I shall
not bring a blush upon that cheek. I have always been in mischief, but I have not done much harm. I go wherever the whim
takes me. I am sometimes in the heart of the *demi-monde*—
though you don't know where that is—and sometimes in a great
lady's boudoir, and sometimes in a girls' school. You may wonder
how I got here ; but my certificates were perfectly good, and no
one had a word to say against me. The *demi-monde*, you know,
either in London or Paris, has no connection with Watcham
School.'

'Oh, I wish you would not tell me any more—please don't tell
me any more !' cried Mab, rising up (though still deeply sensible
that it was too abrupt after the apple), 'for,' she added, in her
trouble, 'I don't know at all what you mean.'

' But my dear young lady,' said Mrs. Brown, ' you have neither
told me how you liked my apple, nor what you wanted me to do.'

' Oh,' cried Mab, arrested and feeling all the weight of that
sin against the hospitality she had accepted.   Her honest little
face grew crimson-red, and her eyes sank for the moment before
those bold and keen ones that seemed to read her very soul.
' The apple was very nice, thank you,' she said, faltering, ' I—
never tasted any like it: but—mother will be waiting for me for
her dinner—I—think I must go.'

' Tell me first,' said Mrs. Brown, ' what you wanted me to do.'
Mab had very seldom been silenced or daunted in her life, or
kept from saying out what was in her mind.   For once she had
been overcome—chiefly by the apple and its effects, the sense of
familiarity and obligation thus brought into her embarrassed mind
—but such an embarrassment could not last, nor was she cowed
except for a moment by Mrs. Brown's personality—potent though
it was.

' I wish,' she cried, ' you had not told me these things.   You
put a weight upon my mind, for, of course, I cannot tell them to
anybody, and I shall have to carry them all about as if they were
secrets of mine.   It was not just or fair to tell me—when I can't
tell them again or free myself from knowing, or forget for a long
time what you have said.   And as for what we wanted you to do
—it was when we thought you were only Mrs. Brown, a lady that
was poor, and obliged to put up with the school to get her living.
Which did not matter to anybody—but now—now——'

' You are disappointed in me,' said Mrs. Brown.   ' You think
I am not a lady, or obliged to get my living—and you think you
had better say no more about it.   You are quite right, for I should
not have done it whatever you had said to me.   I have a great
curiosity, however, I confess, to know what it was to be.'

' Please !' said Mab, ' of course I know you are a lady, but it
is all different ; they thought you might have done—Lady Macbeth—or something.   But all that doesn't matter now.'

' Lady Macbeth—or something.   What other thing did their
wisdom think could go beside Lady Macbeth ?   No, my dear Miss
Pakenham, I will not do Lady Macbeth—or anything.   Tell the
ladies I make my courtesy down to the ground,' she did so as she
spoke with the greatest gravity, while Mab followed her every
movement fascinated, ' for their kindness and for their thought that
I was good enough to exhibit myself among them.   You know now
that I am not good enough.   I am not a decayed gentlewoman
that has known better days ; but don't hesitate on my account to

clear your bosom of that perilous stuff. Tell it out, my dear, run home and tell it all to my lady, your mamma.'

She stopped short suddenly, but as if she would have said a great deal more. Mab seemed to stop short, too, in the hot tide of her interest as the schoolmistress paused. It was as if some swift career and progress of horse or man had been drawn up and cut short in their midst. Mab's breath, which she had held in the great fever of her interest, burst from her with a kind of gasp. She seemed to herself to have been stopped short on the edge of some precipice.·

'Did you know,' she said, hesitating, and thinking over every word, ' my—mother—*too* ? '

Mrs. Brown apparently did not expect this question. She stared at her for a moment, and then burst into an uneasy laugh and turned away.

'Sarah, Sarah,' she cried, clapping her hands, ' it is almost time for school ; come and clear these things away.'

Mab went home from her visit to Mrs. Brown a very different girl from that little person who had run off from the group of her friends to ask the co-operation of the schoolmistress—which had seemed to her a very amusing mission. She had wondered much how it would be taken—with satire or with pleasure. Mrs. Brown's tongue was one which could sting, Mab knew; but a tongue is all the more amusing for that, when its sting is not for one's self. Mab rather liked to hear her sending her arrows from right to left. She had thought that probably it was misfortune that caused this, and the sense which people who have seen better days are apt to entertain that it is somehow a wrong to themselves that other people should be prosperous. We are all, unfortunately, too apt to feel so. Blatant prosperity, smiling and smooth, how hard it is for the rest of us not to hate its superior well-being, even if we do not think that it is something taken from ourselves. But that was a very different thing from the dreadful confidences which Mab had received, and which made of her, even herself, who had certainly nothing to do with Mrs. Brown's sin, a heavy-laden and burdened spirit. Little Mab, who had run down to the schoolhouse as light as a feather—though she was not, as the reader is aware, one of your thread-paper girls—came back from it as if she had carried that pack upon her back which Christian had in the *Pilgrim's Progress*. The pack belonged to Christian himself, and he had a right to bear it; but, I repeat, Mab had nothing to do with Mrs. Brown's sins. And I am not at all sure what Mab conceived these sins to be; she knew nothing about them: they were something vaguely terrible, vaguely yet frightfully guilty to her childish sense of purity and rectitude. And yet Mrs. Brown was the schoolmistress, the woman who had all the Watcham girls in her hands; and Mab alone, of all the parish, knew that she was not fit to be trusted with that charge. She

walked home with the tread and the air of a woman of fifty, her
soft brow lined with prodigious scores of thought, her spiritual
back bent under this burden. Mab knew, while all the parish
lay in darkness. And Mab, the Rector's niece, and a district
visitor, and Lady Bountiful from her cradle, had a duty to the
parish which a person less bound with ties of duty might not
have thought of. There was her duty to the parish, and, on
the other hand, there was her duty to her penitent; for, though
she had not asked to have that high office, still Mab felt that she
had been adopted as the confessor of the sinner. Sinner was a
better name for her than penitent, for she was not penitent; but
yet she had trusted Mab. And what was the person so trusted to
do?—betray it to the parish, or to any one in the parish? Oh,
no, no! And yet was not that to betray the parish and its trust
and confidence in herself? If you can imagine any subject more
likely to score with wrinkles a brow of seventeen, such a divina-
tion is beyond my powers. Mab thought and thought, turning
the question over and over in her mind with more curiosity than
if she had been a philosopher in search of a new theory. What
it is right to do between two conflicting duties is a question for
a moralist more than a philosopher, if there is, indeed, any
difference between the two. It was a tremendous question.
She did not see her friend, the General, though he took off his
hat and waved it in cordial greeting as she passed his garden
hedge; nor Miss Grey, who had run after her, but finally gave up
the chase, unable to make Mab hear her call. Lady William
was waiting, though not impatiently, for the mid-day meal, which
was the chief repast in the cottage, when Mab reached home: her
mother called out to her to make haste, for Anne in the kitchen
was apt to lose her temper when her ladies were unpunctual. But
Mab was too much confused to make haste. She did not come
down for a quarter of an hour, until Anne was half-wild, and
Patty in the highest agitation. The dinner had already been sent
in, which should have pacified Anne, but she was something of an
artiste, in feeling at least, and could not bear her dishes to be
spoiled. Mab heard her voice from the depths of the kitchen
intoning comminations, and saw that Patty had tears in her eyes,
though they sent out pretty sparks of satisfaction at sight of the
laggard.

'Oh, Miss Mab, the soup's cold,' she ventured to say, even
Patty thus raising a protest.

But Lady William was not very severe. 'You little sluggish
thing,' she said. 'What have you been doing? Patty and I

have been suffering much from Anne. And I fear the soup will be quite cold.'

'Oh, that's all the better,' said Mab, trying to pluck up a spirit, 'for it's a very warm day.'

'I am glad you find it so,' said Lady William, with a shiver. 'May is seldom so hot in England as to make cold soup desirable. And how did the practice go off, and where have you been? for I saw Emmy and Florry go home a long time ago.'

'I have been to Mrs. Brown. They wanted her to act something. She is a very funny woman. She was at her lunch, or dinner, or whatever she calls it. She gave me an apple, which she called *Pomme au sucre*, and I never tasted anything so nice.'

'Oh, she is like that, is she?' said Lady William; 'the woman who has seen better days.'

'Yes, mother, she is like that,' said Mab; even to say so much as this relieved her mind a little, though she had no idea what was meant by the question or reply.

'And is she going to—act? To act, did you say?—that will be an odd thing for the schoolmistress to do.'

'They thought — she might do Lady Macbeth — or something.'

'Or something!' said Lady William, just as Mrs. Brown had done : 'that will be still more odd,' she added, with a laugh. 'And is she going to do it, Mab? I shall see this woman, then, at last.'

'No, she is not going to do it, mother. She laughed at the idea. She said, " Lady Macbeth—or something," just as you did. She is a very strange woman, but I don't think that you would like her.'

'Probably not,' said Lady William. 'It is, perhaps, unkind to say it, but I am not very fond of the decayed gentlewoman in general. It would serve me right,' she said, with half a smile and half a sigh, 'to end like that myself.'

'But how could that be?' said Mab. It was one of those questions to which there is no answer possible. Nor did she expect an answer. But it brought a little cloud over Lady William's brow. Indeed, it was all Lady William could do to keep her face tolerably unclouded, and her conversation as cheerful as usual for Mab's sake. And this struggle on her mother's part kept Mab's unusually serious face from being noticed as it otherwise must have been. After that there were no further questions asked about Mrs. Brown, and Mab went out to her gardening and the many other occupations which filled up her time. But whatever she was doing this heavy question hung upon her mind, and she carried with her the burden that was like Christian's, yet which she had not, like him, any right to bear. Her duty to the parish was to denounce the woman who ought not, with her mysterious guiltiness, to have the training of the girls of Watcham. And her duty to her penitent was to keep everything jealously within her own breast which had been confided to her, so to speak, under the seal of confession. Mab had, as was natural, a tremendous sense of her responsibility to both, but how she was to reconcile the two was more than she could think of. She determined at last upon a compromise, which was not indeed half sufficient to meet the case, but which was the only thing she could think of. She herself, she concluded, would for the future go constantly to the school, and thus neutralise any evil that might be produced by Mrs. Brown. She would go and watch over the girls, and see that their morals were all right, and that nothing was said or done to lead them astray. By dint of thinking it over the whole afternoon, shutting herself up alone to wrestle with it, refraining even from tea in order that her deliberations might be unbroken—this was the middle course to which Mab attained. She could not betray Mrs. Brown. That was out of the question : and it was also dreadful to think of betraying the parish, which, alas! if it knew what Mab knew, would not continue Mrs. Brown in her place for a single day ; but if Mab took it upon herself—her little innocent self—to watch over the girls, to be there early and late, guarding them from every allusion, from every lesson that could hurt them—would not that make up for the silence? She would watch the children as nobody else could watch. She would have eyes like the lynx and ears like those who heard the grass growing. This was what Mab determined upon in the anxiety of her soul.

She had persuaded her mother to go to the entertainment, though it was a dissipation to which Lady William was noways inclined. But Mab, notwithstanding the sad check that had been put upon her by the forenoon's proceedings, was very anxious about the delights of the evening, which were of a kind unusual in Watcham, where there was so very little going on. A concert was of the rarest occurrence. A little comedy had once been known to be played in the large room of the 'Blue Boar' by a strolling company, and, as we are aware, there had been a dance at General FitzStephen's. But the occasions that occurred in Watcham of putting on a best cap or a flower in your hair and sallying forth in the evening without your bonnet, to meet other persons under the same beatific conditions, were so very rare that nobody wished to miss the curate's entertainment. There had been very grave and serious questions among the ladies as to the point of costume, some being of opinion that as the entertainment was primarily for the working people, it would be 'better taste' on the part of the ladies and gentlemen not to go in evening dress, or at all events to shroud their glories in bonnets on one side, and great-coats on the other. This, however, had been boldly combated by Mrs. Plowden, who maintained that it would be much better for 'the poor things' to have the exhilarating spectacle for once in a way of ladies in their evening toilettes, and gentlemen with shirit-fronts that could be seen half a mile off. It would do them good, the Rector's wife said, to see that the best people were ready to mingle with them thus on a sort of equal terms, coming to enjoy themselves just as the boatmen did. And it was absolutely necessary that the young ladies who were to perform should be arrayed and made to look their best; it would have been very hard upon them to step down from the platform amongst a mass of bonnets, and thus be made conspicuous in the assembly even when they had finished their exertions in its behalf. I don't think that Mrs. Plowden had the least difficulty in bringing the others to her opinion, and accordingly the front seats in the school-room where the performance was to take place, were peopled by a small, and select, but distinguished audience, which rather over-shadowed, it must be allowed, and put out the homely ranks behind, and made the curate gnash his teeth when he saw immediately in front of his presiding chair all the shining shirt-fronts and frizzed or smooth locks, or lace-covered heads of the familiar little society of Watcham. Poor higher classes! They wanted a little amusement to the full as much, or perhaps more, than the boatmen and their wives from Riverside. And, perhaps, had they been at the back and the others in front, Mr. Osborne would not have minded. As it was, perhaps in this as in greater matters all was for the best—for General FitzStephen's high head prevented the curate from seeing how old George from the landing yawned over the quartette of the violinists from Winwick. Breeding is everything in such cases, for the General was quite as much bored as old George; yet he applauded when it was over (partly in thankfulness for that fact) as if he had never heard anything so beautiful before.

As for Mab, she was able to forget for the moment her interview with Mrs. Brown. Not only was it pleasant to be out in the evening—though only in a white frock high up to the neck, which was in reality a morning dress, but quite enough in Lady William's opinion for such an entertainment; but the excitement of feeling that she had really a part in the performance through the songs of Emmy and Florence, and the recitation of Jim, enlivened her spirits and raised her courage. The Rectory girls sang two duets, far better in Mab's opinion than all the other performers, and she felt sure that if Florence, whose voice was so much the strongest, had but had the courage to sing alone— ! But this was a suggestion that Florence had crushed at once. It was bad enough to stand up there in face of all these people with Emmy to support her : but alone !

'Don't you think it was rather silly of Florry to be so particular,' whispered Mab, 'when they have all known her—almost since she was born ?'

'No. I don't think it was silly,' said Miss Grey decisively.

'Oh ! but you never think any one silly,' said Mab.

'Don't I !' said Miss Grey, with a truculence which left all the swearing roughs of Riverside far behind. 'I know who I think silly,' said that enraged dove.

Mab's eyes ranged over all the people on the platform in astonishment, to see who could be the object of this outburst.

'Not poor Jim ?' she said, faltering.

'Jim is worth a dozen of him,' said Miss Grey.

There was only one face that was not friendly and bright. And that was, Mab supposed, because Mr. Osborne was so anxious that everything should go off well. Florence, the duet just over, was standing within three steps of him, with a little group about her congratulating her on her success, and the sound of the applause behind was still riotous in the room. Old George was very audibly exclaiming at the top of his gruff voice : 'That's your sort now ! that's somethin' as a man can understand ;' while some of the Riverside lads, the people Mr. Osborne had been so anxious about, kept on clapping their big rough hands persistently, when everybody else had stopped, not daring to cry encore to the young ladies, but signifying their wishes very clearly in that way. The two girls hesitated and lingered, kept by their friends from retiring while this noisy but timid call went on, which presently was joined in by all the front benches, under the leadership of the General, who was not at all shy, and cried 'encore' lustily. Mr. Osborne grew more gloomy than ever, and called imperiously for the next performers. 'We must stick to the programme,' he

cried; 'we shall never get done at this rate,' and the Winwick
amateurs came up again with their fiddles, while Emmy and
Florry stole away, escaping abashed from their friends, who were
discomfited too. It was then that Miss Grey said between her
closed teeth, 'I know who I think is silly;' as if she would have
liked to crush that person in her little hand which (in a very
ill-fitting glove) she clenched as she spoke. If he had been a
butterfly he would have had no chance in that clenched fist of
Miss Grey.

And then Jim came up smiling and delivered his 'Ride,' and
was applauded till the roof rang, chiefly, however, because he
was Jim, and there was something about racing horses in what he
had read. 'That's your sort,' old George said again, but more
doubtfully; 'though I'd like to have known a little more about
them horses,' he added; and shortly after the entertainment came
to an end. There was no doubt it had been a great success.
While the common people streamed out, not sorry to be able to
stretch their limbs and let loose their opinion, and indemnify
themselves for having been silent so long, the audience in the
front benches lingered to pay their respects and congratulations,
and to assure the curate that everything had gone off beautifully.
'I hope the Riverside people enjoyed it. I am sure *I* did,' said
General FitzStephen. Mr. Osborne looked at that gallant officer
as if he would have liked to knock him down. He could not
have shown a more angry and clouded face had the entertainment
been a failure. 'Oh yes. I suppose it has done well enough,'
he said. Mab, who did not know what all this meant, but who
was able to perceive that something was wrong, was fixing her
wits upon this mystery, and very anxious to know what it meant,
when she suddenly heard a little cry from her mother, whose eyes
were fixed upon the last stragglers of the crowd going out, and
who suddenly broke off in the midst of a conversation, and with
every appearance of excitement suddenly rushed out after some
one—Mab could not tell whom. Mab rushed after her mother
full of astonishment and eager curiosity, but only to find Lady
William standing outside looking vaguely round her with an
anxious, bewildered look upon her face. 'What is it, mother?
Who is it?' Mab cried. 'Do you want to speak to somebody?'
'I am certain,' cried Lady William, 'I saw her in the crowd.
She turned round for a moment and I saw her face.' 'Who is it,
mother? Who is it, mother?' cried Mab. But Lady William
did not make any reply to her. She turned round to another
who had rushed after her ('*That* Leo Swinford, of course,' Mab

said to herself) and put out her hand to him, as if he, and not her child, could help her. 'I have seen her, I am sure I have seen her!' she cried—and she repeated in a tone of rising excitement what she had said before—'with a black veil over her head. She turned round as she went out of the door; and there was Artémise. Oh, find her for me; find her, Leo!' Lady William cried.

NEXT morning, however, there came a crisis which drove all thought of anything else for the moment out of Lady William's mind.

It came in the shape of a letter laid upon her innocent breakfast table, along with the little bunch of correspondence, very small, and very unimportant, which was all that the post generally brought to that peaceable house. Lady William had, of course, a friend or two with whom occasionally she exchanged those utterly unimportant letters which form so large a portion in the lives of some unoccupied women. It would be hard to grudge these poor ladies so innocent a pleasure, but their letters were not exciting enough to make a woman like Lady William, who felt that she had herself a great deal to do, and did not want that gentle stimulant, very impatient for the arrival of the post: and her mild correspondence waited for her quite contentedly on both sides till she had performed various little morning duties, and was ready to sit down to breakfast. The long blue envelope, however, alarmed her a little whenever she saw it, and yet there was nothing so very alarming in it, for it was a similar envelope, directed in the same writing, as that which brought her the cheque for her quarterly allowance, which, as it happened, was now a little overdue. She lingered, however, over the letter—though it did enclose a cheque, which she took out and laid upon the table—much longer than she was wont to linger over the letters of Messrs. Fox and Round. She read it carefully over, and then she folded it up, put it in its envelope, and poured out the coffee. But before she touched her own cup, returned to the letter; took it once more from its envelope, read it all over again, and put it back once more. Mab had a little letter of her own to read, all about nothing, from a girl of her own age, so that she did not for a minute or so observe these proceedings of her mother.

But she very soon did so, and divined not only from them, but
from the manner in which Lady William swallowed her coffee and
pushed away the innocent rolls on the table as if they had done
her some harm, that all was not as usual.   When Lady William
spoke, however, it was in a voice elaborately calm.

'Are you going out this morning, Mab?'

'Yes, mother—I am going——' Mab paused a moment.   She
had got up that morning with her mind full of the weighty
determination of last night; but it seemed to her that if she said
she was going to the school it might partly betray the secret
which was not hers, but which lay so heavy on her soul.   'I
think,' she went on, correcting herself, 'I will run over and see
how they feel at the Rectory, now it's over, about last night.
And I will probably look in at the school,' she added, for to have
a secret from her mother was dreadful to her, 'before I come
back.'

'If you are going to the Rectory,' said Lady William, 'tell
your uncle James that I should like to see him, Mab.'

'Yes, mother;' but Mab could not help glancing aside at the
letter with an awakened interest, and wondering what Uncle
James, so infrequent a visitor on ordinary occasions, could be
wanted for—again.

'You are right, Mab,' said her mother, 'it is about business
and about this letter in particular.   And if you can give him my
message without anybody else knowing, I shall be all the better
pleased.'

'Is it about—Uncle Reginald, mother?'

'About Reginald!   Oh no, you may make your mind easy.
It is not about Reginald.   It is,' she said, with a sudden desire
for sympathy, 'something much more important to you and me;
but I cannot tell you now,' she added, remembering herself, 'you
will know of it all in time.'

'Is it from Mr. Leo, mother?' said Mab, growing very pale,
and towering over the table as she looked at her mother, with
severity, yet terror, as if she had suddenly grown a foot in stature.
Lady William, altogether engrossed in other thoughts, gave her a
look of astonishment which was balm to Mab's soul.

'From Leo!' she said, amazed.   'Why should it be from
Leo?   I told you,' she said, with a little impatience, 'that it was
a letter of importance, which none of his little communications
could be.   Tell your uncle,' she continued, falling into her usual
tone, 'that I have received a letter on which I wish to consult him.
Remember that I have no secrets,' she said, suddenly looking up;

Y

'I don't want you to make a mystery; but if you could see him
—by himself, to give him my message——'

'Oh yes, I can do that easily,' said Mab, in the relief of her
mind. 'I want to say something to him about Mrs. Brown.'

'I must see this Mrs. Brown,' said Lady William, with a
smile. 'She seems to have a fascination for you, Mab.'

At this unexpected and most unintentional carrying of the war
into her own country Mab flushed crimson, and cried quickly:
'Oh no, nothing of the sort. I don't even *like* her. She is not
like any one else I ever saw.'

'I must see her—one of these days,' said Lady William
vaguely: and then the faint smile died off her face, and she turned
to contemplate the long blue letter which lay by her plate. It
looked a dangerous thing among the little inoffensive white and
gray envelopes. Lady William's letters were chiefly gray, written
upon that ugly paper which people, and especially ladies, use out
of economy, and which is one of the additional (small) miseries of
life.

Mab felt much ashamed of her foolish question as she went
out, but hoped her mother had forgotten, or had not attached any
meaning to it. It was all the fault of the horrid people who
talked—as if there was anything strange in Mr. Swinford's visits.
'Where else should he go?' Mab said indignantly to herself.
'To the FitzStephens or the Kendalls, who are six times as old as
he is? or to the Rectory, where Aunt Jane would talk to him all
the time, and the girls never could get in a word? How different
mother is! I don't think I have ever seen any one so nice as
mother! Well, of course, she is mother, which is a great thing
in her favour; but not, perhaps, in the way of society. Emmy
and Florry are very fond of Aunt Jane. She is very nice and
kind if you are ill, and all that; but I am sure they would rather
talk a little themselves sometimes, rather than just listen to her,
especially when it is Mr. Leo.' This was the result of Mab's
unprejudiced observation, and she was much ashamed of herself
for having been moved to ask the very inappropriate question
which her mother had not paid any attention to, thank heaven.
Mab, as good luck would have it, met the Rector at his own door,
and conveyed her message in the most natural way in the world.
'Mother would like to see you, Uncle James. Would you go
into the cottage as you pass? She has got a letter.'

'Oh, she has got a letter?' said the Rector.

Mab longed to say, 'Not a letter from Leo Swinford, an
important letter, a letter about business,' but she restrained her

inclination.   Probably Uncle James had never thought upon that other subject.   She went on quickly to the Rectory, in order to carry out her own programme which she had in a way bound herself to by announcing it to her mother.   But she did not find the girls at the Rectory very anxious to talk over the events of the previous night.   Mrs. Plowden, indeed, had no objection to discuss it fully; but it was in its connection with Jim that she thought of it most.

'If it had not been for Jim,' Mrs. Plowden said, 'Mr. Osborne might just have kept all his music and his things to himself.   Oh yes, I daresay, the Fitz-Stephens, and Kendalls, and ourselves, and those people from the villas would have come; but, as for the men from Riverside, they came for Jim, not for him.   And did you hear, Mab, what a noise they made with their cheers and their clappings after Jim's piece?   They thought that the gem of the whole evening.   They came chiefly to hear that.   As for Mr. Osborne, with his little speeches and his fiddles from Winwick——'

'Oh, mamma,' cried Emmy, 'the violins were a great treat. We have not heard any music like that in Watcham for ever so long.'

'Well, you may say what you like about fiddles,' said the Rector's wife, 'but there's always something a little like a village fair in them to me.   And the poor people were bored beyond anything.   They liked your songs, girls, and wanted to encore them if Mr. Osborne would have allowed it; and they liked that piano bit, with the tunes from the *Pinafore*.   They understood that, and so do I, I allow; but what do they care for a classical quartette? I don't myself, and I know more about music than they can be supposed to do.   But a fine, stirring thing like Jim's "Ride to Aix"——'

'It was Mr. Browning's "Ride to Aix," mamma.'

'As if I did not know that!   But, all the same, it was Jim's ride to me.   Don't you think he did it great justice, Mab?   I never heard it come off so well.   The people were so attentive. That and the duets were certainly the success of the evening; and what it would have been without them I can't tell.'

'It would have been much more satisfactory without them, mamma,' cried Florry, half turning a shadowed countenance towards her mother.   'Mr. Osborne did not want mere amusement for the people—he wanted them to take pledges, and turn from drinking.   That was his object, don't you know—and a far better object than hearing two poor little country birds like Emmy and me sing. And I approve of it,' said Florence a little loudly, as if she would have liked all the world to hear.

Mrs. Plowden looked at Mab and shrugged her shoulders behind her daughter. 'I can't think what has come over Florry,' she said. 'She has grown so domineering of late—I dare not say a word.'

What Mab thought was that poor Florry looked dark, and pale, and out of heart—she seemed to be losing her good looks and her merry ways. It was rare, very rare, when she put forth any of her old arts of mimicry which the elders laughed yet pretended to frown at, and which all the young ones delighted in ; but I will not have it supposed that Mab was so precocious as to divine what was the matter with Florence—for this, to tell the truth, never came into her unconscious thoughts.

The Rector hurried along to see his sister after he had received Mab's message. He was anxious and disturbed about the state of affairs, and very desirous to find some way of setting his poor Emily straight, and making her independent, as she would be gloriously, did this great fortune come to Mab. If, perhaps, he was at the same time not quite sorry that she had been brought to see she was not so able to do everything for herself as she supposed, and had it proved to her in the most effectual way that to have respectable relatives to fall back upon was the greatest blessing a woman could have, it was no more than natural : and certainly above all, his desire was to be able to help her, and 'pull her through :' but it would be uphill work he felt, and require all the efforts that he himself could make. His brow was full of care when he went into the room in which she sat expecting him ; not, indeed, looking so serious as he did, but, still, with work enough for all her thoughts.

'Well ?' he said, as he drew a chair opposite to her, and sat down on the other side of the table at which she sat at her work. He bent forward across this little table, fixing upon her a look of such solemnity that Lady William's first impulse (though, heaven knows, she was not in a merry mood) was to laugh at his portentous looks, which would have been very inappropriate and improper, and would have shocked Mr. Plowden more than words could say. As she checked herself in this impulse there burst from her instead something which was half a sob and half also a chuckle : but he took it as a sob, which was much the best.

'My dear,' he said, 'my dear !' putting his hand upon hers, 'it can't be so bad as that you should cry about it. We will stick to you, whatever happens. Come, Emily, take heart, take heart!'

'I am not losing heart,' she said. 'I have expected it, you know. It is a distinct demand for my certificates. And now the moment is come when I must decide what to do.'

'Is this the letter?' he said. It was lying on the table between them, and Mr. Plowden took it up and read it over with great care, making little comments of distress with his tongue against his palate, 'Tchich, tchuch,' as he did so. Lady William went on with her work, raising her eyes to him from time to time as he read. His arrival and his tragic looks had amused her for the moment, but those distressful, inarticulate remarks acted after a while on her imagination and nerves.

'You think it a very bad business, James? How I wish,' she said, 'that John, who never was a friend of mine, could have lived for ever, or carried his dirty money with him to the grave!'

'I don't think that is a very Christian wish, Emily.'

'What, to wish him alive and in enjoyment of all he ever possessed?'

'Oh, well, perhaps that is one way of looking at it,' said the Rector, 'but, my dear, the noble family to which in fact you belong——'

'And which show their belief in me so nobly,' said Lady William, this time permitting herself to laugh.

'The noble family to which you belong,' repeated Mr. Plowden with a little irritation, 'will be very much benefited by this money. That nice young Lord Will as good as said so: and your own daughter, Emily, if all goes well, and we are able to establish your rights——'

'If!——' she cried, with a flash of her eyes which seemed for the moment to set the room aflame.

'You know what I mean. I at least have no doubt what your rights are: the question now is what is the best thing to do.'

'Yes,' said Lady William, 'we are in front of something definite at last. I have done little but think about it, as you may suppose, ever since you brought me that crushing news: and it seems to me that there are several ways that are open to us: the first——'

'Emily,' said the Rector, 'by far the best, and first step to take, in my opinion, is to consult Perowne—which we should have done long ago.'

'What could Mr. Perowne do? He could not rebuild the chapel and restore the books and bring back poor Mr. Gepps to life again. He might put my answer into formal words, but that is quite unnecessary. I have not the least inclination to consult Mr. Perowne——'

'Still, he must know how such things are managed better than we can do,' murmured the Rector.

'Such things—what things? You speak as if this was a common case.'

'No, no, Emily, no, no——'

'When it is, perhaps, such a case as never occurred before,' she said. 'I can answer these men formally to their questions, but to him I should have to go into the whole matter, explaining everything from the first step to the last. No, I will not ask Mr. Perowne for his opinion,' she said. Her countenance, naturally so soft in colour, was suffused with a sudden flush. 'Anything but that,' she repeated, in almost an angry tone.

It is so difficult to be purely business-like in matters where men and women are concerned. Mr. Perowne, the 'man of business' employed by the old Rector of Watcham, the father of Emily Plowden—had taken upon him to admire that young lady, and to make certain overtures which were not received graciously in the days that were gone. Lady William would rather have died than disclose all the circumstances of her marriage, as well as the possible doubt that might be thrown upon it, to her former lover. It was no figure of speech to say this; she would rather have died. But to her brother it all seemed very foolish, and to show an arrogant confidence in her own judgment which he did not share.

'Well,' he said, 'of course, it is your own business, and I cannot interfere with you, Emily: but that lawyer should meet lawyer is surely a much better way than that you should think you could encounter Messrs. Fox and Round—who are, of course, experienced in all sorts of villainy—in your own strength.'

'It is a mere simple statement of fact that has to be made to them,' she said. 'I will write and say I have no certificates, but that one person is still alive who was present at my marriage if she can be found: and that my father——'

'For goodness' sake!' cried the Rector. 'What, what do you mean—you are going to show your hand at once to these men, and let them see that you have no proof at all?'

'My father's diary is the best of evidence,' she said. 'The law is not such a bugbear as you make it out to be. There must be some sense and justice in it: my father's word, a clergyman, and a man of honour——'

'They may say it is a got-up thing, and what so easy as for

me to write that entry in an old book? I write very like my
father.'

'What folly, James! You! as little likely to cheat as my
father, a clergyman, and a man of honour too!'

'We might say,' said the Rector, 'for I have been thinking it
over too, my dear Emily—that you were married at St. Alban's
Proprietary Chapel, Backwood Street, Marylebone, on such a day
and year, by the incumbent, the Reverend T. I. Gepps: and leave
it to them to get a copy of the register for themselves—if they
can,' he added grimly. 'The books, of course, ought to have been
saved, and perhaps some of them may be. It is their business to
find all that out.'

This specious suggestion staggered Lady William for the
moment. 'But when they find out that the church is burnt, the
book destroyed, and the clergyman dead—which is a catastrophe
almost too complete for the theatre—they may think we have
chosen the place on that account, and that we mean fraud and
nothing else.'

'I,' cried the Rector, 'meaning fraud—and you! It would
be just as easy to suppose that I had forged the entry in my
father's diary. I hope we are two honourable people.'

Lady William shook her head.

'I hope so too: but I could not send them on such a wild-
goose chase, which would certainly harm us in the end, without
letting them know the truth.'

'Oh, the truth,' cried the Rector. 'Isn't it all the truth, both
one thing and the other? The truth is all very well and can't be
altered were you to harp upon it for ever, but what they want
and what we want is the proof.'

LEO SWINFORD had been during all these proceedings haunted
with a sense of a visitor about the house, whose comings and
goings were kept secret from him.   Those who were concerned
were much too clever to permit this to be known or suspected by
the risks of absolute meeting, by sudden withdrawal into corners,
whisking past of clandestine shadows in the dark.   It was not
that he ever met Mrs. Brown on the stairs or in the hall, or just
missed meeting her, as is generally the case under such circumstances.   She had, as has been said, an entrance kept for herself,
which opened upon the back part of the house, where there was a
thick shrubbery, and where it would have been as impossible to find
a fugitive in the dark as to find the proverbial needle in a bottle
of hay.   And Artémise was far too deeply learned in all the lore
of evasion to be caught within the house.   Nevertheless, he was
well aware that the place was haunted by a personality very, perhaps unjustly, disagreeable to him, and with which he associated
all those vague suspicions and troubles which haunt the mind of
a child brought up among family secrets and discoveries.   He
had been accustomed all his life to this uncomfortable sense of
some one about who was not seen, who had presumably unac-
knowledged errands of mischief-making, and whose presence,
whose very existence, was inimical to family peace.   That Leo's
thoughts went a great deal too far, and that this curious secret
agent and confidante exercised, in fact, no evil influence, but had
in many cases held the side of honour and justice, was a fact
that Leo was not only quite unaware of, but totally incapable of
believing in.   It had always been, indeed, a sort of consolation when
there was anything equivocal in Mrs. Swinford's proceedings, to
be able to think that it was not his mother who was to blame.
but that wretched Artémise.   Leo's father, so long as he lived,
had laid that flattering unction to his soul, and during his life-

time the appearance of Artémise had always been the occasion of domestic trouble. It was natural that Leo in his youth should have had no such right or reason to object or interfere ; and he had not even been of his father's faction in the house until that father was dead, and a natural compunction towards a man not happy in his life nor lamented in his death, awoke his sense of reason, and of right and wrong in this matter. But he had always had an instinctive dislike to Artémise. She had teased and sneered at him as a child, which is a recollection seldom altogether forgotten, and she was his mother's evil genius in life—or so it gave him a certain relief to believe.

The commission given him by Lady William to find this woman, so strange and incomprehensible a commission, and which was not explained in any way, roused all the indefinite feelings of disgust, and a kind of despair which had filled his mind from the moment of her reappearance (after a long interval, in which he had been of opinion that she was permanently shaken off) in the house. He had expressed to his mother so distinctly his objection to her presence, that it was difficult for him to reopen the subject, and still more difficult to suggest, as he was tempted to do, that since Mrs. Swinford could not live without her, it would be better on the whole that she should come to live in the house than haunt it clandestinely. Difficult, however, as these overtures were, he felt the necessity of making them, as soon as he understood that the finding of Artémise was necessary to his friend. What would not he have done to serve her, to please her ? The laugh with which she had turned off his offer of service, the suggestion that such offers belonged to the regions of fairy tales, had scarcely been necessary to show Leo how futile, so far as she was concerned, was his devotion. But this conviction rarely puts an end to devotion, and it must be said that as there is fashion in all things, it was not disagreeable to Leo's fashion of man to entertain a devotion of this kind, however hopeless, for an older woman, whom it was, in the nature of things, impossible that he could ever marry. In the nature of things as seen by her, that is to say, and which he clearly divined. His double breeding as Frenchman and Englishman did him service in this complication of fate. As an Englishman he was aware that such relationships as are possible to a Frenchman's ideal, without apparently injuring it in his standard of honour, were here as impossible as that the sky should fall : while as Frenchman he was not so determined on that strong step of marriage which seems the foregone conclusion of love in an Englishman's eyes. He was willing to be utterly devoted to this lady of dreams who was not for him, and to ask no more, seeing that more could not be—but that her wishes should be obeyed and her commissions executed at whatever cost, was the thing most certain to his mind.

'Mother,' he said, on the first occasion when he had the possibility of an interview, for Mrs. Swinford, after the little controversy over Lord Will, had exercised her usual caprice, appearing only when she pleased at the common table, and 'was not well enough' to receive even her own son in her boudoir, 'you have, I think, a very frequent visitor.'

'I—have very frequent visitors! Where do I find them? I should be glad if you would tell me, Leo.'

'I have no desire to be disagreeable, mother—you have Artémise.'

'Ah, Artémise! Yes, fate for once has been a little favourable to me. To keep me from dying of England, and your village, and all the exciting circumstances of my life. I have Artémise—that is occasionally. You know that I am not permitted to have her here.'

'Mother!' he said; then subduing himself, 'You are very much attached to this woman, who has never done anything but harm, so far as I know.'

'Well,' said Mrs. Swinford, 'and what then? Is it not permitted to me to love as well as to hate? Artémise is the nearest to me in blood of any one in the world.'

'You forget your son, it appears.'

'My son—ah, that is a different matter. Sons have a way of being in opposition to their mothers. Besides, isn't there a high authority which says that a mother is no relation, so to speak—an accident? It is so in English law.'

'English law has little to do with you and me, or any law. Mother, if you prefer this Artémise to every one, why have her pay you visits clandestinely like——'

'Like a lover!' she said, with her tinkling laugh. 'Well, say she is my lover and I like it; have it so.'

'Such a simile is insulting,' he said. 'I resent for you that you should even yourself say it.'

'Ah, but I do not resent; I like the simile. The thing itself might not be so impossible. But you are a Puritan, Leo, like your father. I have tried to prevent it, but one cannot stop the course of nature. Fortunately, my own constitution is not so.'

He rose in impatience, as was generally the result of these conversations, and paced the long dining-room from end to end.

Then he returned to where she sat with her back to the fire, which she still insisted on, though it was now May. He stood half behind her, leaning on the mantelpiece. It was better, perhaps, than being face to face.

'What I mean,' he said, 'is, that if your comfort so depends upon this woman—whom I don't pretend to like, as you know; but that does not matter: if your comfort depends upon her, mother, or if she is some pleasure to you, it would certainly be better to have her here, living with you, than skulking to and fro like a——'

'Lover!' she said again, with a laugh to madden him. Then she turned round upon him, as he stood with his head bent regarding the glow of the fire. 'I don't say that you've made your offer an insult, Leo, which would be the truth—but what is the cause of such a change? You have a motive. Ah! I think I see it!'

He looked up with a more profoundly clouded brow than had ever been seen in Leo before.

'What do you see?' he said.

She laughed again. Any one who has ever listened to the dreadful endless tinkling of an electric bell at a foreign railway station will understand how Mrs. Swinford laughed, and how it affected the nerves of those who listened.

'Ah! I think I see!' she repeated.

Perhaps it was because he was used to these *agaceries* that he bore it so well. What tempests of impatience were in his heart! He did not move. He remained as still as if he had been made in bronze, leaning against the mantelpiece till the laugh ceased. Then he said coldly:

'I have expressed myself willing to give up what may be my own prejudice on your account, mother. I think it would be more dignified, more fit and becoming for you that your visitor did not come by stealth. What motive you credit me with I can't tell. If you do not think fit to adopt my suggestion, so be it; but at least let her come openly, not by stealth.'

The tinkling began again with that supreme power of exasperation, and she said amid her laughing, every word coming tinkling out:

'That you may have her at hand and within reach when she is wanted, eh? I divine you, my Leo. What is becoming for the mother who is so little capable of understanding that for herself, is a beautiful pretext—what is convenient for some one else——'

'Who is the person,' he said, suddenly lifting his eyes, 'to whom it will be so convenient to know where this woman is?'

He did not shrink or show any consciousness as he thus carried the war into the enemy's country. Leo, after all, was a man of the world, and his mother's son.

'Ah!' she cried, stopping in her laugh, which was always a gain. 'I congratulate you, my son, upon your *aplomb*. But don't you know you take away all grace from your offer, if there were any in it, when you say *this woman?* How dare you speak of your mother's dear friend and relation as *this woman?* It is an affront I will not bear.'

'Mother, this is a subterfuge,' said Leo indignantly.

'And is not your proposal a subterfuge? Understand that I will manage things in my own way, Leo. Artémise shall come to me how she and I please. She shall stay with me if I wish it, and she consents to it, as would have been the case whatever you had felt on the subject. I am not here, you understand, as your housekeeper,' she laughed scornfully, 'or your dependent; I am, while I am here, the mistress of the house: and shall invite whom I please. If you think your order to shut her out affected me, any more than your order to admit her does now—I think we have said enough on this subject. You can give me your arm upstairs.'

She held out her arm, imperiously rising from the table, and Leo obeyed. They presented a group full of natural grace, as he led her carefully upstairs, subduing his steps to hers. She, wonderful in all her laces and draperies, a *marquise*, a lady of the old *régime*, exacting every sign of devotion; he, not made of velvet or brocade, as her cavalier ought to have been, but in the spare and reserved costume of modern days, with a manner very grave, very self-controlled, full of care, and attention, and duty. There was nothing in it of that pretty gallantry, so charming from a son to a mother, of which Leo for years of his life had been an example, but a serious care of guidance and protection, which was as different as night from day. They went upstairs thus, she leaning all her weight upon him, he careful above measure to keep her foot from stumbling even upon her own too ample skirts. When he had placed her in her favourite chair, and seen that she had everything she liked near her, he stood gravely by her side.

'Is this your last word, mother?' he said.

'It is quite my last word. Should Artémise come here, I shall expect you to be civil to her. Should she not come, you will be careful to let her alone.'

'I must act in that matter according to my own judgment,' he said.

He could hear the tinkle of the laugh as he went away. That

laugh !—it had been compared to silver bells *dans les temps*.   It
was not that now, but an electric jar or vibration that got on the
nerves.   Mrs. Swinford's son did not think of this, or feel any
pity for the woman who had descended thus from the poetic state
of compliment and adulation.   Sons, perhaps, rarely consider that
downfall with any sympathy.   And Leo was too angry to make
any sentiment possible for the moment.   He was all the more
angry because of his own undisclosed motive, which his mother
had been so quick to discover.   Had he been quite single-minded,
desiring only his mother's comfort and honour, things might perhaps have gone better ; but he was not single-minded.   And now
the question was, not how to justify his mother, but to discover
for Lady William the woman she wanted—to secure her, wherever
she was, and whatever might be the motive for which she was
sought.   He did not very clearly know what that was, nor was he
sure as to the previous connection of Artémise with Lady William's
history.   But his mother's revelations to Lord Will had helped
the vague recollections in his own mind, and he divined something
of her possible importance—importance most probably (he thought)
more fancied than real, for it would be in the nature of a woman
to give weight to a personal witness of the marriage, above all
papers and records.   Importance or not, however, real or fancied as
might be the need of her, it was enough that Lady William wanted
her to make Leo's action certain.   She must be found, he said to
himself, as he went downstairs.

He questioned Morris that evening carelessly : ' Do you
remember a lady, Morris, who came here one evening in the
dusk ?   A lady—who insisted on disturbing Mrs. Swinford.   Don't
you remember ?   And by dint of insisting was allowed to go in ?'

'Remember 'er, sir !' said Morris, with much emphasis.   ' I
should just think I did—as well as I remember my own name.'

' She has never,' said Leo, carelessly aiming at a ball on the
billiard table, ' been here again ?'

He spoke in so artificially careless a tone to convey no suspicion
of any special meaning in the question, that Morris would not have
been a man and a butler had he not been put upon the alert.

' Oh, 'asn't she, sir !' said Morris.   ' I should say, sir, as she's
here most days, is that lady ; as if the house was her own——'

' I have never seen her,' said Leo, with as natural an expression
of surprise as he could put on.

' No more haven't I,' said Morris.   ' Never ; and how she gets
in and goes out is more nor I can say ; but she's favoured, sir, of
course, in the 'igher suckles ; that we know.'

'Morris, my man,' said Leo briskly, 'you forget yourself, I think. I asked you if a lady, who is a friend of my mother's, had been here again : and you take it upon you to talk of how she comes into the house without attracting your intelligent attention, which was not the question at all.'

'I 'umbly beg your pardon, sir,' said Morris ; and here the conversation stayed. Leo felt that he had done as much as in the meantime it was possible to do. His own faculties alone must arrange the rest. Those faculties, thoroughly awakened and put to the sharpest usage that was in them, were, however, of but little use to Leo for a day or two. There could be no doubt, he felt sure, that Artémise was continually in the house. But it was impossible for him to storm his mother's apartments in search of her, and equally impossible to show himself to a keen-eyed houseful of servants as in waiting to trap her near his mother's door. The situation was one of the utmost difficulty, and demanded extreme caution, and the only result he attained after twenty-four hours' sustained observation was that it was possible from Mrs. Swinford's rooms to reach, without going near the formal entrance, a servants' door, apparently little used, and which opened at an unfrequented angle of the house, quite apart from the noisy and populous kitchen entrance. He had made up his mind to post himself in the shrubbery close to this door at the hour of dinner, when his mother would imagine him to be occupied with his meal. She had sent down word that she herself was not coming to dinner, and the opportunity seemed propitious. Leo was pondering upon this resolution, and how to carry it out, as he returned from the village, where Lady William had told him that the need for finding Artémise was greater than ever. It was a hazy, rainy evening, not dark, but growing towards dusk, as he walked home soberly under his umbrella, full of this intention. And he had just passed the glimmer of the lake, all dimpled with the circlets of the falling rain, when a movement in the shrubbery behind caught his eye. The bushes were thick there, a heavy *bosquet* of all the flowering shrubs that make spring delicious, a thicket of lilac and syringa, which extended along the further side of the pretty piece of water. Leo scarcely paused to think, but, putting down his umbrella, and pulling himself together, started at full speed for the house to intercept the visitor who, on whatsoever errand, was making her way towards the back entrance : probably only a servant using the legitimate way. He was not near enough, nor was there light enough to make out absolutely who it was, or, indeed, more than that the figure was that of a woman, covered from head to foot with one of the shapeless garments, ulster or waterproof, which are the habitual wear of a humble class of the community. He managed so well that he reached the neighbour-hood of the house sooner than this gliding figure, who was more a movement than a being, and whom, in a less excited state of his nerves, he would probably not have noticed at all. He made for the little entrance which he had discovered and arrived there before her. Would he be convicted of spying by the astonished eyes of some innocent maidservant? Or would he———? What was that? Certainly the movement had been there for a moment in the bushes, and there had been a pause—a pause was it of consternation to see him on the watch? A moment after, he perceived that the almost imperceptible quiver of the pale lilac, washed almost white with the rain, had gone further off; the visitor had retreated. He hurried along in the track, his heart beating. Certainly it was retreating. Down again along the edge of the little lake he followed, cautious, tracking the faint swaying in the branches. If the evening had not been perfectly still, he could not have noted any progress at all, the path of the fugitive was so judiciously chosen. Then he gave almost a shout of satis-faction; skirting among the bushes became no longer practicable, and, trusting to the dark and the rain, an indistinct form suddenly appeared in the open, moving like a shadow, but with great speed, over the grass. He uttered a cry, almost without knowing it, and launched himself forth in pursuit.

HE had almost stumbled in his haste and perplexity upon another figure all cloaked in waterproof and sheltered under an umbrella near the Rectory gate. By this time it was quite dark, and the rain, small and soft but persistent, had increased so much as to be almost blinding. A faint exclamation—'Oh, Mr. Swinford!'—greeted him as he was passing.

'Miss Plowden,' he said, 'I beg your pardon,' and then he added, breathlessly, 'I am running after a lady—don't laugh—an old friend of whom I had a sudden glimpse. I have pursued her all the way from the lake, and thought I had kept her well in sight, but at last I have lost the track. Have you met any one? Excuse me for keeping you in the rain.'

'A lady?' said Emmy. 'No, I have seen no one—that is, no one that is not well known in Watcham. I suppose it was a stranger?'

'How can I tell?' said Leo in his perplexity; 'a slight woman, exceedingly swift and energetic—witness, I have not been able to make up with her all this way—in a cloak—impermeable—what do you call it?—like what you wear.'

'In a waterproof!' said Emmy. 'No one has passed me but the schoolmistress. It could not be the schoolmistress?'

The idea was so ludicrous to Leo that he burst into a laugh in the midst of his wretchedness and perplexity.

'That does not seem likely,' he said.

'No one else has passed,' said Emmy; 'but there are some lanes, if the lady had wanted a short cut to the station, for instance.'

'That is exactly what I should expect.'

'Then if you will turn down to the right the first opening you come to, and afterwards to the left, and then—— The quickest way,' she said suddenly, with a blush and a laugh, 'would

be to show you; for I fear I am not clever enough to describe it.'

'Not in this rain?'

'Oh, I don't care for the rain. We are out in all weathers;
it will not take ten minutes.' She had already turned and was
hastening on in the direction she had indicated with a friendly
desire to serve him, at which Leo admired and wondered.
'Besides, I don't call this bad rain,' said Emmy cheerfully, 'it is
so soft and warm. But for habit I should prefer to have no
umbrella. But you, perhaps, would like a share of mine?'

'Thanks, it would do me no good and hamper you. I am as
wet as I can be.'

'Yes, you are very wet I see. Well, there is one good thing,
you cannot be any worse now, and you must change as soon as you
get in. When one is only a little wet one does not see the need,
but when it is as bad as that you must. This way: I am afraid
it is a little dirty, Mr. Swinford,' said Emmy, with a tone of
apology, as if it were somehow her fault.

'It is not very clean,' he said, with a laugh, 'but it is worse
for you than for me. I have an object, but you have none, save
kindness,' he added, with a grateful look that pleased Emmy.

'If it were kindness,' she said, 'that is the best object of all.
But I can't claim that, for it is a pleasure to help a—friend if one
can, in such a very little thing.'

'You hesitated, Miss Plowden, before you said a friend.'

'Yes,' she said, with the faint little laugh of embarrassment,
'I was not sure that I knew you enough to use that name.'

'I hope,' cried Leo, 'you will never doubt that again after all
the rain and mud you have faced to help me.'

'Oh,' said Emmy, 'I would do as much for any one—if I had
never seen them before: I should be a poor creature indeed if I
took credit for this. Is that your lady, Mr. Swinford, running
down the lane to the station? I am afraid she will be late for her
train. Run on, please—never mind me—I'll follow and see if you
find her, though,' she called after him cheerfully.

It was the pleasantest little excitement to Emmy, even had it
not been Leo Swinford about whom she had once entertained so
many romantic dreams. These dreams had faded away in the
most wonderful manner in the light of reality—though they still
kept a little atmosphere of romance about him. But it was
perfectly true that she would have done this little service for any
one, and would have felt the exhilaration of a small adventure in
doing it, and the same curiosity to see how it ended. She went

on accordingly smiling under her umbrella : her hair was touched here and there by the raindrops, and shone in the light of the lamps, and her walk and the little excitement had given her a pretty colour.   All the likeness to Lady William, of which Emmy was so proud, came out in the pleasant commotion in which she stood on the opposite side of the platform to look if Mr. Swinford had found his friend.   But his friend, as the reader knows, was not bound for the station, and was, indeed, at that moment secure in the last place in the world where he was likely to look for her, shaking the rain from her cloak, and changing her shoes with the sensation of warmth and comfort which dry garments give after a drenching.   Mrs. Brown had on the whole rather enjoyed the stern-chase, in which she felt herself quite safe : for she knew that she could elude her pursuer one way or the other—either by allowing him to overtake her, in which case she was confident that her own wits were quite equal to any encounter with Leo—or by vanishing into some side way by which she could gain her school-house—the last place where he would seek her.   Artémise was quite invigorated by the incident, which kept up, perhaps, an interest which was slightly flagging in her continued visits to Mrs. Swinford.   If she were to be pursued every time, it would give to these visits a wonderful zest.

Leo came across the railway with a sensation of pleasure, for which he was quite unprepared, to give his guide the information that he had failed in his search.   Emmy had always been pensive and stony when he had seen her before, a pale resemblance, like a half-faded photograph, of her aunt.   Now her bright interest and readiness to listen and sympathise warmed him almost as much as the dry shoes which Artémise was luxuriously putting on by her little kitchen fire.

'No,' he said, 'she is not there.   Perhaps she felt that I was likely to go to the railway, and so avoided me—to take, perhaps, a later train.'

'Oh,' said Emmy, 'did she want then *not* to be found ? '

There was a slight unconscious tone of suspicion in this which was very flattering to the young man.

'She wanted to avoid me—yes,' said Leo.   'She knows that I don't love to have her in my house.   She is an old friend,' he added, 'I am not sure what — but a sort of relation of my mother.'

'Oh,' said Emmy.

This very English exclamation, which is so often laughed at, has, according to the intention—or sometimes contrary to the intention—of the speaker, a wonderful deal of meaning in it. In the present case it meant surprise, mingled with a sort of disapproval, and almost reproof. An old friend, a relation, and yet you don't like to have her in your house! This was all expressed in Emmy's tone. She would not—I need scarcely say—have put such a sentiment in words for the world, and had not the least intention of expressing it even in her astonished 'Oh!'

'You think that strange?' said Leo.

'Oh—no,' said Emmy, hesitating slightly. 'I—don't know any of the circumstances,' she added hastily, with a sudden blush. 'Please, don't think for a moment, if I knew them all, that I would set up myself for a judge.'

'Why not?' he said. 'You are as well qualified to judge as any one I know; and even your surprise throws a little new light for me on the situation. It is always good to see a thing through another pair of eyes. However, what I want to find this lady for, is to prevent a wrong thing being done—which she could set right, but I fear does not want to set right. So I must find her.'

'Certainly in that case——' said Emmy. She added, 'I wonder if I could help you—if there was any place here where you think she might have gone!'

'She may, perhaps,' said Leo, with a laugh, 'have doubled like a hare, and got safely into my mother's room after all, while I have been hunting her here.'

'Into—your——!' Emmy was so bewildered that she could not keep in these astonished words, which were out of her mouth before she felt that here was some complicated matter with which she had no right to interfere. 'Oh, never mind,' she cried, 'never mind! I did not mean to be so impertinent as to make any remark.'

'Well,' said Leo, 'perhaps I did not mean to say so much: but I must tell you now, Miss Plowden——'

'Oh, nothing, nothing, please,' said Emmy in distress.

'That my mother and I don't look on the matter in the same light. She takes one view, I another. We need not enter into the question, but that is the fact. It is permitted to a man to differ with his mother in judgment when he is as old as I am.'

'One cannot help it sometimes,' said Emmy, in a low tone, with a slight bowing of her head. 'It is very painful, but I suppose God never meant that we were not to exercise the faculties He has given us. We may keep the commandment all the same. It says "honour." It does not say always agree. The Bible is always so reasonable, don't you think?'

'Oh! I don't know that I have very much considered that question, Miss Plowden.'

'Never anything excessive that would be a burden,' said Emmy, with the grave simplicity of assurance. 'Perhaps if you could give me any indication, Mr. Swinford, I might think of a place to look for her, being on the spot, and knowing all the people.

'Indeed you must go in at once out of the rain—with my most grateful thanks for what you have done.'

'To be sure,' said Emmy, 'no lady would be likely to stay out in such a wet night—but there are two or three people who keep lodgings in Watcham where I could inquire for you—or I could go to the early train and see if she goes by that. But you must describe her—what she looks like, and what I should say——'

'And you would really take all this trouble for me?'

'Oh, for any one!' cried Emmy. Then she laughed, and added: 'That does not sound very civil. Of course I should do everything I could—a great deal more—for you, who are a— friend. But I mean I would do that much—or any of us would do it—for any one. You know my father is the Rector. It is in a kind of way our business to be of any use we can—especially,' she added, 'when it is a question of right and wrong.'

'You are too good,' said Leo. 'You are too systematically good. I don't want to be helped merely because I am a fellow-creature, which I fear is what it comes to. I should like—very much—to be helped—because it was me——'

'And it would be because it was you,' said Emmy. These words were far more pleasant to hear, on both sides, than it is to be feared they were intended to be—but they were even upon Leo's part perfectly sincere. He wanted to be more than merely any one, to be helped and served for his own sake, and perhaps it did not occur to him that to an unsophisticated girl like Emmy (of whose romance, to be sure, he was profoundly ignorant) such words as those meant more than they did to him.

'You are very wet,' she said suddenly; 'will you come into the Rectory and get dried? Perhaps you could wear some of Jim's things. You ought not to be so long in your damp clothes.'

This motherly solicitude amused Leo much, and, to tell the truth, he began to forget the annoyance of his unsuccessful quest and to feel very uncomfortable in his wetness, and disposed towards a little light and warmth. He hesitated for a moment.

'It would be wise to go home at once,' he said, 'and change my wet things there.'

'Oh!' said Emmy, who had indeed expected no favourable answer to her invitation, 'I am sure mamma would be very sorry if you went away that long walk without resting. She would ask you to share our dinner and go home in the fly—for it means to rain on, I am sure, all night.'

'Do you think Mrs. Plowden would be so very good?' Leo said.

I do not deny that dreadful questions ran through Emmy's mind about the dinner. She did not know in the first place what it was, for Mrs. Plowden was severely determined on the point of retaining the housekeeping in her own hands : nor was she quite sure that she would escape a lecture for bringing him in upon them like this without notice, a man accustomed to a French cook. But Leo was town-bred—Paris-bred, and not accustomed to long expeditions in all weathers, and it was clear that he was beginning to shiver in the persistent though softly falling rain.

'I am quite sure mamma would never forgive me if I let you pass the door,' she said, leading him in through the damp garden, where already the rain began to form little pools.

Emmy felt no cold as she went in by the side door, which was always on the latch, leading her captive. Her cheeks had never glowed with such a rosy colour ; her eyes had never shown so like two stars. She slid off her cloak in the passage, and stood dry and trim underneath in her little gray dress as if she had come straight from her toilette. When she pushed open the drawing-room door the light flashed about her in a sudden warm dazzle, shining in her eyes, and in those raindrops that were like pearls in her hair.

'Mamma,' said Emmy, in a voice that had never before sounded so soft, 'I have made Mr. Swinford come in with me, he is so wet ; and I have told him you will make him stay to dinner ; and that he must put on some of Jim's clothes.'

'Which will be much too long for me,' said Leo ; 'but if you will really be so charitable as Miss Plowden says——'

What a sudden sensation it made in the drawing-room ! Mrs. Plowden sent Florence upstairs flying, to put a match to the fire in Jim's room.

'It is all laid ready ; it is no trouble,' she explained breathlessly ; 'but Florry will do it so much quicker than ringing the bell. And Emmy, call Jim—he is in the study with your papa—to get everything comfortable for Mr. Swinford. You are wet

indeed.   I will not even keep you downstairs to give you some
tea.'

'Perhaps,' said Emmy modestly, 'a little wine or something,
mamma, to keep him from catching cold——'

'And what do you take to keep you from catching cold?' he
said.   'Am I supposed to be more delicate than you?'

'Oh,' said Mrs. Plowden, sending Emmy off with a look,
'they are used to it; they are accustomed to our climate.   How
glad I am you came!   This is the way, Mr. Swinford; let me
show you the way.   You must excuse me if I don't take you to
one of the best rooms, but only to Jim's, which will be the most
homely; for I think comfort is the thing to think of when one is
wet and cold.   Oh, here you are, Jim.   I will just go with you
to see that the fire is burning—and you must get out dry things
to make Mr. Swinford comfortable.   Have you lighted the candles,
Florry?   And is the fire burning up?   Oh, well, then I will leave
you with Jim.'

Thus the whole family ministered to Leo, who, half-horrified,
half-amused to see the two girls sent flying in different directions
for his comfort, and Jim much puzzled and flurried, extracted
from the dreadful depths of the study—submitted himself to these
attentions with the best grace in the world.   If he had fathomed
Jim's dreadful perplexity as to whether he should offer the brand-
new coat which he had got for the FitzStephens' ball, or his old
one, which he believed in his heart would be a better fit, he could
not have spoken more wisely than he did on this subject.

'Give me an old coat,' he said, 'one you had before you had
grown so big.   You are a head taller than I am.'

The whole house was stirred by this unexpected visitor.   Mrs.
Plowden downstairs was eager in her questions to Emmy.

'Where did you meet him?   What made you think of asking
him?   What a good thing that we have such a nice dinner—
really too nice a dinner to eat by ourselves to-day.   I said so to
cook this morning.   Those beautiful chickens Mrs. Barndon sent
us, and a piece of salmon, and—— Really, a dinner for a dinner-
party.   What a very lucky thing it was to-day!'

Even the Rector came forth from his study to hear what the
commotion was about.

'Emmy brought in Mr. Swinford to change his wet clothes
and dine.'

'*Emmy* brought him in?   Why, you must be dreaming,
Jane!'

'And why shouldn't Emmy bring him in?' cried Mrs.

Plowden, triumphant; 'indeed, what could she do else on such a wet night?'

Thus, instead of dining mournfully alone, with Morris behind his chair, in the great dark dining-room with the mock marble pillars, Leo sat down with the cheerful Rectory party around the severe but shabby mahogany, upon a chair covered with horse-hair, to a dinner cooked by a plain cook. He was more amused than words could say, and delighted with the new scene, the kind people, and, above all, the contrast of the family party with his solitude, and the *bourgeois* comfort with his own elegant and fas-tidious fare. The chickens, carved anxiously by Mrs. Plowden with 'Just another little piece of the breast,' in addition to the well-developed wing, were so good, and everything was so warm and bright, so honest and simple, that his amusement soon grew into pleasure. What a contrast! He told them even his story with judicious elisions.

'I cannot think how I lost her,' he said, 'even if she did not want me to find her : and where she disappeared I cannot tell.'

'I came all through the village,' Emmy explained, to add to the tale, 'and no one creature passed me but Mrs. Brown, the schoolmistress, flying along in a great hurry to get out of the rain.'

Jim looked up at these words with a little start, but took care not to say anything, as may well be believed.

'Perhaps,' said Leo, with a laugh, 'it might be Mrs. Brown, the schoolmistress, whom I was pursuing all the time. She might be paying an innocent visit to some friend in the servants' hall. In which case she will think me a dangerous madman, and I owe her an apology.'

'Oh, she's not one of that sort!' cried Jim. He said it under his breath, and fortunately nobody heard him but Florence, who gave him a look of inquiry, but no more.

'So I might have saved myself the trouble—and the wetting,' Leo said.

As it happened, however, there were several people much occupied
about Mrs. Brown on the morning after that wonderful chase with
all its consequences. Mab, under one pretext or another, had
spent most of the previous day in the school. She had heard the
bigger girls say their lessons; she had hovered about the classes
taught by the schoolmistress; she had watched over the course of
instruction in general with anxious eyes. Was there any tamper-
ing with the morals of the girls of Watcham? Were the little
ones taught their hymns and collects? Were the big ones kept
up to their catechism now that the time for their confirmation
began to approach? Mab had never hitherto felt herself one of
the clergy of the parish, as the Rector's niece might have been
permitted to do. But now she was torn with those sensations
which we may suppose to be felt by a priest who has received
under the seal of confession a new light upon the proceedings and
motives of an important official. This is a drawback of the
priestly office which has rarely struck the general observer. To
know that a man who is largely influential in life, who has important issues on hand, is using his powers for evil and not for
good, and yet to be powerless to do anything, to prevent anything,
to give any warning on the subject! Many a good priest no
doubt has been bowed down under this unthought-of weight.
And so was Mab, whose young shoulders were quite unfit for the
part. Should she tell it all to Lady William, this knowledge
that was too much for her to bear? Should she give her uncle a
hint that she had discovered something which made the schoolmistress unfit for her place? Mab felt that in all likelihood
Uncle James would laugh at her discovery, and to repeat Mrs.
Brown's confidences, even to Lady William, would be a breach of
trust. Thus the only thing Mab could do was to come in, in her
own person, to hold Mrs. Brown (perhaps) in awe, to watch over

the instruction, to correct what was wrong, to see how far it might be her bounden duty to interfere. One wonders how a priest would act in a similar case, or whether the possession of many secret responsibilities in his consciousness may perhaps neutralise the weight of each. Nothing neutralised this dreadful weight in Mab's case. She watched Mrs. Brown as a cat watches a mouse. She did not like to let that enigmatical person out of her sight. She even followed down .the ranks of the girls whose heads were bent over their copybooks, to see that the line so beautifully written in round hand at the head of each page was orthodox. Mab gave herself a great deal more to do than if she had herself been the mistress of the school. She asked the girls all sorts of unexpected questions to test their views of morality.

'What would you do if you saw somebody take something out of a shop? Suppose you saw a very poor person take a loaf from the baker's?' said Mab, with an anxious pucker in her forehead.

'Oh, miss!' cried two or three girls together; 'tell Mr. White that minute, and if he runned away, catch him up.'

'But if he were very, very poor—starving?' said Mab.

There was a pause, for of course all the girls studied her countenance to know what she wished them to reply; and Mab's little round, blunt-featured face, with an anxious cloud upon its childish brow, was void of all expression that could be taken as guidance.

'If we knowed the man we could tell after—when he was gone,' said one Jesuitical little person.

'And then 'e could run after 'im to 'is 'ouse — or send the police,' cried the rest. The idea of sending the police was the most popular. It seemed somehow to take off the responsibility. But the girls soon perceived that this was not the solution required.

'If you please, miss,' said a sharp little girl who was well acquainted with Mab's ways, 'if I 'ad a penny I'd pay instead of 'im, and then it wouldn't be stealing at all.'

This was received, however, by a spontaneous groan from the class. 'Oh, Lizzie Jones! that would be cheating as well.'

'And it ain't likely as I'd 'ave the penny,' said Lizzie meekly. She drew from Mab's countenance the consolation that, after all, it was she who had answered the best.

To describe the delight with which Mrs. Brown looked on and listened to all this would be difficult. She read little Mab like a book, and her sense of humour was tickled beyond description.

That she was herself upon her trial, and that the sentiments of
her scholars were to be considered in justification or condemnation
—while, at the same time, Mab was covertly consulting their
ignorance and (supposed) spontaneousness of perception like an
oracle, was as clear as daylight to this clever woman. She had
never met anything so funny in her life; and it delighted her as
a good joke delights people who are given that way, whether it is
against themselves or not. But the gravity of her aspect was
equally beyond description. She seemed to take this question in
ethics with the most perfect good faith and all the seriousness in
the world.

'If the man was starving,' she said, taking up the argument,
'and Lizzie Jones had not a penny, as is most likely, and he was
known not to be a dishonest man, but only driven mad by the
poor children hungry at home——'

'Yes, teacher,' said Lizzie Jones, who felt that she herself had
thrown most light on the subject.

'Well,' said Mrs. Brown, 'of course it is never right to shield
a wrong act.'

This was so unlike what the girls expected after her exordium
that there was a little cry of surprise, swiftly modified into one of
cordial assent.

'But,' said the schoolmistress, 'knowing that this is so—which
you must never forget—I'll tell you what this young lady would
do. She would go after the man to his house—which most
likely she would know: and I'm not sure that she would not
stop and buy some things on the way — at the butcher's,
perhaps——'

At this the girls manifested a little doubt; while one murmured
'Tea, teacher,' and another said 'Potatoes' loud out that she
might not be overlooked; at which the class, consulting Mrs.
Brown's face by a lightning glance, burst into a laugh.

'Hush!' said Mrs. Brown. 'This is a very interesting question
that is set to us—as good as a story; but you mustn't laugh.
The young lady would go to the man's house, and she would probably see the children devouring the bread; and she would ask a
number of questions—far more than she has asked you to-day,
though she has asked a great many. She would discover there
was no fire (supposing it to be cold, which it isn't to-day) and
nothing to eat in the house, and that the man was out of work
and the wife ill and the children starving. She would immediately
send off for all that was wanted——'

'Please, teacher,' said Lizzie Jones, holding out her hand,

'she'd give 'em a coal ticket, and a bread ticket and bid 'em send one of the little ones up with a basket for the pieces.'

'Well, perhaps she would do that. And when she had supplied their wants, she would take the man aside, and she would say to him, "I saw you steal that loaf at Mr. White's."'

There was a long breath and a cry of 'Oh!' from the girls, and Lizzie Jones, who was soft-hearted—or was it only that she was forward?—began to cry.

'"Now,' the young lady would say, "come back with me and pay for it. You're going to get work again presently, and the children shall not starve; but you must not have anything against you when you get work."'

There was another very large round 'Oh!' from the girls, who turned their eyes with one accord from Mrs. Brown's to Mab's face.

'I don't know if I would do that,' said Mab.

'Neither do I,' said Mrs. Brown; 'but judging by what I know of your character, Miss Pakenham, that is what I should expect you to do.'

This happened on the morning of the day after Leo's chase in the rain. Mab went home very soberly when the children were dismissed for dinner and in a very uncertain state of mind. She did not know how to take Mrs. Brown's apologue, which already was being circulated through the village in a dozen different versions as a thing which Miss Mab had actually done, until it came to the ears of White, the baker, who contradicted it indignantly, and declared that he'd give a stale loaf as soon as look at it if the children were starving; but let a man off as stole it because he come and offered to pay up after was what he wouldn't never do.

In the meantime Leo had been turning over in his mind that idea of Mrs. Brown, the schoolmistress. At first it amused him to think that so harmless a visitor to the servants' hall might have been the object of his very unnecessary pursuit, and in this sense he laughed at the situation, which was so ludicrous, and longed to cross over to the cottage in the rain, when he left the Rectory, to make Lady William the partaker of so good a joke. But as he drove home in Jim's clothes and the sober Watcham fly, which Mrs. Plowden, in her motherly care, had ordered for him, a different view suddenly occurred to Leo. The joke was good, but not good enough to last out that slow drive through the deep dark and the falling rain. It occurred to him as he thought of it that a visitor to the servants' hall might, indeed, be disconcerted by the curiosity of the master of the house, but would not, unless she had some very dishonest meaning, turn back and fly. Why should the schoolmistress, probably acquainted with the housekeeper and entertaining a very good opinion of herself, fly from Leo? There was no reason in the world why she should fly. She would probably have quickened her steps, and arrived at the little side entrance puffing and blowing, but chiefly with indignation, and given very warmly her opinion of the young master who spied upon the back-door visitors. But to turn back at the sight of him and get herself out of the way meant something more than a respectable visit to the housekeeper. What did it mean? A village schoolmistress was not one to visit the young maids, or get them into mischief; but why, why did she turn and flee? It was impossible to assign a sufficient reason for this to himself.

And then there was suddenly shot into his mind, as our best intuitions come, suddenly and with a sharp shock—almost a pang—the question, Who was the schoolmistress? Artémise was nothing if not a woman of variety. He had himself known her go through the most extraordinary transformation; one time dazzling in splendour, the next almost a beggar. Why should not she herself be the schoolmistress? There could be no such concealment, no such unlikely place to look for her, as in the parish school of Watcham. There she would be at his mother's very door, accessible on every occasion, ever within call. He had thought it scarcely possible that she could come constantly from London and disappear again unseen; but if she were in Watcham, at hand, in such a place, where nobody could think of looking for her, the difficulty would disappear. And she was an excellent actress; a woman to take anybody in, not to say an unsophisticated and artless company like the Rector and his churchwardens. He could scarcely help smiling to himself in the dark as he suddenly thought of the perfect representation of a model schoolmistress which Artémise would get up for the edification of the authorities. No schoolmistress in the world was ever so excellent a type of the class as Artémise would make herself look—her voice, her gestures, her demeanour would be all perfect. And she would have the satisfaction of being perfectly safe, for who would think of looking for her there?

But then there were the ladies, who were different. Would she take in the ladies, too? Would not they suspect the representation to be too complete? And then Lady William—Lady William could not have been deceived. She must have recognised at once the woman of whom she was in search. Leo did not know Lady William's peculiarity about the parish. He was aware that Mab knew everybody and all their circumstances, and it did not occur to him that her mother would hold apart.   This seemed to cut the ground from under his feet again.   But he determined to see for himself next day who the schoolmistress was.

Next day, however, was a half-holiday, and he did not reach the school till the afternoon, when all the children were dispersed and the house shut up.   Mrs. Brown, he was informed at the nearest cottage, where it appeared her little maid-servant lived, had gone away for the afternoon, so that his inquiries made no further progress that day.   He went to tell his adventure to Lady William, and, if not to suggest this solution, at least to ask what she knew of Mrs. Brown.   But Lady William also was out of doors, and nothing more was to be done.   He hesitated whether he should not go to the Rectory to make a call of thanks, and to see (perhaps) if Emmy Plowden resembled her aunt as much by daylight as she had done in the unusually favourable circumstances of last night.   But this intention he did not carry out.   Unfortunately for romance, Leo was so ungrateful as to recall what he called the *bourgeois* dinner, the drab-coloured comfort, the petty little anxieties and cares (chiefly on his own account) of the Rectory party, with more amusement than admiration, though with a compunction, too.   Kind excellent people!   How abominable it was to laugh at them !   But his laughter was not checked by the compunction—it only gave a certain piquancy to all that was ludicrous in the picture.

The third person whose mind was full of Mrs. Brown was Jim Plowden.   He had seen her little of late, partly that the many calls Mr. Osborne made upon him left him less time for those strolls about the village, which had ended so often in the 'Blue Boar,' but sometimes, to his advantage, in the schoolhouse ; partly because, now that the evenings were so much lighter, he could not go there unseen.   This reason had acted with the others in the partial reformation of Jim.   It was scarcely possible to go into the 'Blue Boar' in the lingering daylight while all the village folk were about.   Had he been altogether uninterrupted in his former habits, it is possible that by this time he might not have cared.   But Mr. Osborne's warm and exacting friendship had begun with the lengthening days, and after an interval, even of a week or two, such a hindrance told.   On this occasion, however, Jim felt that he must risk a little danger for the sake of a woman who had been kind to him, who had certainly amused him, and, he sometimes began to think, had done him good.   It could be nothing to her advantage to have a visitor such as he was.   She had done it, he thought vaguely, out of kindness, and now he

would risk something for kindness too ; and then he could always
say he had brought a message about the school from his father, or
Florence, who took an interest in the school, or Mab, or somebody.
Fortified by his good intention he walked into the schoolmistress's
house about six o'clock that evening when all the people were
about, several of whom stared, he could see, at Mrs. Brown's
visitor—in which, however, I need not say, Jim deceived himself,
for the village people were already aware that he visited Mrs.
Brown, as well as that he visited the 'Blue Boar,' and held these
secrets in store against the time when they might be of use either
for or against the Rector's son.   He went in, however, boldly, to
the surprise of Mrs. Brown, who did not expect him, and who was
engaged in some sort of operation that looked very much like pack-
ing.   She invited him to come in, and cleared one of the chairs
from a number of miscellaneous articles with which it was covered,
and which she was putting away.

  'You are not—going on a journey ?' he said, alarmed.

  'Oh no, not that I know of; but you know, Mr. Jim, a
woman in such a humble position as mine, with so many people to
please, has but an uncertain tenure.   I am putting some old things
in order, so that should anything untoward happen——'

  'But I hear nothing except praise,' said Jim ; 'they say no
one ever kept the school in such order, or the children so bright,
or——'

  'Do they really say so ?   How truly good of them !' said Mrs.
Brown, with a laugh.   It was a laugh of so much amusement
that Jim, who did not see the joke, was disposed to be angry, but
she ended by shaking her head and putting on a comically doleful
look.   'But I do not please everybody,' she said ; 'oh, far from it.
Your friend, Mr. Osborne, does not like me : and your cousin,
Miss Mab, is full of suspicions.'

  'Mab,' said Jim in high disdain, 'as if it mattered what Mab
thought !'

  'Don't you know,' said Mrs. Brown, 'that Miss Mab will probably be an heiress one of these days, and that it will matter a
great deal what she thinks ?'

  'Nonsense,' cried Jim, 'as much an heiress as I am !   We
have no rich relations, alas ! to leave us money.'

  'But she may have,' said Mrs. Brown, 'and if you will take
my advice you will go in for your cousin, Mr. Jim ; that would
make everything straight if you got a nice little bit of money with
your wife.'

  'Nonsense,' cried Jim, becoming scarlet, and feeling the very tips of his ears burn. 'Besides,' he said, 'if I ever have a wife I'd rather keep her than that she should keep me.'

'A very excellent sentiment,' said his adviser, 'but I don't quite see how you are going to carry it out.'

'I shall carry it out by having no wife at all,' said Jim : and then he added hastily, 'that's not what I came to tell you. Have you any reason for not wanting Swinford to know that you are here?'

'For not wanting—Swinford—to know——?' A little colour seemed to rise, too, in her dark countenance. 'This change of subject,' she cried, 'takes away my breath. You are too quick for me. Have I any reason——? It is Leo Swinford you mean, at the Hall?' As if she did not know who it was! Even Jim was clever enough to perceive that she was simply gaining time. 'No,' she answered slowly, 'I have no particular reason. I do not, perhaps, in a general way wish—to receive—friends who have known me elsewhere, here——' She looked round upon her little room, with a laugh. 'You may, perhaps, if you think of it, understand why. Have you come to warn me that I am found out?'

'Oh no,' said Jim. 'And I'm sure I don't want to interfere ; but he was at the Rectory last night. He said he had caught a glimpse of a lady he knew, and had followed her all the way down to the village to speak to her, and she had disappeared. Some one said that no one had passed but Mrs. Brown. And then he laughed and said, "Perhaps it was Mrs. Brown he had seen going to pay a visit to some one in the servants' hall."'

A sudden flash shot out of Mrs. Brown's dark eyes. 'I hope,' she said, 'you encouraged the idea that I paid visits in the servants' hall?'

'I didn't say anything—good or bad,' said Jim.

Which was not strictly true ; but then nobody heard him, which came to the same thing.

'Good friend,' said Mrs. Brown, 'true friend! but you can tell Leo Swinford when you see him again that one of these days Mrs. Brown is coming to call on him, with important information, at the Hall, and he will never need to hunt her through the rain any more!'

WHAT a contrast from the little schoolhouse, though it was so much more decorated than a schoolmistress's little sitting-room has any right to be, or from the drab drawing-room at the Rectory! The more one became acquainted with Mrs. Swinford's boudoir, the more exquisite it appeared. Those little water-colours which were hung on the walls were worth a small fortune, and a crowd of collectors would have appeared like ravens on the scene if it had been suggested that they could be sold : and the little Italian cabinets between the windows, with their delicate inlayings of ivory—not like the untrained beauty of the East, but fanciful and varied as a dream—were almost as valuable. And then the tempered, delicious warmth, and the softened, delightful light! Yet I think (though, of course, she would not have endured them for a day) that the roughest wooden furniture, and the shabbiest surroundings would have been a sort of relief—for the moment at least—to Mrs. Swinford. She surrounded herself with all these beautiful things, and then she hated them. They never varied, they were lovely and novel for a moment, and then there they hung for years, and never changed. How tired she was of them all! To have broken the delicate frames, and torn up a picture here and there, which was only a piece of paper after all, would have given her a sensation. And yet that would not have done much good; it would have left a visible blank on the wall, which it would have been necessary to fill up, searching far and near through all the studios to find something that would fill its place —which would keep a little movement in life for a short time. But it would be ludicrous to tear up a picture for that reason, and ridicule was more unbearable even than weariness. On this particular occasion, however, the room looked brighter even to her than usual. It was again an evening of soft-falling spring rain. The skies had been one unbroken gray all the afternoon. The soft small flood fell almost unseen over the country, making the young foliage, which did not dislike the wetting, glisten, and washing the colour out of the lilacs, and covering the ground under the fruit-trees with fallen white petals, almost like snow. A day which the lonely lady thought, if ever by chance she glanced from her window, was enough to account for any suicide. And she had been reading the greater part of the day, reading, save the mark! exciting French novels, in which all the ways of breaking the seventh commandment were dwelt upon to the sickening of any appetite. Even Mrs. Swinford, who considered that the chief occupation of life, was a little sick of one after another. The delicacy of the analysis of sentiment, etc., palled upon her after hours of such reading. She would have liked, perhaps, even at her age, if some gay Lothario had entered her boudoir, and led her, or tried to lead her, into those paths which relieve the idle soul : but only to look on while one woman after another was led astray ! The books were like the room, her habitual reading as it was her habitual scene ; and she would have declared it impossible to exist without the one and the other. But even to her accus-tomed faculties it became sickening at the last. Was that life any more than the boudoir was life? It was impossible for any drudge to have been more sick of her toil and wretchedness than Mrs. Swinford was of her existence, if this were all.

But at the moment of distraction Artémise arrived, and every-thing for the moment became tolerable. She had thrown off her cloak and overshoes in the other room ; that the shock of seeing a damp woman, who had walked through the rain, might not be given to the delicate lady within. And Artémise truly enjoyed the difference in the atmosphere, and held her feet to the fire, and breathed in the warm and balmy air with genuine pleasure. 'How comfortable you are !' she said.

'Comfortable ! I am miserable—always and always !' the great lady cried.

'My dear, many people would be very glad to have the half of your misery,' said Mrs. Brown, 'though I confess I agree with you more or less. It would bore me to death. A fight with Mrs. Jones on the question whether or not Lizzie is getting on with her lessons as well as she ought, for the great sum of fourpence a week, is more agreeable to me.'

'Are you going on with that dreadful work for ever, Artémise ?'

'No, I am afraid not. It is not that I dislike it, however. It is great fun. You should see little Mab Pakenham, who has conceived some doubts of me from what I have told her—so it is entirely my own fault—coming down as grave as a judge to superintend the moral effects of my teaching. She would not betray me for the world, but she is afraid of me lest I should teach the girls principles unknown to Watcham.'

'The little impertinent! She ought to look at home—— !'

'She does look at home, and that is what makes her so staunch. She comes and superintends, but betrays me, never! However, as my morals might prove too great a charge for little Mab, and as your son Leo has got on my track——'

'What, Leo—has got on your track, Artémise?'

'Yes, that was rather fun, too. I saw him the other day watching me through the bushes, and as I did not want to fall into his arms at that little side door—which is so convenient—I turned and dodged him. His patience was wonderful; he was resolved to have me. We played an amusing game through and through the shrubbery, and then I took to the open, thinking I was lost. But the rain was blinding, I suppose, and the dark coming on, so I got off safe. Were you aware that he dined at the Rectory one night?'

'I heard he did not come in for dinner. I was not downstairs. It did not concern me. At the Rectory—with that Plowden woman——'

'And that Plowden girl. Do you know one of them is like her aunt? How should you like it if Leo——'

'You insult my son, Artémise.'

'Ah well! There is never any telling; since he cannot have one, he may content himself with the other. I have seen more wonderful things before now.'

'Who is the one he cannot have?'

'My dear Cecile, why this tone of surprise? I told you before. Leo thinks Lady William the most attractive woman he ever saw, and I do not wonder. She was always attractive, even as a silly girl.'

'How you insult me, Artémise!—a woman I hate, who has no right to that name, and will soon be proved the impostor I have always known she was.'

Mrs. Swinford sat upright on her sofa, with a glow of anger on her face.

'Then I had better hurry off,' said Mrs. Brown composedly. 'If she is to be attacked, it is evident I cannot stay here.'

'But you said it was the safest place,' cried Mrs. Swinford in alarm, 'that nobody would think of looking for you in Watcham.'

'It is no longer safe now that Leo is on my track, and little
Mab full of alarm as to my morality. She will not betray me, that
little thing; but some time or other she will make her mother
come with her, to judge if my teaching is all right.'

'Then you must go, Artémise—you must go at once; though
how I am to live, in this dreadful place, with no one to care
whether I am alive or dead——'

'Yes,' said Mrs. Brown solemnly, 'I have thought of that.
You want somebody to look after you. You will have to make
up your mind between two things, between the two greatest things
in the world—love and hate. If you hate her more than you love
me, I will go. But you must remember, it is not going to come
back. I will have to disappear so entirely, that no one will ever
hear of me more. I can't turn up again when you want me, even
by stealth, as I do now.'

'Why, why?' said Mrs. Swinford, who had uttered this
question again and again, while Mrs. Brown was speaking. 'Why
should you disappear entirely? When it has blown over, when it
is forgotten—everything is forgotten after a while.'

'Do you think Emily will forget a thing that means her
honour, and her child's inheritance?—you have not forgotten, and
it ought to be nothing to you.'

'Nothing! You know what it is to me, Artémise.'

'Yes, I know what it is to you. It is hate and revenge—
and do you think your motives are stronger than hers? You want
to pay off an old score, but she wants to live respected and to
provide for her child. She will send detectives after me everywhere as soon as she knows. She will have you watched so that
I shall never be able to approach you. It will be good-bye for ever
between you and me, Cecile, if I am to carry out that rôle——'

'Artémise, you are too cruel! You know that I cannot live
long without you. You know that seeing you, having you at
hand, is my only comfort. I live only while you are here; for the
rest of the time I only exist, I vegetate, and hate the light——'

'I know,' said Mrs. Brown, in a slightly softened tone, 'that
you are fond of me, Cecile; that I have been more or less necessary
to you ever since I was born. You must make up your mind,
however, soon, for it will certainly be as I say.'

'No, no!' said Mrs. Swinford, rising from her sofa, trailing her
long skirts after her from end to end of the beautiful room. 'No,
no! We will leave this place; we will go to Paris, where we can
be secure. There are places there no detective would think of.
Detective — an English detective'—she laughed her tinkling

intolerable laugh. 'Bunglers all! what do they ever find out? I tell you, Artémise, we can live there in perfect safety, you and I together—and see our friends—and amuse ourselves. All with you! Fancy what a changed life!'

'On the edge of a volcano—for me.'

'On the edge of no volcano—what could be done to you? Nothing! It is no crime—and she would give it up very soon. She could not help herself, she would have no money. These people will take even her allowance from her—she will have nothing, nothing—not a penny, not a name; she will have to work —she will not think much of detectives then; she will not be able to go to law. No, Artémise; we shall live together, and you will be safe, safe as a child.'

'My dear Cecile! In the meantime if all this should come to pass, Leo will marry Lady William, who will have no alternative but to accept him, and it will be she who will have the revenge, not you. Stop a bit—and he has plenty of money, and will never rest till he has found me out. He will know well enough where to look. All that you know in Paris, and more, he knows.'

Mrs. Swinford had kept saying 'No, no, no!' all the time. Her face flushed, her eyes shone.

'He shall not, he shall not! It will be with my curse. He shall never, never do it,' she cried. 'I would rather he were dead.'

'It does not matter much what you wish—your curse! you have not made your blessing a thing to be desired, Cecile. Oh, I am not blaming you; it is not my affair, but I don't believe in the curse, you know. He will do it, and the woman whom you have ruined will marry him, for she will have no other resource. And Leo will find me wherever you hide me : no, it is for you to choose —between love and hate, Cecile.'

'I will never,' she said between her closed teeth, 'let that woman go.'

'Then you choose hate? I knew you would,' said Mrs. Brown, still perfectly calm; 'and now, my dear, you must hear me. For I never meant to serve your hate all the time; I never meant to let Emily be ruined. If she needs me I shall reappear. Yes, wherever I am. I am going away, but I shall leave my address with Leo, or with Jim, or with——'

'Artémise!' she cried.

It was rarely that the sound of a raised voice was heard out of Mrs. Swinford's room. She had nobody there to excite her to anger, but on this occasion she was no longer the sovereign in her own palace. It was not rebellion that moved her, for Artémise had always retained her independence; nor defiance, for nothing could be more quiet than Mrs. Brown's tone. It was the impatience of contradiction, the surprise at opposition which a woman to whom everybody has yielded feels at the first check, and the sound was so sharp and keen, and raised to such an unusual pitch of surprised exasperation, that when a knock came immediately after to the door, and Leo's voice was heard asking 'May I come in?' it was impossible for his mother to stop him with the languid, 'No, I do not wish to be disturbed,' with which she had often closed the door upon him. Julie, the usual sentinel, had stolen away, believing her mistress to be too much occupied to miss her —unhappy Julie when the moment of retribution came.

There was not a word said. Mrs. Swinford had not recovered her composure when her son opened the door.

'You do not say anything; so I suppose I may come in,' he said.

The man's intrusion was strange in this chamber never intended for him. A man and a son!—that is something different from a man and a brother. Mrs. Swinford gave her visitor a sharp and meaning look, and then said:

'What may you want, Leo, coming upon us in such a sudden way?'

'Was I sudden? I heard you with some one, and I thought I might venture also, as you were evidently talking. And here I find precisely the person I wanted.'

'Leo, you are very ill-bred. When you come to your mother's room, which is not very often, you might pretend, at least, that it was for her you came.'

'That surely goes without saying, mother. I was not aware when I came that there was any one here.'

'And you may be very well assured, Cecile, that at all events it was not for the love of me.'

Mrs. Swinford returned to her sofa with an exclamation of impatience.

'You have all your own objects,' she said, 'you are all pursuing your own ends. There is no one who thinks what is best for me. Leo, we were talking on private matters, women's matters. Now that you have seen Artémise, as you seem to have wished, your good sense will tell you that it is best to go away.'

'It was not from any desire to see her,' said Leo. 'Madame Artémise knows very well what I should be likely to wish in that respect: nor to talk to her, though she is so entertaining, but to know where I may find her, for the sake of others.'

'Oh yes, we all know what you mean. It is Emily Plowden you mean—it is you who have been backing her up all this time against your mother. I know you, Leo—that it should be against your mother, gives it a zest. You make her think—poor thing!—that it is for her, while your real desire is to expose your mother—to build her up in opposition to me.'

'I think you must be dreaming,' he said provoked. 'Madame Artémise, was it you I saw the other night in the shrubbery? Why did you run away?'

'Do you call that running away? I wasn't, however, displeased to have had a little excitement for once. But you see I was not afraid of you, for I have come back.'

'I don't know wherein the excitement lies,' said Leo impatiently. 'I have a message to give you, that is all.'

'You will give no message to Madame Artémise in my room.'

'Are you mad, mother? Why should I not say what I have got to say? There is nothing so sacred in your room. I respect your seclusion, and never interfere; but surely when I find you with your chosen companion——'

'She is my chosen companion. She is the only person who cares for me in the world. She shall come here and live with me, and comfort me for all the evil I have had to bear. She knows how I have been treated here, by those who should have cherished me most. My husband, who never understood me : my son, who has been beguiled from my side by my enemy. Artémise knows all my miseries, every one. She has consoled me when I have been at my worst. She shall come and live with me now, and be my companion, as you say, or else——'

But then Mrs. Swinford paused. There had been a certain pathos and dignity in her complaint. And she meant to add a threat, but instead stopped short and looked her son in the face.

'Mother,' he said, 'you have always been the mistress of your own house, and chosen your own company. You invite whom you choose here——'

'Yes, I will invite whom I choose. Artémise shall stay with me, and we will fill the house. Oh, it is not the time for the country, I know; but later, later. Thank you, Leo, I will trouble you no longer. Send the housekeeper here, I will give my orders; or Julie—Julie will give my orders. You need not take any trouble. And we will not detain you any longer; you must have affairs of your own that interest you more than ours.'

Mrs. Swinford waved her hands and all her rings, dismissing her son, who made a step towards the door.

'Leo will stay a little longer, please. You are speaking very much at your ease—mother and son : are you aware that this is a proposal that has been made before, and that I have never consented to it? No, Cecile, I will not live in your house—nor will I do your bidding, whatever it may be, Leo. The schoolmistress of Watcham has her own humble duties to perform, and she will perform them just as long as she chooses. She is a woman not bound by rules in general, and who does not care for a character from her last place, or anything of that sort. But at present she cannot be spared from her duties, not even for the sake of the best of friends who dispose of her so sweetly. She is not a woman to be calculated upon or to be disposed of, except in her own way.'

'Do you mean to say that you are the schoolmistress, Mrs. Brown?'

Leo had no inclination or desire to thwart her, or to disturb her in her position. He commented to himself with secret satisfaction on the inconsequence of the woman who thus gave herself up, so to speak, into his hands. For all that he wanted he had now discovered, that is, where she was to be found.

'Yes; I am the schoolmistress, Mrs. Brown, whom you scared the other day. Why should I have been scared and fled, and led you such a dance? Because it amused me, Mr. Swinford : and I am here because it amuses me. And I shall go away when I please, probably without giving notice. I think, Cecile, if you will ring your bell, it would probably please Mr. Morris, your dignified butler, to let me out to-night by the great door.'

'It rains,' said Leo. 'If you will permit me, Madame Artémise, I will order the brougham to take you home.'

She made him another curtsey with a merry devil twinkling in her eye.

'The poor schoolmistress ! That will be the best joke of all,' she said.

'MOTHER, I want you to come with me to the school,' said Mab. She had lost no time in carrying out Mrs. Brown's previsions, though she was quite unaware of them.

'Me—to go with you to the school? You know I have never had anything to do with the school. There are plenty of ladies to look after the school.'

'Yes, I know what you always say, mother: and I never asked you before. You will never have anything to do with the parish; but this is not the parish, it is me. Mrs. Brown is a very queer woman. She has them all in the most excellent order; but—I want you to see with your own eyes and tell me what you think.'

'I have a very important letter to write, Mab.'

'You are always writing important letters now, mother. What is it about? You never tell me anything now. I used to know all about your letters, and lately you never tell me anything. You are always conspiring with Uncle James. You never trust anything to me!'

'Poor Uncle James! How much perplexity and trouble I have brought him—and everybody connected with me.'

'You—mother!'

Mab stood and stared at her with wide-open eyes.

'No,' said Lady William, with a blush and a laugh. 'You do well to stare, Mab. I suppose that is one of the conventional things that people say when they are in trouble. No, I have not brought perplexity upon any one, or trouble, for a great number of years; but it is true that I have begun again now——'

'What is it, mother?' Mab came to the back of her mother's chair, put her arms round Lady William's neck, and rubbed her downy girlish cheek against the other, which was paler, but not less soft. Then Mab made a guess at the trouble in the only form that occurred to her. 'Have we been spending too much money?

Have we got into debt? Has anything happened about—Uncle Reginald——'

'Poor Reginald!' cried Lady William. 'That is what it is to be the prodigal of the family—everything is laid upon him. No, it is quite another matter. It is—why shouldn't I tell her? It is your father's brother, who has died and left a great deal of money. And there are things to arrange. If I can settle everything, as I wish—you will be a rich girl. But it is all uncertain, and it has stirred up so much that was gone and past.'

'Then it is about money,' said Mab in a relieved tone. 'And perhaps we may be rich! Well, that is nothing to trouble about, mother. I should like it, on the contrary. Come out, and leave the letter till to-morrow. Come anyhow—whether you come to the school or not——'

'What a little pertinacity you are! But, Mab, there is another side to the question. If it is not settled that you are to be rich— an heiress, as people call it—we shall, perhaps, be very poor, poorer than you can imagine: with nothing—less than nothing!' cried Lady William, thinking with a pang of the good name and honour —the loss of which Mab never could understand.

'Well!' said Mab, with another rub of her cheek upon her mother's, 'that's nothing so very dreadful either. Most people are poor—far, far more people than are rich. We shall be no worse than our neighbours. I daresay we shall be able to do something for our living. We are not useless people, mother, you and me. And now come out, come out, mother dear! You will write your letter much better after you have had a walk. The fresh air puts things into your head, the right things to say——'

'Ah, Mab,' cried Lady William, 'if you only knew how willing I am to be tempted, how much rather I would put it off—for ever if I could——'

'Well, mother, putting it off till the afternoon is not putting it off for ever,' said sensible Mab.

And when Lady William went to get her hat, Mab, who had always a hundred things to do within as well as outside the house, in the course of her moving about as she put things straight upon the table, saw her mother's letter upon the blotting-book, which Lady William had left open. Mab had no idea that she did anything wrong in looking at it. She had had no hesitation in all her life before, about anything that was her mother's, and why now? It began, 'Gentlemen,' which was a queer mode of address, Mab thought, and this was how it went on:

'I had already heard of Lord John Pakenham's death, and expected your letter accordingly. I have no certificates to send you, as it never occurred to me to provide myself with anything of the kind, and circumstances, as I hear from my brother, have occurred to make it somewhat difficult to obtain them; but you will perhaps know better how to act in the matter than I do. I was married on the 13th May, in St. Alban's Proprietary Chapel, Stone Street, Marylebone, by the Rev. Mr. Gepps, who is since dead. And I am informed by my brother that the Chapel was burnt down some years ago. It seems an unfortunate concatenation of accidents, but I don't doubt that you will know how to proceed in the matter. There is no witness of the marriage still alive—except——'

Here the writing broke off, and Mab stopped short with a curious sensation as if she had been pulled up suddenly. It startled her a little; she could scarcely tell why. What did people mean, inquiring into matters so long past? Her mother's marriage! Why, everybody knew all about her mother's marriage. 'Am not I a proof of it? Mab said to herself. 'I hope they don't mean to suggest that I am not my mother's child!' It disturbed her a little, though she could not have told why. Poor mother! she never liked talking about her marriage. Why should she be troubled? Mab had long ago made up her mind that it could not have been a happy marriage, though natural piety (which was strong in her) prevented her from blaming her father. They did not understand each other, she supposed. Many married people failed in that: strange to think how anybody could fail to understand mother, who was so very easy to get on with, not jealous or touchy, or any of those things! And that anybody should worry her about her marriage after all this time when she had been a widow for such years and years! Mab could not bear that her mother should be worried in this or any other way.

'Mother,' she said, when they set out, 'I want to say something to you. I read your letter, you know, in the writing-book——'

'You read my letter, Mab?'

'Well, you never said I mustn't; I never thought you could be writing anything you did not want me to see.'

'And you are quite right, my dear,' said Lady William seriously; but all the same, she asked herself with a shudder, 'How far she had gone, what she had said?'

'And, mother, if they are raking up everything, all those

things you prefer not to talk of, that you have never even told me—because of this money that might or should come to me— mother, I don't want their money. Let them keep it to themselves. I will not have you worried or get that look over the eyes for anything of the kind. I ought to have a say in it, if it is for me.'

'My love, it is very sweet of you to say that—and quite what I might have expected from my Mab ; but unfortunately they, if you mean the lawyers, won't keep it to themselves, nor can they keep it from you, if—— The family would keep it willingly, I have no doubt, but then it is not in their hands.'

'If—what, mother ?'

To think—among all her mother had said—that this little straightforward, practical mind should have seized on the one little word which she had not meant to say ! Lady William was pale, besides having, as Mab remarked, a look over her eyes. 'If—I can settle it all as I wish,' she replied.

Mab gave a dissatisfied look, but said no more on the subject. Lady William's tone admitted of no more questioning, and the little girl knew when to stop. She took her advantage, however, in another direction, and seizing her mother's arm as they reached the village street, said : 'Now, mother, come with me to the school.'

Lady William laughed, and consented. A laugh, an escape from present anxiety, a run with a little coaxing, not-to-be-denied girl through the morning air and sunshine—how pleasant these things are ! She had been a little vexed about the letter, and had checked Mab's inquiries in a manner which does not at all show in print, but which was very effectual, and now she could not fail to make up for all this by giving in to Mab. When they reached the schoolroom, however, it did not present the same aspect of quiet without and occupation within which it generally did. There was a little crowd round the door, in the midst of which were some of the elder girls talking volubly. And at the moment when Lady William and her daughter appeared upon the scene, Mr. Osborne was visible coming towards them on one side and Leo Swinford on the other. What was the matter ? Mab, whom everybody knew, pushed into the midst of the agitated group.

'Oh, Miss, teacher's gone,' the girls cried, hurrying round as to a new listener.

'Gone ! Mrs. Brown !' cried Mab, with almost a shriek of dismay : and then the story was told by half-a-dozen eager voices at once. Mrs. Brown had returned last evening in a grand carriage—the carriage from the Hall—to the wonder and awe of the nearest neighbours who were witnesses of the event; but whether she went away again late that night or by the first train in the morning no one knew. What was certain was that when the children came to school in the morning the schoolroom (oh, joy!) was locked up, and no trace to be found of Mrs. Brown. Later, when the schoolmaster decided upon the strong step of breaking open the doors, it was found that Mrs. Brown's trunks were fastened, her house stripped of all its embellishments, and no sign of her left anywhere. The boxes were addressed to a railway station in London to be left till called for. There was no letter, no statement of any excuse. She was gone, that was all that could be said.

This, of course, was by no means all that was said as the schoolgirls chattered and the women compared notes. A number of them had perceived as something was up. Some had seen from the first as she wasn't the kind of woman for our school, and it wouldn't answer long; though several acknowledged as it must be allowed she pushed the girls on.

'There's my Lizzie,' said an admiring mother, 'passed all the standards and done with schooling, and she but twelve; and the help it is to have her at home!'

'But teacher was allays fond of me, mother,' said Lizzie, 'and pushed me on.'

Then a great many had burst in to declare that teacher was very fond of them individually, and had pushed them all on. A little Babel of talk arose at the schoolroom door, which was only partially stayed when Mr. Osborne arrived, to whom the whole story had to be told over again. And then Mr. Swinford came up breathless, who received the news with more excitement than any one.

'Gone!' he cried, 'gone!' as if he could not believe his ears. 'Have they searched the house?' he inquired anxiously.

'Well, sir, what's the good o' searching the house? She can't be hiding upstairs,' the women said.

Leo was not satisfied with this, however, but ran into the schoolmistress's house with a very white and anxious face, making his way upstairs to her bedroom and into the little kitchen and every corner. He came down again and took Lady William by the arm, leading her aside. He did not even observe the scrutiny of Mab, who, full of curiosity which she herself did not understand, watched and followed them.

'Did you see her?' he asked anxiously.

'See her?' cried Lady William—'the schoolmistress? Mrs. Brown?'

'Then you had not found out,' he said, 'that she was Artémise?'

And then Mab thought that her mother would have fainted. She threw up her arms and cried: 'Artémise!' almost with a shriek. 'And she has been here at my door—here—and I never knew!'

'Mr. Leo,' said Mab, 'mother has been worried until she is almost ill. She has had business and all sorts of things to worry her. Why did you tell her this, whatever it means, to make her worse?' She had drawn Lady William into a chair and stood behind her, supporting her head upon her own breast, with her arms over her mother's shoulders like the wings of some homely angel half-fledged and not in full heavenly state.

'Somebody must go after her,' Lady William cried hurriedly. 'She must not, she must not escape. Here! do you mean to say *here*, at my very door? And I had been told to go and see her, and Mab, my wise Mab, had made me come at last. Oh, child, why was it not yesterday—why was it not——? And Leo, to think you should never have told me. The woman that can make all right, that can save Mab's fortune, and my—— Leo, Leo, why didn't you tell me? Oh, Mab, why did you not make me come before to-day?'

'I only made the discovery last night,' he said, while she sat wringing her hands, 'and that she should fly like this never came into my mind. I was on my way to tell you, to bring you here.'

'Mab did that. Mab, though she knows nothing, understands. And who is to follow that woman and secure her now? Some one must go at once, before the scent is cold, before—before——'

'Dear lady, I am ready to go—wherever you please to send me. I am here only for your service. I will go to where the address is and wait, wait till she comes. It is easy. I will never forgive myself for letting her go last night.'

Lady William had been slowly coming to herself, the giddiness going out of her head, and the dimness from her eyes. When she recovered her composure, she saw that a little crowd had gathered round her—some of the women from outside, one of whom held a glass of water, while another had rolled forward Mrs. Brown's sofa and was entreating her ladyship to lie down; while behind stood two tall figures looking on, Mr. Osborne and Jim. The curate had on that mask of disapproval which he was too apt to show to any weakness. Why Lady William should get up a little faint because this schoolmistress, of whom he himself had never approved, had gone, he found it impossible to divine. A faint ! As if it were anything to her—the schoolmistress ! of whom she had never taken any notice. It was like the folly of women, making a fuss upon every possible occasion. Mr. Osborne did not pause to consider that Lady William was not the woman to faint in order to make a fuss, or even to remember that she had not fainted at all. Such considerations interfere sadly with the solid foundations of tradition. Jim stood beside his friend with a very different expression upon his face. It was anxious, full of sympathy, and of something more than sympathy, eager to interfere, to speak ; but nobody took any notice of Jim.

'Mother, do you think you could walk home now ?' said Mab in her ear. 'Please, please, mother, come away if you can.'

'I ought to go after her, Mab.'

'Dear lady, I will go,' cried Leo. 'Surely you can trust me ?'

'Oh, mother,' cried Mab, more and more impatient, 'come home now, come home.'

Mab could scarcely tell why it was that she was so anxious for her mother to come away. Other people were arriving from moment to moment. Miss Grey, on one of her parochial rounds, startled by the commotion and the sight of so many children about during school hours : and General FitzStephen, who, seeing that something had happened (always such a godsend in a village), had walked over to inquire into it. Mab could not bear that her mother's agitation should be seen by so many curious pairs of eyes. And by Mr. Osborne above all, looking disapproval over the heads of the little crowd.

'There is no train,' she said, 'till the afternoon ; and if the things are not sent off, how can she come to claim them ? And you could not hang about a railway station waiting. Oh, mother, come home.'

'Mab,' said Jim, making his way to her, 'I'll do anything. You can send me anywhere. And let me take Aunt Emily home.'

Lady William rose from among the attendants, recalled to herself by these offers of aid.

'Mab has always the most sense of all of us,' she said with a smile. 'Of course nobody can go when there is no train. Thanks ; but I don't think I need your arm, Jim. No, no ; I am not ill at all. I was only much startled to find that Mrs. Brown, who has just gone away so hastily, was an old friend whom I had many reasons for wishing to see : and I never knew she was here.'

'Do you know,' cried Miss Grey, 'I always thought her face was familiar to me ; but I could not put a name to it. Who was she ? I ought to have known her, too.'

'And she has gone away—without any notice !' said the General. 'I never heard of such a thing. The schoolmistress ! And what is to be done to fill her place ?'

Lady William, under cover of this discussion, which was immediately taken up by the curate and Miss Grey, left the house, which had never before, perhaps, been so invaded by the crowd. The released children were in full *émeute* outside—those who had not already been secured by their mothers—filling the village street with commotion, and sorely trying the patience of the boys on the other side, who heard but could not understand those sounds of jubilee. To think that there were no means of checking the riot, and that half of the children in the parish had thus an unexpected holiday, was grievous to the soul of Mr. Osborne, who formed a sort of committee instantly in the abandoned house over Mrs. Brown's boxes. Miss Grey called to Mab that she would come in the afternoon and tell them how things were arranged, as they went away. That little lay-curate could not imagine, sympathetic as she was, that there could be any question so interesting as this.

And, indeed, nothing had happened in Watcham for years that had been so exciting. The schoolmistress ! without a word of warning, without a thought, apparently, of the embarrassment or trouble it would cause to the parish, without any consideration even of her own interest—for how could she ever obtain another situation, having left her charge like this ? People came out to their doors to ask, as Lady William passed, could it be true? and groups stood discussing the strange event all along the street. The schoolmistress ! that functionary of all others in an English parish is the least apt to be revolutionary. What could this portent mean ?

It was very hard to get rid of Leo Swinford, but Mab succeeded at last. He insisted on walking with Lady William to the cottage, full of apologies and excuses all the way.

'I thought this morning,' he said, 'when I was told she was gone, that it was a dose of chloral. All women like her take chloral, and all women like her are apt to take a sudden disgust with life.'

'Poor Artémise?' said Lady William, who was always fair and rarely unkind. 'Do any of us know what kind of woman she was? She has never had justice all her life, and with all that power and independence and spirit, she would have made a better man than a woman. I cannot think if she had known how much I wanted her that she would have gone away.'

To this Leo made no reply. He thought he knew a great deal better. He thought it was because of a cruel plot with his mother that Artémise had disappeared. But he would not destroy Lady William's confidence, nor did he dare betray how much more he knew about the matter, and the cause of her anxiety to see Artémise than had ever been confided to him. But he walked on by her side repeating what he would do. He would go to London and take the boxes with him. He would wait at the station she had indicated till she came. But she might not come. She might send a stranger.

'*Bien!*' said Leo. 'I will be there. I will follow, whoever it may be. I will not lose sight of her property, her boxes, till I have found her or some clue to her. Dear lady, the boxes —that is the best of guides: for what is a woman without her "things"? Is it not so?'

'You are always safe to have a theory about women to fall back upon,' said Lady William, beguiled into a laugh; and then they reached the door of the cottage, and Leo, who was not invited to cross the threshold, had nothing for it but to go away.

The ladies, however, had another attendant, who was more pertinacious, who waited for no invitation, but stalked in after them as he had stalked along by Mab's side, with a much-troubled countenance but few words, all the way. Jim found himself in the midst of this imbroglio, which he did not in the least understand, not as a spectator only, but as a potential agent with something to say if he could but secure the means of saying it. What the message with which he was charged meant he knew as little as he could comprehend what possible or impossible link there could be between Mrs. Brown and Lady William, the one the symbol of dignity and modest greatness to Jim, the other—— He thought no evil of Mrs. Brown : he thought she was 'queer' though kind : that a woman so old and so clever should be on the terms of a *bon camarade* with himself was astounding to him, but agreeable. There was no harm in anything she had either said or done in his knowledge. But he had known that the ladies of the parish, at whom she laughed so much, would have very little approval of Mrs. Brown had they known more of her—and Lady William was 'a cut above' the ladies of the parish : that she should be so much distressed by Mrs Brown's sudden departure as to faint, or almost faint, when she discovered it, was incredible to him. But things being so, Mrs. Brown's message, which he had thought at the time to be a kind of insanity, began to have meaning in it—meaning still dark to him, but which, perhaps, Lady William would understand. He went into the cottage after them, accordingly, indifferent to Mab's looks, who frowned him back : but Jim was not to be kept back by Mab. When he appeared in the drawing-room, Lady William had thrown herself into a chair, and was leaning back with an air of anxiety and trouble, yet relief to be at rest and unobserved for the moment. Jim's entrance made her start, with a little exclamation of annoyance.

'Jim,' said Mab, 'oh, do go away, there's a good fellow ; don't you see that mother's overdone ?'

'Yes, I see,' said Jim, 'but I've got something to say to Aunt Emily.'

'Oh, what can you have to say ? Something about going up to town. There's a hundred people ready to go up to town — if that would do any good. Please, Jim, please, go away !'

'I have something to say to Aunt Emily,' said Jim, standing first on one foot and then on the other in his embarrassment, but with a dogged look of determination that had never been seen upon his face before.

'Get me a glass of water, Mab,' said Lady William, 'and let Jim alone. It is very kind of him to be so ready to help.'

It did not occur to her, indeed, that Jim could have very much real help to give; but she saw the anxiety in the young man's face, and even (as she was always a person who could be amused at the most unlikely moments) the attitude of her little Mab, determined to sweep this big and obstinate encumbrance out of the way, stirred her with that sense of the humorous which gives so much solace to life. When Mab had most unwillingly gone out of the room, Jim came up, red and eager, and much flustered, to Lady William's chair.

'Aunt Emily,' he said, breathless; 'I know Mrs. Brown. She told me to tell you——'

'What, Jim! she told you—*you* !'

'Never mind that now,' he cried, 'I'll explain after. She said: "If there is any chance of harm to Lady William—it sounds like madness, but I must say it—if she is likely to be overwhelmed, tell her not to be afraid, I'll come." That's what she said, Aunt Emily. I thought she was mad—but then I thought I must tell you——'

'She was not mad. Thank you, thank you, Jim. Don't say anything—to any one. She said she would come?'

'I was to tell you she would stand by you—not to be afraid —if you were likely to be overwhelmed——'

'Here is Mab coming back. Thank you, Jim, I understand, and I believe her—I believe her! You've given me great comfort. Thank you, thank you, Jim !'

Jim did not know why he was thanked any more than he knew what the meaning of his communication was; but he was greatly elated all the same, and felt the clearing up of Lady William's countenance—which was, he said to himself, exactly like the clearing of the clouds from the sky—to be his doing, with the warmest sense of beneficence and pleasure.

'She is ever so much better; she is almost quite right,' he said to Mab, who came hurrying in with a glass of water, and who could not help feeling a little annoyance to be thus assured by Jim of her mother's recovery. By Jim !—with a smirk as if he had been instrumental in the improvement. He went away with that look of complacence and gratification on his face for which Mab would fain have boxed his ears; but at all events he did take himself away, and that was always something gained.

'Now, mother, you will have a little peace,' said Mab. 'Lie down a little on the sofa, and close your eyes. That always does Aunt Jane good, and perhaps it may you. But I don't know what will do you good; you never give me the chance to know.'

'I don't think closing my eyes will do me any good,' said Lady William. 'Give me that work of yours to set right, which you got into such a muddle last night. I am much better; I am almost all right, as poor Jim said.'

'He seemed to think he had something to do with it,' said Mab, with a snort of disdain.

'Poor Jim! and perhaps he had. He brought me a message. You never told me much about Mrs. Brown, Mab.'

'Oh, mother! I told you till I was tired telling you. I told you she was a lady. Well, what business had a lady in our school? But what does all that matter now? Who was she, mother? It is your turn to tell me.'

'An old friend, Mab.'

'Oh, that I know! But something more, surely? or you would not have been so startled to-day, or so distressed to miss her.'

'The distress was selfish,' said Lady William. 'She was with me once, at a most important moment of my life; and she can help me better than any one to settle that question with the lawyers about your money, Mab.'

'Oh!' said Mab. 'She told me she knew my father, and old John, as she called him, and——'

'And you never told me, Mab.'

'It was in a kind of confidence. And she did not say she knew you; and it was all so mixed up with things—that made me think she oughtn't to be there, mother, in our school. And yet how could I tell any one, and make her lose her place? And that is why I wanted you to go this morning, to see what you thought; for you would have known in a moment if there was anything wrong.'

'And that is why you have been so often at the school of late, my little girl?'

Mab nodded her head, slightly abashed, but yet not shaken in her confidence that it was the right thing.

Lady William drew her child into her arms and kissed her. 'My little girl!' she repeated, with a soft burst of laughter. And then she put her handkerchief to her eyes, and pushed Mab away and took the tangled work of last night, in which Mab had come to great grief, into her clever hands.

No doubt, whatever it was that had done it—even were it

Jim—Jim, of all people in the world!—mother was better,
brighter, happier, Mab concluded, half comforted, half perplexed.
For that Jim should have had the power to do that—*Jim !*—
transcended Mab's powers of imagination. Lady William retained
her cheerfulness until the afternoon, when she sat down to finish
that letter which had been left in her blotting-book. But she
made small speed over it, and it appeared to Mab that ‘the look
over her eyes’ came back. If it could be imagined that Mab was
capable of being glad at the overclouding of her mother's face, I
would say she was at least not displeased when this occurred, so
that such a ridiculous instrumentality as that of Jim might be
proved insufficient for the change it seemed to have caused. But
this was a feeling of which Mab was ashamed after the first moment when it flashed upon her. Lady William sat for a long time
over the letter, but she did not add anything to it. She held her
pen in her hand, and on several occasions bent over the paper as if
she were about to write, but always stopped short. What had she
more to say ? She knew now that when these words were written
the all-important witness had been within her reach ; but now she
was as much out of it as Lady William had then supposed her to
be—lost in that big world of London where the most anxious
parent cannot find his child. And who could tell whether Artémise would ever hear how things went, or whether she was
wanted ? The promise Jim brought had consoled her for a moment. It had been like a revelation of comfort to hear that at
least Artémise was on her side. But this did not outlast the
depressing effect of the afternoon—that puller-down of hopes.
Artémise might be on her side, but how, now that she had disappeared again, was she to find her when that moment arrived at
which her word was indispensable ? And then Lady William felt
that this promise of help only in the moment of uttermost need
had something humiliating in it. To keep her in suspense to the
last, trembling with the sword suspended over her head, and then
to step in—no sooner. This was not surely the act of a friend.
And why should Artémise be her friend when Mrs. Swinford was
her enemy ? Her heart sank. The little flush of satisfaction
faded. She threw down her pen, and left her letter unfinished, as
before.

And then Leo Swinford came with his eager proposals to go
to town, to find the runaway at all hazards, until Lady William,
exhausted by many emotions and by that sickening revulsion of
fresh despair after a rising of hope, became impatient, and more
than half resentful of his importunities, which were more ardent

than the occasion required—or seemed so to this fastidious lady, who in the failure of her own confidence was disposed to take umbrage at his—which rested upon the certainty of being able to do himself by his unassisted exertions now, what it would have been so easy, so simple, to do yesterday, and so entirely within his power.

'It scarcely seems to me worth the while,' she said, with a weary look. 'Why should you make a sentry of yourself at that railway? She will send some one for her boxes and elude you, as she has done before.'

This was hard upon poor Leo, who, indeed, had done his best. He was still there when the Rector appeared, who interrupted one of those protestations and entreaties to be trusted, from which Lady William turned so coldly. And the Rector was still more cold.

'If we had but known in time,' Mr. Plowden said. 'I had never seen the lady. If any of those who must have known her had but given us a hint in time.'

It could only be Leo to whom this reproach was addressed, and the Rector did not notice his protest that he had never associated his mother's visitor with the school. Even Lady William was unjust. She said: 'You must have suspected that she had some haunt or shelter at Watcham.' Leo had to fall back upon some of his own general theories about women, that they are always unjust. But he did not go away, which made the Rector more angry still: for Mr. Plowden had come on business. Some days had elapsed since the lawyer's letter was received, and yet it had not been answered, nor had any decision been come to as to what was or was not to be said in the reply. He had come again to-day with the intention of pressing for Mr. Perowne—Mr. Perowne and his firm had known all the secrets of the Plowden family for generations, why should not he be entrusted with this? But Lady William would only look at him with a silent resistance. She would not accept Mr. Perowne, nor would she tell him why.

'I have begun my letter,' she said, 'I will finish it to-night; it is merely to tell them the facts——'

'For Heaven's sake,' said the Rector solemnly, 'don't send it away at least without letting me see it—without taking my opinion at least.'

'There is as much as I have written,' she said, handing him the letter, 'you are welcome to see it, but whatever comes of it I must do it my own way.'

And Leo had the bad taste to sit through this discussion, to remain even while the Rector read the half-written letter, vehemently shaking his head and saying 'no—no—no' as he went on.   It is true that Mr. Swinford went to the other side of the room and talked to Mab, whose presence there her uncle also felt to be *de trop*.   For the room was so small that being at the other end of it only meant that those other two people were some two or three yards away.

'No,' he said, 'I would admit nothing, Emily. You are wrong—you are wrong. You are making no stand for yourself at all. Why tell them about the chapel being burnt down, and why say you don't know where she is——.   It is wrong, I say; it is betraying everything. When they see this, they will have no mercy.'

'You think I should go away?' said Leo to Mab. 'But I have not yet received my orders. Have patience with me a little, and I will go.'

And then, as if there were not already too many, Miss Grey came in, to fulfil her volunteer promise to bring them news of how things were settled.

'Oh, Mr. Plowden, how glad I am to see you,' she said, 'for I am very anxious to know whether you will sanction our arrangement.   Mr. Osborne seemed to think it was all right because Florry—though, as I said to him, Florry is a darling, but she is not the Rector. What an extraordinary business it was, to be sure!'

'Do you mean Mrs. Brown?' the Rector asked, very impatiently: and yet incivility was not possible to Miss Grey.

'What a wonderful thing to do, to shake the dust from her feet, as the Bible says. But we never did anything unkind. I should have laid myself out to be friendly if she would have responded.   But I always felt she was a most unlikely person to hold that position. Did you happen to keep her testimonials, Mr. Plowden, or do you remember who they came from? There should be some inquiry made; and the people who recommended her should be warned of the way she treated us. Not that there was a word to say against her management of the school. Everybody seems to say she did very well there.'

'I don't remember,' said the Rector, more affronted than ever, 'anything about her appointment, Miss Grey.'

'Ah, well! but you remember something about her, Emily. Didn't you say you knew her—under some other name? If it was here, I must surely remember her, too. I always felt that I had seen her face somewhere before. The first time I saw her it made quite an impression on me. I kept asking myself where have I seen that face? But, you know, familiarity breeds—— that is to say, when you get used to a face, you no longer think. Was it in Watcham you knew her, Lady William, my dear?'

'She did not live actually in Watcham,' Lady William replied, with hesitation. 'I saw her—that is, she was present—at my marriage.'

The Rector (for what reason I cannot tell) looked at his sister angrily, shaking his head as if this had somehow been a betrayal of weakness too.

As for Miss Grey, she threw up her hands as if a sudden light had flashed upon her, and cried: 'Ah, to be sure! now I remember—at your marriage! I recollect all about her now: that was where I saw her—and often in Mrs. Swinford's carriage before.'

'That was where you saw her?'

Lady William's bosom heaved with a quick breath; her colour changed from pale to red; she bent forward as if her hearing had failed her. As for Miss Grey, she gave her friend a sudden apologetic look, put up her hands as if to cover her face, and burst into a deprecating laugh.

'Didn't you know?' she said. 'No, of course you didn't know. I kept it to myself, for I had no business to be there. And I was a little huffy that you had not asked me. Yes, my dear, I saw you married,' said little Miss Grey.

Lady William fell back in her chair, and covered her face with her hands. The Rector, for his part, got up and walked to the window, where he stood looking out, 'to see if it rained,' he muttered; though a brighter sky could not be than that which shone in upon the startled group. Mab and Leo, looking on, were as much startled as little Miss Grey herself, by the sensation she had evidently produced.

'You don't mean to say that you're angry,' she said, 'Emily, after nearly twenty years?'

Lady William uncovered her face, from which the blood had receded again, leaving her perfectly pale. She rose up tremulously, and cast herself upon the neck of her old friend.

'Angry?' she said. 'Oh, glad, thankful beyond measure. Why didn't I know it before?'

'Well, my dear, I suppose I was ashamed to confess the liberty I had taken,' said Miss Grey, who was much surprised, and yet pleased by the impression made. 'I may as well make a clean breast of it now, since you're not displeased. I was going up to town that day. I do assure you I was going up on my own business to town. And I saw you at the station, the dear old Rector, and you in a little white bonnet, and another lady. Bless me, to think that should have been Mrs. Brown ! You were looking like a lily flower—paler even than you are now. Ah ! you are not pale now, you are like a rose. Did ever any one see the mother of a big girl like Mab change colour like that before ? I saw you all three get into a cab—and then my curiosity got the better of me. I daresay it was very dreadful. I was too much ashamed ever to tell anybody. I took another cab and followed you. And I crept in behind to the very back of that nasty ugly little chapel, quite furious with the Rector and everybody that you should have had such a wedding. To think how things come out all of a sudden after one has bottled them up for twenty years ! '

WHEN Mr. Osborne found himself alone — the impromptu committee which had hastily discussed the emergency having melted
away, with the understanding that nothing could be done for this
morning, that the holiday must be permitted, and a more formal
meeting held in the afternoon at which some expedient might be
settled upon — he stood for a moment at the door of the schoolhouse looking out upon the emancipated children, and making up
his mind what to do. There was one thing very clear, and that
was that the Rector ought to know. The curate stood and medi-
tated with many things in his mind. He had not gone to the
Rectory for some weeks, not since that disastrous moment when
Florence had spoken her mind. His heart leaped up in his
bosom, and began to beat in a most wild, unclerical, and unjustifiable way, when he saw that it was his duty to go now, and that
there was no one else to do it for him. Jim had gone off in
attendance upon Lady William, which was wholly unnecessary,
seeing she had already her daughter and Swinford with her; but
the fact that he had gone was evident, and more immediately
important than to decide whether he had any right to go. And
there was nobody but the curate to fulfil this necessary duty.
Miss Grey even, the feminine curate, who ought to have been the
first to undertake that mission, had melted away with the rest,
going off to her district—as if her district for once could not wait!
Mr. Osborne looked round him for help, but found none. At last
he buttoned up his coat, which was the same as the Scriptural
preparation of girding his loins, and went forth, hesitating no
longer, but walking with a firm foot, light and swift, up the village
street, resolved to do his duty. His duty was clearly to beard
the lion in his den: no, not the Rector—the Rector was no lion
to this critical young man: the lion whom he felt himself called
upon to beard was a person of very different appearance from that

of the respectable middle-aged clergyman who was Mr. Osborne's
ecclesiastical superior, and whom, with the instinct of the new
generation, the curate was disposed to estimate lightly.   It was a
very different kind of lion indeed—a lion probably in a white
gown, with pretty brown locks a little astray on her forehead, with
a pair of mild brown eyes, that could indeed shine with sacred
fire, as when she dared to discourse to a consecrated priest upon
his duty—his duty ! which was, first of all, by all laws, both of
Nature and the Church, to hold her in subjection and ordain for
her what she was to do—a case which she had taken upon herself
to reverse.   It would be difficult to say why Mr. Osborne should
have concluded that this dangerous animal was the one he would
see at the Rectory and not the true spiritual ruler of the parish
himself, or even the ruler-ess, at whose pretensions the curate
would have snapped his fingers.   No, curiously enough, it was of
neither of these that he thought.   He felt absolutely certain, by
what means I cannot tell, that it was Florence he would see—
Florence, who had so offended him that he had all but insulted her
sister and herself in the sight of the whole parish about their
duet : and now he would have to face her—probably alone.   To
all ordinary calculations nothing could be more improbable than
this—that circumstances should conjoin in such a concatenation
accordingly as that nobody should be in the Rectory to receive Mr.
Osborne but Florence ; that her father should be out—a man
always in his study till luncheon ; and her mother out—a woman
devoted to housekeeping and the cares of her family ; and even
Emmy out, with whom Mr. Osborne had no controversy.   Only
that spitfire, that little dictator, that feminine meddler, who had
taken upon her to give advice to a priest !   Such a contingency
was not to be looked for by any of the laws of probability ; and
yet Mr. Osborne felt certain this was how it would be.   His heart
would not have beat so, his cheek taken such a colour, his head
been held so high, if it had been the Rector he expected to see.
He knew he should see *her*, and no one else ; and he strode along
accordingly, with sensations which were somewhere between those
which moved David when he went out to meet Goliath and those
which might be supposed to inspire a Forlorn Hope.

He did, however, everything he could to persuade himself
that, after all, this was an ordinary visit upon parish business to
the Rector.   He went in by the parish door, which, as has been
said, was a swinging door, always open in case any shy and shame-
faced parishioner should wish to communicate with the spiritual
authorities : but Mr. Plowden was not in his study, as Mr. Osborne

foresaw. As he came out of that room, pretending to himself that
he was disappointed—which he was not—he met one of the
servants, who informed him (what he had discovered without her
aid) that her master was out, and missis was out, and Mr. Jim
was out, but she thought there was some one in the drawing-room,
one of the young ladies, if that would do. Mr. Osborne could not
say to Mary Jane that *that* would not do, that it was the last
thing he wished, though he had been sure of it all along. All
that he did was to nod his head rather impatiently in reply, and
push past Mary Jane. No, he would not have himself announced
by the maid, as if it were quite a usual matter. He waved her
away, and went on by himself and opened the drawing-room door.
How his heart beat, and what a wrathful shining was in his eyes!

And of course his previsions were quite true, true in every
particular : there she sat, looking as if—as if, according to the old
wives, butter would not melt in her mouth. Not with the air of a
lion to be bearded in his den. Oh no! much more like a lamb—
in the white dress which (even that detail!) the unfortunate curate
had foreseen, looking so peaceable and innocent, so—so—sweet,
confound her! Oh no, the curate did not say that. It is I who
say it, in the impossibility of finding words to express his sentiments. It all surged upon him now—much worse even than he
had expected! the abominable impertinence and presumption of
her, the sweetness of her, the everything he liked best, conjoined
with that intolerable something which he could not endure.
Poor curate! He had foreseen it all—but not so bad, not quite
so bad as it turned out. She was seated close by the window, at
one side of the large table which had been thrust into a corner,
but not put away, as being so convenient for work—with a good
deal of white stuff about, cotton from which she was cutting out
various shapes, of which I do not pretend that Mr. Osborne
recognised more than the purpose of them, which was for the
sewing class evidently in the first place, and the comfort of its
members after that. A clergyman—if not celibate, which,
perhaps, is the best—but Mr. Osborne had regretfully allowed the
difficulties of it some months before this—could not well behold in
visions a wife more suitably employed. Florence was so busy
that it did not occur to her to turn round when the door opened.
She was singing to herself in a sort of undertone as she planned
out, and pinned, and cut, not thinking of any visitor. It piqued
Mr. Osborne extremely, as if it were a special little defiance thrown
out at himself, that she should be singing at her work.

'Miss Plowden,' he said.

Oh, then he was revenged for the moment! Florence started
so that she nearly jumped from her chair, and the scissors with
which she was cutting out so carefully gave a long and jagged gash
into the cotton like a wound, and the cheeks and pretty white
throat which were under his gaze suddenly turned red to the edge
of the white dress as if with some ruby dye.

'Mr. Osborne!' she said, with a half-terrified look.

'I am afraid I startled you. I came to see the Rector—to
tell him of a most extraordinary incident.'

Florence uttered a quavering, troubled 'O—oh!' and then she
said, dropping her scissors, 'I hope it is not bad news.'

'Oh, not to any of us,' said the curate hurriedly, 'to the
parish, perhaps; but I am not even sure of that.'

When Florence heard it was only the parish that was threat-
ened, she calmed down immediately; her 'O—oh!' repeated, was
in quite a different tone. 'My father is out,' she said, 'and so, I
am afraid, are mamma and Emmy. It is very seldom,' said
Florence, feeling herself almost on her defence, 'that I am the only
one at home; but I can tell papa—anything——'

Anything? How was it that it occurred to both of them instinctively that there might be things which Florry could not tell
papa—which it would be Mr. Osborne's duty to say in his own
person? If there is anything that it is specially embarrassing to
think of, at any given moment, that, one may be sure, is the thing
that comes into one's head. Anything? If the curate wanted
to ask Mr. Plowden for his daughter, for example, which was a
thing that did not seem unlikely some time ago, though not now
—oh, certainly, not now! This thought in all its ramifications
went like lightning through the minds of both, and made each—
thinking nothing could be further from the ideas of the other—
more confused than words can say.

'It is to ask,' said the curate, recovering himself, 'that the
Rector would call together the education committee at once, if he
does not mind. A wonderful thing has occurred. The schoolmistress, without giving any notice or warning, without a word to
any one, has gone away. When the children went to school this
morning the door was locked, and she was gone.'

'The schoolmistress? Mrs. Brown?'

'I don't know how she was appointed,' said the curate; 'I was
away at the time for my holiday; nor who is responsible for her,
nor what recommendations she had. I had never any confidence
in her, for my own part. She did not at all seem fitted for such
a sphere.'

Florence felt that this was an assault upon her father's judgment, and immediately stood to her guns.

'She was an excellent teacher ; the girls would do anything for her, and the inspector said there was such an improvement.'

'She was not a woman to have charge of the moral training of all those girls.'

'Oh, their moral training ! But it was for the standards that she was there.'

'We need not quarrel over that,' said the curate, as who should say, we have plenty of subjects to quarrel upon, 'the thing is that she is gone. I was going to say bag and baggage ; but that would not be correct, for her boxes are left all fastened up— directed to a distant railway station. She has not even left an address.'

'How very odd !' Florence said. And then there was a little pause : there is nothing so dangerous as a pause in certain positions of affairs.

Mr. Osborne stood in front of the window, and when he came to the end of a sentence looked out upon the garden. Florence, except when she was speaking and was obliged to raise her eyes to him now and then, kept them upon her work. She had not asked him to sit down—partly from inadvertence, partly from embarrassment—and both of them cast furtive glances at the gate, longing for somebody to come. Did they long for somebody to come ? At last the silence became so very appalling that Florence rushed into it, not knowing what might come of that too eloquent pause.

'I am to tell papa that there is to be a meeting of the ·education——'

'I hope you don't think I would send my Rector a message like that ? That, if he thinks well, there ought, perhaps, to be a meeting—for something must be done at once ; the children are all about'—Mr. Osborne added, sinking into a more confidential tone—'we cannot keep the girls' school shut.'

'No,' said Florence, 'oh no ; do you know of any one ? There is Anderson's wife, the schoolmaster. He wanted her to get it, but now she has the infant school. At the worst, don't you think for a day or two we ladies, perhaps ? If you can't hear of any one, I could take the reading and spelling, and perhaps the writing. Having the copylines makes that easy, though, of course, I don't write well enough myself.'

'You might do it, Miss Plowden ; you don't mind what trouble you put yourself to—' He had to pull up sharply, or he did not

know what he might have said.   His voice began to grow rather
soft in spite of himself, which was a thing that could not be permitted to be.   'We might think of Mrs. Anderson,' he said ; 'as
for the other ladies, I don't think it would do.   It is useless
trusting to amateurs.'

'Yes,' said Florence, with humility.   'I never thought, of
course, that I could be much good, or any of us, only for a stop-
gap for the moment.   Mrs. Anderson would be the most hopeful
thing, perhaps.'

'I did not mean to imply that you would be no good.   Quite
the reverse.   I meant——'

'Oh ! I know, I know, Mr. Osborne,' said Florry.   'We need
not stand upon compliments ; we are only trying to think what's
best for the children.'

That was all — what was best for the children — nothing
more.

He stood looking out of the window, and Florence pinned her
paper patterns to new folds of the white cotton.   And there was
again a pause—which Florry this time did not try to break.   It
was he who began.   'Your brother,' he said, suddenly but harshly,
'was so good about that ridiculous entertainment of mine ; I
should never have got those men to come but for him.'

'Jim ?' said Florence.   'I am very glad ; he liked to help ;
but I don't see why you should call it a ridiculous entertainment.'

'I felt it so,' cried the curate fiercely.   'What is the good of
such attempts ?   Perhaps if they went on, like the public-house,
every night, a warm bright place, with ladies to sing, and——'

'Dance !' said Florry, with unsteady laughter, 'as Miss Grey
said.   Well, then, you must start a working-man's club, Mr.
Osborne, and then you can have it every night, and there will
always be a nice bright, light place to sit in, and games, you know,
and papers——'

'And beer ?'

'I have heard people say,' said Florence, 'that it is best to let
them have whatever they would have if it was natural.   But I am
rather on your side about that, and so is mamma.'

'On *my* side ?' said the curate, with a faintness in his voice.

'About the temperance.   But, on the other hand, papa says it
is not having no beer, but having just as much as is good, that is
temperance.'

'None is good,' cried Mr. Osborne impulsively.

'Well,' said Florence, with judicial calm, 'I have said that I
think I am on your side.'

A pause again, and Florence went on with her work steadily. Nobody came—the May sunshine fell over the lawn without a shadow to break it. Would they never come back, Florry asked herself? And yet the present situation was not without its charm. All his displeasure was oozing out of his fingers' ends, all his unwillingness to be dictated to by a girl. He thought he would like it if she would dictate to him again, and tell him what was his duty. No; he did not think this, he only felt it vaguely—touched, he could not tell why, by her avowal of being on his side. Was he not her spiritual superior, and was it not her duty, as soon as she heard his sentiments on the subject, to be on his side? But somehow he did not feel so sure of that position, and rather wanted to hear her unbiassed opinion and what she would say.

'Your brother has been a great help to me,' he said again.

He would not for the world have reminded her of what she had said that day. And, of course, she had said nothing in so many words about her brother. He was by no means sure that it was not a mean thing thrusting this forward to make her think she was obliged to him, but yet—when a man is at his wits' end, what can he say?

'We have all been so glad to see that Jim was beginning—to take an interest——'

'And he knows so much,' pursued the curate, 'more than I do. If we were to get up a club, he might do almost anything he pleased with the men. I have to thank you, Miss Florence,' he went on, finding as he proceeded that it was necessary to be definite if he was to make any impression, 'for giving me a hint——'

'I don't think I gave you any hint,' said Florence, dropping her scissors; while she stooped for them she went on, saying quickly: 'We know what we owe to you; we all feel it. One can't talk of such things, Mr. Osborne, and I was very bold and disagreeable once; but if you think I don't thank you from my heart——'

'Florence!' said the curate.

'Oh, I don't mind, call me whatever you like. You had a good right to be angry, and I took a great deal, a very great deal upon me—but if you knew how we all thanked you from the bottom of our hearts.'

'Florence!' the curate said again; he had got down on his knee on the carpet to look for the scissors too—they were strange scissors to disappear like that—scissors are not round things like a ring or a reel of cotton to run into a corner; yet they eluded both these people who were looking for them, and who, not finding them, suddenly somehow looked at each other, probably for the first time since that day.

I think it highly probable that these young people forgot from that moment that there was a girls' school in Watcham at all, much more that the mistress had ran away from it, or that there was any occasion for moving heaven and earth, as Mr. Osborne had intended when he entered the Rectory, to get a substitute for Mrs. Brown.

L

MR. OSBORNE went off and had a long walk after this little scene, and Florence retreated to her own room. Neither of them for that first hour felt at all disposed to face the looks and possible inquiries of those ridiculously composed and commonplace persons to whom nothing had happened. The presence of these people surrounding them on every side, prying at them, laughing or wondering, or making investigation into their feelings, is at once a trouble and an astonishment to the hero and heroine. On a day which is the beginning of a new life to them, to think there should be so many in the world to whom it was only the fifteenth of May. How grotesque it seems! Only a day like another to be written down quite calmly as the date of their letters, and never thought of more, just the same as the sixteenth or the twenty-second! There are so many stupidities, so much that is dull and common in this life.

And in the afternoon there was that other event, so much less important, but yet meaning much, in Lady William's cottage. That the Rector, after spending all the morning out of doors, should have gone out again in the afternoon was a contrariety which Mr. Osborne for one could scarcely believe. When he came back in the afternoon to see his chief and to tell his tale, the curate's face, on hearing that once more that chief was out, was a study. Astonishment, annoyance, even displeasure were written on it, as well as a subduing consciousness that Florence would laugh, which Florence did accordingly with a strong inclination partially mastered to mimic the curate to his face: an inclination which, perhaps—who can tell?—if indulged in might have been too much for that gentleman, though he was very much in love. She laughed, and explained that poor papa could not mean any offence, seeing he was quite unaware what great intimation was about to be made to him.

2 c

'I tried to keep him,' she said, 'but he had business with Aunt Emily, and frowned upon me when I tried to insinuate that there might be more important business at home.'

Florence had come out to meet her curate at the gate. She put her hand within his arm as they came together across the lawn, and as she said these words she looked up into his face with so exact a representation of the Rector's frown, and his 'Go away, child, don't worry me with nonsense,' that Mr. Osborne, all grave, provoked, and half offended as he was, could not help but laugh.

'Florry, darling,' he said, pressing her arm to his side, 'it is very funny—but when you are a clergyman's wife, you know——' Poor Florry had not had the heart to mimic anybody since that April day : but now she only laughed at the reproof : she was ready to have 'taken off' the Archbishop of Canterbury had His Grace come in her way.

I need scarcely say that the sight of Florry coming across the lawn with her arm within that of the curate, laughing and looking up at him, while he looked down, and shook his head, and had the air of reproving, though with a smile on his face, had the greatest effect upon the people in the drawing-room who saw that scene from the windows.

'Emmy—*Emmy!*' cried Mrs. Plowden to her daughter, who was coming in calmly with the basket of stockings to be darned— and as soon as Emmy was within reach, her mother seized her by the skirts and pulled her forward to the window. 'What does that mean?' cried the Rector's wife. Mrs. Plowden's heart had leaped up into her throat, beating almost as fast and as tumultuously as the curate's heart had done when he stooped down in that very spot to look for the scissors. 'Tell me, *what* does *that* mean?' she said imperiously, while Emmy in consternation gazed out, not knowing what to say.

'Well, mamma, you are not angry, are you?' said Emmy, with a sympathetic jump of her heart, too.

'Angry!' said Mrs. Plowden, and began forthwith to cry ; for though she was fussy, and perhaps commonplace, she was a very devoted mother. And there was not a word to be said against Mr. Osborne—he was tolerably well off, well connected, likely to 'get on,' and an excellent young man—almost too good, if a fault might be hinted ; and Florry liked him ; and, crowning virtue of all, he had been kind to Jim. Afterwards, when the little *épanchement* was over which followed on the entry of these two evident lovers, after she had cried a good deal and laughed a little, and given her consent and blessed them, and retired to see whether Mr. Plowden had returned, followed by Emmy, who thought it would be well to tell the cook to have some sally-luns for tea— Mrs. Plowden expressed her sentiments more freely. 'I should not like to marry him myself,' she said, 'but since Florry likes it, and everything is so suitable, I feel quite sure your father will be pleased.'

'No,' said Emmy thoughtfully, 'he is very nice, but I should not like to marry him.' Which was just as well, probably, since there was no possibility of anything of the kind. Emmy thought of Another, with whom she thought Mr. Osborne could not bear comparison. But, alas! that Other, it is to be feared, was quite as little likely to fall in Emmy's way.

The young pair walked over to Lady William's cottage after a while, with that satisfaction in communicating the fact of their happiness which is natural to well-conditioned friendly young pairs. I am not myself sure that Mr. Osborne, indeed, liked to be led. in triumph even to the house of so near a relation, for he had a secret dread of ridicule, which gave this young man a great deal of trouble. They met Mr. Swinford walking away from the cottage with a grave face, accompanied by little Miss Grey, who was full of excitement. I need not say that by this time, as they walked along in full view of the village, Florence no longer hung on the curate's arm, as she had done while crossing the lawn at the Rectory. On the contrary, they were walking very demurely side by side, with the air of people who had met accidentally in the street and could not help but walk together, little as they liked it, as they were going the same way. Miss Grey's chatter was audible almost before they came in sight of her. Her countenance was wreathed in smiles, her old-fashioned broad hat had got a little to one side, and looked more jaunty and 'fast' than the most fashionable headgear.

'I could have told her years ago if I had thought it would be of any consequence,' Miss Grey was saying; and so much pre- occupied was she, that the unusual spectacle of the curate and Florence walking together, although in the most austere manner, which would have excited her so much on another occasion, did not even attract her observation now.

'Has anything happened, Miss Grey?' Florence asked de- murely, with a secret consciousness which made her heart dance, of all she had herself to tell, and of the very great thing which had certainly happened, far greater than anything else which could possibly have taken place in Watcham. And Miss Grey remarked nothing! The young people gave a glance of amazement at each other, and Miss Grey fell in the opinion of both—but most in that of the curate, who had been so great a friend of hers, and who felt that she ought to have divined him at the first glance.

'I should think, indeed, something *has* happened,' cried Miss Grey. 'I have just been telling your dear aunt Emily, Lady William, that I was at her marriage. And she is so pleased, it has been quite a little *fête* for me. Think of Lady William, the darling, being so pleased that I was there, and I always frightened she should find out, fearing she would think it a liberty! I am sure I might have told her years ago if I had thought she would have liked it. It made quite a little sensation, Mr. Swinford can tell you. It agitated her a little, poor darling, to think of that time at all; and yet she was so pleased.'

'She never speaks of her marriage,' said Florence carelessly. Oh! what waste of sentiment to think of people making a fuss about a marriage of twenty years ago when they might hear at first hand of one that was going to be now!

'No, she never speaks of it; and I had taken it into my head that she did not like to go back upon it. We never knew *him*, and I don't know why people should have taken an unfavourable impression; but to see her agitation and her change of colour when I spoke! Ah, my dear Florry, there are many things in this world that are never thought of in our philosophy! She must have been thinking of him many and many a day when we thought there was no such thing in her mind.'

It surprised Miss Grey a little, it must be allowed, to see that the curate stood by all this time, and did not stalk on about his business, leaving Florry to go also her own way; and afterwards she thought of it with a little surprise and a question to herself. But, in the meantime, she was much more taken up with what was in her own mind.

'I thought,' cried Florry when they had passed on, 'that we carried it written all over us; and yet she never found out anything! Miss Grey, too, who knows so many things.'

'It proves,' said the curate loftily, 'how much more largely the most trivial incident in our own experience bulks in our eyes than the greatest event in another's. I must say I am surprised that Miss Grey should be so obtuse—Miss Grey, of all people in the world.'

He was perhaps, to tell the truth, a little offended, too.

They went into the cottage, where Lady William was in the course of writing a letter, for which the Rector seemed to be waiting

to give it his approval. Lady William was writing hurriedly,
sometimes pausing to listen to something he said, but, I fear, not
giving him the devoted attention which the Rector felt that he
merited. Mr. Osborne was not a very common visitor at the
cottage, and Lady William stopped her writing to give him a
reception a little more ceremonious than usual.

'Will you excuse me for a moment,' she said, ' while I finish a
letter? It is an important one, which must be ready for this post,
and my brother must see it before it goes.'

And then there ensued a curious pause. Mab did her best
to entertain the visitors, discoursing to them on what she in her
innocence still believed to be the principal event of the day—for
Miss Grey's revelation did not strike Mab as particularly exciting,
and she had thought her mother's interest in it quite out of pro-
portion with the importance of the subject. And she felt the
appearance of Florence and the curate together to be another proof
of the momentous nature of the morning's event; for what could
have brought them here but a desire to settle about Mrs. Brown's
successor? So Mab began, thinking, no doubt, this was the chief
matter in their thoughts, to talk of Mrs. Brown.

'I was there yesterday,' she said, ' she might have given me a
hint. I was there almost all the morning; the afternoon was a
half-holiday. She might have said she was going away.'

' My dear,' cried Florry, a little impatient, ' if she had intended
to tell, there were other people whom she was more likely to tell
than you.'

'She told me a great many things,' said Mab, ' and I was interested in her. But, Mr. Osborne, there is a very nice girl, who
was a pupil teacher, in one of the houses down by Riverside. She
would do very well till you can get somebody, if you like to try
her. I meant to have told Uncle James, but Uncle James is so
full of that business of mother's.'

' Just as you are about the schoolmistress, Mab,' said Florence,
with a laugh.

Mr. Osborne did not make any remark, but he, too, thought—
to fuss about Lady William's business, whatever it might be, to
make a commotion about the very ordinary and commonplace fact
that Miss Grey had been present at a certain wedding twenty years
ago—what a waste of emotion, what folly it was, when there was
here, waiting for the telling, a piece of news so much more interesting! He exchanged a glance with Florence, and they both
laughed at human absurdity and the blindness even of fathers and
aunts, the latter especially, who are supposed to have an eye for

events of the kind of which these two were so conscious.   And
then that everlasting affair about the schoolmistress !   To be sure,
somebody must be found and something done ; but to thrust it
upon them *now !*

Lady William had finished the letter, which was the one she
had begun in the morning with the admission which Mr. Plowden
thought so rash of the burning down of the chapel.   She had
struck out the line in which she said 'one witness of my marriage
is alive, but——.'   What she wrote was as follows :

'There are two witnesses of my marriage alive, one Miss Grey,
The Nook, Watcham, who will make an affidavit, or see anybody
you may send to take her evidence ; the other, Mrs. Artémise
Mansfield.   I do not know at this present moment where to find
the latter, but she will appear if necessary.   There is also a record
in a diary of my father's which I am told would hold good in
law——'

'Yes,' said Mr. Plowden doubtfully, ' I suppose that is all
right, Emily ; Miss Grey's evidence, of course, makes all the
difference.   Still, I can't see why you should be so anxious to confess to them that the chapel is burnt down.'

'They would discover that fact themselves : and they might
think we knew it all the time, and had chosen that place on
purpose to have a good excuse.'

'Who is thinking ill of her fellow-creatures now ? ' said the
Rector.   ' Yes, yes, I suppose it will do—with my father's diary
and Miss Grey to back you up, you may say anything you please.
Yes, I think you may send it, and I think I may congratulate
Mab now.   Yes, I believe we may allow ourselves to think that
it is all right now.'   He watched while Lady William folded up
and put the letter into its envelope.   ' Yes, yes,' he said, so as to
be heard by all, ' this has been a very interesting day.   There was
first that untoward act of the schoolmistress going away—which
indeed I must not call untoward, for she was not the sort of person
for the place : but that also had to do with you, Emily : and then
the quite unhoped-for, unthought-of discovery that Miss Grey had
gone to see you married in such an easy, natural way ; and then
the great fact, to be announced to-day for the first time, that little
Mab is an heiress.   Do you hear, Florry ?   Could you have believed such a thing ?   The finest piece of news ! that our little
Mab is an heiress.   She has come into a great deal of money.
She will be able to take her proper position, which is far better
than anything we can give her in Watcham.   Mab,' said the
Rector, rising up and looking round him, as he had a way of doing

when addressing a much larger audience, 'has come into a fortune of fifty thousand pounds—as to-day.'

A little shriek broke from Florence—it came against her will. It was not wonder and sympathy, as might have been expected from her, but an intolerable sense of the contrariety and distraction of things. 'Oh, papa!' There was a protest in it against Mab, Mab's mother, and all that could happen to those secondary persons. What did anything matter in comparison with what she herself had to tell? And they were all in a conspiracy against her to prevent her from getting it out!

At last, however, there arrived a crisis, as the Rector got his hat and prepared to go away. The curate rose, too.

'I'll go with you, if you will permit me. There is something I want to talk to you about,' said Mr. Osborne, with a visible blush, which Lady William, looking suddenly up, caught, and started a little to behold, feeling for the first time some thrill in the air of the new thing.

'Oh yes, to be sure, the schoolmistress,' the Rector said. He gave a little sigh of impatience. 'To be sure, that is a thing that must be attended to,' he said.

'No, it is not the schoolmistress. It is something much more important,' said Mr. Osborne, at the end of his patience. There was something in the tone of his voice this time which made them all look up.

'Ah?' said Mr. Plowden, half alarmed.

'Oh!' said Lady William, sitting upright, bending forward to catch the new light. Mab did not say anything, but her eyes turned upon Florence with a certain illumination too. Florence, excited, exasperated, and worn out with the suspense which had been so little expected, was on the point of bursting into tears. Mr. Osborne took her hand, and pressed it so that she gave another little shriek of excitement and almost pain, as he followed the Rector out; and there was Florence left half sobbing, angry, full of the news which was so much greater than any of the others— even Mab's fortune, which she did not in the least believe in— which nobody would take the trouble to understand.

'Florry, dear child, what is this?' cried Lady William, while the big steps of the gentlemen were heard, one following the other, from the door.

'Oh, what does it matter?' cried Florry, 'you are all so full of your own affairs. We came to tell you, thinking you would be interested; but you would not let us speak; and to see papa standing there talking about the finest piece of news! "Mab, our little Mab, is an heiress,"' cried the irreverent girl, getting up and looking round exactly as he had done, and with all his solemnity, ' " Mab has come into a fortune."'

'Florry, Florry, spare your father !' cried Lady William, with an irrepressible laugh.

And then Florry, who, notwithstanding her white frock, and her agitated heart, and her girl's face, had been the Rev. James Plowden in person for one malicious, humorous, angry moment, dropped into her chair and fell a-crying in her own character and no other.

'Oh,' she cried, ' to think that you should be so stupid, Aunt Emily, you that always see everything.   When we came expressly to tell you !   Good gracious, what are fortunes, or schoolmistresses, or Miss Greys, or anything, in comparison with it being all right, all right and everything settled between Edward and me ?'

NOTWITHSTANDING Miss Grey's testimony and all that had happened to make her quite sure of her position, it cannot be denied that Lady William awaited the lawyers' reply to her letter with some anxiety. How does an uninstructed woman know what lawyers may do? They may find the clearest evidence wanting in something, some formality which may invalidate the whole. Had she not heard a hundred times of the difference between moral certainty and legal evidence? They might allege something of this sort, and perhaps, for anything she could tell, insist upon a trial, and the public appearance of witnesses, and the discussion of her marriage in the papers, a possibility which made Lady William's heart sick. I am not at all sure (but then I know little more about law than Lady William did) that had Messrs. Fox and Round been pettifogging lawyers, and their clients petty and unknown people, they might not have attempted something of the kind; but, as a matter of fact, they had never advised their clients to do anything in the matter, and Lord Portcullis, who remembered his sister-in-law very well, and all the circumstances of Lord William's death, had never entertained a doubt on the subject.

'Certificates?' he said, 'why, I have seen the woman!' as if that was more than certificates; and Lord Portcullis was not a man who was ignorant of the evil that exists in the world, or who was at all in a general way an optimist about women. It had been the Marchioness, more hasty, and more disposed to think that by a bold *coup* anything could be done, who hoped to secure the whole of Lord John's fortune in that way. When she found that this was impossible (though she always retained a secret conviction that Lady William was 'just as much Lady William as my old housekeeper is!') my Lady Portcullis thought of another way—a way, indeed, which had been one of the two things she had thought of in sending her son Will to see into the affair.

'If we can't have it in any other way we might at least marry it', she said to her husband. 'If Will got it in the end it would not be altogether lost.' And this was how it happened that the gay Guardsman, cursing his luck, was sent down again to Watcham to pay a visit 'at that hole of an old Hall, with that dreadful witch of an old woman,' as he expressed it to his friends, in the first burst of the opening season, when everything had a special zest, and all was delightful, fresh, and new. Lord Will's petition to be received so soon again was the first thing which revealed, to the Swinfords at least, that against Lady William there was now no further word to say.

'Why don't you come up to town ?' that young gentleman said at dinner, where Mrs Swinford was not present. 'What good can it do, Swinford, to bury yourself down here ? Why, man alive ! it's not even the country ; it's not much better than a suburban villa. Fine place, I allow, and all that ; curious old relic of grand-papa, don't you know ; but grandpapa is such a very recent relation, it is not much worth your while keeping this up.'

'Thanks for your kindness,' said Leo ; 'I may say, also, if that is not too much, that, had I not been here, it would, my dear Will, have been less convenient for you.'

'Ah yes,' said the young man, 'less convenient, but much nicer, if the truth must be told ; for to come down here a-fortune-hunting, don't you know, is about the last thing in the world to please me.'

'Oh, that is it !' said Leo.

'That's it, to be sure,' said the other. 'A cousin, too ; and it is not such a heavy price to put oneself up for. There's half-a-dozen little Americans about town, or Australians, or whatever you like to call them, that are much better worth than that, if a man is to make a sacrifice of himself,' said poor Lord Will.

'But so long as your brother Pontoon is well and strong, the Americans don't care much, do they, for a courtesy title ?'

'They're getting awfully well up,' confessed the other in a doleful tone, 'got their peerage at their fingers' ends, and care nothing for younger brothers, that's the truth ; and I'm sure I don't want to marry any of them, nor any girl that I know of. I say, Swinford, you don't know how well off you are, you lucky beggar, to be all there is of your family. I don't mean to say that I'm not a bore to Pontoon, and all that, having to be provided for somehow—as much as he is to me, standing in my way.'

'You think it would be a better arrangement having only one son ?'

'One child, that's what I should recommend ; like the French do,' said this victim of English prejudices. He was not aware that his grammar was bad, and would not have cared had he known. There are some people who are above grammar, just as there are many who are below it. He sighed, and added, as if that was a dreadful fact that needed no comment : 'There are four girls, and none of them married.' A second sigh after he had made this announcement was something like a groan.

'They are almost too young for that, as yet,' said Leo, with good nature.

'Too young! This will be Addie's third season, and not so much as a nibble. If you don't think that serious, by Jove, I do —and Betty treading on her heels, and the little ones beginning to perk their heads out of the schoolroom. The poor old mother, it's enough to turn her gray. And when she bids me up and do something for myself, I can't turn on her, Swinford, I can't indeed, though it's hard on a fellow all the same. It ought all to have come to us, it ought indeed—without any encumbrance, the advertisements say.'

'The encumbrance,' said Leo, who was half angry and half amused, 'is not a thing you will find it so easy to reckon with, my poor Will. She has her own ways of thinking, and a will of her own.'

'Ah !' said Lord Will, with much calm. He was not afraid, it would appear, of Mab. He thought of the little roundabout thing whom he had seen on his previous visit, not, certainly, with much alarm, but with a sense that if she resisted his advances (which was so very unlikely) he would not be inconsolable. Anyhow, he would have done what duty and his parents required of him. It was very satisfactory to him that Mrs. Swinford did not come downstairs that evening, for the recollection of his last interview with her was not agreeable to him in the present changed circumstances. How he was to explain to her the *motif* of his conduct now, and how the failure of all her information— her hints and prophecies of evil—was to be got over, did there ever again ensue a *tête-à-tête* between the hostess and her visitor, he could not tell. Mrs. Swinford was much more alarming to Lord Will than the little cousin whom he came to woo.

The first assurance received by Lady William that all was well was thus conveyed to her by the second visit of the young man who bore her husband's name, who came stalking into the cottage alone on the morning after his arrival as if he had been one of the intimates there, and addressed her as Aunt William, to her great surprise and agitation. Not a word did Lord Will say of his uncle's money or the proceedings of Messrs. Fox and Round. Watcham was so handy for town, was what the young man said. It was so easy to run down for a breath of fresh air : and boxed up in town, as it was his hard fate to be, nobody could think what a pleasure it was to get into the country from time to time.

'I had no idea that you were such a lover of the country,' Lady William said.

'Not the country in the abstract,' said Lord Will ; 'but a pleasant little place like this within an hour's ride—with such a pleasant fellow as Swinford always throwing open his doors—a man with really a nice place, and the best *chef* I've met with, out of the very best houses, don't you know.'

'Yes, I see,' said Lady William ; 'I should not think of asking you to meet *my* cook after that.'

'Oh, delighted,' said Lord Will. 'I don't demand a *chef* like Swinford's everywhere ; besides, there's not a dozen of his quality in the world—brought him from Paris with them, don't you know. Women don't often care much for what they eat—but when they do—— !'

'Yes,' said Lady William, with great gravity, 'when women are bad, as people say, they are worse than men ; which is a compliment or not, according as we receive it.'

'There is nothing bad, my dear aunt, in being particular about what you eat.'

'Nothing in the world, or I should be a great sinner. We both like nice things, both Mab and I.'

'Oh,' said Lord Will—'but I am not surprised,' he added—'not even that my cousin should show so much sense : for when she has had the advantage of being trained by such a mother——'

Lady William burst into a laugh. His compliments pleased her, as showing how complete was her own victory ; but be amused her still more.

'Let us hope that Mab will continue to show that she has profited by that training,' she said.

'Oh, ah,' said Lord Will ; 'now, of course, you will take her to town. My mother, indeed, wanted to know if she could do anything for you about that—look out for a house, or see after rooms, or that sort of thing ?'

'Lady Portcullis is very kind. I am not sure if I shall make any move this year. Mab is only seventeen ; there is plenty of time.'

'That is just what my mother thought,' said Lord Will.

Lady William could not restrain another laugh. The kindness of Lady Portcullis, and her desire to be useful, were profoundly amusing to her.

'Your mother is too kind to take my plans into consideration,' she said.

'Well, you see, the mother has girls of her own, and knows all the fuss about introducing them and all that. A girl is ever so much more trouble than sons. We are tossed into the world to sink or swim; but there's all sorts of fuss about invitations and things for them—the right sort of invitations, don't you know, to meet the right sort of people. My mother's deeply up in all that. She could give you a great many wrinkles. That's one reason, I suppose, why women are so pleased when they get their girls off their hands.'

'Is it the result of your personal observation, my dear Lord Will, that women are so pleased to get their girls, as you say, off their hands?'

'Oh, Lord, yes,' cried the Guardsman, with warm conviction; 'to marry them off in their first season is the very best thing that can happen, especially if there's money in the case. You get a lot of fellows dangling about that think of nothing else; and the poor things get ticketed, you know, with their values, and if a man thinks he can let himself go at that price——'

'What a terrible prospect for the girls with money—and their mothers!'

'So it is. And if a decent fellow turns up beforehand who can take care of the girl, don't you know——'

'I see,' said Lady William. 'How good you are to come and give me these hints—to be a guide to my ignorance!'

He gave her a doubtful look; but seeing her perfect gravity was encouraged.

'Well,' said Lord Will, 'some people would think it wasn't my place; but when I see a nice woman like you, Aunt William——'

'Thank you, Lord Will.'

'Oh, you need not thank me; it is a pleasure. When I see you just starting out of this nice quiet place upon the world, and think what a horrid wicked deceitful place it is——'

'My dear Lord Will, you almost make me cry over you in the character of youthful prophet, and myself in that of the inexperienced novice. You are a Daniel come to judgment; but surely you have too bad an opinion of the poor world.'

'I hope you will think so when you come to try it,' he said.

And then looking up suddenly he was caught by the gleam of fun in Lady William's eye.

'I believe,' he said, 'you are laughing at me and my advice all the time.'

'I shall not perhaps require to take advantage of it,' she said evasively, ' till next year : and one can never tell what wonderful things may happen before that time.'

It was Lord Will's decision as he went away that his dear aunt was much 'deeper' than he had given her credit for being, and that perhaps to be chary of advice might be better on the whole. But he came back in the afternoon, and also next morning before he went away, and was very anxious to be permitted to be of use to the ladies when they came to town—if they should come.

'I suppose you'll come up—for the pictures or something,' he said, ' or to go to the opera, or that sort of thing?—when a fellow that knows his way about might be of use. Drop me a line, Aunt William. There is nothing I like so much as being of use.'

'I like a day in town,' said Mab, who this time was present. 'Don't you think, mother, it's a good idea? There are a number of things I want to see. I should like to go to the Row with somebody who could tell me who everybody was. And if Cousin Will can spare the time——'

'I shall take care to spare the time, Cousin Mab.'

'And you can tell me who everybody is ?'

'Oh ! I know a few of the swells,' the young man responded modestly ; and an appointment was accordingly made. But in the evening, when they were alone together, Mab made inquiries into the sudden cordiality of her cousin. 'Why should he have come back again so soon? I am sure you did not wish him to come back : and why should he be so kind? He was not kind like this when he was here before. And you look either as if you were very happy about it, or as if it were a capital joke.'

'It is a capital joke—as it has turned out, Mab ; but I don't know what it might have been if Lucy Grey, devoured by curiosity, had not gone to my marriage without being asked, as she told us the other day.'

Mab opened her eyes very wide.

'What could it matter whether Miss Grey was there or not?'

'I will tell you, Mab—I can't keep secrets. I was married in a great hurry, and got no—certificates, or things of that sort. The church has been burnt down ; the clergyman is dead— accidents which your uncle James thinks have been partly my fault for being married there—and I might have had difficulty in proving my marriage——'

'Why, mother?'

'Well, Mab—— Why, because I had no evidence, don't you see?'

'You had me,' said Mab calmly; 'surely I am evidence. If you had not been married how could you account for me?'

Lady William kept an expression of perfect gravity, though not without some trouble.

'That is an unquestionable proof, to be sure,' she said, bending her head; 'but,' she added, in a lighter tone, 'I could not send you by post to show the lawyers, as I could have done a certificate.'

'A certificate!' cried Mab, with mild disdain, 'as if people would ever ask for certificates from you! But that,' she added, 'anyhow has nothing to do with Cousin Will. Why should he have come back so soon? and why should he be so kind? and why are we asked to lunch with the Marchioness, and all that? I think there must be more in this than meets the eye.'

'You know that you have just come into a fortune——'

'Oh, mother, don't say it is for that,' Mab said, in tones of disgust.

'No, it's not exactly for that. But perhaps your cousin thinks that he might help you—to spend it, or take care of it——'

'Oh!' said Mab. She did not blush, nor was she excited, but a faint movement swept over her round face which indicated that she knew what his visit meant. And not only did she know what it meant, but it gave her a certain satisfaction as clearing up for her a question which had been very puzzling to her little sober brain.

'Oh,' she said again, 'is that what it means?'

'No one can speak quite certainly on such a subject,' said Lady William, 'but I think that is what it means.'

It was some time before Mab spoke again.

'Is it then,' she said, 'a very large fortune, mother?'

'It is fifty thousand pounds.'

'And how much does that mean a year?'

Lady William had a woman's limited understanding of interest, that is, a woman's view who has never had money to invest. She thought it meant something about five per cent, a little more or a little less, and replied accordingly that it meant a little more than two thousand pounds a year.

'That's not so much, is it, for a man like Cousin Will?'

'No, it is not so very much——'

'And a cousin—that would be no fun.   If I were to marry a cousin, I think I would much rather have Jim——'

'Jim!' cried Lady William, with a start.   'Not for the world, Mab! an idle young man, with bad habits—you would never be so mad as that!'

'Everybody is not made exactly alike, mother,' said Mab gravely.   'Jim is idle, it is true, and he always will be idle, should all the Rectory people go on at him till doomsday.   The more reason that he should be married (if he is ever married) to some one who is very steady, and has money enough to live on, and can keep him straight.'

'But, Mab,' her mother said, with a gasp, 'what reasoning is this?   To put a premium on idleness, and save a man from himself.'

'Well, mother, I've heard you say what a pity it was that people were so afraid of responsibility.   I am not afraid of it.   If I were to marry my cousin—which would be no fun at all, in the first place—I should certainly rather have Cousin Jim, whom I could be of most use to, than Cousin Will.'

'So that is all finished and settled and done with,' said Leo Swinford, with no great expression of delight on his face.

'You don't seem to see the great happiness and satisfaction of it,' said Lady William.

'No, perhaps I do not. I had always the hope that I might have been of some use, of some service to you, something more both in importance and use than a mere friend.'

'Is there anything more than a true friend?' said Lady William, holding out her hand.

He took her hand, which was so cool and soft and white—and kind—and indifferent. As kind as could be, ready to soothe him, help him, do anything for him that he needed; and perfectly indifferent, as if he had been the little boy of ten whom Emily Plowden had been so fond of in his ingenuous childish days.

'Yes,' said Leo, 'there is something more——'

'Not according to my understanding of life. Perhaps my experience has not been a very favourable one. I like a friend— one who understands me and whom I understand—who would stand by me in any need as I would stand by him—with a nice wife and children whom I could love.'

'Ah!' said Leo, dropping the hand he had held. After a moment he said, in a different tone : 'My mother has finally made up her mind that she can endure this hermitage no more.'

'And you are going to town? It will be better for you in every way.'

'She is going back to Paris. I have done all I could to persuade her to gather friends about her here—or in London better still. But she will not hear me. Her opinion is that Paris, even out of season, is better than London at its gayest. She will go, perhaps, to some *ville de mer*, and then back in October to her old apartment and her old friends.'

2 D

'And you, Leo?'

'I am an Englishman,' he said, with a little air half of pride, half of self-abnegation, which created in his friend a profane inclination to laugh.

> 'In spite of all temptations
>   To belong to other nations,'

she said.

Leo laughed, too, but not with the best grace in the world.

'It is true that I perceive drawbacks in it,' he said. 'The life is not—gay.'

'No, it is not gay. You must go to town when your mother goes to her *ville de mer*. And in autumn you must fill the house. And then—you must marry, Leo.'

He gave her a wistful, lingering look.

'Whom?' he said, and then he went away.

He went away, going down the village, turning many things over in his mind. It occurred to him to remember that rush down this same street in the rain in pursuit of Mrs. Brown, while he was still fully of the mind that much was in his power to do for the woman who occupied his thoughts—and with the possibility at the end that he might rescue her from undeserved humiliation by the offer of his home and name. And then he remembered the girl whom he had met, who had entered so warmly into his search, and of her eyes shining in the lamplight and the raindrops upon her hair. The raindrops upon Emmy's hair were certainly not moral qualifications like the unfeigned kindness of her look, the instant sympathy with which she had responded to his call, her concern about his condition of damp and discomfort. He thought of her with a rush of kind and almost tender feeling. Certainly she never looked so pretty as on that evening. And she was very like Lady William. When her mind was roused to interest, and what he in his modesty called kindness, there was nothing in Emmy of the vulgarity of her surroundings. Nor was it vulgarity, properly speaking. Mrs. Plowden, good woman, was *bourgeoise*, that was all. And how kind she had been! How she had stirred the whole house to attend to his comfort! Leo saw all the family running this way and that to wait upon him, and Jim turning out his wardrobe to give him whatever he liked. How kind they all were! He had never been in the smallest degree civil to them. None of the entertainments to which Mrs. Plowden had looked forward had been given at the Hall. There had not been so much as a dinner to the neighbours. Mrs. Swinford had put her veto upon anything of the kind, and Leo

had felt it impossible to do anything without his mother.   And
yet how kind, how anxious to serve him they had all been!   Leo
laughed within himself at the race of civility—every one trying
to be agreeable to him.   And then his thoughts turned upon
Emmy, who, after introducing him to the Rectory, had done
nothing—had stood aloof a little from all these attentions.   Why
did she stand aloof?   Perhaps if she had been the kindest and
most active of all, doing everything for him, his vanity would
have profited by that.   It did still serve when he remembered that
she was the only one who stood aloof.   Why?   Was it because
Emmy felt the inclination to be a little more than kind which he
had felt for Lady William?   A very small matter is enough for a
complacent imagination to build upon.   He hesitated, with a half
intention of going to the Rectory, of making a call upon—whom?
His call could not be upon Emily.   It would be upon her mother,
who would receive it as a piece of ordinary civility.   He paused,
lingering at the corner where the road to the Rectory crossed the
high-road in which stood the great gates and chief entrance to the
Hall.

It was at this moment that Jim, feeling himself much 'out
of it,' suddenly loomed in view.   Very much out of it was poor
Jim once more.   Mr. Osborne was so much engrossed with Florry
that he had clean forgotten that Workman's Club which he and
his future brother-in-law were about to begin to organise.   And
Jim was aware that to go to the curate's rooms was unnecessary,
seeing he was much more likely to be found near or about the
Rectory.   And Mrs. Brown was gone.   There was no longer the
alternative of dropping in at the schoolhouse.   What was he to
do with himself these late afternoons when the time for work
was over, and there was nothing to do?   Did he think of the
'Blue Boar' again?   I hope Jim had no hankering after the
'Blue Boar'; but he wanted a little variety—a change, somebody
to speak to who did not belong to him, who would not tell him
over again the same things he had heard at breakfast and luncheon
and tea.   He, too, was wavering, not certain which way to go—
the road that led out to the country, where he could take a walk
—a very doubtful kind of pleasure—or the road that led to the
'Blue Boar.'

No one had ever told Leo Swinford to put forth a hand to
this youth, who was still lingering between good and evil.   No
Florence had taken upon herself to preach to him upon this text.
It was no business of his; he had no responsibility in respect to
Jim; but he suddenly remembered certain things he had heard,

and good-nature and a good heart, which are sometimes even more efficacious, being more spontaneous, than a sense of duty prompted him. It was more self-denying than the curate's interposition, for Leo had no Florry to please; and it was less self-denying, for he had no feeling of repulsion to the careless young fellow wavering between good and evil. He waved his hand to Jim, who was coming slowly towards him, and waited at that corner of the road.

'You are the very man,' said Leo, 'whom I wished to see. Come and dine with me to-night at the Hall, will you, Plowden ? It will be an act of charity, for I shall be quite alone.'

'At the Hall !' said Jim, startled.

'It is far to go for a charitable object,' said Leo, with a laugh.

'Oh, I didn't mean that !' cried Jim, confused. And thus once more the 'Blue Boar' (which was, indeed, quite an innocent beast, and rather relieved than otherwise that the Rector's son entered its jaws no more) was cheated of its prey.

But whether Jim, unconscious Jim, may be the means of bringing together Leo Swinford and the good Emmy, who was so like, and yet so unlike, the other Emily Plowden of the past, is a fact which lies still undiscovered in the womb of time—where also it remains as yet unknown whether the dispositions of Mab in his favour (conditionally) will ever be understood by him or carried out. Should they be, the reader may be sure that the strenuous opposition of Lady William will be a difficulty hard to surmount in the experiences of this young pair.

Mab and her mother, however, spent more than one day in town during that summer—it being decided that the young lady's introduction to society was not to take place till she was eighteen —under the escort of Lord Will: and they went to luncheon with the family, and were most benignly received by the Marchioness, who regretted warmly that she had never up to this time made the acquaintance of her sister-in-law.

'But you see how my time is taken up,' she said, with a significant glance at the four tall girls (all taking after her ladyship's family, and not a Pakenham among them, thank Heaven ! she was apt to say) who assembled at luncheon, the two who were still in the schoolroom looking quite as mature as the two who were 'out.' Mab was the only one who was like Lord Portcullis, ridiculously like, all the family agreed. And one day they went to the Row together, where Lord Will and his sister, who accompanied the party, pointed out everybody who was anybody to Mab. They

pointed out to her many people whose names she knew, and whom
she looked upon with admiration and interest, and a great many
who were to her quite unknown.

'I never heard of them before,' said little Mab, ready to yawn
after a list of such names.   'Who are they?   What have they
done?'

'Oh, you little simpleton,' said Lady Betty, 'they are the
very smartest people in town,' for that odious adjective had just
come into use at the time.

As for Lord Will, he was at that moment engaged in communicating a piece of modern history to the charming aunt, whom
that young man much preferred to her daughter.

'You know the Swinford woman's gone off,' he said.   'What
a release for that poor Leo who was never allowed to stir from her
apron-strings!'

'I don't know,' said Lady William, 'that he will think it such
a release.'

'And, of course, you know why she's going,' said the young
man of fashion.   'The old witch thought everybody had forgotten
her naughty ways.   Well, she's old enough, she might be allowed
benefit of clergy: and she meant to go to the Drawing Room and
get whitewashed, don't you know.   But H.M. has a long memory
—wouldn't have her at any price—asked what they meant by
insulting her Court, bringing such a Person there.   When Her
Most Gracious calls a woman a Person there's an end of *her*.   So
town don't agree with that old lady's health, no more does the
Hall—and she's off to her beloved France, she says, where there's
something like society—society, don't you know, where there's
nobody that has any right to interfere.'

'Is that the reason?' said Lady William—her heart was
touched, though she was aware that she had little cause to love
Mrs. Swinford.   'I have not been very much in charity with her
lately, but she was once very kind.   I am sorry this should have
happened.   Everything that is naughty, as you say, must have
been over long ago.'

'Oh, don't you be too sure of that,' said Lord Will.   'The
old hag, made up for a burlesque, would have flirted with me the
other day, between the showers of the venom she was shooting out
upon you.'

'Did she shoot out venom upon me?' said Lady William.
Her face lighted up for a moment with a gleam of angry indignation.   And then, 'Poor old woman!' she said.

I am afraid Lord Will had no comprehension whatever of this

misplaced pity.   He stared ; and he made up his mind that his
handsome aunt overestimated his simplicity, and intended to take
him in by that show of feeling—which was the most unlikely
undertaking, seeing that Lord Will was a young man about town,
and up, as he himself would have said, to all the dodges.   It was
trouble altogether thrown away in his case.

'What did Will mean by H.M. having a long memory ?' said
Mab, who had overheard part of this talk.

'He means that Her Majesty remembers all about everybody
—it is a point of Royal politeness—and that the Queen will not
receive anybody at Court with a stain upon her name.'

'But that is the very thing she ought to do !' cried Mab.

She was not aware that it was improper to use vulgar pronouns
in speaking of the greatest lady in the land.

Lady William made no reply.   She was thinking of the long
life of self-indulgence, of luxury and pleasure, a life in which no
wish had been allowed to remain unfulfilled, of the woman who
had sentenced herself in her youth, remorselessly, to a horrible
fate—to deception and undeception, one more dreadful than the
other—in order to save her own reputation : and then had turned
upon her and endeavoured to ruin her for having been thus deceived.   Mrs. Swinford had suffered little outwardly for all those
indulgences which she had insisted upon securing for herself, and
for all the wrong she had done to others.   But here, at last, her
lovers, her victims, her husband whom she had deceived, her friend
whom she had sacrificed, were avenged.   By what ?—by the Lord
Chamberlain's wand across that doorway forbidding entrance to
one of the most tiresome ceremonials in the world.

'Poor old woman !' Lady William said.

'I don't know who is the poor old woman,' said Mab, 'nor
what she has done ; but it's grand of the Queen, if she is a wicked
old woman, not to let her in.   So, say poor woman as much as
you like, mother ; I approve of the Queen.'

'I hope Her Majesty may be duly grateful, Mab,' her mother
replied.

I will not say that Mr. Francis Osborne's family were quite
satisfied that he had done as well for himself as he ought by marrying his Rector's daughter.   With his connections and prospects
he might, as they said, have married anybody.   But, at the same
time, for a curate to marry his Rector's daughter is a thing that
is always on the cards, and the Plowdens in their way were unexceptionable ; and then there was that connection with the Portcullis family, which was always something.   So the Osbornes and

the kindred in general exerted themselves, as they had always intended to do on fit occasion, and provided the living which was always understood to be waiting until Francis should have gained a little experience.   There was the prettiest wedding in Watcham Church, which became a bower of flowers, all the old lines of its arches and pillars traced out with lilies and roses, and the dim building made bright with a festal company of old and young, which filled it as if for an Easter or a Christmas service. The procession walked from the Rectory through the little private gate to the church, with all Watcham looking on outside the hedge of the garden.   Fortunately, it was very dry as well as bright, and the most delicate dresses got no harm, and the sight afforded the truest gratification to all the parishioners, great and small.   When Florence had changed her wedding robes for the pretty gray gown in which she was to travel, she lingered in the old room which she had shared for nearly all her life with her sister, and kissed her inseparable Emmy with a few tears.

'If it had not been me, it would have been you,' Florry said. 'One of us was bound to go the first.   And it will soon be your turn, too.'

'No,' said Emmy, 'I do not think I shall ever marry.'

'Oh, what nonsense!' Florence said.   'He has kept beside you all day.'

Emmy disengaged herself from her sister with a gravity beyond description.

'That will never be,' she said.   'You know it was only a girl's fancy, and never, never meant anything.'

'I know nothing of the sort,' Florence said, 'and I think it never meant so much as now.'

'Florry!' cried Emily, in sudden alarm, 'if you ever tell, if you ever breathe a syllable—— !'

'No, I never will!' said Florence, pursing up her lips as if to prevent any treacherous word from coming out.

And, though she had many temptations and struggles with herself, she never did—until there came a time——

THE END

Printed by R. & R. CLARK, *Edinburgh.*

The Eversley Series.

Globe 8vo.   Cloth.   5s. per volume.

Charles Kingsley's Novels and Poems.

WESTWARD HO! 2 Vols.
HYPATIA. 2 Vols.
YEAST. 1 Vol.

ALTON LOCKE. 2 Vols.
TWO YEARS AGO. 2 Vols.
HEREWARD THE WAKE. 2 Vols.

POEMS. 2 Vols.

John Morley's Collected Works.   In 11 Vols.

I. VOLTAIRE. 1 Vol.
II. III. ROUSSEAU. 2 Vols.
IV. V. DIDEROT AND THE EN-
    CYCLOPÆDISTS. 2 Vols.

VI. ON COMPROMISE. 1 Vol.
VII.-IX. MISCELLANIES. 3 Vols.
    X. BURKE. 1 Vol.
XI. STUDIES IN LITERA-
    TURE. 1 Vol.

Dean Church's Miscellaneous Writings.   Collected Edition.   6 Vols.

I. MISCELLANEOUS ESSAYS.
II. DANTE: and other Essays.
III. ST. ANSELM.

IV. SPENSER.
V. BACON.
VI. THE OXFORD MOVEMENT.
    Twelve Years, 1833-1845.

Emerson's Collected Works.   6 Vols.   With Introduction by JOHN
MORLEY.

I. MISCELLANIES.
II. ESSAYS.
III. POEMS.
IV. ENGLISH TRAITS AND
    REPRESENTATIVE MEN.

V. THE CONDUCT OF LIFE,
    AND SOCIETY AND SOLI-
    TUDE.
VI. LETTERS AND SOCIAL
    AIMS.

Charles Lamb's Collected Works.   Edited, with Introduction and Notes,
by the Rev. Canon AINGER, M.A.   6 Vols.

I. THE ESSAYS OF ELIA.
II. POEMS, PLAYS, AND MIS-
    CELLANEOUS ESSAYS.
III. MRS. LEICESTER'S SCHOOL,
    and other Writings.

IV. TALES FROM SHAK-
    SPEARE. By CHARLES and
    MARY LAMB.
V. & VI. THE LETTERS OF
    CHARLES LAMB. 2 Vols.

Life of Charles Lamb.   By ALFRED AINGER.

The Collected Works of Thomas Henry Huxley, F.R.S.   9 vols.
   I. METHOD AND RESULTS.
   II. DARWINIANA.
   III. SCIENCE AND EDUCATION.
   IV. SCIENCE AND HEBREW TRADITION.
   V. SCIENCE AND CHRISTIAN TRADITION.
   VI. HUME. With Helps to the Study of Berkeley.
   VII. MAN'S PLACE IN NATURE: and other Anthropological Essays.
   VIII. DISCOURSES, BIOLOGICAL AND GEOLOGICAL.
   IX. EVOLUTION AND ETHICS, AND OTHER ESSAYS.

The Poetical Works of John Milton.   Edited, with Memoir, Introduc-
tions, Notes, by DAVID MASSON, M.A., LL.D.   In 3 Vols.
   I. THE MINOR POEMS.
   II. PARADISE LOST.
   III. PARADISE REGAINED, AND SAMSON AGONISTES.

MACMILLAN AND CO., LONDON.

The Eversley Series.

Globe 8vo. Cloth. 5s. per volume.

MACMILLAN AND CO., LONDON.

THE GLOBE LIBRARY.

Globe 8vo.   3s. 6d. each.

BOSWELL'S LIFE OF JOHNSON.   Introduction by MOW-
BRAY MORRIS.

BURNS.—COMPLETE POETICAL WORKS AND LET-
TERS.   Edited, with Life and Glossarial Index, by ALEXANDER
SMITH.

COWPER.—POETICAL WORKS.   Edited by the Rev. W.
BENHAM, B.D.

DEFOE.—THE ADVENTURES OF ROBINSON CRUSOE.
Introduction by H. KINGSLEY.

DRYDEN. — POETICAL WORKS.   A Revised Text and
Notes.   By W. D. CHRISTIE, M.A.

GOLDSMITH.—MISCELLANEOUS WORKS.   Edited by
Prof. MASSON.

HORACE.—WORKS.   Rendered into English Prose by JAMES
LONSDALE and S. LEE.

MALORY.—LE MORTE D'ARTHUR.   Sir Thomas Malory's
Book of King Arthur and of his Noble Knights of the Round Table.
The Edition of Caxton, revised for modern use.   By Sir E. STRACHEY,
Bart.

MILTON.—POETICAL WORKS.   Edited, with Introductions,
by Prof. MASSON.

POPE.—POETICAL WORKS.   Edited, with Memoir and
Notes, by Prof. WARD.

SCOTT.—POETICAL WORKS.   With Essay by Prof. PAL-
GRAVE.

SHAKESPEARE.—COMPLETE WORKS.   Edited by W.
G. CLARK and W. ALDIS WRIGHT.   *India Paper Edition.*   Cr. 8vo,
cloth extra, gilt edges.   10s. 6d. net.

SPENSER.—COMPLETE WORKS.   Edited by R. MORRIS.
Memoir by J. W. HALES, M.A.

VIRGIL.—WORKS.   Rendered into English Prose by JAMES
LONSDALE and S. LEE.

MACMILLAN AND CO., LONDON.

English Men of Letters.

In Paper Covers, 1s. *Cloth,* 1s. 6d.

ADDISON. By W. J. Courthope
BACON. By R. W. Church.
BENTLEY. By Prof. Jebb.
BUNYAN. By J. A. Froude.
BURKE. By John Morley.
BURNS. By Principal Shairp.
BYRON. By Prof. Nichol.
CARLYLE. By Prof. J. Nichol.
CHAUCER. By Prof. A. W. Ward.
COLERIDGE. By H. D. Traill.
COWPER. By Goldwin Smith.
DEFOE. By W. Minto.
DE QUINCEY. By Prof. Masson.
DICKENS. By A. W. Ward.
DRYDEN. By G. Saintsbury.
FIELDING. By Austin Dobson.
GIBBON. By J. C. Morison.
GOLDSMITH. By W. Black.
GRAY. By Edmund Gosse.
HAWTHORNE. By Henry James.
HUME. By T. H. Huxley.
JOHNSON. By Leslie Stephen.
KEATS. By Sidney Colvin.
LAMB. By Rev. Alfred Ainger.
LANDOR. By Sidney Colvin.
LOCKE. By Prof. Fowler.
MACAULAY. By J. C. Morison.
MILTON. By Mark Pattison.
POPE. By Leslie Stephen.
SCOTT. By R. H. Hutton.
SHELLEY. By J. A. Symonds.
SHERIDAN. By Mrs. Oliphant.
SIDNEY. By J. A. Symonds.
SOUTHEY. By Prof. Dowden.
SPENSER. By R. W. Church.
STERNE. By H. D. Traill.
SWIFT. By Leslie Stephen.
THACKERAY. By A. Trollope.
WORDSWORTH. By F. W. H. Myers.

MACMILLAN AND CO., LONDON.

MACMILLAN'S THREE-AND-SIXPENNY LIBRARY OF BOOKS BY POPULAR AUTHORS

Crown 8vo.

THIS SERIES comprises over four hundred volumes in various departments of Literature. Prominent among them is an attractive edition of **The Works of Thackeray,** *issued under the editorship of Mr. Lewis Melville. It contains all the Original Illustrations, and includes a great number of scattered pieces and illustrations which have not hitherto appeared in any collected edition of the works.* **The Works of Charles Dickens,** *reprinted from the first editions, with all the Original Illustrations, and with Introductions, Biographical and Bibliographical, by Charles Dickens the Younger, and an attractive edition of* **The Novels of Charles Lever,** *illustrated by Phiz and G. Cruik-*

shank, have also a place in the Library. The attention of book buyers may be especially directed to **The Border Edition** **of the Waverley Novels,** *edited by Mr. Andrew Lang, which, with its large type and convenient form, and its copious illustrations by well-known artists, possesses features which place it in the forefront of editions now obtainable of the famous novels.* **The Works of Mr. Thomas Hardy,** *including the poems, have also been added to the Three-and-Sixpenny Library.*

Among other works by notable contemporary authors will be found those of **Mr. F. Marion Crawford, Rolf Boldrewood, Mr. H. G. Wells, Mrs. Gertrude Atherton, Mr. Egerton Castle, Mr. A. E. W. Mason, Maarten Maartens,** *and* **Miss Rosa Nouchette Carey;** *while among the productions of an earlier period may be mentioned the works of* **Charles Kingsley, Frederick Denison Maurice, Thomas Hughes,** *and* **Dean Farrar;** *and the novels and tales of* **Charlotte M. Yonge, Mrs. Craik,** *and* **Mrs. Oliphant.**

THE

WORKS OF THACKERAY

*Reprints of the First Editions, with all the Original Illustrations,
and with Facsimiles of Wrappers, etc.*

Messrs. MACMILLAN & CO., Limited, beg leave to invite the
attention of book buyers to the Edition of THE WORKS OF
THACKERAY in their Three-and-Sixpenny Library, which is the
Completest Edition of the Author's Works that has been placed
on the market.

The Publishers have been fortunate in securing the services of
Mr. LEWIS MELVILLE, the well-known Thackeray Expert. With
his assistance they have been able to include in this Edition a
great number of scattered pieces from Thackeray's pen, and illustrations from his pencil which have not hitherto been contained in
any collected edition of the works. Mr. Melville has read all
the sheets as they passed through the press, and collated them
carefully with the original editions. He has also provided Bibliographical Introductions and occasional Footnotes.

List of the Series.

VOL.

1. Vanity Fair. With 190 Illustrations.

2. The History of Pendennis. With 180
Illustrations.

3. The Newcomes. With 167 Illustrations.

4. The History of Henry Esmond.

5. The Virginians. With 148 Illustrations.

6. Barry Lyndon and Catherine. With 4
Illustrations.

7. The Paris and Irish Sketch Books. With
63 Illustrations.

THACKERAY'S WORKS—*continued.*

VOL.

8. Christmas Books—MRS. PERKINS'S BALL: OUR STREET: DR. BIRCH AND HIS YOUNG FRIENDS: THE KICKLEBURYS ON THE RHINE: THE ROSE AND THE RING. With 127 Illustrations.

9. Burlesques: From Cornhill to Grand Cairo: and Juvenilia. With 84 Illustrations.

10. The Book of Snobs, and other Contributions to *Punch.* With 159 Illustrations.

11. The Yellowplush Correspondence: Jeames's Diary: The Great Hoggarty Diamond: Etc. With 47 Illustrations.

12. Critical Papers in Literature.

13. Critical Papers in Art; Stubbs's Calendar: Barber Cox. With 99 Illustrations.

14. Lovel the Widower, and other Stories. With 40 Illustrations.

15. The Fitz-Boodle Papers (including Men's Wives), and various Articles. 8 Illustrations.

16. The English Humourists of the 18th Century: The Four Georges: Etc. 45 Illustrations.

17. Travels in London: Letters to a Young Man about Town: and other Contributions to *Punch* (1845—1850). With 73 Illustrations.

18. Ballads and Verses, and Miscellaneous Contributions to *Punch.* With 78 Illustrations.

19. A Shabby Genteel Story, and The Adventures of Philip. With Illustrations.

20. Roundabout Papers and Denis Duval. With Illustrations.

MACMILLAN'S

EDITION OF THACKERAY

SOME OPINIONS OF THE PRESS

EXPOSITORY TIMES.—"An edition to do credit even to this publishing house, and not likely to be surpassed until they surpass it with a cheaper and better themselves."

WHITEHALL REVIEW.—"Never before has such a cheap and excellent edition of Thackeray been seen."

ACADEMY.—"A better one-volume edition at three shillings and sixpence could not be desired."

GRAPHIC.—"In its plain but pretty blue binding is both serviceable and attractive."

DAILY GRAPHIC.—"An excellent, cheap reprint."

PALL MALL GAZETTE.—"The size of the books is handy, paper and printing are good, and the binding, which is of blue cloth, is simple but tasteful. Altogether the publishers are to be congratulated upon a reprint which ought to be popular."

GLOBE.—"The paper is thin but good, the type used is clear to read, and the binding is neat and effective."

LADY'S PICTORIAL.—"The paper is good, the type clear and large, and the binding tasteful. Messrs. Macmillan are to be thanked for so admirable and inexpensive an edition of our great satirist."

WORLD.—"Nothing could be better than the new edition."

BLACK AND WHITE.—"The more one sees of the edition the more enamoured of it he becomes. It is so good and neat, immaculate as to print, and admirably bound."

SCOTSMAN.—"This admirable edition."

LITERARY WORLD.—"The paper and printing and general get up are everything that one could desire."

ST. JAMES'S GAZETTE.—"A clear and pretty edition."

THE

WORKS OF DICKENS

Reprints of the First Editions, with all the original Illustrations, and with Introductions, Biographical and Bibliographical, by CHARLES DICKENS the Younger.

1. THE PICKWICK PAPERS. With 50 Illustrations.
2. OLIVER TWIST. With 27 Illustrations.
3. NICHOLAS NICKLEBY. With 44 Illustrations.
4. MARTIN CHUZZLEWIT. With 41 Illustrations.
5. THE OLD CURIOSITY SHOP. With 97 Illustrations.
6. BARNABY RUDGE. With 76 Illustrations.
7. DOMBEY AND SON. With 40 Illustrations.
8. CHRISTMAS BOOKS. With 65 Illustrations.
9. SKETCHES BY BOZ. With 44 Illustrations.
10. DAVID COPPERFIELD. With 40 Illustrations.
11. AMERICAN NOTES AND PICTURES FROM ITALY. With 4 Illustrations.
12. THE LETTERS OF CHARLES DICKENS.
13. BLEAK HOUSE. With 43 Illustrations.
14. LITTLE DORRIT. With 40 Illustrations.
15. A TALE OF TWO CITIES. With 15 Illustrations.
16. GREAT EXPECTATIONS; AND HARD TIMES.
17. OUR MUTUAL FRIEND. With 40 Illustrations.

MACMILLAN'S
EDITION OF DICKENS

SOME OPINIONS OF THE PRESS

ATHENÆUM.—"Handy in form, well printed, illustrated with reduced re-productions of the original plates, Introduced with bibliographical notes by the novelist's son, and above all issued at a most moderate price, this edition will appeal successfully to a large number of readers."

SPEAKER.—"We do not think there exists a better edition."

MORNING POST.—"The edition will be highly appreciated."

SCOTSMAN.—"This reprint offers peculiar attractions. Of a handy size, in one volume, of clear, good-sized print, and with its capital comic illustrations, it is a volume to be desired."

NEWCASTLE CHRONICLE.—"The most satisfactory edition of the book that has been issued."

GLASGOW HERALD.—"None of the recent editions of Dickens can be compared with that which Messrs. Macmillan Inaugurate with the Issue of *Pickwick.* . . . Printed in a large, clear type, very readable."

GLOBE.—"They have used an admirably clear type and good paper, and the binding is unexceptionable. . . . May be selected as the most desirable cheap edition of the immortal ' Papers' that has ever been offered to the public."

MANCHESTER EXAMINER.—"These volumes have a unique interest, for with each there is the story of its origin."

QUEEN.—"A specially pleasant and convenient form in which to re-read Dickens."

STAR.—"This new 'Dickens Series,' with its reproductions of the original illustrations, is a joy to the possessor."

Complete in Twenty-four Volumes.   Crown 8vo, tastefully bound in green cloth, gilt.   Price 3s. 6d. each.

In special cloth binding, flat backs, gilt tops.   Supplied in Sets only of 24 volumes.   Price £4 4s.

Also an edition with all the 250 original etchings.   In 24 volumes. Crown 8vo, gilt tops.   Price 6s. each.

THE LARGE TYPE
BORDER EDITION OF THE
WAVERLEY NOVELS

EDITED WITH

INTRODUCTORY ESSAYS AND NOTES

BY

ANDREW LANG

SUPPLEMENTING THOSE OF THE AUTHOR.

With Two Hundred and Fifty New and Original Illustrations by Eminent Artists.

BY the kind permission of the Hon. Mrs. MAXWELL-SCOTT, of Abbotsford, the great-granddaughter of Sir WALTER, the MSS. and other material at Abbotsford were examined by Mr. ANDREW LANG during the preparation of his Introductory Essays and Notes to the Series, so that the BORDER EDITION may be said to contain all the results of the latest researches as to the composition of the Waverley Novels.

The Border Waverley

1. **WAVERLEY.** With 12 Illustrations by Sir H. RAEBURN, R.A., R. W. MACBETH, A.R.A., JOHN PETTIE, R.A., H. MACBETH-RAEBURN, D. HERDMAN, W. J. LEITCH, ROBERT HERDMAN, R.S.A., and J. ECKFORD LAUDER.

2. **GUY MANNERING.** With 10 Illustrations by J. MacWHIRTER, A.R.A., R. W. MACBETH, A.R.A., C. O. MURRAY, CLARK STANTON, R.S.A., GOURLAY STEELL, R.S.A., F. S. WALKER, R. HERDMAN, R.S.A., and J. B. MACDONALD, A.R.S.A.

3. **THE ANTIQUARY.** With 10 Illustrations by J. MacWHIRTER, A.R.A., SAM BOUGH, R.S.A., R. HERDMAN, R.S.A., W. M'TAGGART, A.R.S.A., J. B. MACDONALD, A.R.S.A., and A. H. TOURRIER.

4. **ROB ROY.** With 10 Illustrations by R. W. MACBETH, A.R.A., and SAM BOUGH, R.S.A.

5. **OLD MORTALITY.** With 10 Illustrations by J. MacWHIRTER, A.R.A., R. HERDMAN, R.S.A., SAM BOUGH, R.S.A., M. L. GOW, D. Y. CAMERON, LOCKHART BOGLE, and ALFRED HARTLEY.

6. **THE HEART OF MIDLOTHIAN.** With 10 Illustrations by Sir J. E. MILLAIS, Bart., HUGH CAMERON, R.S.A., SAM BOUGH, R.S.A., R. HERDMAN, R.S.A., and WAL. PAGET.

7. **A LEGEND OF MONTROSE and THE BLACK DWARF.** With 7 Illustrations by Sir GEORGE REID, P.R.S.A., GEORGE HAY, R.S.A., HORATIO MACCULLOCH, R.S.A., W. E. LOCKHART, R.S.A., H. MACBETH-RAEBURN, and T. SCOTT.

8. **THE BRIDE OF LAMMERMOOR.** With 8 Illustrations by Sir J. E. MILLAIS, Bart., JOHN SMART, R.S.A., SAM BOUGH, R.S.A., GEORGE HAY, R.S.A., and H. MACBETH-RAEBURN.

9. **IVANHOE.** With 12 Illustrations by AD. LALAUZE.

10. **THE MONASTERY.** With 10 Illustrations by GORDON BROWNE.

11. **THE ABBOT.** With 10 Illustrations by GORDON BROWNE.

The Border Waverley

12. KENILWORTH.   With 12 Illustrations by AD. LALAUZE.

13. THE PIRATE.   With 10 Illustrations by W. E. LOCKHART, R.S.A., SAM BOUGH, R.S.A., HERBERT DICKSEE, W. STRANG, LOCKHART BOGLE, C. J. HOLMES, and F. S. WALKER.

14. THE FORTUNES OF NIGEL.   With 10 Illustrations by JOHN PETTIE, R.A., and R. W. MACBETH, A.R.A.

15. PEVERIL OF THE PEAK.   With 15 Illustrations by W. Q. ORCHARDSON, R.A. JOHN PETTIE, R.A., F. DADD, R.I., ARTHUR HOPKINS, A.R.W.S., and S. L. WOOD.

16. QUENTIN DURWARD.   With 12 Illustrations by AD. LALAUZE.

17. ST. RONAN'S WELL.   With 10 Illustrations by Sir G. REID, P.R.S.A., R. W. MACBETH, A.R.A., W. HOLE, R.S.A., and A. FORESTIER.

18. REDGAUNTLET.   With 12 Illustrations by Sir JAMES D. LINTON, P.R.I., JAMES ORROCK, R.I., SAM BOUGH, R.S.A., W. HOLE, R.S.A., G. HAY, R.S.A., T. SCOTT, A.R.S.A., W. BOUCHER, and FRANK SHORT.

19. THE BETROTHED and THE TALISMAN.   With 10 Illustrations by HERBERT DICKSEE, WAL. PAGET, and J. LE BLANT.

20. WOODSTOCK.   With 10 Illustrations by W. HOLE. R.S.A.

21. THE FAIR MAID OF PERTH.   With 10 Illustrations by Sir G. REID, P.R.S.A., JOHN PETTIE, R.A., R. W. MACBETH, A.R.A., and ROBERT HERDMAN, R.S.A.

22. ANNE OF GEIERSTEIN.   With 10 Illustrations by R. DE LOS RIOS.

23. COUNT ROBERT OF PARIS and THE SURGEON'S DAUGHTER.   With 10 Illustrations by W. HATHERELL, R.I., and W. B. WOLLEN, R.I.

24. CASTLE DANGEROUS, CHRONICLES OF THE CANON-GATE, ETC.   With 10 Illustrations by H. MACBETH-RAE-BURN and G. D. ARMOUR

The Border Waverley

SOME OPINIONS OF THE PRESS

TIMES.—"It would be difficult to find in these days a more com-petent and sympathetic editor of Scott than his countryman, the brilliant and versatile man of letters who has undertaken the task, and if any proof were wanted either of his qualifications or of his skill and discretion in displaying them, Mr. Lang has furnished it abundantly in his charming Introduction to 'Waverley.' The editor's own notes are judiciously sparing, but conspicuously to the point, and they are very discreetly separated from those of the author, Mr. Lang's laudable purpose being to illustrate and explain Scott, not to make the notes a pretext for displaying his own critical faculty and literary erudition. The illustrations by various competent hands are beautiful in themselves and beautifully executed, and, altogether, the 'Border Edition' of the Waverley Novels bids fair to become the classical edition of the great Scottish classic."

SPECTATOR.—"We trust that this fine edition of our greatest and most poetical of novelists will attain, if it has not already done so, the high popularity it deserves. To all Scott's lovers it is a pleasure to know that, despite the daily and weekly inrush of ephemeral fiction, the sale of his works is said by the booksellers to rank next below Tennyson's in poetry, and above that of everybody else in prose."

ATHENÆUM.—"The handsome 'Border Edition' has been brought to a successful conclusion. The publisher deserves to be complimented on the manner in which the edition has been printed and illustrated, and Mr. Lang on the way in which he has performed his portion of the work. His introductions have been tasteful and readable ; he has not overdone his part ; and, while he has supplied much useful information, he has by no means overburdened the volumes with notes."

NOTES AND QUERIES.—"This spirited and ambitious enterprise has been conducted to a safe termination, and the most ideal edition of the Waverley Novels in existence is now completed."

SATURDAY REVIEW.—"Of all the many collections of the Waverley Novels, the 'Border Edition' is incomparably the most handsome and the most desirable. . . . Type, paper, illustrations, are altogether admirable."

MAGAZINE OF ART.—"Size, type, paper, and printing, to say nothing of the excessively liberal and charming introduction of the illustra-tions, make this perhaps the most desirable edition of Scott ever issued on this side of the Border."

DAILY CHRONICLE.—"There is absolutely no fault to be found with it, as to paper, type, or arrangement."

THE WORKS OF

THOMAS HARDY

Collected Edition

1. TESS OF THE D'URBERVILLES.
2. FAR FROM THE MADDING CROWD.
3. THE MAYOR OF CASTERBRIDGE.
4. A PAIR OF BLUE EYES.
5. TWO ON A TOWER.
6. THE RETURN OF THE NATIVE.
7. THE WOODLANDERS.
8. JUDE THE OBSCURE.
9. THE TRUMPET-MAJOR.
10. THE HAND OF ETHELBERTA.
11. A LAODICEAN.
12. DESPERATE REMEDIES.
13. WESSEX TALES.
14. LIFE'S LITTLE IRONIES.
15. A GROUP OF NOBLE DAMES.
16. UNDER THE GREENWOOD TREE.
17. THE WELL-BELOVED.
18. WESSEX POEMS, and other Verses.
19. POEMS OF THE PAST AND THE PRESENT.

THE WORKS OF

CHARLES KINGSLEY

WESTWARD HO!

HYPATIA; or, New Foes with an old Face.

TWO YEARS AGO.

ALTON LOCKE, Tailor and Poet.   An Autobiography.

HEREWARD THE WAKE, "Last of the English."

YEAST : A Problem.

POEMS : including The Saint's Tragedy, Andromeda, Songs Ballads, etc.

THE WATER-BABIES : A Fairy Tale for a Land-Baby.   With Illustrations by LINLEY SAMBOURNE.

THE HEROES; or, Greek Fairy Tales for my Children.   With Illustrations by the Author.

GLAUCUS ; or, The Wonders of the Shore.   With Illustrations.

MADAM HOW AND LADY WHY; or, First Lessons in Earth Lore for Children.   With Illustrations.

AT LAST.   A Christmas in the West Indies.   With Illustrations.

THE HERMITS.

HISTORICAL LECTURES AND ESSAYS.

PLAYS AND PURITANS, and other Historical Essays.

THE ROMAN AND THE TEUTON.

PROSE IDYLLS, New and Old.

SANITARY AND SOCIAL LECTURES AND ESSAYS.

LITERARY AND GENERAL LECTURES AND ESSAYS.

ALL SAINTS' DAY : and other Sermons.

DISCIPLINE : and other Sermons.

THE GOOD NEWS OF GOD.   Sermons.

GOSPEL OF THE PENTATEUCH.

SERMONS FOR THE TIMES.

VILLAGE SERMONS, AND TOWN AND COUNTRY SERMONS.

WESTMINSTER SERMONS.

THE NOVELS

OF

F. MARION CRAWFORD

1. MR. ISAACS: A Tale of Modern India.
2. DOCTOR CLAUDIUS: A True Story.
3. A ROMAN SINGER.
4. ZOROASTER.
5. MARZIO'S CRUCIFIX.
6. A TALE OF A LONELY PARISH.
7. PAUL PATOFF.
8. WITH THE IMMORTALS.
9. GREIFENSTEIN.
10. TAQUISARA: A Novel.
11. A ROSE OF YESTERDAY.
12. SANT' ILARIO.
13. A CIGARETTE-MAKER'S ROMANCE.
14. KHALED: A Tale of Arabia.
15. THE THREE FATES.
16. THE WITCH OF PRAGUE
17. MARION DARCHE: A Story without Comment.
18. KATHARINE LAUDERDALE.

THE NOVELS

OF

F. MARION CRAWFORD

19. THE CHILDREN OF THE KING.

20. PIETRO GHISLERI.

21. DON ORSINO.

22. CASA BRACCIO.

23. ADAM JOHNSTONE'S SON.

24. THE RALSTONS.

25. CORLEONE: A Tale of Sicily.

26. VIA CRUCIS: A Romance of the Second Crusade.

27. IN THE PALACE OF THE KING: A Love Story of Old Madrid.

28. CECILIA: A Story of Modern Rome.

29. MARIETTA: A Maid of Venice.

30. THE HEART OF ROME.

31. SOPRANO: A Portrait.

32. THE PRIMADONNA.

33. THE DIVA'S RUBY.

34. "WHOSOEVER SHALL OFFEND ——"

35. A LADY OF ROME.

36. ARETHUSA.

37. THE WHITE SISTER.

38. STRADELLA: An Old Italian Love Tale.

THE NOVELS

OF

ROLF BOLDREWOOD

1. ROBBERY UNDER ARMS: A Story of Life and Adventure in the Bush and in the Gold-fields of Australia.

2. A MODERN BUCCANEER.

3. THE MINER'S RIGHT: A Tale of the Australian Gold-fields.

4. THE SQUATTER'S DREAM.

5. A SYDNEY-SIDE SAXON.

6. A COLONIAL REFORMER.

7. NEVERMORE.

8. PLAIN LIVING: A Bush Idyll.

9. MY RUN HOME.

10. THE CROOKED STICK; or, Pollie's Probation.

11. OLD MELBOURNE MEMORIES.

12. WAR TO THE KNIFE; or, Tangata Maori.

13. BABES IN THE BUSH.

14. IN BAD COMPANY, and other Stories.

By H. G. WELLS

THE PLATTNER STORY: and others.

TALES OF SPACE AND TIME.

THE STOLEN BACILLUS: and other Incidents.

THE INVISIBLE MAN. A Grotesque Romance.

LOVE AND MR. LEWISHAM. A Story of a very Young Couple.

WHEN THE SLEEPER WAKES.

THE FIRST MEN IN THE MOON.

TWELVE STORIES AND A DREAM.

THE FOOD OF THE GODS AND HOW IT Came to Earth.

KIPPS: The Story of a Simple Soul.

IN THE DAYS OF THE COMET.

TONO-BUNGAY.

By A. E. W. MASON

THE COURTSHIP OF MORRICE BUCKLER.

THE PHILANDERERS.

MIRANDA OF THE BALCONY.

By EGERTON CASTLE

"LA BELLA": and others. | "YOUNG APRIL."

MARSHFIELD THE OBSERVER.

By AGNES and EGERTON CASTLE

THE BATH COMEDY.

THE PRIDE OF JENNICO. Being a Memoir of Captain Basil Jennico.

THE SECRET ORCHARD.

THE NOVELS OF

ROSA N. CAREY

WESTMINSTER GAZETTE.—"A clever delineator of character, possessed of a reserve of strength in a quiet, easy, flowing style, Miss Carey never fails to please a large class of readers."

STANDARD.—"Miss Carey has the gift of writing naturally and simply, her pathos is true and unforced, and her conversations are sprightly and sharp."

LADY.—Miss Carey's novels are always welcome; they are out of the common run. Immaculately pure, and very high in tone."

Over 700,000 of these works have been printed.

1. NELLIE'S MEMORIES. 55th Thousand.

2. WEE WIFIE. 40th Thousand.

3. BARBARA HEATHCOTE'S TRIAL. 35th Thousand.

4. ROBERT ORD'S ATONEMENT. 28th Thousand.

5. WOOED AND MARRIED. 38th Thousand.

6. HERIOT'S CHOICE. 27th Thousand.

7. QUEENIE'S WHIM. 32nd Thousand.

8. NOT LIKE OTHER GIRLS. 41st Thousand.

9. MARY ST. JOHN. 27th Thousand.

10. FOR LILIAS. 26th Thousand.

11. UNCLE MAX. 34th Thousand.

12. RUE WITH A DIFFERENCE. 24th Thousand.

THE NOVELS OF

ROSA N. CAREY

Over 700,000 of these works have been printed.

13. THE HIGHWAY OF FATE. 23rd Thousand.
14. ONLY THE GOVERNESS. 40th Thousand.
15. LOVER OR FRIEND? 29th Thousand.
16. BASIL LYNDHURST. 24th Thousand.
17. SIR GODFREY'S GRAND-DAUGHTERS. 27th Thousand.
18. THE OLD, OLD STORY. 27th Thousand.
19. THE MISTRESS OF BRAE FARM. 30th Thousand.
20. MRS. ROMNEY and "BUT MEN MUST WORK." 14th Thousand.
21. OTHER PEOPLE'S LIVES. 5th Thousand.
22. HERB OF GRACE. 25th Thousand.
23. A PASSAGE PERILOUS. 22nd Thousand.
24. AT THE MOORINGS. 21st Thousand.
25. THE HOUSEHOLD OF PETER. 21st Thousand.
26. NO FRIEND LIKE A SISTER. 21st Thousand.
27. THE ANGEL OF FORGIVENESS. 17th Thousand.
28. THE SUNNY SIDE OF THE HILL. 18th Thousand.
29. THE KEY OF THE UNKNOWN. 15th Thousand.

THE NOVELS AND TALES OF

CHARLOTTE M. YONGE

THE HEIR OF REDCLYFFE. With Illustrations by KATE GREENAWAY.

HEARTSEASE; or, the Brother's Wife. New Edition. With Illustrations by KATE GREENAWAY.

HOPES AND FEARS; or, Scenes from the Life of a Spinster. With Illustrations by HERBERT GANDY.

DYNEVOR TERRACE; or, the Clue of Life. With Illustration by ADRIAN STOKES.

THE DAISY CHAIN; or, Aspirations. A Family Chronicle. With Illustrations by J. P. ATKINSON.

THE TRIAL: More Links of the Daisy Chain. With Illustrations by J. P. ATKINSON.

THE PILLARS OF THE HOUSE; or, Under Wode, under Rode. Two Vols. With Illustrations by HERBERT GANDY.

THE YOUNG STEPMOTHER; or, a Chronicle of Mistakes. With Illustrations by MARIAN HUXLEY.

THE CLEVER WOMAN OF THE FAMILY. With Illustrations by ADRIAN STOKES.

THE THREE BRIDES. With Illustrations by ADRIAN STOKES.

MY YOUNG ALCIDES: A Faded Photograph. With Illustrations by ADRIAN STOKES.

THE CAGED LION. With Illustrations by W. J. HENNESSY.

THE DOVE IN THE EAGLE'S NEST. With Illustrations by W. J. HENNESSY.

THE CHAPLET OF PEARLS; or, the White and Black Ribaumont. With Illustrations by W. J. HENNESSY.

LADY HESTER; or, Ursula's Narrative; and THE DANVERS PAPERS. With Illustrations by JANE E. COOK.

MAGNUM BONUM; or, Mother Carey's Brood. With Illustrations by W. J. HENNESSY.

LOVE AND LIFE: an Old Story in Eighteenth Century Costume. With Illustrations by W. J. HENNESSY.

UNKNOWN TO HISTORY. A Story of the Captivity of Mary of Scotland. With Illustrations by W. J. HENNESSY.

THE NOVELS AND TALES OF

CHARLOTTE M. YONGE

THE ARMOURER'S 'PRENTICES. With Illustrations by W. J. HENNESSY.

SCENES AND CHARACTERS; or, Eighteen Months at Beechcroft. With Illustrations by W. J. HENNESSY.

CHANTRY HOUSE. With Illustrations by W. J. HENNESSY.

A MODERN TELEMACHUS. With Illustrations by W. J. HENNESSY.

BYWORDS. A collection of Tales new and old.

BEECHCROFT AT ROCKSTONE.

MORE BYWORDS.

A REPUTED CHANGELING; or, Three Seventh Years Two Centuries Ago.

THE LITTLE DUKE, RICHARD THE FEARLESS. With Illustrations.

THE LANCES OF LYNWOOD. With Illustrations by J. B.

THE PRINCE AND THE PAGE : A Story of the Last Crusade. With Illustrations by ADRIAN STOKES.

TWO PENNILESS PRINCESSES. With Illustrations by W. J. HENNESSY.

THAT STICK.

AN OLD WOMAN'S OUTLOOK IN A HAMPSHIRE VILLAGE.

GRISLY GRISELL; or, The Laidly Lady of Whitburn. A Tale of the Wars of the Roses.

HENRIETTA'S WISH. Second Edition.

THE LONG VACATION.

THE RELEASE ; or, Caroline's French Kindred.

THE PILGRIMAGE OF THE BEN BERIAH.

THE TWO GUARDIANS ; or, Home in this World. Second Edition.

COUNTESS KATE AND THE STOKESLEY SECRET.

MODERN BROODS ; or, Developments Unlooked for.

STROLLING PLAYERS : A Harmony of Contrasts. By C. M YONGE and C. R. COLERIDGE.

STRAY PEARLS. Memoirs of Margaret de Ribaumont, Viscountess of Bellaise. With Illustrations by W. J. HENNESSY.

Works by Mrs. Craik

Olive: A Novel. With Illustrations by G. BOWERS.

Agatha's Husband: A Novel. With Illustrations by WALTER CRANE.

The Head of the Family: A Novel. With Illustrations by WALTER CRANE.

Two Marriages.

The Laurel Bush.

King Arthur: Not a Love Story.

About Money, and other Things.

Concerning Men, and other Papers.

Works by Mrs. Oliphant

Neighbours on the Green.

Kirsteen: the Story of a Scotch Family Seventy Years Ago.

A Beleaguered City: A Story of the Seen and the Unseen.

Hester: a Story of Contemporary Life.

He that Will Not when He May.

The Railway Man and his Children.

The Marriage of Elinor.

Sir Tom.

The Heir-Presumptive and the Heir-Apparent.

A Country Gentleman and his Family.

A Son of the Soil.

The Second Son.

The Wizard's Son: A Novel.

Lady William.

Young Musgrave.

The Works of Dean Farrar

SEEKERS AFTER GOD.   The Lives of Seneca, Epictetus, and
  Marcus Aurelius.
ETERNAL HOPE.   Sermons preached in Westminster Abbey.
THE FALL OF MAN : and other Sermons.
THE WITNESS OF HISTORY TO CHRIST.
THE SILENCE AND VOICES OF GOD, with other Sermons.
"IN THE DAYS OF THY YOUTH."   Sermons on Practical
  Subjects.
SAINTLY WORKERS.   Five Lenten Lectures.
EPHPHATHA ; or, the Amelioration of the World.
MERCY AND JUDGMENT : a few last words on Christian
  Eschatology.
SERMONS & ADDRESSES DELIVERED IN AMERICA.

THE WORKS OF
Frederick Denison Maurice

SERMONS PREACHED IN LINCOLN'S INN CHAPEL.
  In five vols.
SERMONS PREACHED IN COUNTRY CHURCHES.
CHRISTMAS DAY : and other Sermons.
THEOLOGICAL ESSAYS.
THE PROPHETS and KINGS of the OLD TESTAMENT.
THE PATRIARCHS AND LAWGIVERS OF THE OLD
  TESTAMENT.
THE GOSPEL OF THE KINGDOM OF HEAVEN.
THE GOSPEL OF ST. JOHN.
THE EPISTLES OF ST. JOHN.
THE FRIENDSHIP OF BOOKS : and other Lectures.
THE PRAYER BOOK AND THE LORD'S PRAYER.
THE DOCTRINE OF SACRIFICE.   Deduced from the
  Scriptures.
THE ACTS OF THE APOSTLES.
THE KINGDOM OF CHRIST ; or, Hints to a Quaker re-
  specting the Principles, Constitution, and Ordinances of the
  Catholic Church.   2 vols.

By J. H. SHORTHOUSE

JOHN INGLESANT: A Romance.

SIR PERCIVAL: a Story of the Past and of the Present.

THE LITTLE SCHOOLMASTER MARK.

THE COUNTESS EVE.

A TEACHER OF THE VIOLIN.

BLANCHE, LADY FALAISE.

By GERTRUDE ATHERTON

THE CONQUEROR.

A DAUGHTER OF THE VINE.

THE CALIFORNIANS.

By HUGH CONWAY

A FAMILY AFFAIR.

By W. CLARK RUSSELL

MAROONED.

By ANNIE KEARY

A YORK AND A LANCASTER ROSE.

CASTLE DALY: the Story of an Irish Home thirty years ago.

JANET'S HOME. | OLDBURY.

A DOUBTING HEART.

THE NATIONS AROUND ISRAEL.

By THOMAS HUGHES

TOM BROWN'S SCHOOLDAYS.

TOM BROWN AT OXFORD.

THE SCOURING OF THE WHITE HORSE.

ALFRED THE GREAT.

By ARCHIBALD FORBES

BARRACKS, BIVOUACS, AND BATTLES.

By MONTAGU WILLIAMS

LEAVES OF A LIFE.

ROUND LONDON.

By E. WERNER

FICKLE FORTUNE.

By W. E. NORRIS

THIRLBY HALL.

A BACHELOR'S BLUNDER.

The Works of SHAKESPEARE

VICTORIA EDITION.   In Three Volumes.

Vol. I. COMEDIES.   Vol. II. HISTORIES.   Vol. III. TRAGEDIES.

UNIFORM EDITION OF THE

NOVELS OF CHARLES LEVER

With all the Original Illustrations.

1. HARRY LORREQUER.   Illustrated by PHIZ.

2. CHARLES O'MALLEY.   Illustrated by PHIZ.

3. JACK HINTON THE GUARDSMAN.   Illustrated by PHIZ.

4. TOM BURKE OF OURS.   Illustrated by PHIZ.

5. ARTHUR O'LEARY.   Illustrated by G. CRUIKSHANK.

6. LORD KILGOBBIN.   Illustrated by LUKE FILDES.

By W. WARDE FOWLER

A YEAR WITH THE BIRDS.   Illustrated.

TALES OF THE BIRDS.   Illustrated.

MORE TALES OF THE BIRDS.   Illustrated.

SUMMER STUDIES OF BIRDS AND BOOKS.

By FRANK BUCKLAND

CURIOSITIES OF NATURAL HISTORY.   Illustrated.   In four volumes:

FIRST SERIES—Rats, Serpents, Fishes, Frogs, Monkeys, etc.

SECOND SERIES—Fossils, Bears, Wolves, Cats, Eagles, Hedgehogs, Eels, Herrings, Whales.

THIRD SERIES—Wild Ducks, Fishing, Lions, Tigers, Foxes, Porpoises.

FOURTH SERIES—Giants, Mummies, Mermaids, Wonderful People, Salmon, etc.

Works by Various Authors

Hogan, M.P.
Flittors, Tatters, and the Counsellor
The New Antigone
Memories of Father Healy
CANON ATKINSON.—The Last of the Giant Killers
—— Playhours and Half-Holidays; or, further Experiences
   of Two Schoolboys
SIR S. BAKER.—True Tales for my Grandsons
R. H. BARHAM.—The Ingoldsby Legends
REV. R. H. D. BARHAM.—Life of Theodore Hook
BLENNERHASSET AND SLEEMAN.—Adventures in Mashona-
   land
LANOE FALCONER.—Cecilia de Ncël
W. FORBES-MITCHELL.—Reminiscences of the Great Mutiny
REV. J. GILMORE.—Storm Warriors
MARY LINSKILL.—Tales of the North Riding
S. R. LYSAGHT.—The Marplot
—— One of the Grenvilles
M. M'LENNAN.—Muckle Jock, and other Stories
G. MASSON.—A Compendious Dictionary of the French
   Language
MAJOR GAMBIER PARRY.—The Story of Dick
E. C. PRICE.—In the Lion's Mouth
LORD REDESDALE.—Tales of Old Japan
W. C. RHOADES.—John Trevennick
MARCHESA THEODOLI.—Under Pressure
ANTHONY TROLLOPE.—The Three Clerks
CHARLES WHITEHEAD.—Richard Savage

ENGLISH
MEN OF LETTERS

EDITED BY JOHN MORLEY.

Arranged in 13 Volumes, each containing the Lives of three Authors.

I. **Chaucer.** By Dr. A. W. WARD. **Spenser.** By Dean CHURCH. **Dryden.** By Prof. SAINTSBURY.

II. **Milton.** By MARK PATTISON. **Goldsmith.** By W BLACK. **Cowper.** By GOLDWIN SMITH.

III. **Byron.** By Professor NICHOL. **Shelley.** By J. A. SYMONDS. **Keats.** By SIDNEY COLVIN.

IV. **Wordsworth.** By F. W. H. MYERS. **Southey.** By Prof. DOWDEN. **Landor.** By SIDNEY COLVIN.

V. **Charles Lamb.** By Canon AINGER. **Addison.** By W. J. COURTHOPE. **Swift.** By Sir LESLIE STEPHEN, K.C.B.

VI. **Scott.** By R. H. HUTTON. **Burns.** By Principal SHAIRP. **Coleridge.** By H. D. TRAILL.

VII. **Hume.** By Prof. HUXLEY, F.R.S. **Locke.** By THOS. FOWLER. **Burke.** By JOHN MORLEY.

VIII. **Defoe.** By W. MINTO. **Sterne.** By H. D. TRAILL. **Hawthorne.** By HENRY JAMES.

IX. **Fielding.** By AUSTIN DOBSON. **Thackeray.** By ANTHONY TROLLOPE. **Dickens.** By Dr. A. W. WARD.

X. **Gibbon.** By J. C. MORISON. **Carlyle.** By Professor NICHOL. **Macaulay.** By J. C. MORISON.

XI. **Sydney.** By J. A. SYMONDS. **De Quincey.** By Prof. MASSON. **Sheridan.** By Mrs. OLIPHANT.

XII. **Pope.** By Sir LESLIE STEPHEN, K.C.B. **Johnson.** By Sir LESLIE STEPHEN, K.C.B. **Gray.** By EDMUND GOSSE.

XIII. **Bacon.** By Dean CHURCH. **Bunyan.** By J. A. FROUDE. **Bentley.** By Sir RICHARD JEBB.

THE GLOBE LIBRARY

Crown 8vo. 3s. 6d. each.

The volumes marked with an asterisk (*) are also issued in limp leather, with full gilt back and gilt edges. 5s. net each.

*Boswell's Life of Johnson. With an Introduction by MOWBRAY MORRIS.

*Burns's Complete Works. Edited from the best Printed and MS. Authorities, with Memoir and Glossarial Index. By A. SMITH.

*The Works of Geoffrey Chaucer. Edited by ALFRED W. POLLARD, H. F. HEATH, M. H. LIDDELL, and W. S. McCORMICK.

*Cowper's Poetical Works. Edited, with Biographical Introduction and Notes by W. BENHAM, B.D.

Robinson Crusoe. Edited after the original Edition, with a Biographical Introduction by HENRY KINGSLEY, F.R.G.S.

*Dryden's Poetical Works. Edited, with a Memoir, Revised Texts, and Notes, by W. D. CHRISTIE, M.A.

*The Diary of John Evelyn. With an Introduction and Notes by AUSTIN DOBSON, Hon. LL.D. Edin.

Froissart's Chronicles. Translated by Lord BERNERS. Edited by G. C. MACAULAY, M.A.

*Goldsmith's Miscellaneous Works. With Biographical Introduction by Professor MASSON.

Horace. Rendered into English Prose, with Introduction, Running Analysis, Notes, and Index. By J. LONSDALE, M.A., and S. LEE, M.A.

*The Poetical Works of John Keats. Edited, with Introduction and Notes, by WILLIAM T. ARNOLD.

Morte Darthur. The Book of King Arthur, and of his Noble Knights of the Round Table. The Original Edition of Caxton, revised for modern use. With Introduction, Notes, and Glossary. By Sir E. STRACHEY. [by Professor MASSON.

*Milton's Poetical Works. Edited, with Introduction,

The Diary of Samuel Pepys. With an Introduction and Notes by G. GREGORY SMITH.

*Pope's Poetical Works. Edited, with Notes and Introductory Memoir, by Dr. A. W. WARD.

*Sir Walter Scott's Poetical Works. Edited, with Biographical and Critical Memoir, by Prof. F. T. PALGRAVE. With Introduction and Notes.

*Shakespeare's Complete Works. Edited by W. G. CLARK, M.A., and W. ALDIS WRIGHT, M.A. With Glossary.

*Spenser's Complete Works. Edited from the Original Editions and Manuscripts, with Glossary, by R. MORRIS, and a Memoir by J. W. HALES, M.A. [edges. 4s. 6d.]

*Tennyson's Poetical Works. [Also in extra cloth, gilt

Virgil. Rendered into English Prose, with Introductions, Notes Analysis, and Index. By J. LONSDALE, M.A., and S. LEE, M.A.

ILLUSTRATED
STANDARD NOVELS

Crown 8vo. Cloth Elegant, gilt edges (Peacock Edition).
3s. 6d. each.

Also issued in ornamental cloth binding. 2s. 6d. each.

By JANE AUSTEN

With Introductions by AUSTIN DOBSON, *and Illustrations by*
HUGH THOMSON *and* C. E. BROCK.

PRIDE AND PREJUDICE. | MANSFIELD PARK.
SENSE AND SENSIBILITY. | NORTHANGER ABBEY,
EMMA. | AND PERSUASION.

By J. FENIMORE COOPER

With Illustrations by C. E. BROCK *and* H. M. BROCK.

THE LAST OF THE MOHICANS. With a General Introduction by Mowbray Morris.
THE DEERSLAYER. | THE PIONEERS.
THE PATHFINDER. | THE PRAIRIE.

By MARIA EDGEWORTH

With Introductions by ANNE THACKERAY RITCHIE, *and Illustrations by* CHRIS HAMMOND *and* CARL SCHLOESSER.

ORMOND. | HELEN.
CASTLE RACKRENT, AND | BELINDA.
THE ABSENTEE. | PARENT'S ASSISTANT.
POPULAR TALES.

By CAPTAIN MARRYAT

With Introductions by DAVID HANNAY, *and Illustrations by*
H. M. BROCK, J. AYTON SYMINGTON, FRED PEGRAM, F. H.
TOWNSEND, H. R. MILLAR, *and* E. J. SULLIVAN.

JAPHET IN SEARCH OF | JACOB FAITHFUL.
A FATHER. | PETER SIMPLE.

ILLUSTRATED
STANDARD NOVELS

By CAPTAIN MARRYAT—*continued.*

MIDSHIPMAN EASY.
THE KING'S OWN.
THE PHANTOM SHIP.
SNARLEY-YOW.
POOR JACK.

THE PIRATE, AND THE
   THREE CUTTERS.
MASTERMAN READY.
FRANK MILDMAY.
NEWTON FORSTER.

By THOMAS LOVE PEACOCK

With Introductions by GEORGE SAINTSBURY, *and Illustrations by* H. R. MILLAR *and* F. H. TOWNSEND.

HEADLONG HALL, AND
   NIGHTMARE ABBEY.
MAID MARIAN, AND
   CROTCHET CASTLE.

GRYLL GRANGE.
MELINCOURT.
MISFORTUNES OF ELPHIN
   AND RHODODAPHNE.

BY VARIOUS AUTHORS

WESTWARD HO! By CHARLES KINGSLEY. Illustrated by C. E. Brock.

HANDY ANDY. By SAMUEL LOVER. Illustrated by H. M. Brock. With Introduction by Charles Whibley.

ANNALS OF THE PARISH. By JOHN GALT. Illustrated By C. E. Brock. With Introduction by Alfred Ainger.

SYBIL, OR THE TWO NATIONS, ETC. By BENJAMIN DISRAELI. Illustrated by F. Pegram. With Introduction by H. D. Traill.

ADVENTURES OF HAJJI BABA OF ISPAHAN. By JAMES MORIER. Illustrated by H. R. Millar. With Introduction by Lord Curzon.

THE NEW CRANFORD SERIES

Crown 8vo, Cloth Elegant, Gilt Edges, 3s. 6d. per volume.

Cranford. By Mrs. GASKELL. With Preface by Anne Thackeray Ritchie and 100 Illustrations by Hugh Thomson.

The Vicar of Wakefield. With 182 Illustrations by Hugh Thomson, and Preface by Austin Dobson.

Our Village. By MARY RUSSELL MITFORD. Introduction by Anne Thackeray Ritchie, and 100 Illustrations by Hugh Thomson.

Gulliver's Travels. With Introduction by Sir Henry Craik, K.C.B., and 100 Illustrations by C. E. Brock.

The Humorous Poems of Thomas Hood. With Preface by Alfred Ainger, and 130 Illustrations by C. E. Brock.

Sheridan's The School for Scandal and The Rivals. Illustrated by E. J. Sullivan. With Introduction by A. Birrell.

Household Stories. By the Brothers GRIMM. Translated by Lucy Crane. With Pictures by Walter Crane.

Reynard the Fox. Edited by J. JACOBS. With Illustrations by W. Frank Calderon.

Coaching Days and Coaching Ways. By W. OUTRAM TRISTRAM. With Illustrations by H. Railton and Hugh Thomson.

Coridon's Song; and other Verses. With Introduction by Austin Dobson and Illustrations by Hugh Thomson.

The Fables of Æsop. Selected by JOSEPH JACOBS. Illustrated by R. Heighway.

Old Christmas. By WASHINGTON IRVING. With Illustrations by R. Caldecott.

Bracebridge Hall. With Illustrations by R. CALDECOTT.

Rip Van Winkle and the Legend of Sleepy Hollow. With 50 Illustrations and a Preface by George H. Boughton, A.R.A.

The Alhambra. With Illustrations by J. Pennell and Introduction by E. R. Pennell.

MACMILLAN & CO., LTD., LONDON.

J. PALMER, PRINTER, CAMBRIDGE.　　20 . 11 . 13

www.ingramcontent.com/pod-product-compliance
Lightning Source LLC
Chambersburg PA
CBHW020858130726
47900CB00014B/1015